WOLFHAMPTON

WOLFHAMPTON

JAY FITZPATRICK

Hard Pressed Publishing
New York

Hard Pressed Publishing

© 2019 JAY FITZPATRICK

All rights reserved.

ISBN-13:9780578576022

ISBN Ref: 10:0578576023

Library of Congress Control Number: 2019913996

LCCN Imprint Name: HARD PRESSED NYC

For Me

America is a country of inventors, and the greatest inventors are the newspapermen.
    —Alexander Graham Bell

The stock market is a house of cards built on idiocy, stacked on spider webs, hanging tenuously from the Hindenburg. — Lee Camp

The tiger and the lion may be more powerful, but the wolf does not perform in the circus.
    —Ramarghya Banerjee

The Fake News Media nowadays not only doesn't check for the accuracy of the facts, they knowingly make up the facts. They even make up sources in order to protect their partners, the Democrats. It is so wrong, but they don't even care anymore. They have gone totally CRAZY!!!!
    —Donald Trump

This is a work of fiction.

A satirical look at President Trump, Congress,

Russia, and the 2020 presidential election.

SUMMER 2020

The wooden train trestle spanning the estuary one hundred feet above was eerily quiet and still. The 5 pm train heading east to Montauk had just passed and the noise and steel track vibration had ceased. Two young girls were sitting on the tracks with their legs dangling precariously over the creosote-soaked wooden railroad ties, looking down at the shimmering incoming tide below.

"It's either something or it's nothing," said the blond.

"It's something," said the brunette.

"Look no one…"

"Look where?" interrupted the brunette.

"What?"

"You said 'Look'. What am I supposed to be looking at?" said the brunette.

"It's just an expression."

"Well stop it. 'Look – Listen - At the end of the day - To be honest', are all stupid ways of beginning a sentence. So please just stop it," said the brunette.

"With all due respect…"

"Just stop it," interrupted the brunette again.

"Okay but it's still either something or it's nothing. My monies on nothing."

"You haven't got any money — neither do I, but if I did it would be on something," said the brunette.

"Oh, you think there is light at the end of the tunnel? Your life is going to flash before your eyes? Mom and dad are going to be there to welcome you? Well, they are not. It's nothing. You die and it's over. No spirit, no pearly gates, no second chance, no nothing."

They looked at each other and smiled - not a happy smile. They joined hands, leaned forward and let go.

Chapter 1

When the village police arrived on the scene, they found the girls under the bridge. It was getting dark and the sky was turning red and pink. The tide was out, and both bodies were splattered on the rocks just beneath the low water line.

"Who called it in?" asked Detective Mutteo Rossi.

"A couple of boys taking a shortcut home from school," replied Sergeant Jeffery Jaworski.

"It's almost 8 pm and they called it in about an hour ago. That's a long, late shortcut from school."

"Yeah. Well, they said they had jug."

"What the fuck is jug?"

"That's what they call detention at Bishop McGann High School — 'Justice Under God'. It's a Catholic thing."

"Shit. So, what do we got?" asked Rossi.

"Suicide plain and simple. Two young local girls. Both 17 and both from Hampton Bays," said the sergeant.

"They had ID's?" asked Rossi.

Before the sergeant could answer, Detective Rossi looked up at the train bridge and saw two seagulls sitting on the tracks. The two seagulls, in tandem, pushed what looked like a large rock off the bridge. It landed and smashed on the rocks below not ten feet from the bodies.

"Get two uniforms up there and tape off the bridge," ordered Rossi.

"You gonna stop the trains?"

"No. I'm gonna let them run through the crime scene. Of course, I'm gonna stop the trains running through my crime scene, you fucken cretino. And keep the seagulls from using my crime scene as a fucking clam opener."

"Look…"

"Will you please stop starting every sentence with 'Look.' Obama is no longer president, so you can stop it. Bafangu!"

"No, look," he said and pointed. "The medical examiner is coming up."

"Suicide plain and simple, right doc?" asked Rossi.

"Maybe - maybe not," said the medical examiner, already out of breath after walking up the embankment.

"What?" asked Rossi.

"Murder."

"Murder? You think they were pushed?" asked Rossi.

"No. I don't think they were pushed, but they were both pregnant. When they hit the rocks, they landed on their backs and kind of exploded. Looks like they committed suicide, but the fetuses were partially forced out and they kinda look… well, both look like little doll heads."

"Doc, they were pregnant and depressed. Sounds like suicide to me," said Rossi.

"Don't you have to be alive to kill someone? They were dead when they hit the rocks, how do you figure murder?" asked Jaworski.

"That will be up to the district attorney to decide; I just report. They both looked like they were over five months pregnant and if the coroner finds saltwater in the baby's lungs then that means each drew a breath, and if they drew a breath, then they were alive. The girls committed double suicide, but they may have also committed double homicide."

"Merda," swore Rossi.

Chapter 2

Tom Halsey heard the 10-79 code, "Notify Coroner", on his police scanner. That could be anything from a traffic accident to a drowning. Either one would be front-page news in Wolfhampton. Halsey had some cop and detective friends that he liked and who trusted him, but the detective talking to the sergeant wasn't one of them. He stopped behind a clump of trees when he saw the medical examiner approach the detective and sergeant. You never know what you can pick up. He missed most of what was said but heard the last part.

"...the girls committed double suicide, but they may have also committed double homicide."

Then he heard the detective's response, 'Shit.'"

Tom Halsey was born and raised in Southampton, just a few miles east. He could trace his lineage back to his great, great, great...grandmother Mrs. Thomas Halsey listed in the Southampton Colony town records as having been the first recorded death; she was scalped by the Pequot Indians in 1649. There have been many Halseys since then: sea captains, revolutionary war soldiers, builders, farmers, Civil War, WWI, WWII, Korea, Vietnam veterans and so on. After graduating from the University of Kansas, with a journalism major, he continued the patriotic family tradition as an Army Ranger officer in Afghanistan.

Captain Thomas Halsey received the Silver Star, the third-highest valor award. The Army veteran had spent two years with the 75th Ranger

Regiment and commanded a joint task force in Afghanistan. His next two years were with Delta Force and were classified.

During an enemy engagement on April 04, 2010, Halsey, "selflessly and with little regard for his own personal safety, exposed himself to enemy fire several times in order to retrieve a casualty, suppress the enemy by direct fire and called-in several dangerously close aerial munitions," according to the citation.

His actions allowed the assault force to eliminate the enemy and move the unit to the helicopter landing zone to be flown out.

At exactly six feet tall, he had dirty blond hair and always a two-day growth on his face. He just turned twenty-eight and has been with *The Wolfhampton Press* for three years and as an investigative reporter for the last two. Halsey had a few offers to leave for the bigger up-island papers but decided Wolfhampton was where he belonged. He was good-looking, hardworking and proving to be a good, pain in the ass, aggressive reporter. All he needed was a crime.

The next day, while walking down Hampton Road, heading for Starbucks, Halsey bumped into Wolfhampton Village Patrol Officer Michael Denison who had stopped for coffee at the Sip N' Soda. Halsey went to high school with Denison and the two had remained friends. After a few pleasantries, Halsey's reporter instinct kicked in.

"What are you hearing about the divers?" asked Halsey. The unofficial code for the two girls who committed suicide from the bridge.

"I knew them, Tommy. My sister Sara's daughter went to school with them and I chaperoned a few events at their school. I've seen them in the village and around town. Tommy, they were good girls."

"They couldn't have been that good, Michael."

"Yeah well, they didn't deserve what happened to them."

"So, what did happen?"

"I'm not on the case, or did you forget I'm just a lowly patrol officer? Moving violations, noise complaints, that sort of thing. The brass and detectives use me to get coffee. Which reminds me, they're waiting." He motioned towards his patrol car indicating he had to get going.

"So, nothing?"

"I saw them two weeks ago."

"Who?"

"The two girls, Olivia and Zoe. They were in the parking lot behind Citarella's having, what appeared to be, an altercation with an older guy."

"Who?"

"Didn't see his face and it just lasted a minute, so I didn't interfere."

"Michael, an older guy having an argument with two young pregnant girls who are now both dead. I'm thinking this is important," said Halsey with an incredulous stare.

"Tommy, I know that. I told my sergeant, and he said he would run it up the pole."

"There's got to be some cameras covering the parking lot that you could…"

"I've already interviewed shop owners who have cameras, and have some good video. I passed it on, but I think I know who the guy is."

"Thought you didn't see his face?"

"I didn't, but I saw the car he drove away in."

"What?"

"A 2019 black and red Bugatti."

"I always knew you were a knucklehead but didn't know you were a Euro knucklehead. A Bugatti, even here in the Hamptons among all the Ferraris, Porsches, Range Rovers, and Bentleys, would definitely stick out. You didn't happen to get a plate number did you?"

"Yeah. New York vanity tag. 'WOLF.'"

"What the fuck is that supposed to mean? Another hedge fund clown?"

"Remember the movie from the '60s, with Alan Arkin and Jonathan Winters – *The Russians Are Coming-The Russians Are Coming*?'"

"Yeah."

"Well, they're here."

Chapter 3

The eastern end of Long Island splits into a fork, manifesting into a north and south peninsula. The north is quiet, unpretentious and known for its vineyards, lavender festivals, and open farmland. The south, after separation by a geographical and social canal, is loud, pretentious, and known for its traffic, horse show and expensive real estate. Between Southampton and East Hampton lies the incorporated village of Wolfhampton, the most exclusive, expensive, and scary 'Hampton'.

Dmitriy Volkov loves America. He is six-two, trim, hazel eyes, just under 40, slicked-back thick black hair and a chiseled more than handsome face. He loves young American girls, expensive American real estate, American style, and American money; he's worth over $6.9 billion. The only thing he doesn't like is American cars. Dmitriy Volkov loves European sports cars, namely: Koenigseggs, Lamborghinis, and Ferraris. He has several of each, but his current love is his black and red Bugatti Chiron Sport. It's the fastest, most powerful, and exclusive production super sports car in Bugatti's history. A unique masterpiece that generates an incredible 1,500 hp. Zero-Sixty in 2.5 seconds, and it only cost 401,464,800,000 Russian rubles. He purchased it as consolation for losing out on a bid for the one-off Bugatti La Voiture Noire that went for 11 million Euros before fees and taxes.

Volkov aka Wolf, some say because of the loose translation of his surname Volk (Волк, Wolf in Russian) others because of his anger issues, lives in a 19th-century Gothic Revival mansion. When Dmitriy's grandfather purchased the estate, it was considered too large and vulgar to mention square footage. The broker did, however, list one of the many outbuildings, a small guest house, as having 24 rooms and 8,000 square feet of space. The main house, or the 'cottage' as it was referred to by the 19th-century summer colony gentry, was more than imposing. The cold façade ascended upward with its champagne and pink extruded brick, and limestone reliefs, turrets, ramparts, and chimneys. Its attics had attics and looked entirely comfortable with its given name — Wolfhall. The interior has 100 rooms, 23 bathrooms and a 30-foot ceiling grand hall with a fireplace right out of a Dracula movie. It is all grand, if rather gloomy thanks in part to its gothic style and materials, and in part for the need to keep the blinds down to stop the wallpaper, paintings, and carpet from fading. The property sits on 85 walled acres abutting the Atlantic Ocean, includes a 9-hole golf course, tennis court, and many outbuildings. Volkov's and his lessor endowed neighbors call this small Hampton hamlet wedged between Sagaponack and Southampton, their country home.

The residents seceded their hamlet from Southampton and with incorporation came the power to establish zoning and other ordinances along with a police department to enforce them. New building lots were now required to be large enough and therefore costly enough to keep the less privileged from moving in. Access to the coastline was now tightly controlled, in part by prohibiting parking on their village lanes and no public access to the beach.

Because of the amount of privet surrounding all the mansions, the residents originally suggested incorporating as the village of Hedgehampton. Others, however, felt that the name would enforce the impression of having too many Wall Street hedge fund managers in residence. They decided, instead, on the name Wolfhampton, an Americanize adaptation of the English village of Wolverhampton. The Russian community, however, claimed it was in honor of their most visible resident Volkov and Wolfhall manor.

Setting back by the tennis court, Dmitriy and a few of his friends watched a singles match between two world-class tennis pros. In keeping with his nom de guerre, Dmitriy had two black Siberian wolves flown in to add some color and tighten-up security. A slight disturbance behind him causes several large security operatives to close, but Dmitriy waves them back and gave a nod for his gorgeous eye candy Riana to give him some space. But the wolves, male brothers Hammer and Sickle stayed close and scrunched their muzzles, a prelude to baring their fangs.

Wolfhampton Police Chief Ed Daly, tall, dashing and looking every bit a tony Hampton police chief, guided by Sergey Galkin, head of Volkov's security and former Colonel in the KGB, cautiously approached and whispered into Dmitriy's ear, "There's a reporter and one of my patrol officers sticking their noses in where they don't belong."

"Who?"

"Halsey. Tom Halsey with the *Wolfhampton Press*, and PO Denison. They have been seen talking, and now they are asking a lot of questions."

"Do they have anything or are they just digging?"

"Denison found some private exterior security cam vid of you and the girls, turned it over to Detective Rossi, but the vid seems to have disappeared. The reporter has nothing."

"Good. You make sure the vid stays disappeared and keep an eye on your boy, maybe have a talk with him. Leave the reporter to me," said Dmitriy and with a nod dismissed the chief.

Kahbib Nurmodov, a frequent guest of Dmitriy, and UFC lightweight champion that chocked-out Conor McGregor in the fourth-round title fight, came over and Dmitriy gave him a man-hug and invited him to sit.

"How is our friend?" asked Dmitriy while Hammer and Sickle bared their fangs and let out a long low guttural growl. Something about Nurmodov didn't sit right with them. Volkov didn't silent them because he felt the same.

Kahbib is the undisputed UFC Lightweight Champion and best pals with Russian President Vladimir Putin. "He is well and asked me to give you a message," said Kahbib.

"Which is?"

"He wants you to come back. He said all is forgiven."

"Yeah heard that before. You training here or back in the city?"

"Here."

"Good. There's a reporter I want you to talk to," said Dmitriy.

"You know I'm not good with interviews Dmitriy. All they want to talk about is my fight after the fight with Dan Dillon. They still can't get over their 'Notorious' losing to me. Dana White and Fertitta told me to keep my mouth shut and talk to no one. Whatever I say always seemed to come out the wrong way and gets me in trouble."

"This is a different kind of interview, Kahbib. The kind you don't have to answer any questions."

Chapter 4

Michael Denison's a good police officer. He and Tom Halsey went to high school together, but Halsey went on to college, Army Rangers, and became a reporter. Denison, on the other hand, went to shit.

Denison married his high school sweetheart, almost got arrested for DUI, pot was found in his car, drank too much, gained weight, gained a reputation as a bully, cheated on his wife, got divorced, and was finally knocked senseless by his younger brother John. He left for a year to backpack through Europe and upon his return was able to get his act together. With Halsey's help, he was able to get into the Wolfhampton Village Police Department; he never looked back. Now a trimmed down 180 lbs. and 5'-11" and 28 years old, Denison was determined to be a good cop and become a great detective. The cop part was working out, but for the detective part, he needed to be noticed — he needed a crime.

Denison, like most of the Wolfhampton: police, civil servants, and workers, didn't live in the village and had to commute to work each day from Hampton Bays unless they were lucky enough to score an apartment rental over one of the local shops or bars. Denison had a small apartment over a restaurant in Southampton and commuted to work each day on the only east-west highway connecting the towns and villages of the Southfork; a narrow two-lane throwback from the '40s. He arrived for his morning shift ready to protect and serve...coffee.

"Morning Detective Rossi. You get a chance to look at the vid?" asked Denison.

Detective Mutteo Rossi is one of two detectives on the Wolfhampton Village Police Force. He's 53, married with three kids, seriously in love with his wife Vicky, looks like and acts like Clemenza from the *Godfather*. He also moonlights, as do many on the force, for Dmitriy Volkov.

"The vid? Oh, you're not gonna see that no more," said Rossi.

"What do you mean?"

"What do you mean, detective."

"Sorry, what do you mean Detective Rossi?"

"I mean there is nothing on the vid that helps the investigation either way."

"But the vid showed the girls having an argument with this older guy in the parking lot, timed stamped two weeks before they died."

"Yeah, but you can barely see the guy's face, so it's nothing. Anyway, it's gone, but nice try kid."

Denison knew when to stop, and decided that retreat was the best option. He was not permitted to make copies of evidence, but he had. Tonight, he would watch the vid again and decide his next move.

Chapter 5
MOSCOW

"Who is this person?"

"President Trump?"

"Yes, but who is he?"

"His first wife called him 'The Donald'."

"Like the duck?"

"No, that would be Walt Disney."

"Disneyland?"

"Sort of, but…"

"But what does the name Trump mean?"

"It is a good name, but can mean different things. A winning card like in a gambling card game, or it could mean getting the better of someone, or it could mean a drum or trumpet."

"Good family name. Yes?"

"Yes, but that may not be his name. Some say his ancestors changed the surname from Drumph."

"So, Trump is a fake name?"

"Could be."

"What about their American economy?"

"It's driven by gambling. They are addicted to buying and selling stuff and taking chances. Their Wall Street is like a big casino full of gamblers always gambling. Nothing but a big 'Ponzi' scheme."

"Who's Ponzi?"

"Madoff — a rich guy in jail."

"Only the rich can gamble in this Wall Street casino?"

"No. Everyone can play, even the poor, but the house always wins."

"But their economy is doing well, no?"

"If you think a trillion a year deficit and $22 trillion in debt a good economy, I salute you."

"They don't care that their children and children's children will have to pay all this debt back? They, how do they say it, just keep 'kicking the bottle down the prospekt.'"

"The rich white and their politicians don't care anymore. Their children will be taken care of. Besides, whites aren't having any more children, and if they keep 'kicking the can down the road' the only ones left holding the bag, so to speak, will be a country of new immigrants."

"So, it's a fake economy?"

"Could be. They pretend to have such great traditions, but they are, how do you say detskiy - Infants. Their country is only a little over 200 years old, and it is not even their country; they stole it from the Indians."

"Indians? But don't Indians live in India."

"Yes, Americans were a bit confused about that."

"So, it's a fake country?"

"Could be."

"What about his children?"

"He has three sons and two daughters by several wives."

"The youngest, the tall lanky boy?"

"Barron."

"Is he a baron? Royal blood? Like a duke or earl?"

"No. His given name is Barron."

"So, he's not royal. Not a real baron?"

"No."

"So, he's a fake kid?"

"Could be."

"Trump says they have fake news. Now: fake name, fake economy, fake country, fake kid. We need to move now. It's time to turn out their lights and shut down their Wall Street casino."

"What about the boy?"

"Everything in America is fake. It's all an illusion, yes? The boy Barron, let's make him an illusion; make him do the Houdini."

"It's time we talk to the 'Pale Moth.'"

Chapter 6
THE WHITE HOUSE

"How do you stand it Dad?" asked Eric.

"I could say 'consider the source', but it's more like 'in one ear out the other,'" said President Trump.

"If you go there, Schumer, Pelosi and the media will kill you. They will be relentless," said Don Jr.

"Like I said. 'In one ear out the other.'"

"Dad, he's a Russian," said Ivanka.

"Yeah and I'm a McFritz, and Melania is a slob. So?"

"You mean Slav," said Jared.

Trump looked at his son-in-law, Jared Kushner, with disdain and thought of what Sony said to Carlo in the Godfather, *'We don't discuss business at the table'*, but he let it go because of Ivanka.

"Look. I'm not going to East Hampton for God's sake. I might take a side trip to Southampton, but we're going to spend most of the time at his Wolfhampton estate. We can take Marine One in and out. A short motorcade from East Hampton Airport to Wolfhampton."

"That's not your base Dad," said Don Jr.

"Why set yourself up for all this abuse, Dad? The media will…"

"Let's give them something to talk about…," said the president, interrupting Ivanka.

"You have thick skin Dad," said Eric.

"Not worried about my skin. I just need to breathe. I need to get out of the swamp."

Wolfhampton

"I got some good news and some bad news. I just heard from his chief of staff. He accepted," said Colonel Galkin.

"What's the good news?" said Dmitriy with a chuckle.

"Funny. You know Putin's gonna be pissed-off."

"Better than being pissed-on."

When Halsey checked online, the Wolfhampton police blotter had the girl's murders still listed as double suicides. The Suffolk County Coroner & Medical Examiner office had decided the girls' family's and the public, in general, couldn't stomach the truth; it would have been too gory a tale to take further.

His cop friend Denison said everything on the girls' investigation had shut down but wants to meet him.

Halsey was not going to let this die. The girls' were pregnant and Volkov or Wolf or whatever his name was is the father, and wouldn't admit it, or help them, which led them to jump.

Yesterday a bruiser showed up and scared the shit out of him. Didn't say anything, just got in his face, did a thumbs up with his fist then a sweeping motion across his neck, like cutting a throat. Scary dude. Anyway, that's yesterday's news. Halsey just got an *AP* wire that President Trump is coming to Wolfhampton for the 4th of July weekend and staying with Dmitriy Volkov. *What's the expression 'Wag the Dog'? If Volkov thinks having Trump at his estate for the weekend will make everyone forget about the girl's murder he's sadly mistaken*, thought Halsey, *but how do I get an invite?*

Chapter 7

A presidential protection Secret Service and FBI team, from NYC and Long Island, arrived uninvited at Wolfhall for a preliminary security evaluation.

"You can check and secure the guest house where they will be staying, and the adjacent grounds but not Mr. Volkov's house," said Colonel Galkin.

"We have to check and secure everything, including the main house. Just a precaution, you understand, SOP. They will, I assume, be entertained there," replied FBI Agent Bob Bates, SAIC out of the NYC office.

"Yes, and you will accidentally scatter a few bugs while you're at it, SOP. I don't think so, Agent Bates."

"It's not really up for discussion Colonel Galkin. It's our job and we must check and secure everything and everywhere the president and his family venture. If we can't secure it, he can't come," said Secret Service Agent David Orange out of the Melville Long Island office.

With that, the colonel turned his back on both agents and proceeded to the main house.

"Colonel. Where are you going?" asked Orange.

Without turning back, the colonel said over his shoulder, "I am going to inform Mr. Volkov that the president's Secret Service detail said he won't be coming."

"Colonel. A moment please?" asked Agent Bates as he moved towards Galkin.

Galkin stopped and turned. "May I address you formally, agent?"

"If you must," answered Bates, knowing what was probably coming.

"Master Bates," began the colonel smiling and stringing his title and surname together, "there are six levels including the sub-basement and attics. You have six men. No phones. No anything, just the clothes you're wearing. You will be escorted by six of my men; one team per level. You will be given floor plans. You can check off each room as visited, secured or stopped by. I don't care. You have one hour."

The colonel departed and Bates made his way back to where Orange and the rest of the team stood. "Did you hear what the colonel said?" asked Bates.

"Yeah, every word Master Bates," said Orange with a snicker and added, "but it's bullshit. I got pictures of the interior from Sotheby's. The place looks like a freaking Dracula movie set. I'll bet there's a dungeon, sliding bookcases, and hanging paintings with eyes that follow you."

"Okay, Agent Orange," said Bates, similarly stringing his name together, associating it to the famous Vietnam war poison defoliant, "pick four guys and you and I will make it six. I'll take the main floor. You take the basement. We'll just do the best threat assessment that time allows and run it up the flagpole. If Washington wants to take it further, they'll let us know. Let's highlight, on all the plans: ingress, egress and regress and any possible hidden corridors, trap doors and spooky paintings. You check to see if there are any workmen or contractors scheduled to do any repairs to the main house before the 4th?"

"Saw in the service gate log a painting contractor is scheduled for tomorrow."

"Follow up on it and see if it's the main house and if he'll corporate."

"You thinking to have him plant some bugs?"

"No. He'll be searched."

"What about Alexa, Google Home, Echo, or Smart TV mics?"

"We can try but Colonel Galkin is ex-KGB and I'm pretty sure he has top security protocols in place. No, what I'm thinking about, is switching out the painting contractors paint for a new conductive paint developed by the National Science Foundation. I was at a convention a few weeks ago and they have developed new conjugated polymers that feature novel chemical building blocks and inorganic elements. These pi-ways, or the double bonds in the chain of chemical molecules, create a pathway or flow for electrons through the paint. These special pi-ways produce the light-emitting effects in the new field of organic light-emitting diodes-OLED's," said Bates.

"How would you explain that to a 10-year-old if you had to?" asked Orange.

"Instead of buying a big TV for your wall, you buy paint and make your wall a big TV."

"And what do you do for power? Plug the wall into the wall?" asked Orange.

"It generates its own power from ambient light. Sort of solar-powered."

"Thank you, but won't the great Colonel Galkin find it when they do their daily sweep?"

"I don't think so. The conductive material in the paint is a new nano-technology conjugated polymer, and supposedly there is no known sweep signature yet."

"Let's hope Volkov picked a stock color."

Chapter 8

MORNING JOE SHOW – MSMBC

"…yes, but why would President Trump, among all this controversy, among the latest Mueller testimony in front of Congress, and all this whistleblower cover-up, want to spend the 4th of July weekend with a Russian?" asked Mika Brzezinski.

"Better than spending Independence Day with the Brits, but a few adjectives come to mind: insensitive, ignorant, inconsiderate, oblivious, self-absorbed, just to name a few," answered Joe Scarborough.

"Willy, take us home with the last thought."

"Whatever mischief President Trump is up to, endearing himself to Dmitriy Volkov will be at the peril of President Putin. Using Independence Day to fire a shot at Putin and Russia may very well be the 'shot heard round the world,'" finished Willy Geist.

The show's lights dimmed and with the cameras and sound off Joe said, "I would like to be a fly on Volkov's wall when he sits down for that private conversation with Trump that you know is coming."

"Can any of us get an invite or do we know anyone who can?" asked Mika.

"It will have to snow in Palm Beach before any of us will get another invite from Mr. Trump," said Joe.

"I may know someone. A friend of mine has a summer house in the Hamptons and mentioned a reporter who she is friendly with. Want me to make inquiries?" asked Willy.

"Do it. What can it hurt to have a local on our team?" suggested Joe.

Chapter 9
MOSCOW

"He treats me like this? He wants to run with that wolf?" said President Putin aka Pale Moth. "Venezuela then withdrawing from the Intermediate-Range Nuclear Forces Treaty, and he's blaming us. Now I will move forward with our hypersonic mid-range missile." He tossed the *AP* wire onto his desk.

Sanctions Lifted

Washington, DC- June 23, 2020, 7:02 AM ET

By Alex Mutter Associated Press

The Trump administration announced on Wednesday that it intends to lift sanctions against the business empire of Dmitriy Volkov, one of Russia's most influential banished oligarchs, after an aggressive lobbying campaign by Mr. Volkov's companies.

The decision by the Treasury Department, which had been postponed for months, was both politically and economically sensitive and drew criticism from some Democrats and foreign policy analysts that the administration was sending the wrong signal to Moscow about its conduct toward its neighbors and the United States.

The companies are among the biggest in the aluminum industry, and questions about their fate had roiled global metals markets. Mr. Volkov's unsure stature in Russia made any decision seen to be in his favor tricky for the administration at a time when President Trump is under investigation by the special counsel in connection with Russian interference in the 2016 election.

Mr. Volkov and his businesses — including the world's second largest aluminum company, Rusal — were hit with sanctions in April in retaliation for Russian interference in the election and other hostile acts by Moscow.

Volkov owns large stakes in aluminum, power, insurance, and auto companies. He also employed Paul Manafort, who even offered to give him personal briefings about the 2016 presidential election.

"When the sanctions are lifted, we'll just take back ownership of all of Volkov's companies. What can he do, complain to the Better Business Bureau? Trump is doing everything he can to bring the Bear and Dragon together; tariffs, Venezuela, and now this Syria thing," said Putin.

"Then we can take Trump out, Comrade Putin?" asked Ministry of Defense General Sergey Shoygu.

"No, we take the boy when the Trump family is partying with Volkov in Wolfhampton. It will happen on Volkov's watch and Trump and Melania will blame him."

"Comrade Putin, who do we use?"

"The mafiya, perhaps," said Putin.

"The American Italian mafia, Comrade Putin?"

"No, you imbecile, our American mafiya; the Rossiyskaya mafiya or maybe we throw a monkey in the wrench, as our American friends are fond of saying, and have our beloved Dagestan mafiya do the deed," said Putin.

"Yes, Comrade Putin. That takes care of Volkov, he'll be kicked out of America and blamed for the abduction. That leaves Trump and the American economy."

"Trump will fall when their economy crashes," said Putin.

"But their economy is unflappable, Comrade Putin," said Ministry of Finance Anton Siluanov.

"You are wrong, Comrade Siluanov. Many cities, especially New York, are close to bankruptcy. They are careening closer to all-out financial bankruptcy for the first time since Mayor Abraham Beame ran the city more than 40 years ago. Overtaxed businesses and individuals are fleeing the city in mass, and city public spending is surging into the stratosphere, they are perilously near total fiscal disaster."

"You are correct, Comrade Putin, and the rest of the world's economy isn't in much better shape. With help from our Chinese friends, we can start the disinformation and begin the crash," said Siluanov.

"Comrade Siluanov, with a little help from our RBN cybercrime group, and China's PLA Unit 61398 cyber warfare force, we can speed the crash up a bit," added Foreign Intelligence SVR Director Sergey Naryshkin.

Chapter 10

Grey Care Investment Club LLC out of Avalon NJ, comprised of six sep-
tuagenarians hovered around, not *THE NEW YORK TIMES*, but three
large, interactive, wall-mounted monitors and one plasma screen. They
are logged onto their E*TRADE account busily buying and selling financial instruments (e.g. stocks, options, futures, derivatives, currencies).
Doing what they do best — buy low and sell high.

They started 'Grey Care' to get away from their children and grand-
children, disguising it as a gathering place for seniors to meet each day,
play cards, trade recipes, socialize and have some fun. Their children
thought that it was a wonderful idea until they started losing their built-in
babysitters.

"Vinny is everything moving south on the board this morning, or is it
me?" asked Marge, one of the original founding members.

Vinny turned away from listening to Mornings with Maria on *FOX
BUSINESS*. "Something strange is going on according to Maria. The job
numbers just came in and they were way below expectations; US employ-
ers only added 104,000 new jobs for January, way under what was expected. The market has been up for 25 consecutive days and now it's heading
south. What's happening in Europe and Asia seems to be spreading here."

"Unexpected yes, bummer yes, but why strange?" asked Marge as she
and the rest of the club gathered around Maria while Vinny recapped.

"Strange because she said she had seen the job numbers earlier and they said 304,000 new jobs but it was changed to 104,000. She said the markets opened in Asia and Europe this morning and suddenly everything went negative. It's like all the good news has just turned to bad news."

The Grey Care girls were not as sophisticated as Warren, Carl or George, nor did they have their trading power or that much invested, but they could not afford to lose a penny of a dollar or an ounce of pride.

To them, the market was pure and simple. Buy low — sell high. Two things and only two things moved the market and allowed them to make money; good news and bad news. Pure and simple. It is all about speculation. You buy shares in a company because of good news and you think (hope) the good news will continue, so you can sell for more than you paid. The person who buys your stock believes in exactly the same thing. When people stop believing, the whole thing crumbles like a house of cards.

"The board is showing lots of sell orders, but not many buys. Looks like the speculators are taking a pass, and letting the bottom feeders gorge," offered Marge.

"Switch to CNBC and see if the mad man is on," suggested Vinny.

Cramer was ranting and raving — "...we're back in bizarro land. A world where good news can also be bad news. This is crazy, my friends. We were looking for 300,000 plus new jobs and all we got was 100,000 plus. What happened? Europe and Asia were up, now they're down. The Fed is calling for higher..."

"Everything is tumbling," said Noreen dragging their attention away from Cramer and back to the monitors showing the board, "look at Amazon and Apple, why don't we buy?"

"Because it may go lower and besides, we need to decide what to do with our 50k of stock," said Vinny.

"We don't have 50k in stock now. Ours is crashing along with everything else. We need to get out and fast," screamed Marge.

"No, let's just hold on. It will come back. It always does," offered Dolly.

And that's what they did. They followed Dolly's advice and held tight. But the stock market wasn't bouncing back, and they were hemorrhaging badly. Their initial investment of 12k, two years ago, worth 50k this morning, was now down to 38k. That is if they could find a buyer. With the market closing in less than half an hour, trading was still moving down. After-hour trading will continue for another couple of hours, but they were not sure after that. Will they be closed for the holiday and remain closed for the rest of the weekend giving everyone a time-out till Monday or?

Chapter 11

President Trump, just back from the G20 in Riyadh, the capital of Saudi Arabia, and his second historic meeting and weekend in Pyongyang North Korea with Kim jung-un, topping his historic walk into North Korea the year before, boarded Marine One at JFK Airport with Melania, and Barron along with their personal security detail, for their 30-minute flight to East Hampton for their 4th of July holiday weekend in Wolfhampton. It will be a visit that will forever change the president's life, America and the world.

Ten minutes into the flight, the president finished his McDonald's lunch and started tweeting.

Donald J Trump
@realDonaldTrump
I hope the people over at the Fed won't overreact and make yet another mistake. Also, don't let the market become any more volatile than it already is. Hold on. Will bounce back Monday, don't just go by meaningless numbers. Good luck!
11:30 AM - 3 July 2020

Looking at her husband with the phone in his hand Melania said, "Darling, please. We are officially on vacation."

"Not till we land," answered President Trump, but put the phone down anyway.

"Dad, does he have real wolves?" asked Barron.

"What? Who told you that?" asked Trump looking at his head security agent.

Secret Service Special Agent Michael Mick Collins, the president's head of security, just nodded and shook his head, yes, not wanting to commit verbally.

"Well if he does, they are in a cage, like in the zoo," said Trump, again looking towards Agent Collins who this time shook his head no and rolled his eyes.

"I'm sure they're well-trained," offered Melania.

The president looking to change the topic said, "Who should play me?"

Melania didn't understand the question at first, but Agent Collins ventured an opinion. "Not Baldwin — He's a fookin' eejit." Adding the last part in a heavy Dublin brogue hopefully unrecognizable to Melania and Barron.

"Of course, he is, and he's not funny. His dying mediocre career was saved by his terrible impersonation of me on SNL. Now he says playing me was agony. It was agony for those who were forced to watch. They should bring back Darrell Hammond, funnier and a far greater talent!

I'll tell you who should play me. Christopher Walken that's who," said Trump.

"Who's Christopher Walken?" asked Melania.

"He's an Academy Award-winning actor. *Deer Hunter*, *The Dogs of War*, *King of New York*. A lot of big films. He was born in Queens just a few miles from Mr. Trump and even speaks like him and has the same accent," offered Collins.

"It's called speech elocution," offered 14-year-old Barron, "a style or manner of speaking. Fookin' eejit," mumbled Barron looking towards Collins.

Barron didn't like Collins. He thought Collins condescending, crude and felt he treated him like a child. He had his own dedicated security detail who accompanied him to school and such but had to put up with Collins when he was traveling with his mom and dad. He was constantly trying to get a one-up on Collins and give him the slip.

Trump shook his head but let it go, "Right. As Mick said, we're both from Queens and about the same age and we grew up in the '50s. His family is from Scotland and Germany like mine. Plus, he kind of favors me, if he fixed his stupid hair."

"So, you're thinking of a movie about your presidency?" asked Melania.

"No, the whole thing, soup to nuts, like Lincoln or Kennedy. We'll get Tony Schwartz who helped me write *The Art of the Deal*. Get Clint Eastwood to direct it. It will be huge," said Trump.

"So, who would play you when you were first starting out, and who would play me?" asked Melania.

"I think DiCaprio for the younger me then Walken later. Anyway, you know you could play yourself, and maybe I should play myself — wouldn't that be something both of us getting Academy Awards for best actor and best actress?"

Chapter 12

Tom Halsey was sitting outside having lunch with Michael Denison at Bobby Van's in Bridgehampton, about the same time Trump was approaching East Hampton Airport aboard Marine One.

The restaurant tables outside started to vibrate "What the hell!" exclaimed Denison just as he finished taking a bite of his burger.

"It's Marine One on approach," volunteered Halsey then took a bite of his turkey club.

"Jesus that's loud. No wonder we get so many noise complaints. You must be used to that after Afghanistan."

"Yeah, I've been on a few choppers, not that model, but yeah. You got the vid?"

Denison took a sip of his Coke, then reached into his pocket and pulled out his cell phone, fiddled with it then turned the screen towards Halsey. The vid was in black and white and no sound, and Denison didn't bother to provide color. He just let Halsey watch it.

"What reminds you of the war? Backfires, guns?" asked Denison while Halsey was watching the vid.

"No nothing like that, more like the smells of dirt, diesel fuel, the sound of helicopters and that," answered Halsey pointing to what Denison was drinking.

"Coke?"

"Yeah Coke, but in a can."

"My uncle used to say the same thing about Vietnam, only the coke was in a bottle then," offered Denison.

"Nothing really changed since Vietnam. 'Same, same.'" said Halsey. "Again. I want to see it again."

Denison turned the screen back towards himself, touched the screen and returned it to Halsey.

Halsey watched the store security camera film show Dmitriy Volkov arguing with the two girls, Olivia and Zoe. He was attempting to grab Zoe when Olivia seemed to push his hand away. Volkov appeared to be yelling.

"Wow," said Halsey, "that's a smoking gun." The camera barely captures his face but no sound. "Too bad we can't hear what they're saying."

"I might be able to do something about that if I can. I'll text you later," said Denison.

"Do they know you made a copy?"

"No, and they seemed to have lost the original."

"E-mail me a copy then delete yours; that way you can claim plausible deniability if they ask."

State police motorcycle cops were flying up and down the street right in front of them closing off side streets, while tow trucks towed away parked cars whose owners neglected to heed the "No Parking Today" signs. The sound of sirens could be heard in the distance getting closer.

"We got front row seats," said Denison, "too bad my shift starts in about an hour. I have to go get in uniform."

Halsey told Denison to take off and that he would pick up the check.

After Denison left, Halsey checked to make sure he received the incriminating vid, got up from the table and started to leave when his cell rang. He looked at the caller ID, smiled and set down again. It was Abby Adams, his on and off girlfriend.

Abby's parents have a house on Gin Lane in Southampton Village. Abby works on Wall Street and comes out whenever she gets the chance — whether her parents are there or not. Abby, like Tom Halsey, is a runner and they run together, train together and run marathons together whenever their schedules permit. Abby, a few years younger and a few inches shorter than Halsey, is a trim, surfer girl, no need for make-up beauty, with long natural dusty blonde hair, a few freckles, and smart. They also fit in sex whenever they can.

"Hi, Tommy. Got a minute?" asked Abby.

"Yeah. You coming out?"

"That's why I'm calling. Any chance you can get us on the guestlist for the big cocktail party tonight at Volkov's?"

"Why do you care? You're not a Trump fan."

"I don't and I'm not, but Willy Geist, a friend on Morning Joe, is looking to hook up with a local reporter."

"I know who he is, and I can guess what kind of story they plan on doing. No thanks. Anyway I don't think that's going to happen. My editor tried, I tried, everybody tried, including the rags and tags from the city. Volkov's security is not letting anyone in, and Trump's Secret Service won't let any media near Wolfhall."

"What's all the noise?"

"Hold on. Trump's motorcade is coming by now. One second."

A half dozen motorcycles appeared leading and flanking the lead Secret Service Suburban. The presidential motorcade followed. Several black Suburbans came into view, then "The Beast," a huge black bullet and bomb-proof Cadillac shielding the 'First Family' from virtual harm, and actual reality. About 12 vehicles in all, including more security, healthcare, the press, and route-clearing vehicles. Small, as most presidential motorcades go, but they only had to go a few miles either way, and it's the Hamptons after all.

There were no cars parked in front of the restaurant and few pedestrians who bothered to interrupt their busy important schedules, to gawk. Just before 'The Beast' got to Bobby Van's, Halsey stood up, came to attention and saluted.

The motorcade slowed and stopped, not two doors down, from where he was standing, in front of the Candy Kitchen. Suburban doors opened and Secret Service agents started piling out up and down the motorcade. Halsey realized something must have happened and felt stupid standing there saluting like a boy scout. He lowered his hand and started looking up and down the street for the threat and was pissed because neither his Ranger nor reporter instincts kicked in and picked up on it. When he turned back to his left, he saw the president walking toward him.

"Oh shit," he whispered.

President Trump walked directly towards Halsey. He had a dark blue suit on with his signature red power tie, and at 6'-2" he was two inches taller than Halsey, but his girth made him seem like a huge man. He stopped directly in front of Halsey while his Secret Service agents formed a circle and stared intently at Halsey.

"Marine or Ranger?" asked Trump.

"75th Ranger Regiment. Tom Halsey, sir," said Halsey as he saluted again.

President Trump returned the salute and said, "I had an opportunity to study a lot of men in uniform lately and the way they salute kind of gives them away. You still in?"

"No, sir. Two tours in Afghanistan, got out about five years ago. I'm a reporter for the *Wolfhampton Press* now."

President Trump turned and looked at an aid standing close by and asked, "Fake news?"

The aid answered, "The *Wolfhampton Press* is pretty much down the middle."

Turning back to Halsey he asked, "You covering my visit?"

"Yes and no, sir."

Dozens of reporters and film crews jumped off the press van and were now recording the president's and Halsey's interaction.

"What exactly does that mean?"

"It means sir, I intend to write about your visit, but we tried to get an invite, but were not able to get inside or even near the estate. I have some sources, so I'll put something together."

"See all these reporters?" Trump said, turning and pointed at the gaggle of reporter and camera crews now surrounding them, "well none of them, except for those guys," pointing to the White House and Fox crews, "are getting near Wolfhall either. They're fake news. Are you fake news 'Ranger Reporter Halsey?'"

"I call it as I see it, Mr. President."

"Does that mean you'll tell and report the truth?"

"I don't have an agenda if that's what you're asking, Mr. President."

"Can I ask you another question and will you tell me the truth?"

"Yes, sir. Rangers don't lie," said Halsey immediately regretting his childish reply.

"I'm not worried about the Rangers, it's the reporter in you that I'm worried about. Did you vote for me?"

"I did not sir."

"But you saluted me when I went by."

"I saluted the flag on your car fender and the office of the president, sir."

President Trump smiled and said, "I like you 'Ranger Reporter Halsey'. How would you like to be the only reporter allowed full access to me for this entire weekend?"

"Uncensored, sir?"

"As long as you tell the truth."

"So help me God."

President Trump laughed put out his hand which was accepted. "See you at Wolfhall tonight for dinner. You married or have a girlfriend?"

"No, sir. Well…"

"Well bring a date or one will be provided," interrupted President Trump with a wink, then he turned and headed back towards his ride.

Tom Halsey was immediately mobbed by reporters, heard static distant yelling, and ducked into Bobby Van's, where the door was then closed and blocked by the maître d'. The yelling was now louder when Halsey remembered he left his phone on, and who was on the other end.

"Thomas Halsey, what do you mean you don't have a girlfriend? What am I?"

"You heard that?"

"I heard it all, Mr. Ranger Reporter."

"You're my girlfriend?"

"Yes."

"How fast can you get out here?"

"In a limo now and on my way."

"What should I wear?" asked Halsey.

"Your usual. Khakis, polo shirt, Topsiders, and blazar for tomorrow, but tonight for dinner, a black suit."

Halsey looked up at the TV above the back bar and watched a *CNN* 'Breaking News' clip of himself talking with the president outside just minutes before in his khakis, polo shirt, Topsiders, and blazar. *Abby must be watching the same channel*, he thought.

The consensus from the mainstream reporters present seemed to be that this guy was just some local yokel reporter who wouldn't know what to do with a real story. That hurt but he continued watching the TV as President Trump got into the big black Cadillac. Halsey caught a glimpse of Melania and thought, *there goes Beauty and the Beast.*

Chapter 13

Back in the Beast, Melania asked, "Donald, can we please just get there?"

Trump looked directly across the salon at his head of security, Secret Service Special Agent Mick Collins, sitting next to Barron and said, "Mick."

"Yes, boss?"

"Put a tail on Ranger Reporter Halsey. Check him out, and if he's a good guy let him in."

He turned back to Melania, "We'll be there in a few minutes." He then took out his phone and speed-dialed White House Chief of Staff Mick Mulvaney, "Mick get Mnuchin, Kudlow, Coats, and Haspel on the line and get right back to me."

After a minute Mulvaney was back on with Secretary of the Treasury Steve Mnuchin, National Economic Council Director Larry Kudlow, Director of National Intelligence Daniel Coats, and Central Intelligence Agency Director Gina Haspel.

"What the hell is going on Steve?" asked Trump.

"Mr. President, we're still in a downward spiral despite good economic news. Investors worldwide seem to be feeding on disinformation."

"We're in a near panic mode," interrupted Larry Kudlow. "We close in a few hours, but with after-hour trading, we..."

"Mr. President," continued Mnuchin, "we are in big trouble. No one is buying. Not even Chinese bottom feeders."

"Okay. Let's close the market today at 4 pm and halt all after-hour trading. Keep it closed for the entire 4th weekend and open it Monday. Get the exchange president, what's her name?"

"Stacey Cunningham." replied Kudlow.

"Get her on board and tell her to make the call. Calm the market or some such bullshit, but get it done so we can open fresh on Monday. Dan and Gina, are you on?"

"Yes, Mr. President," they both acknowledged.

"We had better have all this sorted out, or we're gonna have a lot of pissed off ex-billionaires and 401k holders up our asses."

"Were on it," said Haspel, "but we're being hunted. Both Russia and China are hacking us."

"Tell me something I don't know. You two got four more days to turn it around. There is but one rule?"

"Mr. President?"

"A great man once said, 'There is but one rule, hunt or be hunted.'"

"Darwin?" suggested Haspel hoping Trump was finally broadening his horizons.

"No. Frank Underwood, House of Cards — Mick, you get my tweet?"

"Yes, Mr. President."

"You know what to do."

"On it, Mr. President," answered his COS Mick Mulvaney.

Ten minutes later, the motorcade pulled up to Wolfhall's main gate and rolled right through, all except for two vehicles containing the press. It seemed like a quarter-mile drive up to the circular drive, and what they saw as they arrived impressed even the president. Wolfhall was a huge rambling Gothic castle with stone walls, turrets, and dozens of chimneys, perched precariously on a cliff overlooking the Atlantic Ocean. They drove into and under a massive stone porte-cochere, stopped and doors started opening. The visible protection detail, not the hidden sniper's hundreds of yards away, all jumped out of their Suburban's, surrounded the Beast and gave an all-clear before Collins opened the door, got out, satisfied himself that all was secure then signaled the family out.

Barron smiling, and seemingly enjoying the outing said, "Dad, this looks like a Tod Browning movie."

"What?"

"You know. Bela Lugosi?"

"Who?"

"For God's sakes Dad, Dracula!"

"Oh yeah, the movie. Melania, you must feel at home here."

"What on earth are you talking about, Donald?"

"You know. Being from where you're from and all."

"You mean Slovenia."

"Slovenia, Romania, Transylvania aren't they all the same?"

Not knowing if her husband was joking or just plain ignorant, Melania said, "You know Donald, I wonder about you sometimes."

"Let's go meet the count," said the president.

Standing at the top of the entrance steps, Dmitriy Volkov and his girl-friend, Riana Yale, a young Christie Brinkley clone, a top Ford model with long blond hair, sparkling blue eyes, trim, young and beautiful; very young and very beautiful. Volkov tells everyone she's 20 but she looks 17.

They walk together down the stone steps, which were larger and wider than those of the White House, to meet and greet the President of the United States, The First Lady, and the Third Son.

"President Trump, First Lady Melania, Barron, welcome to Wolfhall," said Volkov.

"My God Dmitriy. I thought Mar-a-Lago was big; this is just plain huge. You know I built a castle once in Atlantic City, Trump Castle; but mine had electricity not candles," said President Trump with a big laugh.

The President and Volkov shook hands and embraced. Then Volkov shook hands with Melania, followed by air kisses. Volkov then introduced Riana; the president introduced Barron, and more handshakes ensued. With no mainstream media, and only a small White House and *Fox* crew, the atmosphere was very casual; but if one didn't know better, one might mistake Volkov and Melania as a couple, and Trump, Riana, and Barron as a dad with his two kids.

The president's security detail had done their final preliminary sweep of Wolfhall, the guest house, and grounds. Collins, the head of the president's security detail along with Colonel Galkin, head of Volkov's security, followed Volkov and his guests inside.

They walked into an enormous hall the size of a football field with a fireplace as large a Manhattan one bedroom. Volkov led his guests towards a roaring fireplace, which in this huge hall with the air conditioner on full blast, did not seem weird or warm. Defining the fireplace was a beautiful large brass fireplace fender, anchored by two huge wolf sculptures.

Barron stopped in his tracks when he realized that the sculptures were watching him. A moment later, Collins realized it too and stepped in front of the president and started to draw his SIG Sauer until Volkov intervened, "Agent Collins, there is no need for concern. Hammer and Sickle are Siberian wolves, well-trained and well-behaved."

When they turned back, Barron had approached closer and was within five feet of Hammer.

"Barron," barked Volkov, "'Doveryai, no proveryai.'"

Barron stopped in his tracks and looked back at Volkov.

"It's a Russian proverb…" said Volkov.

"I am aware of the proverb Mr. Volkov," interrupted Barron, who also speaks Slovene and Russian, "but I don't sense fear or aggressiveness from either Hammer or Sickle."

The tension broke when two waiters brought in flutes of champagne, sparkling water and one with Diet Coke.

"To good weather, a good foursome this afternoon and tomorrow, and to good friends," said Volkov after the flutes were in hand.

Barron held up his flute of sparkling water and added, "'Trust but verify.'"

He may be useful after all, thought Volkov.

My handsome, brilliant son, thought Melania.

They teach Russian in school now? thought Trump.

Smartass, thought Galkin, and Collins.

Chapter 14

"Tommy, this is Karen Dunn. She's an old friend of mine and has worked on several cases with the Suffolk County Police Department."

"Nice to meet you, Karen. Is being called a lip reader 'PC' nowadays?" asked Halsey.

"Speech reader, lip reader, same thing," replied Karen.

"Ready?" asked Halsey.

Denison dimmed the lights in the *Wolfhampton Press* conference room and turned towards the large wall-mounted plasma TV. An enhanced version of the store exterior surveillance camera vid showing the confrontation between Volkov and the two girls, Olivia and Zoe, appeared.

Karen watched and took notes as the store security camera vid showed Dmitriy Volkov arguing with the two girls, Olivia and Zoe. She watched Volkov try to grab Zoe while Olivia pushes his hand away. Karen watched as Volkov appeared to be yelling. The entire recording lasted less than a minute, and Karen asked for several replays, then asked for several more zooming in on Volkov's face.

"Okay, I think I got it. The two girls are Olivia and Zoe, right?"

"Right. Olivia is in jeans and Zoe has a skirt over tights," answered Denison.

"He says to the girls, 'Calm down.' Zoe says, 'Calm down? You shit. You bailed on us, and want us to calm down?' He reaches for Zoe and Olivia pushes him away saying, 'Haven't you hurt us enough? We're gonna go to the cops. You promised us.' He starts to yell, 'You ungrateful little bitches. I'm not your daddy. No one will believe you, so you better get abortions, or you'll be sorry. I don't want to see your sorry asses again, and if you go to the cops, you're dead,'" revealed Karen.

"Holy shit," said Halsey.

"Are you sure?" asked Denison.

"I'm positive," answered Karen.

"How can you be so sure?" asked Denison.

"Ah… because there is no way that these tire marks were made by a '64 Buick Skylark convertible. These marks were made by a 1963 Pontiac Tempest?"

"What?" asked Halsey.

Karen looked at Denison and they both laughed, "I'm sorry," she said, "I just thought we were doing a My Cousin Vinny bit."

"What?" asked Halsey again.

"Nothing — not important. What I lip read from this vid is what I just told you. I'm positive," said Karen.

"Jesus, Denison," said Halsey, "will this hold up in court? I mean is a lip reader like a lie detector test or better?"

"Karen?" asked Denison.

"It's a science and admissible in court, but it doesn't always hold up."

"Why?"

"Because the defense will usually counter with their own lip reader who will come up with a different read."

Halsey thanked Denison and Karen and promised to keep both their names out of the paper. Denison drove Karen home while Halsey headed to his apartment on Main Street to change before he met Abby. A black Suburban followed him.

It was 5 pm by the time Halsey pulled up in front of Abby's parents' home on Gin Lane; an hour before they were expected at Wolfhall. Abby had stopped at her parents' house to change into a black cocktail dress. Halsey had changed into a black suit, white button-down shirt, and black and silver rep tie. His khakis, polo shirt, Topsiders, blazer, underwear, and dob kit were in his overnight.

"You look terrific," said Halsey.

"You scrub up pretty well yourself, Mr. Ranger Reporter," said Abby as she came forward and gave him a hug and a kiss.

"Are your parents' home?"

"We can catch up after dinner if that's what you mean."

"Should we bring anything?" asked Halsey.

"You mean like a bottle of wine or Lysol disinfectant wipes?" asked Abby.

"True, and after what I'm about to tell you we'll need plenty of both."

They walked over to Halsey's black Range Rover, got in and headed east to Wolfhampton. Halsey watched as the black Suburban followed. The usual summer traffic on 27, the only two-lane highway east-west on the Southfork was bumper to bumper. Because the president was in town the normal summer five-mile 30-minute drive would now take an hour.

"Have you heard about the two young girls who committed suicide?" asked Halsey as they waited in traffic.

"From my parents, and there was something on Page Six in the *Post*. So young and so sad. Both pregnant. Where were the shithead fathers when the girls needed them?"

"Fathers? How about singular?"

"You mean one shithead got both girls pregnant and left them to what, take care of it themselves?"

"Yeah."

Just then a loud chirping sound came from behind them. Halsey looked through his rear-view mirror while Abby turned around.

"What the hell!" exclaimed Abby.

A black Suburban with flashing light bars pulled into oncoming traffic alongside Halsey's Range Rover, the passenger's window rolled down, and a man indicated for Halsey to do the same.

"Follow us," was all the man said.

Halsey pulled out of the stalled eastbound traffic and followed the black Secret Service Suburban with light bars flashing and blaring siren into the head-on traffic at an almost reckless speed. Cars were ditching into the shoulder to get out of the way.

"I'm impressed, and I can just see the headlines. 'Local reporter gets Secret Service escort to meet the president.'"

"And the shithead," added Halsey.

Chapter 15

Their hour drive which, would normally take 30 summer minutes, now took only 20. State and Suffix County police cars were all along the highway attempting to keep traffic moving and seeing another black Suburban chirping with flashing light bars to and from Wolfhampton was not unusual. Not unusual but a real pain in the ass for anyone trying to get from Southampton to East Hampton.

"So, the president's host for the weekend is the shithead — pedophile — rapist?" asked Abby.

"Add Russian billionaire and that about sums him up," answered Halsey.

"The president knows this."

"I don't think so. Volkov made sure the story and evidence never went anywhere. The suicides happened in Wolfhampton and he owns the village police."

"Does he own your paper?"

"I don't think so. At least I haven't been told to stop. My boss knows I'm working on it and that I have a vid of all three of them together. He's hoping that my getting this invite for the weekend party will open more leads. I've also talked to the girls' parents who are clueless, but Olivia and Zoe's siblings and friends know something but won't talk. They're scared to death of someone, and that someone has a lot of power."

"Anything interesting?"

"Yeah. Our boy has been busy. Apparently, there are more girls — many more."

"You have been busy. There is more action out here than in the city."

"Speaking of the city, how are things on Wall Street?"

"I'm just on the legal side but have never seen it this bad. If the windows weren't sealed, traders and investors would be jumping. They closed the exchange for the entire holiday weekend to stop further hemorrhaging. That's the main reason Willy Geist called. He needs someone inside; a fly on the wall with Trump and the Russian."

"If you think I'm gonna be 'Deep Throat' for Morning Joe, you're sadly mistaking."

"Never thought you would, but here we are, aren't we? – having dinner with the First Family."

"And?"

"And, I was listening to this online show the other day called *Redacted Tonight* with Lee Camp and a guy named Tan Liu making a case that the stock market is nothing but a 'Ponzi Scheme.' I got a lot from Champ and Liu, and I believe these guys. He says, and I agree, that the exchange is the central nervous system of our economy, and it's estimated worth is around $30 trillion. And I know that when it tanks, the lives of millions of Americans are wrecked, ruined and upended. I know that when that happens, the powerful millionaires and billionaires who caused the destruction, grab their money first and make a run for it," said Abby.

"I have a 401k, and I'm worried the entire thing is a gigantic fraud. My parents are mildly invested, but they say it will come back. It always does," said Halsey.

"That's what Bernie Madoff thought," said Abby.

"Right. The money you, me, and all the little guys make from stocks, if we make money, is coming from other investors pumping new money in, and if there aren't any new investors willing to buy your stock, then we're all just screwed," offered Halsey.

"I don't have any problem with gambling. If you want to gamble at a casino, then gamble your little heart out. Stay up all night until you're on your taped out. The house always wins, but yeah go for it. But at least the casinos are honest with you and tell you it's gambling," added Abby.

"I lost 50k to Madoff through a feeder fund. I got most of it clawed back from multiple account investors, but the whole thing scared the shit out of me, and I took what little I had left and put it under the mattress," said Halsey.

"Someone's spreading a lot of bad news and misinformation on social and mainstream media and people are listening. Whoa! I think we're almost there," said Abby.

A 'Rally to Save America, Stop Hate', a peaceful protest event, hosted by Progressive East End Reformers/NYPAN, was gathered on the Water Mill Green yelling and flashing signs at motorists as they passed by. Other groups included: Centro Corazon De Maria, East End Action Network, East End Women for Change, Indivisible North Fork, Let's Visit Lee Zeldin, Long Island Activists, Long Island Network for Change, NY 2nd Democrats, NISI: Neighbors in Support of Immigrants, Resist and Replace, ShowUpLI, Suffolk Progressives, and Together We Will LI joined the rally. Antifa, a left-wing, autonomous, militant anti-fascist group was there also, but did not see the president's visit as 'a peaceful protest event.'

After passing the protesters, they entered the small village of Wolfhampton and at the light, which was recently installed and timed to benefit locals, turned right onto a narrow lane framed with nothing but 10-foot-high hedges, white driveway gates, and herringbone cobblestone aprons. It took almost another 10 minutes to get through the crowds of reporters and TV satellite trucks.

"Slow down," said Abby as they came abreast of the *MSMBC* truck. Reporters started to converge on them as their guiding Suburban put it in reverse and headed back to rescue them.

Abby rolled down the passenger window and saw Willy Geist and a producer approaching.

"Abby, what the hell?" asked a surprised Geist.

"I didn't get a chance to tell you we got invited but wanted to stop and say thanks for reaching out. I owe you."

With that, she rolled the window up and Halsey gunned it to the surprise of his escort, who quickly reversed his direction and led Halsey's Range Rover through the now open estate gate as Abby watched, in her side-view mirror, Willy Geist become the story.

Chapter 16

They pulled up under the huge portico, sat there and took it all in.

"My God. Are you seeing what I'm seeing?" asked Abby.

Halsey had seen it before, at least from the beach, as a kid before they put all the no-access laws in place and was busy checking his *Circa News* feed on his iPhone.

> *Circa News-Market continues to plunge overseas despite the halt in US trading. No buyers in site while President Trump spends the 4th in Wolfhampton with his Russian pal.*

> *Circa News-Wolfhampton Press reporter Tom Halsey is new best friends with President Trump gets Secret Service escort to the dinner party.*

> *Circa News-Wolfhampton girls' double suicides linked to President Trump's weekend host. Unconfirmed source...*

Halsey didn't need to finish reading the last blurb; he knew what it said. He was, after all, the source. He fringed amazement to Abby's take on the place and answered. "Wow." He put away his phone, reached for the door handle and thought about the three news blurbs he just read. '*...two out of three ain't bad' according to Meat Loaf.*

"Wow is right!" said Abby, "This place is something else. It looks like Harry Potter's Hogwarts school. Can't wait to see inside."

They opened their doors and stepped out onto the Versailles like pea stone driveway. From all directions, Secret Service agents appeared. One took the Range Rover away; two others asked if they would agree to a wand search. Halsey was an approved reporter, so he was allowed to keep his phone. Abby objected, but was relieved of hers. From different hidden observation ports, Volkov's head of security Colonel Galkin, Wolfhampton Police Chief Ed Daly, Secret Service Special Agent Michael Mick Collins, and Kahbib Nurmodov — all exceptionally dangerous men, secretly watched their prey. When cleared, Abby and Halsey were escorted up the steep white steps and into the deep dark past.

A set of huge doors open; and then they were escorted down a long hallway into a magnificent hall with stone and wood parquet floors and 30 foot ribbed and groined vaulted ceiling. A massive crystal chandelier with LED flickering bulbs, imitating gaslighting, added a turn of the century ambiance. As they entered, they were announced.

"How did they get my name? Did you tell them?"

"The president said, 'bring a date,' so I did. His SS must have taped my phone while the president and I were talking earlier today outside Bobby Van's."

"Wow," said Halsey, this time meaning it. There were about a dozen couples in dinner attire, scattered throughout, with the president and first lady holding court by the roaring fire. The president, tanned as always, was also wearing a black suit, black and silver rep tie, but with a flyaway collar white shirt. He must have heard Halsey had arrived, because a waiter came over, offered drinks, and directed them to join the president.

As they walked over towards the president and first lady Abby said, "She's more than beautiful; she's gorgeous."

"Glad you could make it, Mr. Halsey," said the president, reaching out his hand to welcome his guest, "my wife Melania."

"Mr. President - Mrs. First Lady," said Halsey, with a head bow to Melania, "may I introduce Abigale Adams."

Abby seemed overwhelmed, not at all by the present company, but by the huge hall and over-the-top Gothic architecture. The president took her wide-eyed amazement for that of a star-struck kid and offered her his hand while the first lady smiled and nodded.

"Welcome, Abigale," said the president with his charming smile and wink in an effort to ease her misinterpreted anxiety, "where are you from?"

"Manhattan, Mr. President, but originally Weymouth Mass."

"What do you do in the city?"

"I work on Wall Street, Mr. President."

"Well, Abigale, looks like you're in the middle of this whole stock market mess."

"Yes, Mr. President, but please call me Abby."

"I was going to say Abigale is a funny name. I don't believe I ever knew an Abigale."

"My parents felt compelled to name me after my ancestor's wife."

"Oh," said President Trump, seemingly not grasping the magnitude of what Abby just said.

Melania, however, got it and whisked Abby away to hear all about her family. It seemed to go right over Trump's head as he looked at Halsey and asked, "You gonna do the right thing by me?"

"Mr. President, do you mean am I going to tell the truth? Give me a good story and I'll write it. If not, I'll end up doing a puff piece on Mr. Volkov and Wolfhall for *Architectural Digest*."

The president chuckled, put his hand on Halsey's shoulder and said, "I like you Mr. Ranger Reporter." And on cue, Dmitriy Volkov stealthily appeared behind Halsey.

"And this must be our famous *Wolfhampton Press* reporter Thomas Halsey."

Halsey turned to see Volkov smiling and dressed completely in black looking eerily like the late Karl Lagerfeld. Beside Volkov was a very pretty and very young girl. Behind Volker was a handler with Hammer and Sickle in the sit command. Many guests now gathered round to see

President Trump, their host Dmitriy Volker, Lolita, Hammer and Sickle, and Halsey.

Mick Collins was at the president's side as always, but Police Chief Daly and Kahbib Nurmodov remained in the shadows.

In lieu of offering his hand, Volkov bowed from the waist. If Volkov was waiting for a reaction to his performance, he didn't get one. Halsey just looked at him and the young girl but said nothing as The First Lady and Abby, now accompanied by Barron, rejoin the group.

If Volkov took an affront to Halsey's coolness he didn't show it. "I hope you will stay and join us for dinner Mr. Halsey, and perhaps on the golf course tomorrow."

"Thank you, Mr. Volkov," said Halsey feeling Abby's hand insert itself around his arm, "Abby and I are looking forward to dinner tonight but I'm not much of a golfer. Perhaps you'll allow us to ramble through Wolfhall tomorrow. We're both architectural buffs and would love to do a photoshoot for *Architectural Digest*," Turning to the president and adding, "unless something better comes along."

"Nothing better's gonna come along," said Trump "unless my tee shot tomorrow inadvertently beans Jim Acosta in the fookin head," said Trump with a big smile.

Colonel Galkin seemed to have something important to tell his boss and tried to get his attention, but Volkov was on a roll and waved him off.

"Now there's the rub," said Volkov laughing and placing his hand on his head imitating Acosta in pain.

Everyone but Halsey seemed to find this funny. "Interesting choice of words Mr. Volkov," said Halsey.

Volkov stopped his pantomime. "Excuse me?"

"'There's the rub,' isn't that from Shakespeare's Hamlet where he reflects on the possibility of suicide as a means to an easy end?"

"What's your point, Mr. Halsey?" asked Volkov with fire in his eyes.

"Suicide," said Halsey.

Trump had been briefed a few minutes earlier about Volkov's possible connection to a double suicide involving two young girls. But apparently, Volkov hadn't yet gotten the message. Colonel Galkin wasn't persistent enough. Trump, however, saw the hatred in Volkov's eyes and knew Halsey now had his story and he now had Volkov by the balls.

Volkov abruptly broke off the conversation and left the hall followed by his entourage - President Trump gave Halsey a wink. Abby, into Halsey's ear, whispered "Shakespeare?" Halsey whispered back, "John Adams?" Kahbib Nurmodov pulled out his cell phone and punched the speed dial for Pale Moth. Then the lights began to flicker on and off.

Chapter 17

MOSCOW

Vladimir Putin aka Pale Moth had just finished addressing the nation. His message to the United States and to President Trump was direct and powerful. "Moscow will match any United States move to deploy new nuclear missiles closer to Russia by stationing own missiles closer to the United States and by deploying faster more powerful missiles."

It had been a long day for Putin. After a long previous night, he rose late in the morning and played with his badly-behaved dogs, a black Labrador named Konni, an Akita named Yume, and a Karakachan named Buffy. He took breakfast around noon which consisted of a big bowl of porridge, with some quail eggs and fruit juice on the side and coffee.

After breakfast, he exercised starting with a two-hour swim, then an hour lifting weights in the gym. He showered, put on his black Brioni with a white shirt and dark tie, headed to his office in the Kremlin, and sat down at his desk to begin reading briefing notes a little after 4 pm. These included reports on domestic intelligence and foreign affairs, as well as clips from the Russian press and the international media and the ongoing investigation into alleged collusion with President Donald Trump's campaign. He worked into 'the cold hours where everything is clearer.'

Putin, like he nemesis Trump, and unlike former President Boris Yeltsin, abstains from alcohol except for formal receptions. Projecting the optic of teetotaler helped his political image.

Just after 10 pm, Putin asked, "Where are we?"

Ministry of Finance Siluanov began, "Comrade Putin, our disinformation rolled out on their social media and echoed by their mass media is beyond successful. Their stock market is all doom and gloom. Everyone including Europe is tumbling over themselves to sell. Everyone, that is, except China and Mother Russia. The New York Ponzi Exchange is sinking quickly. When their markets open Monday morning, it will be a disaster."

Foreign Intelligence SVR Director Naryshkin concurred adding, "Comrade Putin, the lights on Long Island have started to trip thanks to our RBN cybercrime group, and China's PLA Unit 61398 cyber warfare force. They hacked into the main power station in Northport and smaller sub-stations in Southampton and Bridgehampton and halted the flow of natural gas which fuel emergency generators. Tonight, we'll turn them off for a few hours then turn them back on. In Wolfhampton we'll turn them off for good and leave Trump and Volkov in the dark. We'll leave the power to the rest of Long Island and Manhattan on, so they can all watch the fireworks Monday, as their economy collapses."

"Excellent," said Putin. "Then the Trump boy. As Comrade Trotsky famously divined, 'When one runs with the wolves, one must howl with the pack.'"

Chapter 18

Barron Trump was in heaven. He loved the castle, the wolves, and was fascinated by Riana Yale, whom he assumed was Volkova's daughter but was about to learn otherwise.

Barron at 14 was just over 6', and Riana, who looked to be only a few years older, were talking when Halsey walked over and introduced himself.

"Good evening and excuse me. I'm Tom Halsey with the *Wolfhampton Press*; mind if I ask you a few questions and take some notes?"

Riana started to walk away, thinking the reporter wanted to talk to the president's son.

"Please don't go," said Halsey, "It's you I would like to talk to."

Riana stopped, but then Barron turned and excused himself.

Halsey asked if he would stay knowing that it would seem more appropriate to be seen with the two of them. Security for both was near but did not interfere.

Barron knew what the media was capable of, but also knew his father somehow trusted this man, so he stayed.

"I am doing an article about the party and the guests and would love to include something about you. May I have a photo of you both together?" He snapped a photo with his phone, then asked, "You're Riana Yale, correct?' Riana nodded. "And may I ask how long you have known Mr. Volkov?"

"We have been dating for a while."

Barron did a double take, but it went unnoticed.

"You're very lovely. Are you a model? And may I ask your age?"

"I'm with Ford and I'm 20."

"Lovely. I take it you're from the city?"

"Yes, I go to Convent of the…"

She stopped abruptly when she realized she said too much and when she noticed her security handler giving her a hard stare.

"I'm sorry Mr. Halsey, but I really have to go," said Riana and walked away.

"That went well," said Barron.

"Yes, I seem to have the same effect on certain people. I'm better around guys and thanks for sticking around. By the way. How does one address the president's son?"

"Mr. Trump or Barron. I prefer the latter," adding, "She's nice, but too young for Mr. Volkov."

"Barron, you have no idea," stated Halsey.

"I think I do, Mr. Halsey. I read your article."

Agent Collins stepped a bit closer.

"What's with him?" asked Halsey nodding towards a man he remembered seeing earlier with the president.

"He's a fookin eejit," said Barron.

Just then the dinner bell rang, and the guests began heading towards the dining room.

"May I have a copy of the photo?" asked Barron.

"Sure. What's your email or phone number?"

Just then Halsey's phone pinged, and Barron's cell phone number appeared on his screen.

"How did you do that?" asked Halsey.

"You need to be more careful Mr. Halsey; you left your Bluetooth on."

Chapter 19

The lights flickered again giving the room, a huge glass greenhouse dining hall reminiscent of London's King's Cross Train Station, a scripted Hollywood effect. Every surface that wasn't marble was carved polished mahogany bookcases or walls displaying 19th-century paintings, cavalry kits, and accouterment. Magnificent, cut-glass chandeliers cast a golden sheen across the wood parquet floor.

It was close to 8 pm and the guests began searching the 40-foot-long dining room table for their seating place cards when a bright flash of lightning illuminated the large room, followed shortly by a loud crash of thunder. A pelting rain signaled a summer storm that came rolling in from the Atlantic.

The seating was formal and staggered, except for the host, his date and the guest of honor. Behind each guest was a personal waiter dressed in formal black Victorian servant kit. Champagne, mineral water, and Coke were poured in anticipation of a toast. At the head of the table sat Dmitriy Volkov, to his left Riana and to his right Melania, Barron, President Trump, and Halsey. The rest of the guests including bankers, arms dealers, hedge fund managers, money launders, politicians, tech titans and their wives, husbands, and dates filled out the table. Abby was seated directly across from Halsey.

A clinking of metal on glass brought everyone's attention to the head of the table, Dmitriy Volkov.

"Mr. President, I would like to propose a toast to you and your family's good health and to the good health of this great country on this special holiday weekend."

A lot of hear-hears and cheers were sounded around the table.

President Trump, without missing a beat stood, raised his crystal Coke filled flute and added, "We made America great again. We made America wealthy again and with your help, I will win in 2020. We'll take back the House, retain the Senate and then we will 'Keep America Great.'" He sat down to more hear-hears and cheers.

Volkov and his guests liked President Trump's 2020 slogan 'Keep America Great'. He simply stood and said, "Na Zdorovie!"

"I thought it was Dostrovia," said President Trump to Halsey.

"It's actually nostrovia but that's a miss-pronunciation of Russian word na zdorovie," said Halsey.

"You sure? I could swear he said dostrovia."

"I heard na zdorovie?" said Halsey.

"No. Not him. I'm talking about Christopher Walken in The Deer Hunter. He said dostrovia. I'm thinkenabout having him play me in my movie. I'm also thinkenabout playing myself. What do you think?"

"What movie?"

President Trump apparently didn't care to elaborate and asked, "Hey, you got something on Volkov with those little girls? He didn't seem to appreciate your interrogation earlier. I saw it in his eyes; you hit a nerve. He's not good at hiding things — like me, especially when you get ambushed. He can't even hide his money. He got caught in that 'Panama Paper' thing and had to move his money to Cyprus. Then he got caught again in that 2015 Cyprus thing. Then, in 2016, the dumb fuck moved most of his money to India and lost his shirt in the India thing."

Halsey was lost on Trump's rambling, made a note about Volkov hiding money and instead asked, "How do you do it, Mr. President? How do you take all the negative press? The never-ending Mueller Investigation. Your detractors: Pelosi, Schumer, Schiff, and Blumenthal? Your turncoat Cohen. How do you not blow up?"

"The mainstream media has never been more dishonest. *NBC* and *MSNBC* are going crazy. They report stories, purposely, the exact opposite of the facts. They are truly the opposition party working with the Dems. May even be worse than fake news *CNN*, if that is possible.

"Senator Burr, Chairman of Senate Intelligence, said that after an almost two-year investigation, he saw no evidence of Russia collusion. No collusion!

"As far as High Tax and Nervous Nancy Pelosi, Crying Chuck Schumer, and Sleazy Buzz Schiff are concerned their all a bunch of losers— hypocrites. They make $174k a year yet they're all multi-millionaires. What does that tell you? And Da Nang Dick Blumenthal! I've spent more time in Vietnam than he did.

"Cohen is a lying lawyer — a disbarred lying lawyer, and now he's a disbarred lying lawyer in prison. Take a bullet my ass."

"Why do you keep calling on Acosta?"

Ignoring Halsey's question Trump said, "Halsey, are you related to Admiral Halsey?"

"My Grandfathers' cousin. I don't know what that makes me?"

"The Gallant Hours."

"Excuse me?"

"The movie, The Gallant Hours; back in the '60s. You're too young to remember. Good movie. Cagney did a great job playing your cousin Bull Halsey."

"I'm not sure he was my..."

President Trump cut him off, "Listen, my whole life has been heat. I like heat. Crazy Jim Acosta of Fake News *CNN* is unbelievably rude. I call on Crazy Jim because I've got this ongoing battle with *CNN*, and by calling on Acosta I get a chance to let everyone see the truth: that reporters are bad people, they're the enemy – and, just to prove it, look how obnoxious this guy Acosta is. He never disappoints.

"They all hate me. The Russia thing - it's all a hoax. Now they are coming after my presidential life, my business life and my personal life. God help them if they go after my family life. But I have lots of loyal people in the White House. You know everyone wants to work there. You know why? Because I make all the decisions."

"Apparently not everyone, Mr. President: Kelly, Haley, Sessions, Tillerson, Bannon, Scaramucci, Spicer, Flynn, Omarosa to name a few."

Before the president could respond or in spite of it, sheets of rain again began bearing down on the windows and glass ceiling followed by bright flashes of lightning then loud claps of thunder that made Hammer and Sickle skittish and guest dash to the windows to watch the stormy ocean waves crash against the cliff. Halsey excused himself and walked over to the far wall near Barron who was in deep conversation with Riana. The president and first lady were having an intimate moment when the lights flickered again, then went out, sending Hammer and Sickle into a howling frenzy over something unseen.

Chapter 20

Servants began lighting candles, supplementing those already on the dining table, while security tried to calm everyone down. Mick Collins and his agents were forming a circle around the president and first lady.

"What's going on?" asked the president.

"We need to move. We don't think the lights going out had anything to do with the storm. We're getting reports... Hold a second. Say again - Jesus Christ!" yelled Collins.

"What's wrong?" asked the president with Melania attempting to break out of the circle.

Collins in a clear voice said into his collar mic, "Blowtorch to Horsepower call in a code two. Mogul and Muse secure. Prince is missing. You copy?"

"Horsepower to Blowtorch, Lima Charley," was the New York office loud and clear reply. New York and Washington would soon be sending in the cavalry.

"We have to move, Mr. President," said Collins as he and several other agents began corralling the president and first lady towards a secured exit.

"Where is he? I'm not going anywhere till we find Barron," said President Trump.

"Where is my son?" demanded Melania.

"He probably ran to another room. We're searching now and we'll be bringing in more lights, but we have to get you out of here first."

"We're wasting time," said Melania as she and her husband pushed away and started searching for their son.

Halsey had been watching Volkov when the lights first flickered then went out, he saw him head for a door and decided to follow. It was dark but fortunately, there was a torch in its charger which he took with him. Down some steps to a landing, down more steps, through another door and down a long brick tunnel.

Halsey came to the end of the tunnel when Volkov stepped out in front of him. "You following me, Mr. Halsey?" asked Volkov.

"Yes," said Halsey.

"You think I snuck away so I could visit my teenage sex slaves in the dungeon?"

"Something like that."

"Then keep following me. Mr. Halsey and you might learn something or ..."

"Or end up in the dungeon?" interrupted Halsey.

"You're not my type and despite what you think you know nothing about me."

"I know enough and I'm learning more every day."

"Regardless Mr. Halsey I really don't care but since you're here I could use your assistance."

Volkov continued down another shorter tunnel, two torches now increased their visibility, Halsey followed cautiously until Volkov opened a large metal door that unsealed a large brick room with two huge pieces of equipment. Volkov then lit several vintage oil lanterns, enough for Halsey to see an amazing sight.

"Do you know what these are Mr. Halsey?"

"I'm guessing some sort of steam engines," said Halsey.

"Very good Mr. Halsey. They are not steam engines but much more. These are two Jumbo Dynamos, originally fired by coal, but my father updated the fuel supply to oil about fifty years ago before we had gas-fired backup generators installed. Each of these Jumbos produces about 1,100 kilowatts, for a direct current system capable of powering-up my entire estate. In fact, I could provide electricity for all Wolfhampton, but I won't."

"So, why didn't your emergency generators kick on?"

"Not sure, but I suspect foul play. Either someone sabotaged the system or they're not getting gas from the provider. I suspect the latter. Someone, I'm afraid, is messing with the utility companies providing our electric and gas."

"Why?"

"To embarrass President Trump, or something more sinister. Give me a minute, then I'll need your help starting these up."

Volkov turned a few valves, then hit a spark switch, and they heard the noise of fuel igniting. He repeated the process on the other Dynamo.

Shortly, steam started escaping from the first Dynamo and Volkov closed the valve. "Come over here and help me turn this flywheel."

After several turns, the flywheel started to turn by itself and they repeated the process on the second Dynamo.

"Let's give it a second or two."

"See this switch? Go find it on the other Dynamo and flick it when I say so."

Halsey did as directed, and on Volkov's say so they flicked the switches. Lights within the room started to flicker. Volkov made a few adjustments and the room lit up like Broadway.

"That should do it, Mr. Halsey. We best be returning to the party before Colonel Galkin and Agent Collins get worried."

Walking back through the tunnel Halsey asked, "Those Dynamos must have been installed before your grandfather's time."

"My grandfather said the original owners had them installed in '84."

"They still work. Whoever design, built and installed them must have known what they were doing."

"Yes, that's very true. My grandfather told me two men were responsible for most of the installation, a boss and his young assistant. They were here every day for two weeks — slept in the guest house. You might have heard of them. Two chaps — Edison and Tesla."

Chapter 21

The lights and air conditioner came back on and everyone and everything seemed to calm down; the guests, the wolves and the storm.

But the dining room was a mess. It looked more like a New Year's Eve party had just ended. Guests were scattered all over the room. Some had left, as did some of the servants, but Volkov's security and Collins team were rounding them up. Not long after they realized Barron was missing, it became clear that three more guests were unaccounted for. Riana, Volkov, and Halsey.

That cleared up a little when Volkov and Halsey came back into the dining room sandwiched between two agents who ran into them somewhere in the tunnel as they were returning. Meeting security put a halt to their conversation.

"I'll assume you want to finish this conversation later," said Volkov.

"You can count on it," answered Halsey.

"Where the Hell have you been Halsey?" asked Collins. Colonel Galkin knew better than to ask his boss. He suspected, when the lights came on, where he might have gone. No one else, not even Galkin or the head groundskeeper, had access to the Edison room and there was only a vague rumor of what was in the room.

"What did I miss?" asked Halsey as he watched more Secret Service agents coming in the dining room and the president and first lady running out.

"The young girl and Barron are missing. You didn't happen to see them on your travels?"

"They were both here together just before the lights went out. The room was full of guests, agents, and Volkov's security and staff. Where the Hell were you?" asked Halsey as Collins stormed away.

The agents assigned to watch over them were in the hot seat, especially Secret Service Agent Nora Pound assigned to Barron aka Prince. She had a lump on her head and said the last thing she remembers was the lights flickering on and off before her lights flickered out.

The president and first lady returned to join Collins, Volkov, and Halsey and were followed by a gaggle of agents. Collins was looking around the room with another agent holding an iPad.

"This is the wall that was painted," asked Collins.

"Painting? What do we care of painting? Find my son," demanded Melania.

Disregarding the first lady SAIC Bates answered "Yes. That entire wall above the wainscoting."

"Okay. Activate it and see if you got anything."

Agent Bates held his breath and clicked the on the button. The wall turned on. They stood there looking at an entire plasma TV wall with themselves looking back.

Colonel Galkin looked at Bates and said, "Impressive Agent Bates. You'll have to give me the name of your decorator."

"Take it back to before the lights went out," continued Collins.

Just like on a smart TV, Bates, who had originally set the wall to record mode shortly after it was painted, took them back in time to about five minutes before the power and lights went out. The wall froze then came alive with the sight and sounds of the storm, rain lightning and loud claps of thunder. Hammer and Sickle were by the fireplace growling, guests moving about the dining room reacting to the storm, Halsey was seen walking over to the far wall near where Barron was talking with Riana. The president and first lady were having a conversation.

"Freeze it," said Collins. "Can you zoom in on Barron and Riana?"

Bates did as directed and not far from the two kids, Agent Pound could be seen in the corner watching Barron, but there was someone watching Pound.

Bates zoomed in on the party crasher. Without hesitation, Colonel Galkin volunteered, "Kahbib Nurmodov."

"Where did he come from?" asked Collins.

Halsey recognized him as the throat cutter from town but thought it better to let Galkin sort it out.

Looking at Volkov for a nod before he proceeded, Colonel Galkin answered, "He's a guest."

"I thought he was part of your security," said Collins.

"Hardly," replied Colonel Galkin.

"Where is he? Is he here?" asked President Trump.

"He's not here. At least he's not in this room," said Colonel Galkin.

"Do a screenshot and get it to everyone. Find him," ordered Collins.

"What the hell is all this bullshit? We're watching TV instead of looking for my son," said the despondent father and president.

"Boss, the house is sealed off. The property is sealed off. The Hamptons are sealed off. I have Secret Service and state and local police swarming all over Wolfhampton. The FBI and Homeland are on the way. Everything's shut down; nobody's going anywhere. He's in the house and in a moment, we're going to see where. Pan right to the boy," said a frustrated Collins.

Bates toggled the screen view to where Barron and Riana were standing, studied the frozen frame for a minute then clicked play. The two were facing each other against the back wall near the fireplace and in close conversation; oblivious of Agent Pound and her watcher watching. Reliving again what happened only a short time ago was like being in H. G. Wells time machine. The lightning flashes were seen, and the thunderclaps heard, and the interior dining room lights flickered. Then the lights went out and the screen went eerily dark, but on the screen, two pair of yellow eyes could be seen through the darkness next to the bookcase and the audio picked up their howling frenzy. The plasma wall continued recording because it made its own power.

Chapter 22

MOSCOW

Foreign Intelligence SVR Director Naryshkin announced, "Comrade Putin, the lights in Long Island's Wolfhampton have gone out."

"Excellent," said Putin.

Ministry of Finance Siluanov began, "Comrade Putin, the algorithms have clicked on and the stock market is devouring itself.

"Excellent," said Putin.

General Shoygu said, "Comrade Putin, the Trump boy has been taken."

"Excellent," said Putin. But something in Shoygu's eyes begged Putin to ask, "Is there anything you would like to add general?"

General Shoygu knew the next words he uttered to Pale Moth would mean the difference between him and his family's continued bureaucratic survival or death to himself and disgrace and banishment to Siberia for his family.

Washington

SOT Steve Mnuchin began, "The algorithms have clicked on."

"And the stock market is devouring itself," finished NEC Director Larry Kudlow.

"Oh, that's brilliant," said COS Mick Mulvaney.

"The lights in Wolfhampton have gone out," announced DNI Coats.

"Is it weather-related or something nefarious?"

"The latter we believe. An effort to embarrass the president or worse."

"Amazing," said Mulvaney adding, "Worse? What could be worse?"

"Actually, Mick there is something. The Prince is missing," said DCI Haspel.

"What? What are you talking about?" for a moment thinking Haspel was referring to the dead singer. Then he realized what Haspel was saying, closed his eyes and said. "Explain."

Wolfhampton

The only image on the plasma wall were the dining room candles, which were soon augmented by several battery lanterns that started to appear here and there. But it was a clear enough picture to see that Prince and Riana were no longer there.

"Where did they go?"

"I should have let you insert a GPS tracker chip in his arm as you suggested," said the president.

"I did anyway," answered Collins, "that's how I know he's still in the house." *Or at least his arm is*, he thought.

Collins walked away from the wall, followed by the president, Melania, Halsey, Bates, Volkov, and Galkin, over to where the Barron and Riana were last standing before the lights went out. In his hand, he had a small receiver and held it against the wall and started moving it around and up and down. The receiver, which was picking up a very low sporadic tracker signal before was now beeping consistently louder.

"You think he's inside into the wall?" asked Melania.

"I'm getting a strong signal from his tracker."

"This place is loaded with hidden rooms, secret stairways, shafts, closets in closets, tunnels, and dungeons. Some I found, many I wouldn't know where to look," admitted Volkov.

Proud of the wall was a bookcase bump - which was mirrored on the opposite side of the fireplace.

"Bookcases in a dining room?" asked Bates.

"Yes, well this is not your average castle," answered Volkov.

A light sconce protruding from the case pilaster was slightly askew and like in the movies when Collin's aligned it the bookcase popped forward giving witness to a small dark room behind.

"What one man can invent another can discover," said an impressed Colonel Galkin.

"Elementary," exclaimed Collins.

Chapter 23

Just as the lights went out, Barron had felt a strong arm around his neck from behind and was pushed into a room that, until that moment, he hadn't realized existed. The room was dark but then, after what sounded like a door closing, the room became dimly lit by a battery torch and Barron heard Hammer and Sickle's muffled howls. Barron now saw a lone man and Riana. It was not unusual in practice drills for agents to surround him and direct him to safety but instinctively he knew this was no exercise and this man was too scary to be an agent.

Kahbib Nurmodov, in the security of the hidden room, put duct tape on both their mouths but didn't bother to secure their hands. He then pulled out his cell phone and punched the speed dial for General Shoygu. "I have the boy and Volkov's Lolita. What do you want me to do with the girl?" asked Kahbib in, Russian.

"Why do you have the girl?" asked Naryshkin.

"She was there with the boy. I had to take them both."

"She is a lia...You must..." The call was breaking up because of the storm.

"Please general, say again. You're breaking up."

But then the call went dead. Kahbib speed-dialed again but nothing. He had no signal.

"Shit," said Kahbib knowing he was now on his own.

Barron heard and understood the one-way conversation but was not sure if the man got his answer. He heard enough, however, to have concern for Riana. He figured, correctly as it turned out, that it was Secret Service protocol that blocked all non-proprietary cell communication, not the storm.

In English, Kahbib looked at Barron and said, "Tracker."

Barron took out his cell.

"Give it."

Barron handed over his cell phone.

"Your tracker. Where is it?"

Barron pointed to his cell.

Kahbib removed the SIM card and smashed it. He then pulled out a small black box, smaller than a pack of cigarettes, turned it on and said again, "Where's tracker?"

Barron suspected what was coming next but gave up nothing and just grunted through the duct tape.

Kahbib started waving the black box around Barron's upper body and listened to the beeping increase as he settled near his right arm. He then ran the box over the rest of Barron's entire body as a double-check.

"Remove jacket and shirt," demanded Kahbib.

Barron hesitated, then Kahbib slapped him across the face.

"Take clothes off now."

Barron removed his suit jacket, undid his tie, unbuttoned and removed his shirt. Kahbib grabbed Barron's right arm and ran the black box in a circular motion. The beeping increased to a steady buzz as he raised Barron's arm. There, just under the skin, between the elbow and armpit, was a small bluish capsule about the size of a vitamin pill. Kahbib removed a box cutter and slid the razor blade forward with his thumb.

Riana, with fear in her eyes, produced a muffled scream. Barron did not fight what he knew was inevitable. Kahbib made a small incision and when blood began to ooze, he retracted the blade and pocketed the box cutter. Then, with both hands, he squeezed the tracker out through the incision.

If Barron felt pain, he didn't show it or couldn't because his mouth was taped. "Put your clothes on," said Kahbib. Then he turned to Riana.

Kahbib removed the duct tape from Riana's mouth, held the bloody capsule to her face and said, "You are Volkov's little whore. I know you know how to swallow."

Riana screamed and punched straight out with her fist landing a cracking blow to Kahbib's eye. Only his pride was hurt as he slapped her and grabbed her mouth and forced the capsule in, then covered her mouth and nose until she swallowed.

Barron pulled off his duct tape and rushed Kahbib, punching him in the same eye. Kahbib turned and swatted Barron hard in the chest, plowing him back against the wall. He then replaced the duct tape over her mouth, added a strip over her eyes and bound her hands with plastic ties and repeated the process on Barron.

Chapter 24

Collins entered first followed by Bates. Other agents kept everyone out of what was possibly going to be a crime scene.

When Riana heard the wall open, she moved away from the sound and assumed a defensive position as she expected the Russian had returned for her.

"Riana. Take it easy. I'm Agent Collins. You're safe now." Turning to his other agents he said, "It's just the girl. Bring in more lights and start looking for how they got out."

More lights arrived carried by two anxious parents, Donald and Melania.

Everyone started looking for another exit from the room, but nothing was obvious. No doors, no vents, the ceiling, and walls were plaster. The floor was of old wood planks which became the focus of their attention.

Collins carefully stepped towards Riana, trying to unbind her while not disturbing evidence.

"Mr. President, please stop where you are," requested Agent Bates. But they could see that Barron was not there and Melania let out a depressing disheartening sigh.

Collins removed the tape from Riana's eyes, then mouth and clipped off her hand tie with his pocketknife. "Riana, are you alright? Where's Barron?"

"I don't know. He put tape over my eyes before he left. I heard something open and close then they were gone."

"Jesus! How long ago did they leave?"

"About twenty minutes ago."

"We're still getting a strong signal from Barron's tracker," said Bates.

"You don't know what he did to me. He made me…"

"That okay, you're safe now Riana," interrupted Collins, thinking she had been sexually assaulted.

"No, it's not okay. Listen to me. He cut he tracker out of Barron's arm, and then made me swallow it," said Riana.

"Shit. They played us for twenty minutes. There must be an opening in the floor. Get the house, the property, Wolfhampton, get fucking Long Island sealed off. But it all starts here. Find that opening," yelled Collins.

"Did he say anything?"

"He made a phone call but spoke in Russian."

"How do you know it was Russian?"

"Dmitriy speaks Russian all the time. I don't understand him, but I know it's Russian."

"Have you seen this man before?"

"Yes, Kahbib something, everyone refers to him as the Hawk. He's a friend of Dmitriy's."

Collins turned to look at Dmitriy Volkov who stood in the room entrance.

The president and first lady also turned towards Volkov and one of them said, "If he hurts my son, I will kill you."

Chapter 25

Patrol Officer Michael Denison was one of many Wolfhampton, Southampton, East Hampton, Suffolk County Police, Sheriff's and State Police officers encircling the Wolfhall estate. They all received a screen-shot photo of Kahbib Nurmodov aka Hawk, a status report of the abduction, and an immediate situation text through a proprietary emergency IM.

Denison was positioned at the base of a high rocky bluff where Volkov's estate ran to the ocean. He was 100 yards distant from the next officers on either side.

All the officers were aware of the seriousness of the situation, especially those by the beach like Denison because of all the Coast Guard ships and helicopters patrolling just offshore. But it was now clearing up after the storm. It was turning into a warm 4th of July weekend evening and Denison had other things on his mind.

Back in the main house Volkov and Riana were under house arrest and being questioned by the FBI. Secret Service and FBI agents were swarming all over the main house and all the outbuildings while Collins, Halsey and an FBI Special Weapons and Tactics team aka SWAT were through the wood floor and into the tunnel chasing the Hawk and the Prince.

"He's got almost an hour on us," said FBI SWAT team leader SAIC Edgar Vaccaro aka Hoover for two obvious reasons.

"We had this property locked down minutes after the lights went out, but it took us ten minutes to find out how to open the fucking trap door in the floor. We have had men where we think this tunnel ends since we found it heading south," answered Collins as they moved swiftly but cautiously through the tunnel.

Halsey was going to say something about his Edison tunnel experience but thought better of it.

"The brief didn't mention him being armed," said Hover.

"Right. We do know he has a box cutter, but regardless, we know he's a very dangerous man."

"We know him. He's a combat sambo mixed martial artist and UFC Lightweight Champion," said Hoover.

"What's that?" asked Collins.

"That's a bad dude," answered Hoover.

They had been in the tunnel moving south for 15 minutes when Hoover called a halt. "You hear that? You smell that?"

A few yards ahead they came to a stop. The tunnel floor was gone and in its place was a ten-foot-long chasm as wide as the tunnel, 20-foot-deep with tidal seawater at the bottom. A wide bridge had been pulled back to the far side preventing further pursuit. The chasm and the bridge were obviously built years ago as a 'draw bridge and moat' enabling family a way to escape pursuers.

"What now?" asked Collins.

Hover and his team were studying options, like tossing a rope across and snagging the bridge but there was nothing to snag it on when Halsey suggested he jump across.

"The ceiling is only seven foot high. I don't think an Olympic long jumper would try that," said Collins.

"You're right, he would smash his head. I'll jump sideways. My intermural sport in college was parkour."

"Want a rope around your waist?" asked Hoover.

"No. It would tie me down so to speak. Toss it across now and if I miss, it could be my lifeline."

"You know you're not in Kansas anymore, Toto," said Collins.

"You really did do your homework," said Halsey.

Everyone cleared back as Halsey started his diagonal stride from the left tunnel wall. He picked up speed and a foot from the hole he went horizontally airborne, if that's even possible, with his right foot making contact with the wall and pushing out hard to provide the momentum to traverse the chasm. He landed hard but his Airborne Ranger training rolled him upright.

"If you think I'm going to follow you over you've got to be crazy," said Collins.

"You're right. I'll just go after them alone or I could tie the rope to the bridge, and you could pull it back over," said Halsey adding, "Fookin eejit," in a brogue that he hoped only Collins understood.

Chapter 26

Kahbib and the boy reached the end of the tunnel, but Kahbib had to wait for the next phase of the escape plan to materialize. Barron no longer blinded by duct tape but still bound hand and mouth, looked out through a small opening at the beach below, the dark ocean beyond, and the cloudy sky above, and wondered where it would all end.

Detective Mutteo Rossi had just checked on Patrol Officer Denison, then moved down the beach to the next posted officer. Denison with his back to the ocean thought he saw something in the eroded bluff overhead. It was dark but through the sand dune, tall seagrass, and exposed smooth rocks and boulders, Denison saw a flicker of light. He pushed his mic button and spoke carefully and softly, "POD to Red Bank, I have them."

Back at Wolfhall, the FBI continued the questioning of Volkov, The Secret Service continued securing the president and first lady and coordinating the search for Hawk and Prince.

The president and first lady were exhausted from searching and worrying. They, along with Agent Bates, and Melania's new best friend Abby, moved into the library and found comfortable couches onto which to sit and organize their thoughts.

Possibly to alleviate her concern or in spite of it, Melania offered, "He is a very strong-minded, very special, smart boy - he's independent and can take of himself." Then she added, "Who would do such a thing? Why?

Who hates us? Who hates you Donald so much to do this to you, me, us, America?"

"Melania, many people hate us - hate me. Hell Pelosi, Schumer, and Waters hate me, but they wouldn't kidnap my son. Soros hates me but he wouldn't either - he might finance it though."

"The fibbies are sweating Volkov now, he's about to move up from a person of interest to suspect. Kahbib Nurmodov's his buddy and invited a guest. We'll know something soon," said Bates.

"It's not Volkov. He's being set up," said the president.

"Then how would this Kahbib Nurmodov guy know all the hidden rooms, secret tunnels, and get invited without Volkov involvement?"

"I don't know, maybe it's about money."

"You think someone did this for a ransom, Mr. President?"

"Could be."

"Mr. President, there are a lot of low-profile billionaires out there to kidnap if someone just wanted money, and they wouldn't have to endure the kind of unrelenting heat the United States has to throw at them," offered Abby.

Seeming to ramble the president added, "Putin hates me."

"Is that why?" asked Bates.

"That's the real question, isn't it? Why? The how and the who is just scenery for the public...Why? Why am I here in Wolfhampton on the 4th of July weekend with Volkov? Why was Barron taken here and now? Why is the stock market and our economy crashing now? Who has the power to cover it up?"

That would be you Mr. President, thought Bates but instead said, "I agree this is political, and I wasn't thinking about connectivity. It may be a stretch, but you might be on to something. Linking, then unlocking a chain of coincidences."

"I don't believe in coincidences," said the president, "and neither did Donald Sutherland."

Just as Bates thought the president was making sense again, he realized the president was just playing Sutherland in his movie mind.

A black and white police SUV came quietly down the beach and stopped. The driver, a female, was on the radio but watched Patrol Officer Denison, with pistol drawn, leading a cuffed man and a boy down the bluff towards the vehicle.

"Get in," said Denison to the man. He opened the back door and guided Kahbib Nurmodov's head with his hand, closed the door, holstered his pistol, and guided Barron to the driver's side, and had him slide in the back seat next to Kahbib Nurmodov.

The driver slid over to ride shotgun while Denison got in the driver's seat. He picked up the radio handset, made a call and started moving silently down the beach.

Barron was still bound and had the tape over his mouth because, as the police officer explained he needed to "Preserve evidence." *I'm so glad it's almost over*, thought Barron, *but something just doesn't feel right.*

Then it became clear. "Mikhail, razblokirovat' manzhety," said Kahbib Nurmodov thrusting his cuffed hands over the seat and through the opening in the partition cage.

"That's not the plan. You stay cuffed until we're clear of the last checkpoint," said Denison.

"Der'mo," uttered Kahbib Nurmodov.

Oh shit, thought Barron.

Chapter 27

Collins, Halsey, Hoover, and team saw the moonlight at the end of the tunnel and smelled the salty sea air, but the Hawk and Prince were gone. There were three sets of tracks leading down the bluff towards the ocean, but there was no one in sight. Collins got on the horn and reported the situation and in less than a minute — the time it took them to get down to the beach — a police vehicle came smartly towards them from the west.

"Get yellow tape and secure this area," said Hoover to one of his team while Collins was on another call.

"I thought there was supposed to be a cop posted here?" asked Halsey to no one.

The area they taped off had two fresh sets of vehicle tracks coming from the east; the first continuing West the other turned around and headed back east. Three sets of footprints led to the latter.

"That's exactly what I said. Hawk had a vehicle waiting for him and they took off east," said Collins into his cell phone as a police vehicle stopped and two men got out and approached the taped off area.

A helicopter swooped low over the beach and hovered blowing sand and evidence away and Coast Guard boats, 100 yards offshore, powered on their searchlights.

"Where's the cop who was supposed to be manning this post and has anyone called in a sighting or arrest?" asked Collins to the man who identified himself as Detective Rossi.

"He was here 15 minutes ago when I was checking lines, and except for you, our radio frequencies have been silent," said Rossi.

"Are these your earlier tracks?" asked Hoover.

"Yeah. I stopped to talk to the officer then continued on to the next post about 100 yards up the beach."

"Well, where's your guy and whose tracks are these?"

Rossi pulled out his radio. "Denison - Denison, where the fuck are you?" He switched frequency and continued. "This is Detective Rossi. Hawk and Prince are on the beach heading east, possibly in a police vehicle. Stop anything and everyone until I tell you different. BOLO for PO Denison - he's MIA."

"We've searched the area and your officer is not here. It looks like your Officer Denison may be involved in this one way or the other," said Hoover.

"What do you mean by that crack? Denison's just a fuck-up."

"Maybe, but he's either a fucked-up captive or..."

"Or what?"

"Or a fucked-up captor," said Collins. "Hoover get on the horn and get that helicopter out of here before his sandstorm turns into a shit storm and tell the Coast Guard boys to belay the searchlights; they're blinding us. Get them heading east to stop anything walking, on wheels or that sinks or floats."

Halsey, who had been somewhat quiet, was now overloaded with blurred thoughts about his friend's safety or loyalty. Also, about reporting on and now being part of the most sensational story ever. About how Collins, the Secret Service, the Wolfhampton PD, and the FBI were acting more like the keystone cops than America's finest. He finally exploded, "Let's stop the bull shiting and follow the money. I'm done talking." He then ran to Rossi's police SUV, got in and started driving east.

"What the fuck you doing? That's my ride, stop," said Rossi.

Halsey drove right past Rossi but stopped next to Collins and asked, "You coming?"

Halsey and Collins took off east down the beach in the borrowed police SUV. Collins told Halsey he was aware of his friendship with Denison. Halsey had no reply.

Hoover and his team moved out down the beach, in line formation, following the tire tracks while Rossi and his partner Sergeant Jaworski got into an argument about having their SUV borrowed and ended up in fisticuffs falling over the yellow tape and being arrested, by one of Hoovers stay behind SWAT guys, for destroying evidence.

Chapter 28

President Trump hadn't been in Wolfhampton only a day when the village locals noticed all the additional FBI, cops, helicopters, Coast Guard, and roadblocks. On Main Street and in the one coffee shop, they were wondering and starting to talk. Something was going on and rumors were spreading. It didn't take long before the news media turned the rumors into facts and attributed them to unnamed sources then took them live.

"How did *CNN* find out?" asked Kellyanne Conway after reading a 'Breaking News' text on her phone. She and Mick Mulvaney, the president's COS, just landed aboard Marine Two, on one of Volkov's many huge lawns.

"They're just tossing shit out to see what sticks. Locals may know something's going on but the media's just sniffing. All the extra feds, choppers and roadblocks aren't helping," said Bates. His phone rang, he picked it up and answered. After listening and uttering one word, "Understood."

Everyone in the library including the president, first lady, Kellyanne, Mulvaney, and Abby waited for the news.

"They're out of the tunnel and on their trail. Collins said they're heading east on the beach and they have blocking forces in place. It's only a matter of time before they have them," said Bates not conveying Collins true message and concern.

Abby was listening and wished she had her phone so she could find out from Tommy what was really going on.

A knock on the door and an agent stuck her head in and got everyone's attention, "Agent Bates, Mr. Volkov's here to see the president."

"Not now," said Bates.

"Not ever," said Melania.

"No, said President Trump, "let him come in."

Volkov looking fresh, for having been sweated for an hour, entered the room, "Didn't expect to need permission to enter my own room."

"Did you escape through one of your own tunnels?" asked the president.

"Hardly. The feds released me as a person of interest. I've been out of circulation for a while. What's new with the Hawk and the Prince?"

Melania lost it, "Stop calling my son a Prince. He's a Barron."

Volkov looked generally hurt and said, "Yes of course. Any word on Barron?"

Bates looked at the president and got a nod. "We found the tunnel and followed them to the beach, we think they're in a four-wheeler heading east. The Hawk, excuse me, your friend Kahbib Nurmodov may have an accomplice, be we have them trapped."

"He's not my friend and never was. He's Putin's friend and sent here to spy on me and more. Obviously."

"So, you think Putin is behind this?" asked the president.

"Yes, and I think I know why."

Bates cell rang and he picked up, listened, said okay, and disconnected. "They think they have them trapped but the beach is rugged and dark. They're bringing in tracking dogs."

"Tracking dogs," said Volkov, "Hammer and Sickle hate that bastard. I'll let them loose, they'll find him fast and we don't even need his clothing to pick up the scent. Hammer and Sickle like Barron so he'll be fine. All I have to do is say Kahbib's name and my wolves will catch the bird, but it's not gonna be pleasant! They'll find him, catch him, and kill him."

"I like it Quint, but try not to kill him; this ain't Amity," said the president in his movie mind.

Twenty minutes later, on the beach a half a mile from Wolfhampton village, and just past the blockades, the wolves found him. The guttural screams from both the Hawk and the wolves could be heard on the beach 100 feet below the small hollow in the bluff above. By the time Collins, Halsey and Volkov reach the hollow, Hoover and his team had their torches lighting the gruesome scene. Kahbib Nurmodov aka Hawk was torn up bad.

"Jesus," said Volkov, "the president told us not to kill him."

Kahbib Nurmodov's throat had been ripped out, his nose, one eye, and both ears were gone. His intestines and privates were ripped out and on the dirt near his body. Hammer and Sickle were in a corner of the cave. Only their chomping and yellow eyes gave them away. One of Hoover's men shined a torch at them revealing another gruesome site. Their muzzles were soaked with blood. Blood was dripping down their throats onto their chest. Hoover added his torch, and both wolves dropped what they were gorging and snarled reveling their blood-red incisors and canines while blood bubbles popped from their snouts.

"They finished him," said Hoover.

"What?" asked Volkov.

"Your wolves finished him. They didn't kill him." Hoover bent down and rolled Kahbib Nurmodov's head over to reveal a small hole in his temple. He lifted his head and brain and blood seeped from an exit wound. He was shot point-blank. He was bleeding out when they got to him. He would have only lived a few minutes more," said Hoover.

"Thank God," said Volkov, "the president is pissed enough at me already."

"Where's the kid," asked Halsey as he began photographing the carnage.

"With the shooter," said Collins.

"Where's the shooter?" asked Halsey, now having a bad feeling about his friend Michael Denison.

"I was hoping you would know," said Collins.

Chapter 29

Bates relayed, to the group in the library, Collins report to him from the beach in a less descriptive manner. He also left out Collins lamenting not staying with the president but instead sending him into the tunnel.

The president and first lady were beyond themselves. "Agent Bates, they took my son, you said you had them trapped. The kidnapper, this Hawk person, is dead but where's my son?" asked an exasperated first lady. Then turning to her husband added, "Donald?"

"Kellyanne, turn on *CNN* they must have something," said the president.

Even though it was getting late Wolf Blitzer was still in the Situation Room surrounded by five quest analysts all giving their opinions about this and that.

> "...and why would President Trump be spending the 4th of July weekend with a such a controversial Russian oligarch as Dmitriy Volkov when Hong Kong and China are close to war, Iran has shut off the oil spigot and hit Kuwait oil fields, Turkey is attacking the Kurds, Spain and Greece are about to be kicked out the European Union — Europe is coming apart — Gloria?"

"Come on. This is absurd. Give me a break here. The president driving through the Hamptons to Volkov's castle was like a crown prince arriving for his coronation. But Wolf there were no crowds lining the streets. No well-wishers or babies to be kissed. Just an unknown reporter who got his 15 minutes," said Gloria Borger.

"Thank you, Gloria. Interesting observation. Let's go live with Jim Acosta in Wolfhampton, Jim."

"Wolf, the thing that has to be noted and we would be remiss if we didn't note it, is the amount of extra security and the baring of the media from covering this event. I have seen here more police, FBI, Secret Service, helicopters, Coast Guard ships in the ocean, barricaded streets than I have seen surrounding the American Embassy in the middle of a coup. Sources are telling me more is going on here than they are letting on. Helicopters are flying in and out and the White House is not returning calls. Wolf, I was on the beach, or as close to it as I could get, and it looked like the Marines landing on Iwo Jima, and to top it off I heard human screams and wolves howling." As if on cue lightning flashed and the producer held the shot until the thunderclap. "Jim Acosta, *CNN* in Wolfhampton. Back to you Wolf."

"Thank you, Jim, and be careful. David, what do you make of all this?"

"It's obvious, Wolf. Someone very important is meeting with the president. My sources say it may be Putin for a high-level summit in Wolfhampton..."

"Turn it off!" yelled the president.

Moscow

"We still haven't heard from the Hawk," said General Shoygu, "and Director Naryshkin has informed me that something has gone wrong with his meeting with the SVR team."

"What were you going to do with the boy anyway? Bring him here to Russia?" asked the Minister of Finance Siluanov.

"My dear Comrade Siluanov: Kahbib Nurmodov, Mikhail Denisov and the boy were to be waylaid by Director Naryshkin's SVR covert team working in the United States. Kahbib Nurmodov and Denisov were to become, as our American friends say, collateral damage and we would rescue the boy and deliver him to President Trump courtesy of the Russian Federation, and thus seal Volkov's fate," said Putin. "But our Colonel Galkin has just reported that everything has gone to shit. Kahbib Nurmodov is dead, Denisov has gone rogue, and Volkov is no longer a suspect."

"But if Kahbib Nurmodov is dead why are we still receiving his embedded GPS tracker signal showing him still moving all over the beach and estate?" asked General Shoygu.

Knowing what he knew about Kahbib Nurmodov's death and Volkov's wolves, Putin instead ignored general Shoygu's obliviousness and instead said, "Another Americanism best describes our situation, FUBAR! Yes, Director Naryshkin? Your and Colonel Galkin's plan has seemed to backfire and for his sake and yours I hope it doesn't come back and, like the wolves, bite us in the ass."

Wolfhampton

Collins was in the library updating President Trump on their new suspect, Mikhail Denisov aka Michael Denison and what they had learned so far from his apartment computer and phone records, giving Halsey and Abby a chance to corner Volkov. "Everything is not as it seems Mr. Volkov. My friend Wolfhampton Police Officer Michael Denison is really Mikhail Denisov and is somehow involved in this mess up to his eyeballs. So, I now feel that he may have unfairly accused you of the girls' suicides."

"I have been trying to tell you and anyone who would listen just that Mr. Halsey," said Volkov.

"But I watched the parking lot surveillance tape of your encounter with the girls. We had a lip reader dub in your and the girls' words. You said some horrible things to them," said Halsey.

"There's no secret I have a fondness for youth, and I did have an encounter with the two young girls in a parking lot, but I can assure you I did not have sex with either," said Volkov.

"And how's that?"

"Because Mr. Halsey, I am gay."

Both Halsey and Abby took a few seconds to digest that but then Abby asked, "What about Riana?"

"Ah, Riana, she's gorgeous, isn't she? Riana is a boy, a transgender boy who identifies as a girl. Perfect for my situation wouldn't you say?"

He waited for that to sink in before he added, "Those two girls were scared, I could tell. Someone sent them to set me up — to try and blackmail me, but I wasn't haven't any of it. I don't know what your lip reader told you I said, but I just wanted to get away from them. The last thing I remember saying was I didn't want to see them again, and if I did, I would go to the police."

"Riana dresses like a girl for appearance sake — to hide that you're gay?" asked Halsey as Abby rolled her eyes.

"For appearance sake? Yes, you could say that but not for the reason you mentioned. I like young boys to appear as young girls so yeah I guess in a way it's about appearances."

Chapter 30

President Trump had had enough and began venting his frustrations, "I built the biggest, most successful hotels and resorts in the world and now I can't even build a fucken wall. I'm the President of the United States with the most powerful law enforcement agency in the world at my disposal and they can't even find a 14-year-old boy.

"Two years in and I have done nothing. No wall, no infrastructure. Only a sinking economy and a crashing stock market, a world that is falling apart, a witch hunt and a kidnaped son.

"Why would they take my son? Why are they fucken with our lights and our economy? What's their end game? Eric and Don Jr. want to come out and help but I'm afraid for their safety." Looking at Halsey, President Trump added, "We can't let any of this get out."

It was July 4th, and the sun was a few hours old and the tragedy of the previous evening was only a few hours older. Earlier, the president and the first lady retired to their guest house for a few hours of sleep and to shower and change clothes before returning to the library to continue their vigil. Everyone else grabbed a few hours of sleep here and there, but there was work to do and other agents kept the investigation and pursuit moving while sleep was had when and where possible.

Hoover's team found the abandon police SUV just before 1 am, way past the blockades, had it dusted and towed off the beach. Three sets of matching prints were quickly acquired: Kahbib Nurmodov aka Hawk, Michael Denison aka Mikhail Denisov and Barron Trump aka Prince. It took a while longer, but Denison's partner Sally Dunn's prints were identified, and she was named as an accomplice. Her apartment was tossed and everything and everyone she ever knew was being accessed and interviewed. It would only be a matter of time.

The president was having his first Diet Coke when Halsey's cell rang. Halsey looked at the caller ID stood up raised his hand to get everyone's attention and shouted, "Denison!"

The FBI techs in the corner started a recording and trace. Colonel Galkin, who had been talking to Volkov got up and excused himself, whereupon Agent Bates blocked his exit and asked him to remain seated and nodded to another agent to keep an eye on him.

Halsey turned up the volume and pushed speakerphone. "Michael, I have you on speaker. I'm with the president, first lady, and federal agents. Where's the boy?"

"Tommy, good to hear your voice. It's been a rough night. The boy's fine. I'm sure you're putting a trace on my phone, but you won't find me I'll be long gone. But you have to know this is not what it seems..."

"I don't care about any of that," interrupted the president standing up and moving closer to Halsey, "I want my son back now."

After a moment of silence, Denison continued, "You'll have your son back and soon, Mr. President, today in fact, but you need to hear the truth..."

"Enough of this!" yelled Collins, "where's the boy?"

"No. Let him finish!" yelled Halsey.

"You want answers?" asked Denison.

"I want the truth," answered Halsey.

"You can't handle the truth!" cried the president.

Everyone became rather still and quiet while the embarrassed president, realizing his movie mind had involuntarily escaped, sat back down. Another moment went by before Halsey continued, "Just tell us what happened and give us the boy."

"I'm what you call a sleeper cell. Remember my backpack trip through Europe years ago? I was radicalized, communized if you like. Anyway, I was recently awakened and assigned to help pull this kidnapping off."

"Why did you shoot Kahbib Nurmodov?" asked Halsey.

"I didn't."

More silence. "Go on."

"We rendezvoused with the people we were to turn the boy over to, and Kahbib went to discuss the exchange. A shot rang out and I floored it. Someone chased me but couldn't approach the roadblocks and backed off. Because I was in a police SUV and they knew me, we passed right through.

"Why it all turned to shit, I don't know. From what Kahbib told me this was all part of a bigger plot to destroy the economy, Volkov and President Trump. Perhaps you can ask Colonel Galkin; it was his plan and his SVR boys we met with."

Colonel Galkin was asked to stand, scanned, handcuffed, and led out of the library.

"Are you and the boy safe now?"

"For the moment, yes, but it's just a matter of time. Kahbib said they have assets in the Secret Service and FBI. I just want out of this and out of here."

"Alright. How do we get the boy?" asked Halsey.

"Two million in 20s-50s and 100's in two airline carry-ons. Non-marked, untraceable and no funny exploding dyes. I need a stake to get away from these guys. I will call you in two hours with a location for the switch. You show the money, I show the boy, then we make the switch."

Halsey looked towards Collins, but the president held his hand up and said, "Deal."

"Okay. Did you hear that? Anything else?" asked Halsey.

"One more thing. I want the president's word that neither he or any of federal, state, private, military or allies' agencies will pursue me or my associate, Sally Dunn."

"You have it," said the president.

"Mr. President one second..." said Collins.

"We have a Deal—you have my word on it," interrupted the president.

"Thank you, Mr. President. But I need something better than that."

"What?" asked an exasperated president.

"I need you to tweet it."

Chapter 31

Halsey became the de facto 'go-to guy' at the detriment of both Collins and Bates but it's what the president wanted. The following two tweets appeared on the president's Twitter account:

Donald J Trump
@realDonaldTrump
To Russian President Putin: NEVER, EVER THREATEN THE UNITED STATES AGAIN OR YOU WILL SUFFER CONSEQUENCES THE LIKES OF WHICH FEW THROUGHOUT HISTORY HAVE EVER SUFFERED BEFORE. WE ARE NO LONGER A COUNTRY THAT WILL STAND FOR YOUR INTERFERENCE AND MACHIAVELLIAN BEHAVIOUR. BE CAUTIOUS!
12:45 PM - 4 July 2020

Donald J Trump
@realDonaldTrump
As President of the United States, I grant Michael Denison and Sally Dunn full pardons for any and all crimes committed and they have my word that neither I nor any federal, state, private, military or allies' agencies will pursue you.
12:50 PM - 4 July 2020

While the news media and most of the civilized world were trying to understand the president's latest tweets, a call came in at 1 pm from Denison instructing Halsey to come alone to Manhattan with the money. He would then be given further instructions when he arrived. A woman and Barron could be heard talking in the background.

"I'm going with you, Tommy," said Abby.

"I don't think so. He said to come alone and I'm not going to screw this up."

"But I think he has Sally Dunn with him."

"So, I'm supposed to ask the president if you can come so we can have a double date?"

A leased helicopter arrived at the East 34th Street Heliport in Manhattan at 2:10 pm with four passengers aboard: Halsey, Collins, Bates, and Adams.

Halsey's phone rang. "Where are you?"

"Just landed at 34th Street."

"Take an Uber down to the South Ferry entrance and get out with the suitcases."

Traffic was a nightmare and competition getting an Uber was worse, but Abby managed to remember the lost art of hailing a cab and they were soon on the FDR Drive south to the ferry.

The ride down was slow, but it gave them an opportunity to see hundreds and hundreds of pleasure boats in the East River and beyond. They were overcrowded, partying and getting ready for the coming 4th of July festivities. Collins and Bates had an unmarked waiting and followed discreetly behind.

Halsey's phone rang again. "Alright stop across from the heliport about 300 meters before the ferry. Walk across the drive with the suitcases. Keep your phone on."

Halsey did as instructed and wheeled the two carry-ons precariously across the unusually slow-moving FDR Drive to the Liberty Helicopter Pier and into the parking lot.

"Go over to the Grady White tied up to your starboard and hand the luggage down."

Halsey went over to the only Grady White tied up and hailed the captain. The woman he remembered as the lip reader appeared with Barron. He handed the two suitcases down. She opened and inspected both, opened a lazarette hatch, tossed them in and secured the hatch. She helped Barron up to Halsey's outstretched arms and the exchange was complete. Sally Dunn untied the port lines, gave a pumping motion and the 30-foot Grady White powered out into the East River and into the confluence with New York Upper Bay towards Liberty Island. Halsey's phone was still on and faintly heard Denison say, "Goodbye, my friend."

Collins was on the phone with the president and the first lady telling them they had the boy. Bates was on the phone with his agents and the Coast Guard alerting them on the boat's movement. Halsey, Abby, and Barron stood on the heliport dock and watched the Grady White power out into the East River where it was joined and absorbed into dozens of other small boats, heading out to the Liberty Island festivities. Then it exploded.

Chapter 32
MOSCOW

"It's done," said Foreign Intelligence SVR Director Sergey Naryshkin.

"Colonel Galkin?" asked Putin.

"Under arrest," said Naryshkin.

"The boy?" asked Putin.

"With his mother in New York," said Naryshkin.

"Volkov?" asked Putin.

"Completely exonerated of the boy's abduction and of the girl's suicides," said Naryshkin.

"The stock market?" asked Putin.

"International trading has leveled off, and the American market and is about to open. They are still predicting a down opening but the Wall Street, stock market, Ponzi scheme will not be the freefall we had anticipated," said Ministry of Finance Anton Siluanov.

"Our one mild success, Comrade Siluanov. You have done well for an opening salvo," said Putin, "and if the actualization of this unraveling is the destruction of President Trump you will be greatly rewarded," said Putin.

"For myself nothing, Comrade Putin, but for my family a…"

"Don't be so modest Comrade Siluanov," interrupted Putin, "a nice dacha in Plyos next door to Medvedev would be good. Yes?" asked Putin.

"You are too kind, Comrade Putin."

"As to the other matter, Volkov may be exonerated but he's tainted and will soon be ostracized and made redundant by Trump. He will come crawling back to his Mother Russia. The boy is back home, which is what we intended, but not how we intended. Our embedded agents in both the FBI and Secret Service are now at risk and we are in President Trump's crosshairs. So, for you Comrade Naryshkin, a nice dacha in Siberia, yes?" said Putin.

Chapter 33

It was Monday, July 6th and the long 2020 Independence Day holiday was over. There had been no parade, no fireworks, and no presidential foursome in Wolfhampton.

The first lady and Barron were back and safely ensconced in Trump Tower, contemplating a near averted tragedy.

Volkov survived, but just barely. He went from an 'A-list' hipster to an 'F-list' fibster overnight. He may have been exonerated of any wrongdoing but he would not be invited to the White House any time soon and without that kind of influence and exposure, he was just another rich ass hole in the Hamptons.

Both Collins and Bates were fearing reassignment pending an internal review currently underway within both the Secret Service and FBI. Both agencies were doing extensive audits for embedded Russian SVR agents.

What remained of the Grady White was bagged and tagged including two bodies, or parts thereof, of Sally Dunn and John Doe. The official cause of the explosion was an accidental fuel leak. The actual cause of the explosion was attributed to the detonation of a thermobaric warhead fired from a rocket launcher in an adjacent boat. The FBI later found a Russian RPO-A Shmel Bumblebee portable rocket launcher in an abandoned boat by the Bayonne docks in New Jersey. Michael Denison aka Mikhail Denisov and the two carry-ons were never found. The Grady Whites aft deck containing the lazarette into which the carry-ons were tossed survived and was found to have a self-activated trap door opening directly to the water below. The FBI is investigating.

The president had kept his word and didn't bother Denison, but it wouldn't be long before *The Washington Post* would soon put the boating "accident" and the president's tweet together.

Tom Halsey walked along Main Street and accepted the stares that came with his new celebrity status. The further east in the Hamptons he traveled the harder the stares became, while Abby Adams walked along Wall Street and wondered if she had lost her man.

The stock market was about to open, but President Trump's boys and girls had done their jobs. Coats, Haspel, Mulvaney, Pompeo, Kudlow and Cunningham, and their staffs had had a long painful 4th of July weekend but were able to put things right. The disinformation was halted, nerves calmed and the big boys, day traders and bottom feeders returned to the market with gusto buying stocks at rock bottom prices from the poor stiffs who couldn't find buyers or just plain held on. All these poor stiffs, the small investors, 401k holders, Moms and Pops, and Grey Care all aka 'The last man out', now decided not to go back in.

Halsey wrote his story and it was and picked up by the wire services and all the major papers. He wrote about the president, first lady, and the third son. He wrote about Wolfhall, Volkov and Riana, the dinner, the storm, the wolves, and the Edison room. Upon the request of the president and the first lady, Secret Service and FBI, Halsey omitted any mention of the abduction but inserted a white lie about a body found on the beach that was currently under investigation. A side piece he did about a local cop who disappeared and was being sought as a person of interest in a recent double suicide was not picked up and was only read by locals. He was invited onto the top Sunday TV shows and was skewered. His work was touted as less than credible even for a local cub reporter. George Stephanopoulos called it a puff piece. Chuck Todd accused him of treason. His editor knew he was holding back, couldn't take the heat and fired him. Halsey had his 15 minutes, watched his dreams of a Pulitzer blow up, and watched as Wolfhampton went back to normal or at least summer normal.

Chapter 34

The New York Times

July 17, 2020, United States Senator Kamala Harris and her running mate, South Bend, Indiana Mayor Pete Buttigieg, were nominated as the Democratic presidential and vice-presidential candidates at the Democratic National Convention in Fiserv Forum in downtown Milwaukee, Wisconsin last night. Harris and Buttigieg will meet the Republican incumbent ticket President Donald Trump and Vice President Mike Pence in the general election on November 3, 2020…

A little over a week had passed and Melania and Barron were still safely tucked away in Trump Tower, his other boys and youngest daughter's trip to Africa; Eric and Don Jr. to hunt in Tanzania, Tiffany to visit friends in Nigeria, were canceled, and Ivanka continued working on her book. After what happened to Barron, President Trump wanted to keep his friends close and his family closer.

The economy was doing better; stocks, bonds, and commodities were all up as consumers' confidence built. It looked like President Trump was making America great again - again, but Europe and Asia were not doing so well. Russians RTS Index and China's Shenzhen Stock Exchange never took a hit and were doing well.

While Congress renewed their efforts to finish off President Trump, Trump planned his revenge on Congress and anyone and everyone who stood on the left side of the aisle.

He sat behind the 1880 English oak partners desk made from the timbers of the British Arctic exploration ship HMS Resolute, looking past the younger Bush's couches, the Reagan rug, towards the fireplace with Rembrandt Peale's portrait of General George Washington over the mantel. Portraits of Andrew Jackson looked over his left shoulder while Jefferson looked over his right.

The three Trump kids and their Dad were discussing the just-announced Democrats nominees for president and vice president Senator Kamala Harris and Mayor Pete Buttigieg.

Then the president went off, "That's the best they can do? I already beat a girl-boy team — Crooked Hillary and Less Able Kaine. Now a Jamaican dot Indian Harris and Little Bo Peep Buttigieg? I'm not even going to waste my time on them. Harris and Buttigieg? They're both too normal. It has to be Biden, Warren or Sanders. Who else could follow someone like me? The fake media and their ratings will demand it. It has to be someone of equal entertainment value. A Sleepy Creepy, 'Beat me like a drum' Joe and all his gaffes. Pocahontas, a goofy carbonated doppelganger or Crazy Bernie the socialist millionaire. The media will need it, the public will demand it. I'm not going to debate her, she's not on my level. If they demand a debate, we can have tweetabate." The president then withdrew and became very quiet.

"Dad?" asked Don Jr, "Dad?"

The second time seemed to snap the president out of his daze and into focus came three of his children. "Even after Mueller said, 'No collusion,' they still won't let it go. No obstruction — no collusion. This witch hunt has killed our resorts, our hotels, our name — our brand. We have to do something — something big."

"What do you mean Dad?" asked Ivanka.

"He means they suffer from collusion delusion," said Eric.

"No, not that. What do you mean by 'something big'?" asked Ivanka.

"Just when I thought I was out they pull me back in," said the president going off again into a thousand-yard stare.

"Dad, what's wrong?" asked Don Jr.

"What's wrong? I'm the most powerful man in the world but here in my own country, I can't even build a wall. I can't close the border, I can't do anything without Nervous Nancy Pelosi, Fake tears Chucky Schumer, Buzz Lightyear Schiff, Crazy Maxine Waters, Fat Jerry Nadler, the 9th Circuit Court and the rest of them shutting me down every step of the way.

"The way I see it, I have three options. First, I run and win in 2020. Whoever they throw up against me will make no difference. Crazy Bernie, Sleepy Creepy Joe or even Pocahontas would have been fun, but Reggae Harris? We probably won't win back the house and another four years of this shit, especially as a lame duck. No way I'm gonna put myself and my family through that unless I let Pence take the heat, keep us out of wars, and I play golf for four years.

"Option two, I say I'm gonna run, build up the economy back up and rebuild our brand and then at the last minute we sell everything. Go from hard assets to cash to gold then I bow out. The Republican party is screwed, they'll have no one. Pence can't win. With me out, the country, hell the world will know a bunch of Socialists will be running, ruining the country and the markets and the economy will tank. But this time, it will be for real and bad. But we, our family will not only survive, but become the richest family in the world. 'Gold will be King.'"

"You're not a quitter Dad—none of us are. You want to be a one-hit-wonder like Carter and Bush?" asked Eric.

Ignoring Eric, the president continued, "I'm surrounded by pussy's and wussy's, so my third option is I replace most of my weak Cabinet and advisers with fighting men: Jim Jordan, Rand Paul, Steve Scalise, Dan Crenshaw, Lindsey Graham, Lee Zeldin. Bring back Trey Gowdy if I have to and add a non-family consigliere and we go to war. I run and I win, but instead of having to deal with Congress, federal judges, I get rid of them all and do what Daniel Dravot did."

"Dad, I thought I was your advisor, your consigliere," said Don Jr.

Disregarding his son, the president turned to Ivanka, "When we make our move, you're going to be my right-hand man but not consigliere. Don is no longer consigliere. He's going to run the businesses. That's no reflection on Don it's just the way I want it."

"Dad, why am I out?"

"You're not a wartime consigliere, Don. Things could get rough with the move I'm making."

Eric, Don Jr. and Ivanka each had the WTF look. Then, Eric spoke up, "Dad, what are you talking about?"

"What didn't you get? I said I have three options. First, I run…"

"No, no not first. Third, third. What's the third thing? What are you talking about and who's Daniel Dravot?" asked Eric.

"Daniel Dravot and Peachy Carnahan, and they say I don't know history."

"Danial and Peachy?" asked Ivanka.

"The two ex-soldiers in India when it was under British rule. They figured that their country did a number on them, so they decided to head off to Kafiristan in order to become Kings in their own right."

"Dad, are you talking about Rudyard Kipling's 'The Man Who Would Be King?'" asked Don Jr.

"Yes, but it was John Huston if I'm not mistaken, and Daniel Dravot goes on and becomes king."

"Melania is not going to go along with this. She's not going to be your Peachy," said Don Jr.

"Of course not. She'll stay in Manhattan with Barron."

"So, who's Peachy?" asked Eric.

"I need someone I can trust, but not family. I need a soldier."

"Dad, do you remember how it ended," asked Don Jr.

"Yeah, Daniel becomes King."

"No Dad, the final ending. The one where Peachy leaves a bag on the table for Rudyard Kipling or John Huston. What do you think happened to Daniel? What do you think was in the bag?" asked Don Jr.

Chapter 35

While the president was writing his screenplay for revenge, Speaker of the House Nancy Pelosi and Senate Minority Leader Chuck Schumer were in the Willard Hotel, just across the street from the White House, ensconced in their congressional safe room, planning their strategy. Chief Concierge Robert Watson had ushered them in through a secret entrance, into a private elevator and would see to it that they were not noticed or disturbed.

"Why don't we make a deal with him? Give him the wall and some infrastructure if he agrees not to run in 2020 and agrees to hold off appointing any further Supreme Court Judges," suggested Schumer. "Anything to get rid of him."

Ignoring the suggestion, Pelosi asked, "Do you believe that newspaper articles about what happened in Wolfhampton?"

"Not for a Humpty Trumpty minute. I heard rumors as I'm sure you have. His son went missing," said Schumer.

"Yeah, but we can't touch that, at least not together. We don't need another American Gothic optic of you and I together speculating about the Trump family," said Pelosi.

"Do we think she can beat Trump?" asked Schumer.

"No, I don't think she can. I wish it was Biden, but Joe's got too much splainin to do. The old 'My son did nothing wrong, I did nothing wrong,' line isn't going to cut it."

"How so?"

"Forget the billion Hunter made, I'm more concerned about that touchy-feely thing he does, and all his gaffes? I'm a member of the straight-arm club...I just pretend that you have a cold and I have a cold..."

"Nancy, I have no idea what you're talking about," interrupted Schumer, "but that would be my guess. It would have been fun to watch two Septuagenarian white men, Humpty Trumpty and Crazy Uncle Joe going head-to-head," said Schumer.

"That's funny, head-to-head. One with a comb-over, the other with hair plugs going head to head," said Pelosi, "Oh Chuck, I'm sorry. I didn't mean..."

"On second thought, I don't see it," interrupted Schumer pretending not to have heard the slight. "To win we need another O to run and it isn't O'Rourke."

"You mean Michelle?"

"She would definitely bring out the black vote. Hillary didn't, Harris might."

"Michelle would tear him a new one but it's not going to happen. Let's face it, there's no one strong enough to run and beat Thump, especially not Kamala and Pete. She's tough enough but too normal. He's going to get another four years unless we neutralize him."

"We have 23 governors and they have 27. There are 14 governorships at stake over the next two years. If we can maintain ours and take theirs, and we will have 37 states to their 13. Thump can use his executive power all he wants, but the states will just ignore or block him at every turn."

"Can you take back the Senate Chuck? If you do, we own him, if not, we neutralize him."

"I can't take another four years. We can't afford another four years. America and the world can't survive another four years of Trump, I'm sorry. What do you suggest Nancy?"

"What Schiff heard from his sources is that the Russians took the boy. What I suggest is next time they aim a little higher — if you get my drift."

Chapter 36

Tom Halsey hadn't been back to Manhattan for several years, and in that time, neighborhoods can change — pharmacies replace Spanish bodegas, nail salons replace Greek coffee shops and banks replace everything and on every block. Restaurants seem to last ten years or so, but on the Upper East Side, Halsey's old haunt, two favorites still live: JG Melon and Le Steak. Out the corner window of Le Steak, on 75th and 3rd Avenue, the views were typical New York City: cars, cabs, and people. Tom Halsey and Abby Adams weren't there for the view, they were there for the memories, food, and commiserate.

"Have you heard from him since the rescue?" asked Abby as she took a sip of her martini.

"Not a word; and I don't expect to. I've had my 15 minutes. It's a wonder you didn't catch what I have and lose your job."

"The markets are rebounding so I'm needed."

"Nice to be needed."

Abby decided to let it go and picked up the menu, and on cue, the waiter came over to their table.

"Would you like to hear our specials?" asked the waiter.

"No, I think we know what we want," said Abby. "We'll both start with the house salad and I'll have the Scottish Salmon."

"I'll have the Filet Mignon, charred and medium-rare, fries and extra mustard sauce, please," followed Halsey.

The waiter topped off Halsey champagne and left to place their order.

"I have been looking forward to this meal and your sleepover tonight for some time," said Abby.

"Me too and a 10k run around the park in the morning, I need to clear my mind."

"You're so romantic Tommy," said Abby as the waiter brought over the salads.

The salad, meal, martini, and champagne were delicious, as usual. The conversation was interesting and romantic. Finally, the waiter asked if they would like to see a dessert menu which was declined, and Halsey asked for the check.

"It's been taken care of Mr. Halsey," said the waiter.

"By whom?" asked Halsey as he looked around to see if he knew anyone and not believing he still had friends.

The waiter was about to answer when Halsey's phone rang. He put his finger up to the waiter asking for his indulgence while looking at the caller ID displaying unknown and said, "Hello."

"Hello, Mr. Halsey, my Ranger reporter. My scouts told me you and Abby finished dinner, but now I need your help," said the president.

"Mr. President. At your service. What can I do for you?" asked Halsey looking at Abby and the waiter with a perplexed expression.

"I need you here at the White House."

"Okay. Can I ask why?"

"Not on the phone. I need you here tonight.

"But I'm here with Abby and…"

"Bring Abby. You can spend the night in the Lincoln bedroom. By the way, how's the food there?"

"The best salad, steak, fries and mustard sauce ever."

"They do take out?"

"They used to."

"Put the waiter on, and I'll see you in a few."

Chapter 37

"Good morning. How was the Lincoln bedroom?" asked President Trump as Halsey joined him in the Oval Office.

"Good morning, sir. I would say it was memorable."

"So, you and Abby had great sex in Lincoln's bed or what?"

"As I said, Mr. President, it was memorable and it's not actually Lincoln's bed. In fact, it's not even his bedroom; it was his office. His actual bedroom is now the first lady's bedroom."

"God! Don't tell my wife that, or she will differently freak out."

"How was your dinner, sir?"

"Last night it was terrific. I had leftover steak and fries smothered in delicious mustard sauce with my eggs this morning. Gave a sample of the sauce to my chef and he's gonna make up a batch."

"Good luck trying to duplicate it, sir. It's a tighter held secret than Coke. Believe me, I've tried."

"He'll send it off to the FDA and they'll unearth the exact ingredients and exact proportions. I'll have him make a batch for you. Where's Abby?"

"Taking a tour of the White House, sir. We went running earlier."

"Where did you run?"

"Over the Roosevelt Memorial Bridge, up the Heritage Trail, back over the Francis Scott Key Bridge, down some more river trails, and back home so to speak. About 10k."

"You should have told me. I could have had my guys drive you."

"Believe me, they were with us, Mr. President. Four agents running a few yards ahead and behind. We enjoy running. We enjoy the high it gives us and the time to think and to just leave your body."

"Your body? All my friends who work out all the time, they're going for knee replacements, hip replacements — they're a disaster. I exert myself by standing in front of an audience for an hour. Now that's exercise!

"I guess you're wondering why I asked you here."

"You watched me get assassinated on the talk shows, felt empathy and heard I got fired?"

"Assassinated? That's a funny choice of words to use when you're talking to a president. Lincoln, Garfield, McKinley, and Kennedy all got assassinated, but only once. I get assassinated every day by the media."

"Sorry sir, I didn't mean…"

"Fuhgeddaboudit. You ever kill anybody? I mean when you were in the Rangers in Afghanistan?"

"No, sir."

"You ever wounded?"

"No, sir."

"You lying bastard. You think I didn't have you thoroughly checked out? I know all about your time with the 75th Rangers in Afghanistan, your medals then your stint with Delta Force special ops performing surgical strikes against high-level targets. Why do you downplay it?"

"Sorry sir, it's my go-to defense mechanism. You tell them you never killed anyone and were never wounded, and they lose interest in you real quick and leave you alone."

"You want me to leave you alone?"

"Not sure. What do you want me to do?"

"Before I tell you, I want you to know it's all about loyalty with me Halsey. Are you loyal?"

"If you will not die for me sir, you cannot ask me to die for you."

"I thought you would say something gung-ho like that. I have loyalty that runs in my bloodstream. When I lock onto someone or something, you can't get me away because I commit thoroughly. That's friendship, that's a deal, that's a commitment. Don't give me paper — I can get the same lawyer who drew it up to break it up. But if you shake my hand, that's for life."

"If we decide to go in different directions, we do it face to face — not on Twitter."

President Trump extended his hand and Halsey took it.

Chapter 38

They were driving a rental car from the airport back to Southampton. A bit of a let down to how they were dispatched aboard a helicopter and escorted by Secret Service agents to Washington. "Well, are we moving to Washington?" asked Abby.

"We?"

"You know sometimes I think you don't love me."

"Abby, I do love you, but I hadn't heard from you for months until just before the president shows up in Wolfhampton."

"We communicate by phone."

"Abby, what are we — Millennials? Anyway, I don't think so. I'm not sure what he wants; maybe he's not sure. He's a mysterious guy who doesn't come right out and tell you anything and although he says he believes loyalty is a two-way street, I think to save his or his family's ass he would throw me to wolves. Which reminds me—he told me something very strange."

"What?'

"He said he was going "full animal" and then he told me he bought Wolfhall."

"That is strange. Maybe he wants you to be his caretaker."

"Funny, but I think he has something else in mind for me."

"Like?"

"You know I was in Afghanistan with the Rangers, but I was never allowed to discuss with you, or anyone for that matter, what I did. And I still can't."

Abby looked across at him and watched as he drifted into his thousand-yard stare and decided his mind was going somewhere and she would have to wait for it to return.

Halsey gazed over the steering wheel and thought of one of many encounters: The story and dossier Halsey remembered from 2015 was that...

Akhtar Omar was a good man, a good father, and husband. He was all these things but no more. He was forty years old but looked older. Three of his four children were now dead, one may still live fighting with ISIS, ISIL, al-Qaeda or the Taliban, he just wasn't sure anymore. His wife was dead as were most of his brothers, sisters, cousins, and friends. He had no political affiliation except to get along with whoever's flag was atop the light improvised fighting vehicle aka 'technicals' which blew through the villages when the Americans weren't around. He now devoted his life to killing the current infidels who murdered his family and friends. Not the British that his great grandfather fought, or the Russians his father fought. No, these infidels, the current invaders, were Americans.

Omar worked as a civilian employee at Bagram Air Base, the largest U.S. military base in Afghanistan. Bagram Airfield was maintained at the time by the 10th Mountain Division in the summer of 2015. It is also maintained by the 82nd Combat Aviation Brigade (Task Force Pale Horse) and 3-10 GSAB (Task Force Phoenix) of the U.S. Army, with the 455th Air Expeditionary Wing of the U.S. Air Force and other U.S. Army, U.S. Navy, U.S. Marine Corps, U.S. Coast Guard, and ISAF units having sizable tenant populations. The base was staffed by civilians.

Omar, a chemist by profession, was for some reason assigned to one of the many gas stations as an attendant. His job was to fill the many vehicles diesel tanks that pull up to the pumps. Humvees, cargo trucks, transport busses and the like.

In his small one-room home, ten miles from the base, Omar worked feverishly converting Semtex 10, a plastic (putty-like) explosive left over from the Russian invaders, into a liquid form. His contribution to the cause would be to add 80oz of Power Service Diesel Kleen Fuel Additive after he finished topping off the tank of the 7:30 am transport bus carrying non-warrior officers and senior non-commission officers from their barracks to work on the other side of the base. He was asked by a friend, why not a vehicle containing troops? His answer was that these men write the orders, push the buttons, and remotely and safely fly the drones.

When the bus pulled up, he opened the gas lid and began filling it with fuel but before it was completely full, he poured in the entire 80 ounces from the Power Service Diesel Kleen Fuel Additive that really contained the liquid Semtex. When he was finished, he collected the pay chit that covered the cost of the fuel and whispered All hu akbar to the driver. He didn't know for sure when it would happen, only that when the diesel fuel, spiked with the liquid Semtex, injected into the combustion chamber began mixing with the super-heated air it would ignite into a tremendous explosion.

Seven minutes later and a mile or so down the road he felt and heard a tremendous explosion and turned to see black and grey smoke rising above the buildings. He would learn later that thirty officers and other ranks and one civilian driver were incinerated within the bus, while dozens of pedestrians were injured.

Halsey thought how he first got involved after the second similar incident occurred when his Delta Force unit was assigned the target. All the intelligence was provided for him. His team was to dispatch Omar. Halsey led from the front and when they arrived at Omar's home very early in the morning, they found the door open and Omar sitting at a table waiting for them. After searching the small two room home, finding bomb-making evidence and checking that Omar was clean, Halsey had his team wait outside and sat down opposite Omar.

Halsey had his 15 round 40 cal. Glock 22 pointed at Omar.

"Do you speak English?"

Omar nodded yes.

"Do you have family?"

Omar nodded no.

"You knew we were coming?"

Omar nodded yes.

"Yet you didn't try to stop us or plant an IED."

"Yes, I knew you would come. I have been waiting many days. My fight is not with warriors."

"Did you do it? Did you work alone?"

"Yes, I am alone."

"I will make this quick. Say your prayers."

"Allāhu akbar," said Omar with a calm face and a defiant stare.

Halsey squeezed the trigger and two 40 cal. rounds barked and double taped through one neat hole in Omar's forehead. The force of the blows knocked Omar and the chair over. Halsey stood up and looked down at the dead man. He looked at the calm face, the long brown hair, and beard, and watched as a halo of blood formed around his head. He knew it was Omar but in death, he looked different — eerily familiar. He knelt, studied the man, and had an epiphany. Today it would all end — this would be his last kill.

Outside Jo Jo, Halsey's 02 assistant team leader, heard the talking, then the shots and went back inside and saw his team leader kneeling over the body with the pool of blood rippling out from his head. "Jesus," said Jo Jo.

"Yes, my thought exactly," said Halsey.

Chapter 39

Even for the President of the United States, a clandestine meeting was nearly impossible; someone was always watching. The best place to have a secret meeting was in plain sight.

It was 7 am when Nancy Pelosi and Chuck Schumer traversed a 761-foot subterranean tunnel from the United States Treasury Building to the sub-basement of the East Wing of the White House. Lyndon Johnson and Nixon used the tunnel to avoid Vietnam War protesters when departing the White House back in the '60s. Pelosi and Schumer were both relieved of their cell phones and body scanned with a tactical wand before being guided by one Secret Service agent to a final short 150-foot tunnel from the East Wing to the Oval Office.

"I haven't slept since the phone call last night," whispered Pelosi.

"What could be so important that he couldn't have tweeted it?" said Schumer.

"Just don't say anything that will come back and bite us in the ass; the room is bugged."

"It's his nickel. I'm going to let him do all the talking."

They arrived at the end of the tunnel and were directed up a flight of stairs and through a door that landed them in the foyer adjacent to the president's Oval Office private restroom. A bit circuitous but it got the job done.

"Good timing," said the president exiting the bathroom while drying his hands. He knew better than to offer his damp hand to 'straight-arm' Pelosi but offered it to Schumer to see if he would take it. He didn't — to the president's surprise and to Pelosi's delight.

Heading through the door that opened into the Oval Office Speaker Pelosi asked, "Mr. President would you mind telling us why we are here and why all the mystery?"

The president went behind his desk and motioned both to have a seat in the two wooden chairs opposite him.

"What I'm about to tell you stays here. Only the three of us know of this meeting and if any part of our discussion and or agreement leaks out then it's one of us who leaked it and then all bets are off. If anything leaks, everything we agree upon this morning is dead. Agreed?"

"So, Mr. President, if you have buyer's remorse tomorrow about what we agree upon today you can send out a tweet and Servpro it, 'Like it never even happened' is that it?" said Schumer.

"I'm not the buyer. I'm the seller, and if anyone has buyer's remorse it will be one of you two.

Look, let's cut to the chase. I have three options. First, I run in 2020, and I win in 2020. Whoever you throw up against me will make no difference. Too bad it won't be Crazy Bernie or Creepy Joe. A socialist and a socializer. Looks like Harris now, but that could change — whoever. They have to run against me and maybe the best economy in the history of our country. I look forward to facing whoever it may be. May the best man win!"

"Woman," said Pelosi.

Ignoring Pelosi's anticipated response, the president continued, "But if I go this route, I'm a lame duck for the next four years of ruling by committee and getting nothing done. Indictments, tax returns, impeachment and on and on. Most presidents would cover it all up with a good war but that's not my style. I could have stayed in Syria you know. But if I have to run again, I'll do it, but I'll let Pence run the whole show while I tweet and golf the time away. Oh, and I may get to appoint one or two more Supreme Court judges."

"God help us. I hope the second option is better?"

"It is and I think you'll like this one. I don't run in 2020. I continue to run, continue building up the economy and then at the last minute, known only to the three of us, I announce I'm out. Hell, you can run your current nominee Harris or even Pocahontas could win."

"You're right; we could and might. We like this option but what's it going to cost us?"

"The cost for me not to run is well worth it. You make my last few months in my first and only tern in office a big booming success, I get my wall finished and we pass a comprehensive immigration bill. We pass a huge bi-partisan infrastructure spending bill. Shore up and do a bipartisan Obamacare health care program. The economy keeps booming, No wars. My ratings will soar."

"That sounds like the down payment. What's the balance due?"

"You two sing my praises, call off your 'Dogs of War': Nadler, Schiff, and Waters. Mueller has spoken; no collusion — drop it. No more whistle-blowers. Get over it. Give the new marching orders to all your embedded news media outlets, stop all the fake news, and no indictments, and no criminal or civil prosecution against me or any member of my family while president or forever thereafter. I go out on top."

"Jesus, anything else?"

"Just two more things. When my family and I leave the White House and are private citizens again, and we can do whatever the hell we want."

"And?"

"And you don't undo, after I'm out, anything we agree upon and everything we accomplish."

"What's behind door number three?" asked Schumer.

"You don't want to make me go there, but so you know, if I do option three, I continue running and win; then replace most of my weak Cabinet and advisers with fighting men: Jim Jordan, Mark Meadows, Rand Paul, Steve Scalise, Dan Crenshaw, Lindsey Graham, Lee Zeldin. I'll bring back Trey Gowdy if I have to and add a consigliere; and for the next four and a half years, the socialists and capitalists go to war.

"We start investigating the investigators. Expose the collusion between the DOJ and the Clintons.

The Steele dossier becomes the Clinton dossier. Brennan, Clapper, Comey and the rest go to jail. Hire special prosecutors to go after the two of you, Nadler, Walters, Biden, Hunter and Schiff. Barr's onboard and says we should go after all of you and I agree."

"Bring it on," said Pelosi.

"What, you want war?"

"No. It's just that it may be more fun torturing you for the next four and a half years, bringing you up on charges, continue the impeachment hearings, then jail, as opposed to letting you off the hook."

"Congress? Both the House and Senate are worthless. You can't agree on anything — let alone get it passed. We need to put you all in a room, Democrats and Republicans, lock the door and not let you out until they reach a compromise. That's the only way to get you to agree on anything.

"Okay. What is it going to be? Lame-duck with at least one more justice? Get rid of me, or war?" asked President Trump.

Reversing their route back through the tunnels Nancy Pelosi and Chuck Schumer walked and talked aloud about what they had just been put through.

"You know everything said in there was recorded. How can we trust him?" asked Schumer.

"It was and we can't, but it would be wonderful if he bows out. We would be rid of him and his family for good," said Pelosi.

"But how can we give him everything he wants, without telling our friends in the House and Senate why we are doing it? It would become clear when he pulls out, but how do we last? We would be declared certifiable and you could be overthrown by AOC and her crowd. This is a devil of a position he put us in," said Schumer.

"Yes. A 'Pact with the Devil', that's what this is," said Pelosi.

Chapter 40

> Pelosi (D-Calif.) told The Washington Post earlier this week that she continues to oppose impeaching the president absent "something so compelling and over-whelming and bipartisan." Trump, the House speaker said, is "just not worth it."

Reading the news flash handed him by his secretary, Madeleine Westerhout, President Trump passed the report to Halsey and said, "It's starting. They took the deal."

Halsey read it and said, "So, what happens next?"

President Trump had his phone out typing away then pushed send.

Donald J. Trump
@realDonaldTrump
I greatly appreciate Nancy Pelosi's statement against impeachment, but everyone must remember the minor fact that I never did anything wrong, the Economy and Unemployment are the best ever, notwith-standing recent Russian interference. Military and Vets are great - and many other successes! How do you impeach a man who is consid-ered by many to be the President with the most successful first three years in history, especially when he has done nothing wrong and impeachment is for 'high crimes and misdemeanors'?"

"Now we just need the other clowns to jump on board," said Trump.

Madeleine Westerhout came into the Oval Office again with another news flash and handed copies to both the president and Halsey.

By Tom Bruntom.brun@newsday.com

@Tom Brun DC

Updated March 2020

WASHINGTON

House Speaker Nancy Pelosi picked up support from a key Democrat on Tuesday in her opposition to any bid to impeach President Donald Trump without bipartisan support for it, prompting some in her party to say they'll proceed anyway. Rep. Adam Buzz Schiff (D-CA.), the House Intelligence Committee co-chairman who in January reopened the panel's investigation into Trump, accused the president of impeachable offenses Tuesday, but added, "I think the speaker is absolutely right." Without broad public and congressional backing, Schiff said, "an impeachment becomes a partisan exercise doomed for failure. And I see little to be gained by putting the country through that kind of wrenching experience."

"Bingo! They do their part and I do mine," said the president.

"You're really going to give up being president that easy?"

"Mr. Ranger Reporter, If you're not a player or an owner, you're a spectator, a fan. You worship the players and the franchise. You are an enabler. It started in Rome with the gladiators to keep proletariate placated; it's all eyewash to keep you content. Everything and everyone is corrupt;

mayors, governors, governments, the United Nations, banks, Wall Street. They're all corrupt. If you're not a player, you're a spectator."

"Got it, but what's that supposed to mean? You're going to sit on the sidelines and watch?"

Trump ignored him.

"Just what am I supposed to be doing here and who do I do it for?"

"Me; but Stephanie Grisham on paper. That shouldn't raise too many eyebrows with your journalistic background."

"Will I last longer than Scaramucci?"

"I sure hope so. He used to be a good loyal man but now he needs attention and he's more of a loose cannon than me if you can believe it. You just help me. Just fly under the radar and you'll be fine."

"Just what am I supposed to be doing here?"

"I want you to start digging. Work with Barr in Justice. He is starting to investigate the investigators. He will assign you as a White House press secretary liaison within the FBI."

"Digging?"

"Yes, like you did in Delta Force special ops. Surgical strikes against high-level targets: Brennan, Clapper, Comey, Pelosi, Schumer, Schiff, Nadler. All of them. I want tax returns, dirt, who they dated in grade school, and what sites they goggle."

"I thought they just agreed with your deal?"

"They did, but Washington politics and politicians have a habit of changing their ways and minds. We have to be ready in case."

"I didn't do the digging in special ops.; they had S2 Intelligence for that, but if you want me to, you need to be more specific."

"Three by eight by six. Is that specific enough for you?"

"A hole?"

"Yes, a hole; a grave actually — many of them."

Chapter 41

"So, where are you? Where are we for that matter?" asked Abby.

"I'm not sure. He speaks in circles. He has his family off-site feverishly rebuilding the brand, while he rebuilds the economy. He has Barr, the Justice Department, the FBI, Homeland, the CIA and all the alphabets secretly working to bring down the left. He wants me to...," trailed off Halsey.

"To what?"

"To dig around for him."

"You'd be like the president's investigative reporter?"

"No, he wants me to be his digger."

"Digger?"

"Like in gravedigger."

Abby just looked at him and Halsey changed the subject and said, "By the way, he wants to have dinner with us tonight."

"Wow. First the Lincoln bedroom now dinner with the president in the White House."

"He wants to go out. Apparently, there's a play and fundraiser tonight at the Ford Theatre and he wants us to be his guest."

Abby had an undergrad history major from Amherst and a graduate degree in astrobiology from MIT asked, "He didn't ask General Milley first did he?"

Not getting the historical implication Halsey just said, I don't think so. Why?"

"Oh, nothing. What's the play? — Oh, wait don't tell me. 'Our American Cousin?'"

"I think that's it."

"That takes balls," said Abby.

"I guess, and we're sitting next to him. Let's take a walk to the wall, I need to pay my respects to some of my and my Dad's buddies."

Later that evening, Halsey and Abby joined President Trump and First lady Melania at the Ford Theatre in the presidential box overlooking the stage. The president sat in the exact location and reproduction chair occupied by president Lincoln 154 years previous. Melania sat to the presidents' right, as did Mary Lincoln before her. Abby and Halsey were next sitting where President Lincoln's guest Clara Harris her fiancée Major Henry Rathbone once sat.

The play was performed in period dialogue and costume and took some getting used to. After the intermission, everyone waited for the famous line delivered by the character Asa Trenchard, "Don't know the manners of good society, eh? Well, I guess I know enough to turn you inside out, old gal; you sockdologizing old man-trap!"

To the disappointment of a few in the audience, nothing happened. Few even laughed at, what at the time, was a very funny line. Despite all the security one guest jumped out of her seat and yelled, "Sic semper tyrannis!" before she was escorted out of the theater.

Unlike the Lincoln's version, the play continued to a standing ovation, but with most of the guests wondering why they were applauding.

The president and first lady, Abby and Halsey were photographed leaving the theater.

"So much for flying under the radar," whispered Halsey to Abby.

The president was hungry and didn't want to stay for the after-party, so they boarded the Beast for a short ride back to the White House.

"I have an unmarked car picking up dinner from McDonald's. Anything particular you want? He's getting burgers, fries, and chicken."

Halsey looked at Abby then back and said, "No, that about covers it. Wouldn't it be a hoot to drive-thru and order yourself? Can you imagine the reaction when you rolled down the window and picked up the order?"

"I did that once and it was a hoot, but Secret Service said that if I did it again, I risk someone spitting in the hamburgers so…"

It was late by the time they reunited in the second-floor dining room. The president was already there and unwrapping a burger while sampling the fries.

Melania came in and was served a salad, not from McDonald's, while Abby and Halsey took seats around the table. It was kind of a buffet, so they just helped themselves.

"So, what do you think, you guys want to watch a movie?"

"Some good stuff on Netflix Mr. President," suggested Abby.

"Never! I banned it. Fake shows. Terrible series. They have all those Sloppy Michael Moore Fahrenheit crap documentaries and The Circus. I turn off the TV until that circus has left town."

"What about the American Dream documentary? I thought that was balanced."

"You know it started out pretty balanced, but they had to turn it to fit their agenda and paint me as who they wanted me to be, not who I am."

"Okay, then what movies don't you like?" asked Abby, seeing as she had him on a roll.

"'A League of Their Own' is a terrible movie and I'm a huge baseball fan, Huge! Baseball is the most American thing ever, so don't insult it by having women playing a man's game! Rosie O'Donnell and Madonna can't act! So bad! And believe me, nobody wants to get to third base with that fat slob Rosie!

"'Deliverance' is tremendously unfair to my voters. I love my mountain men! These are some terrific people, nothing like these toothless, violent losers! Unfair! Look what happens when you ignore real Americans. Sad! And sometimes scary! Okay, so some of these regular American guys are not so innocent. I don't recommend the "squeal like a pig" scene. Believe me, just fast forward!

"'Terminator' with Arnold Schwarzenegger. A terrible actor and low-rated TV host. He talks in Mexican in the movie. Unbelievable! Arnold, learn English or go back to German Austria!

All of them! I like my heroes who are real Americans, okay? Not bodybuilding aliens! Being an action hero is easy. Being president is hard! Arnold can never be president. Just a fake robot with fake weapons. Sad!

My all-time favorite fake movie is 'All the President's Men'. I banned the *Washington Post* for fake news but here they are again reporting the wrong story! Deep Throat is a porn star, not a Washington insider. Not that I would know! One of the few good lines in the movie is "Follow the Money". So true. So unfair to the President! A good guy treated like a bad guy. His staff, so disloyal! The real story never gets told. The Democrats stole information. Republicans just trying to get it back. The leaks are real, the story is fake!"

"What movies do you like?" asked Abby.

"'Goodfellas' has almost a stellar cast, 'The Godfather' is a classic. 'The Good, the Bad and the Ugly', Clint is terrific. The characters are well-developed and sometimes remind me of some of the types I've had to deal with over the years in business."

Abby looked at Halsey then back to the president and said, "Robert De Niro, is in Goodfellow's and in the Godfather."

"I said almost a stellar cast and Punchy De Niro is in the Godfather two, not the classic Godfather one."

Again, Abby looked at Halsey and they both turned and in unison said, "'The Good, the Bad and the Ugly.'"

Chapter 42

USA TODAY **John Jackson and Jack Davison**

WASHINGTON – Congressional Democrats and President Donald Trump agreed to spend $2 trillion on the nation's crumbling infrastructure Tuesday. A plan to pay for that investment was noticeably agreed upon amid an unusual moment of bipartisanship.

"It's clear that both the White House and all of us want to get something done on infrastructure in a big and bold way," Senate Minority Leader Chuck Schumer said after meeting with Trump and House Speaker Nancy Pelosi for about 90 minutes.

Schumer and Pelosi entered the meeting amid an atmosphere and history of mistrust, as Congress hammers the White House for more congressional appearances by former special counsel Robert Mueller, Trump's tax returns, and several other issues.

White House press secretary Stephanie Grisham described the meeting as "excellent and productive" but did not confirm the $2 trillion figure. The number, which would almost certainly be spread out over a decade or longer, represents about half the government's annual budget.

"The United States has not come even close to properly investing in infrastructure for many years, foolishly prioritizing the interests of other countries over our own," Grisham said in a statement. "We have to invest in this country's future and bring our infrastructure to a level better than it has ever been before."

A Democratic source who requested anonymity to discuss details of the closed-door meeting said the lawmakers and the president also discussed immigration, trade and prescription drug prices. Trump pressed Pelosi to support his recently negotiated revised trade deal with Mexico and Canada, but Pelosi said that Democrats remain concerned about enforcing labor and environmental standards, the source said.

Despite the progress on infrastructure, House Speaker Nancy Pelosi was trying but losing her iron hand grip on her House members. On a conference call Monday evening, she and the chairs of several powerful committees discussed Democrats' path forward following the third appearance before the House Ethics Committee of Robert Mueller. Pelosi spoke briefly at the beginning of the call to reiterate her position — stated in a letter to members earlier in the day — that the House should continue committee investigations into the president before deciding on the next steps, according to multiple sources on the call who spoke on condition of anonymity.

One source said it was a "fairly sober discussion," with members generally expressing a "belief Trump should be impeached, but great fear of what the political consequences would be." Lawmakers also acknowledged the Republican-controlled Senate would not convict the president and remove him from office if the House impeached him.

"We have to save our democracy. This isn't about Democrats or Republicans. It's about saving our democracy," Pelosi said, according to a person on the call. "If it is what we need to do to honor our responsibility to the Constitution, if that's the place the facts take us, that's the place we have to go."

Most House Democrats were reluctant to entertain the idea of impeachment, worried that it would further divide the country and hurt Democrats' chances at winning the White House in 2020. But most members on the call appeared to be sobered by the detail provided in Mueller's third appearance before Congress and worried about long-lasting damage to the rule of law.

Back in their private room at the Willard, Pelosi, and Schumer commiserated over their dilemma.

"If I could only tell them about our deal," said Pelosi.

"We swore we wouldn't," said Schumer.

"Even if I could just tell Nadler, Schiff, and Waters they could help me close the deal."

"Yeah, and Waters would be on the 6 o'clock news telling the world."

"For a lousy wall and some immigration laws, we get the dreamers, health care, bi-partisan infrastructure, hold off on any more Supreme Court justice nominees, and best of all, no more Trump. And the cherry is we win 2020. House, Senate, and Presidency and for the next eight years we get to control all future nominees for the Supreme Court."

"Sounds wonderful when you say it, but we also have to give him and his family complete immunity. A get out of jail free card."

"And worth every penny."

"Call him."

Pelosi pulled out her cell and speed-dialed President Trump. After a few rings, he picked up.

"Nancy, what a pleasure. I have a few minutes, but let me call you back."

A few minutes later, Pelosi's phone rang, she heard some clicking which she assumed correctly were security measures to secure the connection and then she heard the president, "Do I have my wall yet?"

"Mr. President, I have spoken to all my House members. It's a tough sell. I might be able to fend off impeachment, but they still want to continue the investigation."

"I thought we had a deal?"

"We do. We will, but I need help to pull it off. I need to bring Nadler, Schiff and maybe one more on board to help me sell it. It's worth everything to the country not to have you run again."

"Your call, but if it leaks then I'm gonna keep running and all bets are off. I'll deny it. I continue to run, I win, and we go to war," said President Trump, and hung up.

Chapter 43

President Trump and Tom Halsey were sitting in the Oval Office discussing Halsey's role, and future when Madeleine Westerhout, the president's personal secretary, rushed in and turned on the TV. "I thought you would want to see this," said Madeleine.

A breaking news banner was flashing on the screen with the camera focusing on Wolf Blitzer.

> This is Wolf Blitzer in the Situation Room. We have breaking news. Democratic Congresswoman Maxine Waters has just come forward with an incredible unsubstantiated story. She alleges a secret 'Devil's Pact', initiated by President Trump, with Speaker of the House Nancy Pelosi and Senate Minority Leader Chuck Schumer in which for major favors, concessions, and immunity, President Trump will not be the Republican nominee in 2020. I stress alleged. Live with reaction to this incredible story is…

"Turn it off," said the president.

Madeleine, accustomed to the president's curt demands, did so and left the office.

"I just wanted to protect my family. That was the only reason I wouldn't seek a second term. What happened to Barron, could happen again to any of my family. I have received death threats if I send the military into Hong Kong or Iran. My family has been threatened over immigration. But now they won't even let me keep my family safe. Now they want war.

"Just when I thought I was out they pull me back in," said the president going off again into a blank stare.

Halsey had seen it many times before in combat soldiers and trapped noncombatants and had been told he had it many times. The thousand-yard stare is a type of look when a person stares far away blankly into the distance. A limp, blank, unfocused gaze of the battle-weary. A characteristic of shell shock, the despondent stare reflects dissociation from trauma and is certainly not unique to soldiers. Anyone experiencing significant trauma from incidences like violent attack, natural disaster, constant danger or phenomenal loss may begin to manifest acute stress disorder or PTSD. He knew two things could happen in the next few minutes. The president would snap out of it or he wouldn't.

Halsey remembered hearing Steve Bannon predicting that now the Russia probe was over, Trump will "come off the chains" and "go full animal" on his political opponents. Maybe that's what this is. Maybe the thousand-yard stare is the prelude of what's to come. Maybe that's why Trump bought Wolfhall in Wolfhampton and kept Volkov, Hammer, and Sickle around. Maybe that's why he wants me, as his 'Grave Digger'. President Trump, who kept us out of wars around the world is now going to war with America—its leaders and its instigators.

"Mr. President," said Halsey.

President Trump, still seated behind Resolve, didn't respond. "Mr. President," said Halsey again, wondering if he should call Madeleine back in and get his doctor. Halsey got up and walked towards the door.

"Where are you going?" asked the president. "Sit back down," he demanded, "we have work to do."

Happy that the president snapped out of it, Halsey did as instructed and waited for the president's orders.

"This has to come from and go through you. Get with David Pecker of the *National Enquirer* and other right-wing rags. Get with Rush Limbaugh, Michael Savage. Beck on the Blaze. Get Sean Hannity, Laura Ingraham, Dennis Prager, Mark Levin, Michael Medved. Hire an opposition research firm.

"I want a Saturday night massacre. Scratch that — that was Nixon. I want a Saturday night lynching. Make it happen in the same time slot as that failed comedy show SNL, and we'll call ours SNL, too. Start this weekend. Pick a victim. I would start with Nadler or Schiff, then Brenan, Clapper, Comey, Waters, Pelosi, Schumer and the rest. Let them sweat who's next. 'One a Day'. I don't care. I want dirt, my gravedigger. Dig up the skeletons. I want something so bad that the Sunday news shows: *Meet the Press*, *State of the Union*, *This Week*, *Face the Nation* and even *Fox News Sunday* choke on it.

"So, I'm what, sort of a buffer?" asked Halsey.

"A what?"

"A buffer. Someone in between you and your investigators. The guy between the diggers and the dirt."

"Oh yeah, a buffer. My administration has a lot of buffers!" said President Trump.

"So, Saturday night we spring the ambush. Sunday, we let the Sunday news shows feed. Monday, we let the water cooler take its toll, Tuesday, they will go on trial, convicted on Wednesday and sentenced on Thursday. Friday they will be executed and Saturday night we start all over again. Is that about it?" asked Halsey.

"Terrific. Except for the water cooler part. You're showing your age. Think Twitter, Instagram, and YouTube," said the president.

"You're showing your age. How about Anchor, Lasso, Vero, Houseparty, Kik, Tik Tok, and Caffeine," said Halsey.

"Touché Halsey," said the president.

"Madeleine," called President Trump on the intercom, "get me the Vice President, Kellyanne, Sara and Rudy." To Halsey, he added, "We do a Bill Clinton. We deny, deny, and deny the 'Devil's Pact' and get our spin out fast."

Chapter 44

It was almost 9 am Sunday morning at "The Wolf House", as Wolfhall in Wolfhampton was now being called by the media, President Trump and Tom Halsey had just settled in in front of the dining room LED wall with their Sausage McMuffin meals from McDonald's to watch Rudy Giuliani on *Meet the Press*.

ANNOUNCER:

From *NBC News* in Washington, the longest-running show in television history, this is *Meet the Press* with Chuck Todd.

CHUCK TODD:

Good Sunday morning. We're going to get to the 3rd edition Mueller report later in the show. But there was a terrible series of additional terror attacks in Sri Lanka this morning. The coordinated attacks across the country again targeted Christian worshippers celebrating the holy days in churches and high-end hotels frequented by foreign tourists. The death toll is going to number into the hundreds. The attacks broke a period of peace in Sri

Lanka established after the Easter Massacre. The country has endured decades of civil war, which had come to an end, or supposed end. But turning now to the home front. Joining me now is the president's personal attorney, Rudy Giuliani. Welcome back to *Meet the Press* Mr. Giuliani.

RUDY GIULIANI:

Thank you, Chuck.

CHUCK TODD:

I intended to start off with some of the front-line conclusions from the latest Mueller congressional appearance, and third Ukraine whistleblower, but what came out from Congresswoman Waters about a Devils Pact the other day and what came from the White House late last night are shockers. First, though, you outed Congressman Adam Buzz Schiff as being gay and that it was his lover who made the claim of beatings and mistreatment. Are you serious? Who is your source, and do you and the president accept this as fact?

RUDY GIULIANI:

First of all, Chuck, we are not making the accusation that Congressman Schiff is gay or that he has a lover. The *LA Times* is, and they are breaking that story today. Someone's personal sexual orientation, as far as we're concerned, is their own business; but when that someone is a high ranking elected official and co-chairman of the House Ethics Committee, well...

CHUCK TODD:

But you did. You leaked the story. You did a parody about it on your new *Saturday Night Lynching* show on *Fox*. Now it's out there. We have no idea if it's real news or fake news.

RUDY GIULIANI:

Fake news Chuck? Oh, now there's fake news you when it suits you? Anyway, you brought it up. Not me. You suggested I outed Congressman Buzz Schiff as being gay. I responded by telling you what the *LA. Times* is reporting. That's one of your fake news outlets, right? *Los Angeles Times* reporter and assistant managing editor, Kristina Bellatori dropped the bombshell, not the White House. We don't believe the story at all.

Bellatori was contacted by a Mr. Smart, who claims to be the gay lover of California Congressman, Buzz Schiff. According to the article, which we received an advanced copy of, Mr. Smart contacted her and told her that he had been neglected and hidden away too long and wanted to speak out. Mr. Smart stated that he has been Mr. Schiff's gay lover for many years and has endured a plethora of emotional and physical abuse and that Mr. Schiff is a hypocrite.

CHUCK TODD:

This sounds like an unfounded rumor to dog Schiff. You say the reporter's name is Kristina Bellatori? But why did you do a skit about it on your SNL?

RUDY GIULIANI:

I didn't and we didn't, but the show did it because that's what your SNL does. Parodies and skits of what or who is in currently in the news. In fact, your SNL has done President Trump many times. I didn't hear you bring that up on your show.

CHUCK TODD:

Why do you keep saying my SNL? I don't have anything to do with the show. Okay moving on. Congresswoman Waters has made some serious accusations about secret meetings between Speaker Pelosi, Senator Schumer, and President Trump...

RUDY GIULIANI:

Let me stop you there, Chuck. That's Mad Max talking trash. The White House has categorically denied her unsubstantiated fabrications. Did Speaker Pelosi or Senator Schumer back her up? No! Case closed; end of story."

President Trump clicked the TV off. "Good job Halsey. Let them chew on that for the week. Mr. Smart? Guess that makes Schiff, Mr. Dumb. Our *SNL's* gonna be huge. Rudy will handle the Crazy Maxine Waters, and I like his nickname for her better than mine. Mad Max!"

Halsey let the praise go but said instead, "This whole story about Schiff stinks. It may not even be true. Sounds made up to me. *Net Spies*, one of our sources, says their source for this Schiff gay lover story is *"Los Angeles Times* reporter and assistant managing editor, Kristina Bellatori". There is no Kristina Bellatori at the *LA Times*. I checked. There is a Christina

Bellantoni, who's *LAT's* assistant managing editor. I haven't seen it yet but there is supposed to be a tweet out by the real Christina Bellantoni claiming that this is '...some very seriously fake news.'"

"Too bad. It's out there now. Let him spend the week defending himself. He's out of the closet now. So now 'fake news' is real? Who's next?"

"Why? Why are you doing this?"

"The real question is why are they doing this? Why did Pelosi and Schumer go back on our deal? Why are they now going full force to impeach me? This is about the takedown of the President of the United States. I accept that they hate me. I don't blame them, I'm everything they're not. The country is doing great; we're not at war with anyone. What's really behind all this hate is that if I get another four years, there is a very good chance that I will get to nominate another Supreme Court Judge. Ginsburg is on her last leg. That would mean six conservatives to three liberals. That's what's eating them. Getting rid of me is just a means to an end. Presidents come and go. Supreme Court judges are for life."

Chapter 45

Barron had accompanied his father to Wolfhall for the weekend, despite his mother's objection. He likes Mr. Halsey and his new personal Secret Service protection agents, Andrea Mancino and Pete Myers aka am and pm.

Despite the media speculation, President Trump kept Volkov around for no other reason than to piss Putin off. Trump's mantra, like Michael Corleone's, "Keep your friends close, and your enemies closer," was "Keep your family close, your friends near, your enemies nearer, your base content and your administration confused."

With Volkov's restoration came Riana, Hammer, and Sickle which delighted Barron to no end. Besides Volkov and some staff, only Barron spoke fluent Russian and that delighted Hammer and Sickle. Together the four of them, along with am and pm spent endless hours exploring Wolfhall and the grounds. Their favorite room was the Edison room but not the tunnel leading to it.

"Dad, can Hammer and Sickle and I go to town? I have leashes for them," asked Barron.

President Trump, not a dog lover, let alone a wolf lover, hesitated but said, "Barron, you and the wolves walking down Main Street might cause a bit of a stir don't you think? After all, they did kill Kahbib Nurmodov or Hawk or whatever his name was. I just don't trust them."

"But this is Wolfhall and were in the village of Wolfhampton. If not here, where? Mr. Volkov could come with us," said Barron.

"I don't want you alone with him. Look, how about taking a walk on the beach to the end of Wolfhampton. That's quite a walk."

"Dad!" exclaimed Barron.

"Okay, but later when we go to town for dinner."

"Thanks, Dad. We'll walk while you eat. Get me five burgers to go, okay?"

"Five?"

"Me, Hammer and Sickle, Riana and am."

The president looked at Agent Mancino and said, "If anything happens…" he stopped, looked at the agent but decided no further threat was necessary. The agent seemed to understand and scurried out of the library after her charge.

"Come on let's go grab an early dinner," said the president to Abby and Halsey. I know the owners of Jackson Hole Burgers and they just opened on Main Street. They're the best and been doing it since the 70s. You can get a pretty good steak out here but a great burger? Fuhgeddaboudit. Having Jackson Hole out here in Wolfhampton is a game-changer."

Donald Trump has always been a meat-and-potatoes kind of guy. He likes his steaks well done and he knows his way around beef on a bun. So, it's no surprise he brought his favorite elbows-on-the-table, saloon-style joint to Wolfhampton. To keep it a pleasant dining experience, a doorman checks guests in on an iPad to keep the non-deplorables at bay.

While Barron, Riana, Hammer, Sickle, and am walked Main Street causing great anxiety among all the tourist and shop owners, President Trump sat at his private table in the back corner with a view of the room and the open kitchen, along with Abby and Halsey, and settled in for what hoped to be an enjoyable early evening dinner.

"Buzz Lightyear Schiff called me a homophobic, can you believe that guy. I kept Volkov here with me so Putin couldn't execute him for being gay. Man-up Lightyear — take your bride out and show her off once in a while. Now you should go after Crazy Pelosi, after her intervention comment and her stammering last week," said the president.

Learning to ignore the president's rants, Abby instead offered, "The market will open down again Monday," said Abby.

But she inadvertently opened another. "Sure, it will. With all the haters coming after me and the fake news, talk of impeachment no wonder. If they keep at it the whole world's economy will tank."

"Tell him," said Abby. She really loved Tommy but knew he wouldn't toot his own horn and had to press him.

Before he could answer a waiter came over to take their orders. The president ordered the cheeseburger platter with steak fries and a Jackson Hole milkshake made with vanilla ice cream, banana, peanut butter, and caramel sauce. Abby ordered the guacamole burger platter with melted cheddar cheese, warm corn tortilla chips, guacamole and sour cream on the side. Halsey ordered the English burger platter served on an English muffin. Both ordered iced tea.

When the waiter left to place the order, Halsey said, "I have an idea how you could end immigration, forgo the wall, make America huge, completely outflank the left and sweep the election — you, the House and the Senate."

"So, you're Secretary of State now? A political strategist maybe?" asked President Trump.

"Why not? You were a TV reality star. Now you're president."

"Show me someone without an ego, and I'll show you a loser – having a healthy ego, or high opinion of yourself Halsey, is a real positive in life. Tell me more Mr. Ranger Reporter."

"An American Union. The AU. A political and economic union of 16 member states including the U.S. Canada, Mexico, Central, and South America. We could also invite the Caribbean, Greenland, and Iceland. We would more than triple our population to almost a billion. That would put us up there with China. We would almost triple our square footage. The Louisiana Purchase in 1803 between the United States and France, gave us approximately 827,000 square miles of land for $15 million. Then we got Florida. In 1848 we stole Arizona, California, New Mexico, and Texas, and parts of Colorado, Nevada, and Utah from Mexico and in 1867 we purchased Alaska from Russia for $7.2 million," said Halsey.

"If I closed my eyes, I would have thought I was having dinner with Crazy Bernie and AOC. You know she's the one who said we don't need farms because we have grocery stores," said the president.

"That was Stacey Abrams," said Abby, "and she didn't actually say that. What she…"

"Doesn't matter," interrupted the president, "it's out there. With this AU we would what, distribute all North America's wealth to El Salvador and Venezuela? Open the borders and replace the dollar with ameros. Ameros for Christ's sake. Press one or stay on the line for Spanish-press two for English. And when this thing goes to shit, like the EU and we want out we'll call for an Axit vote?" laughed the president. He then added, "It didn't work for Theresa May or Boris Johnson and the Brits. What makes you think it would work for us?"

"Because we would be Brussels," said Halsey.

"Hmm…" murmured the president.

Walking out of Jackson Hole President Trump, Abby and Halsey stopped by Barron's Secret Service black Suburban.

The window came down and Halsey passed Barron a take-out bag and asked, "How did it go?"

"Thanks; and great until a very pretty lady with two little white dogs came towards us."

Giving Volkov, who was sitting next to Barron a stern look, President Trump asked, "What happened? They didn't attack the little dogs, or the lady, did they?"

"Dad the crazy little white multi poo and a white fox terrier went wild, barking and scared the crap out of Hammer and Sickle. They pulled me the opposite way down the street to get away from them. I never saw them so afraid. People were laughing and taking pictures. It was embarrassing."

"Where were you, Volkov? You of all people should be able to placate two little white dogs. And, where were you?" asked President Trump now looking at Agent Mancino.

"What," said Agent Mancino aka am with a dumb smile and a hunched shoulder raised arm gesture, "you would have me gun down the woman and her dogs on Main Street?"

Ignoring her antics, the president asked, "Where's Agent Myers?"

"His screws came loose," said Mancino.

"So, I have a comedian and a nut watching my kid?" asked the president.

"Agent Myers is one of the agents who got hurt helping search for Barron during the kidnapping. He broke his jaw and had to have it wired. His jaw screws came loose, and he had to have them tightened," said Mancino.

"Oh," said the president, "That explains it — I thought he was from Locust Valley or went to Yale."

Walking away towards the Beast, President Trump couldn't help but chuckle. He heard snickers coming from Abby, Halsey, and his agents. "You can't make this shit up," laughed the president.

Chapter 46

Once again Pelosi and Schumer were in the Willard Hotel, just across the street from the White House, ensconced in their congressional safe room, planning their strategy.

"Why did you tell Waters for God's sake? Can't you control her?" asked Schumer.

"I know. She gave me her word, but she hates Trump so much she couldn't keep her big mouth shut. I thought I needed her on our side to close the deal, but she hates Trump so much she won't let him off the hook with immunity. She wants him to hang," said Pelosi.

"Look, we have to get this back on track before..." Schumer stopped in mid-sentence as his phone rang. He checked the display and saw it was his Chief of Staff Michael Lynch who had explicit orders not to call. "It's Lynch. He wouldn't call unless it was urgent." He pressed answer. "Better be good Michael."

"Oh, it's better than good. The Summit of the Americas that starts tomorrow attended by Vice President Pence?" said Lynch.

Schumer put his phone on speaker. "Yes and..."

"And... President Trump just bumped Pence and is at this moment aboard Air Force One en route to Orlando with Pompeo, Ross, Lighthizer and another yet unidentified high-ranking administrative official, for to-morrow's summit in Orlando. The Summit of the Americas, which in itself is a big deal has just become huge and brings together world leaders and the most influential CEOs from throughout the Western Hemisphere.

"Aides say the president plans to deliver a sales pitch for the United States as a preferred economic partner, encouraging other countries in the hemisphere to do business with the U.S. rather than "external state actors" such as China. However, an unnamed White House source has leaked that President Trump intends to deliver a different sales pitch and has also invited Canada, the Caribbean, Iceland, and Greenland. A sales pitch with a curve, a fastball, and a change-up all in one. We're told this is going to be a tough sell, but President Trump is promising a game-changer."

"Keep me posted," said Schumer and hung up. "What the hell is he up to?"

"Whatever it is it's not good for us. What could be so important for him to want to deal with Mexico, Central, and South America without even informing Congress? This man is certifiable. I told you he needs an intervention," said Pelosi.

"Not so fast. Immigration, the wall, that's two of our 2020 full house. Without them, we're screwed. If he's meeting with Latin America himself, he's got something cooking. Something big. Because Waters jumped ship, it now looks like Trump is getting ready to send us all to the bottom," said Schumer.

Chapter 47

"What do you think?" asked Halsey sitting across from the president and Pompeo, and next to Ross and Lighthizer in the conference room aboard Airforce One returning from the three-day summit.

"I think they're hot for the deal," said Lighthizer.

"But you think they can keep the oath of secrecy they swore by?" asked Ross.

"Are you kidding? We're dealing with some of the most corrupt politicians in the world. They are meeting right now to see how best to swing this AU to their financial advantage, but they also have big mouths and it's all gonna leak," said the president.

"But if it does leak it will hurt our chances of getting it passed," said Pompeo.

"No," said President Trump. "It will help us because the Dems will have the biggest decision of their lives. Join us or fight us."

"Join us to bring together all North America and Latin America into an America Union like the European Union. That would take the wind out of the left's sails I should think," said Pompeo glancing at both Ross and Lighthizer.

"Exactly. Fight us and they look anti-Spanish, anti-progressive. It's a win-win for us," said the president.

"I think, since we're referring primarily to Mexico, Central and South America it's Latino," said Halsey.

"Spanish, Latino, Hispanic. Why don't they do what we do? You know Whites, Blacks. Why not just Browns or is that not PC?" asked the president.

Ignoring the president, Lighthizer asked, "But how exactly does an AU help us with immigration, caravans, the wall?"

"Because, when we nominate our own president and chief administrative officer of the American Union Council, we'll be Brussels, and we'll rule the Union with an iron hand. All member countries will cooperate fully or suffer the consequences. If one stumbles all fall, except us. There will be a 'No Illegal Immigration Policy' written into the AU constitution. Every county must police their own borders. We'll still have borders but no need for walls. We'll have international passports issued by the AU council member countries which will allow free movement between countries. No passport. No entry. Any country with an exorbitant amount of refugees fleeing their country will be heavily fined," said Pompeo.

"But what about 'Give me your tired, your poor, your huddled masses yearning to breathe free, the wretched refuse of your teeming shore'?" asked Halsey.

"That's the French for you. They tell us what to do on the Statue of Liberty but when it comes to their own country they say 'Non,'" said Pompeo. There's very little in our constitution regarding immigration. Our immigration law is very complex, and there is much confusion as to how it works. The Immigration and Naturalization Act provides for an annual worldwide limit of 675,000 permanent legal immigrants. There is nothing in the constitution protecting or accepting immigrants who come across the border illegally. That's where the states' rights come in to play and they have the right — the duty to protect and secure their borders. Some do and some don't."

"You're preaching to the choir," said Lighthizer.

"All's good. We're investigating the investigators; the impeachment has stalled — again! We hit the street with Pelosi's tax returns Saturday night, and she was grilled all day today. She has a net worth of approximately $120 million."

"In reality, she and her husband made a great deal of that money legally in real estate," said Halsey.

"Yeah, but what about the 2011, 60 Minutes hit segment called "Pelosi Insider Trading." The episode detailed Pelosi's involvement in initial public offerings while having inside information. In one example, Pelosi's profited from an IPO from Visa while regulations on credit card companies were being considered in Congress," said Ross. "Judicial Watch's exposed Nancy Pelosi's corrupt abuse of military aircraft — her numerous requests for military escorts and military aircraft for herself and her family?"

"Again. All of it doesn't matter. She is going to be spending the rest of the week denying and explaining where she got her money from and nobody's gonna believe her and the next pigeon on the roof is waiting for their turn — the next edition of SNL," said the president.

"Our SNL or theirs?" asked Lighthizer.

"Our Saturday Night Lynching. No one watches their SNL anymore," said Trump.

After Lighthizer, Ross and Pompeo left to each secretly leak the president's AU idea to their respective news outlets, President Trump ordered some Diet Cokes and CFC. Halsey then asked, "How come you didn't tell them the AU was my idea?"

"If you wait long enough it will be," answered the president.

"What's that supposed to mean?"

Before the president could answer, the pilot's voice came over the sound system. "This is the pilot speaking. We have visitors. Two UFO's escorting us. One out the port side and one out starboard. Our military fast movers are, as directed, following protocol and keeping their distance. If there is any variance I will come back on the air. Over and out."

Halsey was up and looking out the starboard side at the UFO. It was dark grey and cylindrical in shape. No wings, no windows, no markings, no engines. It was less than 50 yards off Airforce One's nose and cursing at the same speed. Then there was a blur and it was gone.

"Jesus. Did you see that? I saw it. It was a real spaceship. What are we doing about it? It could have shot us down," said an excited Halsey.

"It happens all the time. They just come and fuck with us for a while then go away. We think that's how they get their rocks off. Not to worry, happens all the time," said President Trump.

"We don't tell anyone? — was Area 51 for real?"

"No and yes. They wouldn't believe us any way, and it would just cause fear and world panic. I have my new Space Force all over it. I'll let it out when it's to my benefit."

"You seem to take all this in stride, Mr. President."

"Yeah well, when you get the top job you get the top security clearance and find out things no one else knows. If I told you what really happened to Kennedy, I would have to have you killed," laughed the president. "Anyway, where were we? Oh, yeah, you were asking why I didn't give you credit for the AU idea and I told you if you wait long enough, you'll get it. What I meant was that eventually, most things I touch turns to shit. Casinos, golf courses, wives, friends, Cabinet members, and even ideas. And when this AU idea turns to shit, and it will, you'll own it."

"So, if you think it's going to, as you say, turn to shit, why do it in the first place?"

"Because, my friend, it's all about illusion. I'll be remembered as either the greatest con artist since PT Barnum or as a Megalodon, the biggest, most feared shark ever. But let them have their fun. I'm just a lucky guy from Queens."

Chapter 48

𝕿𝖍𝖊 𝕹𝖊𝖜 𝖄𝖔𝖗𝖐 𝕿𝖎𝖒𝖊𝖘

Making Friends, Chased by Border Troubles, Trump Navigates the Summit of the Americas not with a curve or fast-ball but with a change-up.

By Mark Baker

July 2020

ORLANDO FL — In an unexpected and unprecedented move, President Trump sat down with Western Hemisphere presidents, strongmen, and dictators presumably to discuss the United States becoming a preferred economic partner, encouraging other countries in the hemisphere to do business with the U.S. rather than "external state actors" such as China. However, The New York Times has learned that President Trump had a secret behind closed doors meetings to discuss something entirely different. Three high ranking unnamed White House sources have told us that President

Trump delivered a different sales pitch and had also invited Canada, the Caribbean, Iceland, and Greenland to the summit. He downgraded a meeting with one ally and postponed one with another. He exchanged icy smiles with the prime minister of Canada, who had threatened to skip the summit with the United States and Mexico because of lingering bitterness over steel tariffs.

President Trump was preoccupied with legal clouds back home, after Special Counsel Robert Mueller's fourth press conference, and more Ukraine whistleblowers coming forward, tweeting angrily that nothing changes from the Mueller Report. There was insufficient evidence; therefore, in our country, a person is innocent. The case is closed! Thank you.

Mueller said, "The Constitution requires a process other than the criminal justice system to formally accuse a sitting president of wrongdoing," that he was prohibited to charge the president and therefore not an option he could consider, but he would not proclaim the president's innocence. After Mueller Comments, Nadler Declared, "It's time for Congress to take over."

For Mr. Trump, his first day meetings of the Summit of the Americas industrialized nations in Orlando was a window into his idiosyncratic statecraft after over two years in office. His "America First" foreign policy has now morphed into the "America Union" modeled after the European Union but with a strange patchwork of partners.

President Trump proposed "An American Union, just like the European Union. The AU will be a political and economic union of 16 member states including North America, Mexico, Central, and South America and possibly the Caribbean, Greenland, and Iceland. This unexpected proposal puts the GOP squarely at the forefront of solving immigration and without a wall. We have asked for a response from Speaker Pelosi, but messages and phone calls remain unreturned. We did receive a statement from her office saying that 'President Trump did not discuss this AU proposal with Congress so it's just another reason for treason. President Trump is attempting to sell off the United States to the highest bidder and a smokescreen to cover his crimes against...'

It was 6:30 am and President Trump was sitting at the Oval Office's Resolute Desk, the surface of which is mostly clear, aside from a phone. Trump was leaning backward in his chair reading *The New York Times* article for the second time when Madeleine Westerhout knocked, came in and said, "Mr. Halsey's on line one."

"Put him through Madeleine. Thank you."

"You read the Times?"

"I did sir. Who leaked it?"

"Who do you think?"

"Pompeo, Ross and Lighthizer."

"That's a bingo."

"But you wanted them to, right?"

"Of course. I just didn't anticipate Mueller's latest stunt; pulling a Comey on me."

"A Comey?"

"Yeah. He pronounced Crooked Hillary guilty on live TV but didn't charge her. Seems all these former FBI directors went to the same school.

"It's out there that I want the Western Hemisphere to join us as one. North, Central, and South America. Let the Left join us or fight us. Makes no difference to me. We win either way. As far as Mueller goes, he opened the door for Nadler again, and I say bring it on. It's just going to help us win 2020."

"We still go ahead with the SNL?"

"Of course. Can you move Fat Jerry to the front of the line? Are you still at the Willard?"

"No. We're subletting an apartment in Foggy Bottom."

"If you're free tonight, come on over. We'll have dinner and watch a movie and I'll tell you where all this is heading — what my end game is."

"What's the movie?"

"The Man Who Would Be King."

Chapter 49

Once again, Pelosi and Schumer, only this time accompanied by Jerry Nadler, Buzz Schiff, and Maxine Waters, were in the Willard Hotel, discussing Trump, who else, and planning their strategy.

"This American Union is a crock of shit. He has no intention of going through with it," said Waters. "Low life Trump — lying, crooked, tax evader, porn star fornicator — should take his ridiculous self home, resign, and free us of what we will have to do to impeach him and throw him out of office! He's just prodding us."

"Maybe, but Mexico and the rest of Latin America are loving it. An *NBC News/Wall Street Journal* poll published Sunday put Trump's approval rating at 49 percent among registered voters. Up 5 points since the AU leak. If he comes out with a live address to the nation about his AU proposal, he's gonna have the Spanish, excuse me, the Latin vote locked up. What are we going to campaign on? The economy? Jobs? Immigration? We're left with the 'Green Deal' and that he's a racist and a loony," said Schumer.

"This show on *FOX* going live with their own *SNL* in the same time slot as the real *SNL* is bad. He's making a comedy show out of outing me and Nancy. Who's next?" asked Schiff.

"Is he hosting it?" asked Schumer.

"No! I'm sure he'd like to, but he is staying far away for a change. I'm told he has a buffer," said Nadler.

"Look," said Pelosi, "Chuck and I asked for this meeting because we have to make a decision. We either start impeachment proceedings again and have it drag out into the 2020 elections where Trump uses it against us and wins four more years, or we go back and take the deal.

"For him to drop out in 2020, it's gonna cost us. We must make his last five months a booming success. The wall gets built. A comprehensive immigration bill gets passed. We and the media must play nice and no indictments, criminal or civil prosecution against him or any member of his family while he's in office or out.

"But for that, we get the House, Senate, and Presidency. We get healthcare back, infrastructure, and at least one, possibly two, Supreme Court Judges."

"To put it another way," said Schumer, "For that, you get the head, the tail, the whole damn fish."

"I know how you all feel, and Adam and I have already been lynched. The rest of you are next. But we have got to decide. I want a unanimous binding vote now. Deal or no deal?" asked Pelosi.

Twenty minutes later, Madeleine Westerhout entered the Oval Office and interrupted a phone conversation between President Trump and Equatorial Guinea's leader Teodoro Obiang, with a pantomime routine indicating that Speaker Pelosi was on the other line.

"That was a great story Teodoro, but I have to run. My parting words to you are; when somebody challenges you, fight back. Be brutal, be tough," said President Trump and disconnected.

"Madam Speaker, what a nice surprise," said President Trump.

"Mr. President, I have you on speakerphone. I'm with Chuck, Jerry, Adam, and Maxine in the Willard Hotel, discussing what we talked about last week," said Pelosi.

"The Speaker has me on speaker. Very funny. Madam Speaker I'm not sure what you're referring to, but if it's about solving immigration and border security, you have my attention," said the president.

"If what we talked about is still on the table, I have a unanimous agreement from everyone here to accept it."

"Terrific, but so there is no mistaking this time, write up what it is that you think we discussed and when all five of you sign it, send it over. Time is of the essence and; just so you know, I intend to announce five more campaign rallies in Blue States. Starting in Illinois with First Lady Melania, and Vice President Pence, in Chicago sometime next week. In case you missed it, Melania, at the Albritton Middle School at Fort Bragg, North Carolina, said she's ready to serve another four years as first lady when I'm re-elected. She says, She loves what she does and thinks I'm doing a fantastic job.

"And one more thing Madam Speaker, that two million — in a bag in your room. I'm going in to take a nap — when I wake, if the money's on the table, I'll know I have a partner — if it's not, I'll know I don't," said President Trump and disconnected.

"What the hell!" exclaimed Schumer.

"He's channeling Hyman Roth from the Godfather," said Nadler.

"He's certifiable," said Schiff.

"No, he's a lying, crooked, tax evader, porn star fornicator crazy nut," said Waters.

"Let's sign it and be done with him," said Pelosi.

Chapter 50

President Trump's day began at 5:30 am, and he started making calls around 6 am.

Breakfast consisted of bacon and eggs. Then he spent the rest of the morning *tweeting* while watching *Fox News*, before beginning his official day at 11 am. Starting with the President's Daily Brief, which is a highly classified document prepared by the Director of National Intelligence. It provides the president with sensitive intelligence on international matters and events. The material is available to other very senior officials on a strictly need-to-know basis.

Then the president moved into a series of meetings and events, including a briefing by one of his Cabinet officers and White House staff. He then had meetings with other White House staff and congressional leaders concerning his legislative strategy.

Later, he delivered remarks to several groups of citizens — including a roundtable of educators on raising high school performance, and to businesspeople on American competitiveness and a thank-you to volunteers who responded to a natural disaster.

He held various press scrums where he delivered quick messages to the public on several issues and responded quickly to several press stories. He started to wind down around 6:30 pm and instead of reaching for a beer or a martini he ordered another Diet Coke.

Melania was back in the White House with Barron and was looking forward to a quiet dinner with her family, Halsey and her new best friend Abby. No CFC or McDonalds tonight. She planned a nice semi-healthy meal in the family dining room.

"Smells delicious. What are we having?" asked the president.

"My Caesar salad and Chicken Parmigiana with accouterments and a special chocolate cake courtesy of Jean Georges," said Melania.

"Are they here?" asked Barron.

"They're on their way up," said Melania.

A few moments later. "Hey, Barron. How you doeen?" asked Halsey, imitating Joey from *Friends*, as he entered the dining room followed by Abby.

Barron ran to Halsey and Abby with a big smile on his face, glad to see his friends again.

"Hi, Mr. Halsey. Hi, Ms. Adams. Coming to the game tomorrow?" asked Barron.

"Wouldn't miss it," said Halsey — "Me, too," added Abby.

They spent the next ten minutes, until dinner was served, discussing Barron's soccer team, D.C. United U-14 chances of taking the division title and Barron, a midfielder, chances of getting MVP.

Dinner was delicious. The chocolate cake was proclaimed divine by all who partook. They all retired to the family theater on the first floor for popcorn, candy and to watch an adaptation of Rudyard Kipling *The Man Who Would Be King* starring Sean Connery and Michael Caine.

Only President Trump had seen it before, so it was a new movie for everyone else.

Based on a short story by Rudyard Kipling, the adventure film follows the exploits of Danny Dravot (Sean Connery) and Peachy Carnehan (Michael Caine) two 19th-century English non-commissioned officers stationed in India. Tired of life as soldiers, the two travel to the isolated land of Kafiristan, where they are ultimately embraced by the people and revered as rulers. After a series of misunderstandings, the natives came to believe that Danny was a god and made him king, but he and Peachy couldn't keep up their deception forever. The ending is heroic but sad.

After the movie, Melania and Barron said goodnight, excused themselves and returned upstairs. President Trump, Halsey, and Abby remained it the theater.

"It's a terrific movie. Two great actors. A lot of history and adventure. Did you like it?" asked the president.

"I did like it. It was a great adventure movie. Thank you for the great dinner and a great movie," said Halsey.

"Abby?" asked the president.

"This is the first time I've seen the movie, Mr. President. I did read the short story in high school — a typical Kipling adventure. I thought it was very well done, and well-acted. The moral being ..."

"The moral being," interrupted President Trump, "if you work hard, and be smart, winning takes care of everything!"

"I was going to say something more along the lines of British imperialism, fantasy, racial superiority, arrogance, and friends to the end."

"See! We agree. I want to tell you both a few things. First, that we're not alone. Did Tom tell you about the spacecraft he saw out the window of Airforce One the other day?"

"He might have mentioned it."

"Well, it's real, becoming more frequent, and starting to become a problem."

"A problem? Are they hostile?" asked Abby.

"No, not so far, but they are way ahead of us technically and should they become war-like, we may not be able to stand up to them. We're technically way ahead of Russia and China, so if we can't stop them, they won't be able to help either."

"So, they're seeing them, too?"

"No, they seem to like America. Oh, they have had some sightings but nothing like we're experiencing."

"What about the world coming together like the movie, Close Encounters, and trying to make contact?"

"I have our new Space Force working on just that and a few other options, but there is a bigger problem. If we acknowledge that aliens exist, how will the world's people react? Religions for example. There is nothing in the Bible about Adam and Eve and ET."

"I see what you mean, but I still think this is amazing. Till now it's been books, movies, speculation, and denial. But now it's real. Another civilization, a parallel universe perhaps, and light years ahead of us."

"I have Mike Pompeo secretly working with allied nations on a plan to establish contact and we are meeting with religious leaders throughout the world to get their impute, but it's getting tricky. We are also working on a defensive measure similar to President Reagan's proposed Strategic Defense Initiative (SDI), that would construct a space-based anti-missile system. The SDI was intended to defend the United States from attack from Soviet ICBMs by intercepting the ..."

"I know what SDI was — is Mr. President, but I wouldn't let it out that you are proposing building another wall. This one in space to keep aliens out," said Abby.

"I agree. I can't get one built here and all I need now is to say I have seen aliens. How do you say intervention? Just as well because religious leaders throughout the world are very worried and want us to hold up on any kind of acknowledgment or announcement until they can come to some sort of consensus as to how life on other planets coincides with their belief and teachings."

"In other words, they want to find a way to 'own it,'" said Halsey.

"According to Genesis, the book, not the group, God, on the first day created Earth, Space-Time and Light and on the fourth day, created the Sun, Moon and the Stars but nothing about aliens living on any other planets. So, religions need to find a way to explain that," said the president.

"They did a pretty good job explaining how Cain and Able had kids," said Abby.

"How's that?"

"Well Adam and Eve had two boys; Cain and Able. Somehow, they each found a wife but since God hadn't created other families they went back and gave Adam and Eve even more children which they had forgotten to mention. So, Cain and Able married their sisters and that's how it all started. With incest," said Abby.

"Maybe Earth is a microcosm of the universe. In days of old, the continents were like different worlds inhabited by different races of people. Reds in North America, Yellows in Asia, Whites in Europe, Blacks in Africa and Browns in South America and so on. Not until the invention of ships could all the different worlds be reached by advanced peoples. In most cases, they came in peace but that didn't last long. Soon, the explorers were exploiting the explored. It's always the same. Power, gold, oil, privilege, whatever. So, based on precedence one can assume our visitors, who seem friendly now, will ultimately want something that we don't want to give them and then..."

"And then what, sir?" asked Halsey, interrupting the president.

"Then, if they have advanced military weapons and systems — if they can harness 'Dark Energy', then they could use it against us. Resistance by us would be useless. We would be screwed."

"So, what are you advocating? Roosevelt's 'Speak softly and carry a big stick', or Reagan's 'Trust but verify?'" asked Abby.

"Actually, I prefer Churchill's 'We sleep safely at night because rough men stand ready to visit violence on those who would harm us.'

"You have a graduate degree in Astrobiology. Correct? That's the study of the origins, evolution, distribution, and future of life in the universe. I guess that explains why you're working on Wall Street. How would you like to head up a new department in my new Space Force?"

"I'm not a Roosevelt or Reagan, and certainly not a Churchill. But I could be your Richard Dreyfuss," said Abby.

"See! We agree. Abby, can I steal Tom for a few minutes? Think over my offer. Melania is upstairs in the Trophy Room, I believe, and has something to show you."

"Certainly, Mr. President. Tommy." And with that Abby left the theater.

After Abby left, President Trump said, "Hold on SNL this weekend. I think I have what I want from Pelosi," and went on to tell Halsey all about how he would one day become 'The Man Who Would Be King'.

Chapter 51

"Didn't see that coming," said Halsey.

"What?" asked the president.

"Asking Abby to join the Space Force."

"Jealous?"

"In a way, yes. I'm a gravedigger heading down and Abby is a space cadet heading up."

"Don't worry Halsey; you'll be my Peachy and together we'll rule the kingdom."

"After watching the movie, I'm not sure that's good. So anyway, what did the speaker give you and what kingdom?"

"Freedom. She's going to give me my freedom. She gave me a rough draft but in the right direction. I don't want four more years of this shit. She is going to let me go out on top. I never thought I would win in the first place. It was a publicity stunt to sell books and help my *Apprentice* ratings. You can't rule a country by committee. I had more power back in Manhattan. I did whatever I wanted and answered to no one."

"That sounds like Howard Stern talking."

"He was not too far off the mark."

"My sons and daughter have been building the brand back up and have done a terrific job. The Trump name, real estate, golf courses and some other deals not public, are in huge demand again. The economy is booming again. The market is down slightly because of the tariffs and all the impeachment talk, but they will bounce back once the Fed cuts the rate again. But if something bad should happen to me, everything will dramatically change and very fast.

"If, for instance, I was to join the other four assassinated presidents or even one of the six attempted ones the market and the economy would tank.

"If I continue to run, I'll win, but another four years of their coming after me for my taxes, collusion, impeachment, and tariffs. The market will implode anyway. Tariffs against Mexico? How the hell are tariffs against Mexico going to hurt us? If a consumer used to buy something from Mexico for $25.00 and now, it's $35.00, he-she will either still buy it, or they'll find another resource. Hopefully, they'll go with another resource and Mexico will get the message. What would they prefer? Sanctions? Cut off their aid? We give almost $800 million a year to Mexico, Guatemala, El Salvador, and Nicaragua alone. The money goes to the el-comandante and his junta. Not to the people. All we have to do is threaten to cut it off and the caravans stop dead. You know. What goes up... It's just that my way will happen faster, and I'll go out on top and as one of the richest families in the world. As Mel Brooks said, "It's good to be king."

There was a knock on the side door that leads to the president's bathroom and private area. A Secret Service agent opened the door and said, "They're here and have been sanitized."

"Give me two minutes and bring them in.

"The gaggle is here. I had them come up the Johnson-Nixon Freeway. They are bringing me the revised agreement — signed, sealed, and delivered."

"I should leave," said Halsey and got up.

"No, stay."

In marched Pelosi, Schumer, Nadler, Schiff, and Waters.

"Nancy, Chuck, Jerry, Buzz, Maxine welcome to the Oval Office. This is the first time for some of you. Would you like a tour?"

Ignoring the president's gibe, Speaker Pelosi noticed another person in the room and looked questionably back at the president.

"Oh, this is Mr. Peachy Carnehan. He's my special adviser."

Pelosi did not acknowledge Halsey aka Peachy, but said, "We have nothing. We are shuffled in here through secret tunnels, so no one knows we're meeting. If we do our part but you decide to change your mind we're screwed."

"I'll do my part. I'll announce on live TV that I'm out. I'll make up a good pretext. But I won't until I see you holding up your end by calling off impeachment, building my wall, immigration reform," looking at Nadler, Schiff, and Waters the president added, "and by playing nice."

"What if we give you everything you want but you change your mind and run for a second term anyway?" asked Schumer. Nadler, Schiff, and Waters were told to be good soldiers and listen, but not to say a word.

"As I said, won't happen. But if it did then all bets are off and you all just all start up again making my life, my family's life, and my presidency miserable.

"What if I do my part and drop out, but you change your mind and come after me or my family while I'm finishing off my first and final term, or after I'm out? What's my safeguard?"

Pelosi held out her hand which contained a sheet of paper. President Trump took it and began reading a petition from The Speaker on her personal congressional stationery signed by all present.

Dear President Trump,

For the good of the nation, we, duly elected members of Congress representing the majority of the members of Congress, the will of the American people and all that is good in our country respectfully petition you not to seek re-election for a second term. The country has been put through too much discord and disruption making impeachment imminent and resignation real.

If you agree not to seek or accept a second term, we, Congress, our constituents, supporters including the media will work together in a bipartisan fashion for the rest of your term on building a better relationship with you and building your wall, passing

comprehensive immigration reform, improving and build-
ing upon the American Affordable Care Health Care Act, in-
frastructure and nominating the next Supreme Court Judge
should a vacancy present itself in your remaining term.

We and our congressional heirs further agree to seek no recourse
or repercussions congressional, criminal or civil for any offenses
you may have committed before your administration, during
your administration or after your administration, and will con-
tinue our agreed policies in perpetuity.

Sincerely,

Nancy Pelosi

Speaker of the House

The petition was signed by Pelosi and by each of the other four congressmen and congresswoman present.

The president looked up and smiled, thanked everyone and said he would give it his utmost consideration, but added that barring any unforeseen development it looked promising.

He stood and dismissed the five of them back out the secret tunnel, but before they left, he added, "I'm a superstitious man. And after I leave office if some unlucky accident should befall me or my family, if we should get shot in the head by a police officer or we should hang ourselves while in a jail cell, or get struck by a bolt of lightning then I'm going to blame some of the people in this room."

Before the door closed, he thought he heard Waters say something about his anatomy.

Chapter 52

It was late morning and Halsey was back in the White House with the president. President Trump was agitated and wanted to see how his infrastructure meeting earlier in the morning would be reported and received.

"Turn on *CNN*. Let's see what they have to say," said the president to an a/v tech standing by.

> KAITLAN COLLINS, *CNN* WHITE HOUSE CORRESPONDENT: You read on Twitter every single day from the president, multiple times a day, except this time he said it in person and he singled out Nancy Pelosi, something we haven't seen that much from the president, essentially holding her responsible for the ease in tension between the right and the left.
>
> KATE BOLDUAN, *CNN* ANCHOR: Thanks so much, Kaitlan.John King is going to continue the coverage of this breaking news right now.John.
>
> JOHN KING, *CNN* ANCHOR: Kate, appreciate the toss. Dramatic, breaking news here in Washington playing out, and momentarily we will get the other side of

this promising Oval Office meeting. Nancy Pelosi and Chuck Schumer, the speaker of the House and the top Democrat in the United States Senate about to speak to reporters. You see it on the right of your screen there. The president complimenting the speaker of the House for a bipartisan deal on infrastructure spending. The president walking out of the Oval Office after the meeting into the Rose Garden, praising Democrats for trying to rebuild a bipartisan relationship to get the country moving forward. Let's get the Democratic response. Here are the speaker and Senate Democratic leader with some of their deputies.

REP. NANCY PELOSI (D-CA): Good morning, everyone.

This morning we went to the White House for a follow-up meeting with the president. A follow-up to a meeting we had a few weeks ago where we agreed on a dollar figure.

Today, for the good of the nation, we did just that. In a tremendous bipartisan effort, we found the money to cover the initial cost and have agreed to meet again in two weeks to take another look at immigration and health care; but now we can go forward with infrastructure. The fact is we're hopeful, optimistic and seeing the necessity for a big infrastructure initiative for our country. We went, in the spirit of bipartisanship, to find common ground with the president on this.

I pray for the president of the United States and I pray for the United States of America. I'm pleased to yield now to the distinguished Democratic leader of the Senate, Mr. Schumer.

SEN. CHUCK SCHUMER (D-NY): Well, thank you, Speaker Pelosi. And to watch what happened in the White House today should give America hope. We Democrats and Republicans believe in infrastructure. We believe that our roads and bridges need repair. We believe that rural America, as well as inner-city America, needs broadband. We believe that to bring clean, new energy around the country, we need a power grid modernized and updated. We believe in modernizing our transportation fleet with electric cars. We believe in all these things. And so, despite signals in the previous few weeks that he might not be serious, we went forward. We came here very seriously. The president came in seriously and together, for the good of the nation, we made this happen.We got infrastructure; now onto healthcare and immigration. It's clear that the president wants these, too. Thank you all very much.

(CROSS TALK) KING: Welcome back to the program. You're watching the Democratic speaker of the House, the Democratic leader of the Senate, their key deputies, who were at the White House for a meeting with the president. That meeting didn't last very long. The president walked into the room, said if Democrats want to work together, he and his administration were ready and willing. Twenty minutes later an agreement was reached. I have to say this is a first for me. Could this be the start of the left and the right working together? Coming together on infrastructure and other of the big issues? Let's hope so.

"See if you can get David Greene's Morning Edition on NPR," asked the president.

The a/v tech in another room found the radio station and patched it through.

David Green's voice came on right after a commercial.

> GREENE: Bridges, roads, infrastructure - most of the time, we don't pay attention to any of it until it starts to fall apart, which has been happening for decades. And now in a divided Washington, this could be the issue that brings people together.
>
> Here are some soundbites.
>
> CHUCK SCHUMER: This is a major effort to tackle our nation's most critical infrastructure needs.
>
> BERNIE SANDERS: When we rebuild our infrastructure, we rebuild the middle class.
>
> STEPHANI GRISHAM: I think this is a great place where Democrats and Republicans can come together. They can find some common ground.
>
> GREENE: The voices there, Senate Democratic leader Chuck Schumer, Democratic presidential nominee Bernie Sanders and White House press secretary Sarah Sanders.
>
> Earlier this morning, Schumer along with House Speaker Nancy Pelosi were at the White House for a meeting with President Trump about infrastructure. NPR's Ayesha Rascoe is at the White House, as well, reporting on this. Hi, Ayesha.
>
> YESHA RASCOE, BYLINE: Good morning.

GREENE: So, what happened? Are the two sides coming together?

RASCOE: I don't know if they're coming together, but they were in the same place. We know that the meeting is...

GREENE: That's a start.

RASCOE: (Laughter) That's a start. We...

"Turn it off. This is terrific. A very good start. If it keeps up, I'm gonna be a free man," said President Trump.

"You know you have to do your part. Be nice — no tweets — don't punch back if a junior congresswoman throws you a jab."

"Oh man, I can taste it. I'll get the fuck out of Dodge and I'll never look back."

A knock on the door. Madeleine Westerhout came in and handed the president a couple of press releases. She stood there until the president finished reading.

President Trump heading to Britain for his Second State Visit

WASHINGTON (AP) - It's a unique odd couple: A 94-year-old sovereign who has made a point of keeping her opinions to herself during her long reign is hosting a 73-year-old reality TV star-turned-president who tweets his uncensored thoughts daily to 60 million followers.

For Queen Elizabeth II, Britain's unflappable monarch, the arrival of U.S. President Donald Trump, his family and his armored entourage this Monday means a full day of ceremony and toasts topped by a magnificent banquet at Buckingham Palace.

Yet beneath the pomp and ceremony, there are differences aplenty.

A state visit is a relatively rare honor for a U.S. president, but two? Only Barack Obama in 2011 and George W. Bush in 2003 have received the coveted invitations, which are offered based on advice from British Foreign Office officials, not the whim of the queen.

In another matter, the president said that he intends to kick off major campaign rallies in Chicago and Los Angeles for his second presidential run with First Lady Melania, and Vice President Pence, sometime next week, but continues to avoid any presidential debates with his opponent Kamala Harris.

President Trump Accepting the Presidential Nomination at the Republican National Convention Spectrum Center Charlotte, North Carolina. August 27, 2020

Mr. Chairman, Mr. Vice President, delegates to this convention, and fellow citizens: In 68 days, I hope we enjoy a victory that is the size of the heart of North Carolina.

Melania and I extend our deep thanks to the First in Flight State, where the Wright Brothers first took flight, and to the 'The Queen City' – Charlotte after Queen Charlotte of Great Britain and Ireland and for all its warmth and hospitality.

Four years ago, I didn't know precisely every duty of this office, and not too long ago, I learned about some new ones from the first graders of

Saint Alice School in Upper Darby, Pennsylvania. Little Patty Carr was asked by her teacher, Sister Robert Francis, to describe my duties. She said: 'The President goes to meetings. He plays golf. The President gets frustrated. He tweets a lot and talks to a lot of people at rallies.' How does wisdom begin at such an early age?

Tonight, with a full heart and deep gratitude for your trust, I accept your nomination forthe Presidency of the United States. I will campaign on behalf of the principles of our party which lifts America confidently into the future.

America is presented with the clearest political choice of half a century. The distinction between our two parties and the different philosophy of our political opponents are at the heart of this campaign and America's future. Together we'll Keep America Great.

"Speaker Pelosi is on line one," said Madeleine and left the office knowing the president would take the call based on the last paragraph in the *AP* release.

"Hello, Madam Speaker."

"Mr. President. We have an agreement. What are all these rallies and second term announcements about?"

"Nancy," said the president, being mindful that he could be being taped, "of course we have an agreement. I have been watching all the positive reports about our meeting on infrastructure and I have absolutely no regrets. My second term announcements and rallies are going forward as planned. Another announcement, which you may be more interested in, will follow soon if you and your team continue to cooperate. If you want to talk more, come on over. You know how to get here."

"We are doing our part, you do yours."

"You keep on doing your part Madam Speaker and you can rest assure I'll do mine at the appropriate time," said President Trump and disconnected.

Chapter 53

Several of President Trump's senior advisers and Cabinet members were spending a working weekend in Wolfhampton. A few had summer homes in the other Hamptons; others went for Airbnb, but a few decided to stay in the several guest houses on the Wolfhall property.

After a hard day on the golf course, the president arranged a working dinner.

Volkov cornered the president and said, "He sent you a message."

"What?" asked the president.

"He said he is glad you are running for a second term and offered his help."

"You got to be kidding. And are you guys going steady again? No, that's not what I need now. Better he helps the Democrats."

"He said he is prepared to turn the Internet Research Agency aka IRA loose. All he needs is a nod from you."

"You know what I'm going to do? I'm going to report this conversation to Barr. Is Putin crazy?" Trump's mind ticking a mile a minute. An idea popped into his head and said, "Don't talk about this to anyone. I'll get back to you."

Volkov walked away and Larry Kudlow and Rudy Giuliani came over to the president. "Nice place but a little spooky even for the Hamptons," said Kudlow.

"As your attorney, I have to advise you to stay clear of Volkov or at least have someone with you — namely me," advised Giuliani.

"Can Russians in Russia invest in our stock market?"

"Viktor Vekselberg invests in the U.S. through Columbus Nova, a private investment firm. Vekselberg's company, Renova, is one of Columbus Nova's largest client. LetterOne, the international investment group co-founded by the billionaire owners of Russia's Alfa Group, maintains a U.S. office with over $2 billion of investments in the United States.

"So, the answer is yes, but they have other options. Russia's stock market is now the second best-performing, big emerging market after China. State Russia and State China are avoiding our market. Russia has recently sold off the vast majority of its stash of American debt, but individual oligarchs are still in. It's just too good to resist," said Kudlow.

"There's no law against it, as far as I know," offered Giuliani.

"Is Putin invested?"

Kudlow got the attention of Wilbur Ross, who was talking with CIA Director Gina Haspel and asked both to come over.

"Is Putin invested in our stock market?" asked Kudlow.

"Privately yes," answered Ross, but I'm not sure of the exact amount because he uses an alias and goes through funds. But I do know he's especially interested in tech stock, and he's in a fund that raised $2B and looking for Investment in Artificial Intelligence development."

"Gina?" asked the president.

"The Russian Direct Investment Fund has raised $2 billion from foreign investors and pension funds to support domestic companies developing Artificial Intelligence and has prepared for a meeting with President Vladimir Putin on AI advancement in Russia.

He's secretly trying to get his RDIF invested in Bezos' Blue Origin, or Musk's SpaceX. He's fascinated by science fiction and space."

"What's his favorite movie?"

"ET."

"Interesting. I have a job for you guys," said President Trump.

"Are you all on?" asked the president talking into the speaker.

"We are Dad, and yes, the line is secure. What's up?" asked Don Jr.

"You guys are doing a terrific job. Ivanka give me an update."

"We've sold most everything quietly through third parties. Land, re-sorts, hotels and some other things you know about. All the properties, left in your name, are not for sale and a couple we must keep till the last moment. We spread it out and got terrific deals. Dad, we were worth about 3 billion on paper but now we have over 6 billion in cash, and we are just waiting to dump in all in the stock market as soon as it drops again. Any idea when?"

"I'm afraid I don't but we may be getting some bad economic news sometime tomorrow afternoon, but it will correct the day after, and I'm predicting the market will soon hit 30k. So, tomorrow afternoon may be a good time to buy and 30k to sell. Wonder how *Forbes* will spin it — the net worth gaffe, I mean?" asked the president.

"They won't," said Ivanka, "they need to fire their bean counters, but they won't know a thing till it's over. No one has a clue what we're doing."

"Shit, Bezos' worth 121 billion. The House of Saud is estimated to be worth $1.4 trillion."

"Yes, but they have 15,000 family members that have a share," said Ivanka. "The British royal family has an estimated net worth of $88 bil-lion, but fewer family members."

"Putin has around 200 billion — he's the richest man in the world. Can't have that. We're poor compared to all of them. Where's gold at?" asked the president.

"About $1,335 an ounce and should go to just under $1,100, as the mar-kets get stronger," said Ivanka.

"When the markets crash there will be a colossal move in gold from $1,100, to well over $2,000, an ounce. Timing is everything. When gold hits $1,100, it's showtime. Are your assets putting out a warning to our base and 'Moms and Pops' to stay clear of the stock market?" asked the president.

"Were on it," said Don Jr., "everyone from Beck on Blaze to Breitbart, Drudge, American Thinker to local newspapers, radio and TV stations. The message is subtle but clear; invest at your own risk. The market is rigged so pull your cash and put it under your mattress."

"Okay. They've been warned. As far as my loyal Cabinet, advisors, and friends, I will give them a heads-up now, then a one-hour notice before I'm ready to announce. They are all movers and shakers. They'll figure it out and make the right move or not. But for my loyal 61 million Twitter followers base I'll make it a bit clearer."

Follow @realDonaldTrump The Trump Economy is setting records and has a long way up to go...However, if anyone but me takes over in 2020 (I know the competition very well), there will be a Market Crash the likes of which has not been seen before! KEEP AMERICA GREAT

Chapter 54

President Trump was spending more and more time at Wolfhampton, the Eastern White House or Wolf House as the media had dubbed it, and less time in Washington and Florida, to the detriment of the news media because of access. Nancy and Chuck looked at it as a sign that the end was near.

Gina Haspel, Larry Kudlow, and Wilbur Ross were back again at Wolfhall having touched down on the new heliport behind Wolfhall. They joined the already present advisors who stayed over. The president had to keep Ruddy away this time because of what they were going to discuss.

Halsey met them at touch down, and all four, along with several Secret Service agents walked towards the manor.

Volkov and Barron were having a training session with Hammer and Sickle. The pretty lady and her two little white dogs from Main Street graciously volunteered to help alleviate Hammer and Sickle's fear of aggressive little white multi-poos and fox terriers. It was not working.

"Thanks for coming on such short notice, but things are moving fast," said President Trump as he led the group into the library.

"It's all set up," said Ross. "The family end of the business is in a blind trust, can't touch you or the family personally, and we have in on Blue Origin's IPO next week. The IPO will be underwritten primarily by Credit Suisse, that's our in, and will be valued at an estimated at $20 billion."

"Terrific! That's almost as big as Alibaba's opening and they were up 38% the first day."

"CS's bookrunner is underpricing shares at $60.00 per share. If you're up 38% the first day you could flip it for $83.00 a share. They are offering around 300 million shares and we locked into 20 million shares for about $1.2 billion. You could make $450 million in a few hours if you flip it the first day. Maybe more — you would be a winner."

President Trump looked sternly into the eyes of Ross, one of the richest men in the world, and said, "My whole life is about winning. I don't lose — I never lose."

President Trump had a plan. It was a simple plan in his mind, but Machiavellian none the less to all lesser mortals. To Trump it was as simple as, 'You eat the food, you lose the weight'. A plan that would get back at Putin for all the grief he caused. A plan that would keep Trump, the puppeteer, hidden above the stage while making his family insanely wealthy and topple a lot of rich and powerful people including many politicians. A plan that would set him free.

> Kent, Washington (AP) Blue Origin—the private spaceflight company owned by billionaire Jeff Bezos—announced today that it intends to send its new Blue Moon lander to the lunar south pole and launch its space tourism rocket to fly humans this year. There is a strong rumor that their IPO is back on the launch pad.

President Trump read the *AP* flash on his iPhone and decided it was time to have another chat with Volkov and counter Putin's offer with his own. But first dinner.

President Trump and his guests for the weekend were going to have dinner in Wolfhall catered by The Palm from nearby East Hampton.

Into the same dining room, where only weeks before Barron was kid-naped, the chosen flowed. They were served, by a squad of Navy stewards, anything and everything.

Appetizers
Colossal Lump Crabmeat Cocktail
Carpaccio of Beef Tenderloin
Lobster Bisque
Baked Clams Casino or Oreganata
Classic Caesar Salad
Main Course
Veal Marsala
Prime New York Strip
Atlantic Salmon Fillet
Broiled Jumbo Nova Scotia Lobster
Hash Brown Potatoes
Green Beans and Creamed Spinach
Desert
Key Lime Pie and New York Style Cheesecake
Beverages
Lavazza, Pellegrino, Veuve Clicquo, Pinot Grigio, Châteauneuf-du-Pape,
and Diet Coke

When dinner was through it was declared absolutely delicious by all present.

Although the president didn't smoke or drink, he had no problem with others in his company indulging. A box of Montecristo No.2 was opened and passed around, as was more Lavazza.

"What about Pelosi?" asked Pompeo.

"While I was over in France for 'D-Day' she said she wanted to put me in prison. She said it in private, but she knew it would get out. I actually don't think she's a talented person. I've tried to be nice to her because I would've liked to have gotten some more deals done. She's incapable of doing deals. She's a nasty, vindictive, horrible person, terrible person, and a disaster. I call her 'Nervous Nancy' because she's a nervous wreck. But other than that, she's my newest bestes friend," said the president.

"Pelosi's your 'newest bestes friend'?" asked brand new acting SecDef Mark Esper.

"We're getting things done for once and as long as that continues, we're all going to get along. Kevin?" asked President Trump looking over to his Acting Homeland Secretary Kevin McAleenan.

"The President's tariff threat against Mexico worked brilliantly and Mexico put its National Guard on its north and south borders. It's going to cost us though," added McAleenan with a chuckle.

"You all know that despite the Left's interference the economy is terrific and will stay that way unless something happens to me. I can't foresee the future, and neither can any of you, my trusted friends and advisors, but you need to keep your options open and 'Put your trust in God and keep your powder dry' if you get my drift," said the president.

Many at the table did not get the president's 'drift' and the mention of keeping one's powder dry had a cautionary and ominous ring to it. A few, however, did get it.

"Okay," said the president, "anyone up for a movie?"

Chapter 55

It was getting late and several Cabinet members and advisors flew the president's smaller helicopter to the East Hampton Airport, and boarded their jets for the flight back to D.C., while others retreated to their Hampton homes, Airbnb's, or Wolfhall's guest house. Gina Haspel, Larry Kudlow, Wilbur Ross, Tom Halsey, and Abby Adams, at the president's request, gathered in the library for a midnight nightcap. Abby had accepted a position in the Space Force as director of new projects reporting directly to the president.

"What did you think? Great movie — terrific. Redford and Newman at their best. Nobody does buddy flicks better than them," said the president.

Nods and murmurs of agreement all around. Everyone was getting a bit tired, but Abby, looking at the president added, "Don't forget Connery and Caine, Mr. President."

The president smiled at their private secret then asked, "You guys tired? We have work to do. How old are you Halsey?"

"I'm 28," answered Halsey."

"Right. You're probably a six-thirty. I'm a five-thirty, most 70s are, and Wilbur there is four-thirty, as are most guys in their 80s are. The older you get the earlier you go to bed and the earlier you get up. I get up at 5:30 am, so let's get started. Are we all set with the Blue Origin IPO?"

"All set," said Ross.

"Okay," said the president. "Here's what we're going to do; and I need all your help and discretion to pull this off. The little movie we just watched, 'The Sting' was based on a real-life con, 'The Big Con'. We're gonna do our own real-life 'Big Con.'"

The president pulled out a sheet of paper and read the script, "Following the attempted kidnapping of the president's son, aspiring con man Johnny Hooker aka Tom Halsey teams up with old pro Henry Gondorff, aka me to take revenge on the ruthless crime boss responsible, Doyle Lonnegan — that would be Vlad Putin. Hooker and Gondorff set about implementing an elaborate scheme, one so crafty that Lonnegan won't even know he's been swindled.

"Gentlemen, I give you Blue Origin."

"You're going to get him to invest in the Blue Origin IPO?" asked Kudlow.

"I think we had all better be careful about where this is heading," said Haspel.

"Gina, he tried to kidnap my son. He tried to influence our presidential election. He spawned the Muller Report and all the collusion grief that resulted. You guys pull covert missions all the time without informing Congress. How do you say, 'Plausible Deniability'?

"He may have thought he fooled me. But when the time is right, payback is a motherfucker. Guess what time it is Gina?"

"With all due respect, Mr. President, the kidnapping happened on US soil and was, therefore, FBI and your SS turf."

"True Gina, but you guys missed Russia's interference with our elections and way back your forerunner the OSS then the CIA, in that order, missed or messed up Pearl Harbor, The Bay of Pigs, The Cuban Missile Crisis, TET, The Iranian Revolution, Fall of the USSR, 9/11, WMD, and The Arab Spring, to mention just a few, and don't get me started on the KKK murders."

"The KKK Murders? I think I missed that," said Haspel.

"Missed it? Your shop was up to its eyeballs in the assassinations of Kennedy, King, and Kennedy. Want me to go on?"

"All that happened way before my watch, but yeah, payback would be nice."

"To get that SOB back for all the harm he did to our country, I think I can speak for all of us. We're all in," said Ross. Haspel, Kudlow, Halsey, and Abby Adams all nodded in agreement.

"Okay. Tell us all about Vlad," requested the president.

"Putin is a 'Space Cadet' and into Sci-fi big time. Fav movie is ET. He wants to duplicate our new Space Force. He believes in extraterrestrial — that is life occurring outside of Earth which did not originate on Earth. Russian air space has been visited but unlike us, no real contact has been made — just sightings. He's very interested in SpaceX and Blue Origins, but both are private companies and very security conscious. If, however, one was to go public he would want in big time," said Haspel.

The president looked at Ross and Ross added, "He won't be allowed in the initial offering because he's a hostile foreign national, and Blue Origin's Commercial Space Launch Act agreement with NASA will keep him out. If he tries to get in through a hedge or feeder fund, security algorithms will be in place looking for his fingerprints and he will be blocked."

"But if an initial buyer wants to unload or flip his stock it's a whole new ball game," added Kudlow.

The president nodded towards Halsey. "That's the 'con'. We get Putin to want into the IPO so bad he will be blinded by the light," said Halsey.

"And that light would be?" asked the president.

"That light would be Abby, Space Force, Blue Origin and ET. We leak Blue Origin and NASA have made extraterrestrial contact, and Bezos and Jim Bridenstine, the head of NASA, are putting together a team, just like in the movie, to meet the mother ship. You, Mr. President, want on that team but Bezos at the last-minute turns you down. Your blind trust sells your 20 million shares that same day, assuming they go up as anticipated, and the 'mark' Putin, probably through Russian Direct Investment Fund, Russia's sovereign wealth fund established to make equity investments in high-growth sectors of the Russian economy, buys. The RDIF and its partners, most notably the Russian pension funds, takes the bait and scoops up all of your 20 million shares," said Halsey.

"That's the 'sting'? You get him in the back door of an IPO?" asked a puzzled Ross.

"What? You don't think having Putin pay almost 1.7 billion a few hours after I brought it for 1.2 is not enough?" asked the president.

"No. I think there's more you're not telling us," said Ross.

"We leak that I am going live on TV with a big announcement. We say that it's big news about the FED cutting interest rates and better economic news. He buys the stock thinking it will double."

"And then?" asked Kudlow.

President Trump looked at each of his advisors and said, "And then 'The Sting'."

Only the president's family, Halsey, and Abby knew the sting. Even his advisors and the Frantic Five, the president's group nickname for Pelosi, Schumer, Nadler, Schiff, and Waters didn't know the whole picture — only their part.

The 'Sting' is the moment when a con artist finishes the "play" and takes the mark's money. If a con is successful, the mark does not realize he has been cheated until the con men are long gone.

Some think Putin is the Mark, others think it's Bezos or Pelosi. But only President Trump knows the real 'Mark'.

Chapter 56

It was Monday morning and President Trump was waiting to board Marine One to take him directly from Wolfhall to the White House. Everyone except Halsey and Abby had already left.

Volkov had been waiting for the president to get back to him and was enjoying the renewed intrigue instigated by Putin. He was hoping President Trump would continue the game.

"Dmitriy," said the president, "come over here a second and leave the wolves behind."

Volkov was optimistic because the president rarely used first names unless he wanted something.

"You know Abby, right?"

"Yes, of course. Congratulations on your new job. Sounds exciting," said Volkov.

"Thank you," said Abby.

"I've got to head back to Washington. Abby has to hang back here for a while so please give her whatever help she needs.

"As a friend, tell Putin I appreciate his offer, but I must decline, and tell him I'm not going to report the offer to Barr or the FBI. I'm a shoo-in for re-election. The economy and the markets are booming. There is peace in Dodge, Space Force has some huge announcements coming, and there are many other important things on the horizon.

"With that, I'll take my leave. See you back in DC when you're through Abby," said the president as he walked towards Marine One.

After the president boarded and the hatch closed, Volkov turned to Abby and asked, "Where's your boyfriend?"

"He's in the village running a few errands. Where's yours?" asked Abby.

"They're waiting for me in the house."

"You have more than one?"

"My dear, you have been on Wall Street too long. We're all about identity and pronouns. Come along, Riana is visiting and would love to see you again and have some tea together."

"Us again," said Abby with a smile.

"Touché," said Volkov.

Abby was playing her part like a Broadway actress.

After tea and some catching up, Riana, Hammer, and Sickle left with the trainer to work on their fear of little white multi-poos.

"So, tell me about Space Force and exactly what it is you do?" asked Volkov.

"Mr. Volkov…"

"Dmitriy."

"Dmitriy, most everything we do is highly classified."

"I'm not interested in secrets 'Dear Abby'. Just some juicy gossip. President Trump mentioned some really big announcements coming from Space Force. Just give me a little taste of what's coming."

"The president is like a little boy with a new toy, but you'll have to wait for the big announcement."

"Now you can't leave me hanging. After all, he brought it up."

"I can tell you this much because it's already been reported by *AP* that Blue Origin announced that it intends to send its new Blue Moon lander to the lunar south pole. They're going to launch their space tourism rocket to fly humans this year, and there is a strong rumor that they intend to go public soon."

"I read that but what has the president so excited?"

"He's teasing you. His toy is Space Force and something big has happened, but you'll have to wait for the announcement. But I can say that we, Space Force, Blue Origin and NASA put together a team. The president wants to be on that team but he and Bezos, as is common knowledge, don't get along, so President Trump is looking for some leverage."

"A team — leverage? Come on Abby give me a clue."

"I've said too much, Mr. Volkov. You're a Russian after all and you may 'Phone Home.'"

Chapter 57

"She said exactly that—those exact words 'Phone Home?'" demanded Putin.

"Yes," said Volkov.

"Tell me again about this team."

"She said, "President Trump's toy is Space Force and something big has happened. She said Space Force, Blue Origin and NASA put together a team, and Trump wants to be on it, but Jeff Bezos doesn't want him, so he's looking for leverage. She said he's acting like a little boy."

"I need you here. I will send a jet."

Volkov laughed, "You can't be serious. I come back to Russia and you'll lock the door. You will never allow me to leave."

"You're more valuable to me here than there. Come meet with me and we'll develop a plan. Then you can go back for good. We stay friends."

"Or I come to meet with you, and you'll lock me up in Black Dolphin Prison, torture me, then kill me."

"I can torture you and kill you in America."

"Yes, you could torture me and kill me here in America, but you can't put me in prison, and as they are fond of saying here in the States, 'Two out of three ain't bad'. Look, the media, most law enforcement, and politicians are very suspicious of me now and still think I'm spying. All I need is a trip back to Russia."

"By the way, how is your young beautiful girlfriend, or should I say, boyfriend? It gets very confusing for me — does it for you? I would very much like to meet Riana someday."

"Keep them out of this. I will be your messenger boy, but I will not come back to Russia. You make any more threats and I will cut you off."

"Let's not talk about cutting things off. That would be even more confusing. Just keep me informed on everything about Trump, Space Force, Blue Origin," said Putin and disconnected the speaker on his secure line and turned to his ministers and directors seated around the conference table.

"Our relationship with Washington is getting worse and worse. Trump's administration has imposed dozens of sanctions on us. At the G20 summit in Riyadh, I meet with Trump because he has balls; I'll have to give him that. He tells reporters that our conversation is none of their business. Sounds more and more like me, but our ties remain strained by everything from Syria to Ukraine as well as allegations of our interference in U.S. politics, which publicly I denied. Our blossoming ties with China, a deepening strategic friendship, has alarmed some U.S. policymakers.

"Trump told reporters on Wednesday that he wants to meet with me in Washington, but I told him the meeting was hanging in the air," said Putin to his assembled advisers: Colonel Galkin, recently returned for a diplomat swap from the States, defense-Shoygu, finance-Siluanov, intelligence-Naryshkin, and Dmitry Rogozin head of Roscosmos-Russia's equivalent to NASA.

"Comrade Rogozin, have you heard what Volkov is saying? What is your take?" asked Putin.

"Against all odds, we and the United States have managed to keep things relatively civil when it comes to our relationship in space — particularly with regards to round-the-clock cooperation between NASA and Roscosmos. Space Force is relatively new and Blue Origin private..."

"Excuse me, Comrade Rogozin, I don't need a history lesson. What I need is for you to tell me about this team that Space Force, Blue Origin and NASA are putting together, and why Trump wants to be on it? Why would Special Projects Director of Space Force Abby Adams use the iconic line 'Phone Home' from the movie ET? This is what I want to know from you."

"It is obvious, no? They are going to make another fake movie like the Moon landing," said Rogozin.

"Why did I give you this high position comrade? You oversaw the defense industry, and before that, you were head of Russia's Arctic Commission. Would you like to go back there? Get me some answers. Comrade Naryshkin assist him, please. You are all dismissed except for Comrade Siluanov.

"Did you, at least, do what I asked?" asked Putin when the others had gone.

"I did Comrade Putin. Credit Suisse Group, New York office will be handling the Blue Origin IPO. I have a contact in Switzerland, Albert Zeller, who told me that there is not a chance in Hell of Russia, China, Syria or North Korea getting anywhere near the initial public offering. He said he would check with New York, but he was sure they would say the same."

"So, you're saying that's it? What about getting in through a private equity fund?"

"They won't touch you no matter how much you want to invest. NASA, Blue Origin and Space Force are all locked in together and the algorithms in place will sniff us out and push them out by association. Besides, I'm told that all 300 million shares to be offered are already taken. More may be offered but for now, were locked out. Unless..."

"Unless what?"

"Unless we wait till late afternoon trading and see who's flipping stock for a quick profit and snatch them up. Blue Origin gets its money during the initial sale. When you buy from a flipper the flipper gets the money and Blue Origin and Credit Suisse are out of the picture and could care less who the buyer is. When you buy from a flipper the 'Ponzi Scheme' begins. But why do you want to buy stock in Blue Origin?"

"Trump is a cunning guy. He says and does things to sometimes get, as they say, 'a rise'. The A U for example — joining North and South America? What's his game? Now he wants to be involved with Blue Origin owned by his adversary Jeff Bezos. My suspicion is that Blue Origin has made a 'Close Encounter of the Third Kind' based on the forthcoming supposed big announcement and the 'Phone Home' clue. If I'm right I want to be on that team standing right next to Trump when the hatch opens."

"Open the hatch? Close encounters? I am afraid I don't understand Comrade Putin."

"You don't need to understand that, Comrade Siluanov. What you need to understand, what you need to do, comrade, is purchase enough shares to get me on the team."

"How much are you prepared to invest Comrade Putin?"

"Not me, you imbecile. You will use the Russian Direct Investment Fund money and you will invest whatever it takes for me to have a seat at the Blue Origin table and when you buy from this flipper the 'Putin Scheme' begins."

"As long as you don't end up in prison like Madoff."

"Comrade Siluanov, I intend to make a huge profit while having my 'E.T.' dream come true by investing RDIF in Blue Origin. That is, after all its intended use, no? To support companies developing Artificial Intelligence."

"Domestic."

"Comrade Siluanov our foreign investors and pensioners will benefit from my brilliant investment. If for some reason you bungle it, it will be you, not me, who will go to prison like Madoff."

Chapter 58

Blue Origins stock is soaring on its first day of trading on the New York Stock Exchange

Blue Origins historic initial public offering has gone live trading on the New York Stock Exchange—and its stock shot up.

NEW YORK (AP) — After much hype leading up to the largest initial public offering in five years and after the ceremonial ringing of the NYSE bell by company Blue Origin executives, first official day of trading on the New York Stock Exchange began. Blue Origin garnered investor interest and enjoyed an impressive first-day run. Its stock, which was priced at $60.00, closed up 55%.

"Wow. This is terrific. Closed up higher than expected," said President Trump.

"It went off without a hitch. You are, indirectly, very indirectly, the owner of 20 million shares of Blue Origin. I was just told by Ross that a sell order is now being put on your shares," said Halsey.

"How can we be sure it's Putin on the buying end before we approve the sale?" asked the president.

"That's above my paygrade but Ross and Kudlow say The SEC has rules about how aftermarket offerings of stock in a private company can be made and who may purchase the shares, but nothing like the IPO. It's more for the protection of the buyer and seller, not the company. They have disclosure protocols in place, so we'll know who's knocking before we open the door," said Halsey.

"As soon as the sale is done, and the money is in the bank I'll give Stephanopoulos his interview and then Putin will shit his pants."

"But he will still have the stock and by all accounts, it will stay around $93 bucks a share."

"True, but wait for the sting. 'Pucy, you'll have some splainin' to do,'" said President Trump in Ricky Ricardo's voice.

Later that evening President Trump, Melania, Halsey, Abby were on a herringbone brick path walking past Wolfhall, past the heliport, and past the golf course towards the Clift overlooking the Atlantic Ocean. Barron, Hammer, and Sickle, their trainer and security were behind and to their flank.

"The transcript of my interview with Stephanopoulos should be hitting the *AP* wire about now," said President Trump looking over the horizon. "I can just see Putin's expression when he finds out there is no ET and no team."

"Actually, you're looking towards Bermuda. Russia's over this way," said Halsey nodding to his left.

"What is this shit?" said Putin to Ministry of Finance Siluanov and Dmitry Rogozin head of Roscosmos.

Putin and Siluanov had just finished reading the *AP* wire on Trump's interview with Stephanopoulos, and Rogozin was just finishing it.

EXCLUSIVE: Trump says he doesn't particularly believe in unidentified flying objects

ABC News' George Stephanopoulos talks with President Donald Trump at the White House in Washington

NEW YORK (AP) President Donald Trump said he doesn't particularly believe in unidentified flying objects (UFOs), despite a rise in reports of unidentified aircraft by U.S. Navy pilots.

In an exclusive interview with ABC News Chief Anchor George Stephanopoulos this week, the president was asked what he made of the increased reports.

"I think it's probably -- I want them to think whatever they think. They do say, and I've seen, and I've read, and I've heard. And I did have one very brief meeting on it. But people are saying they're seeing UFOs. Do I believe it? Not particularly," Trump said.

Asked if he thought he would know if there were a case of extraterrestrial life, the president replied, "Well, I think my great pilots would know. Our great pilots would know."

"They see things a little bit different from the past. So, we're going to see. We're watching, and you'll be the first to know," he continued.

Earlier this year, the Navy updated its guidelines for how its pilots report the sighting of "unauthorized and/or unidentified aircraft" due to an increase in the number of reports in recent years.

Navy pilot recalls an encounter with UFO: 'I think it was not from this world'

"There have been a number of reports of unauthorized and/or unidentified aircraft entering various military-controlled ranges and designated air space in recent years," Joseph Gradisher, spokesperson for Deputy Chief of Naval Operations for Information Warfare, told ABC News last month. "For safety and security concerns, the Navy and the [U.S. Air Force] take these reports very seriously and investigate each and every report. As part of this effort, the Navy has updated and formalized the process by which reports of any such suspected incursions can be made to the cognizant authorities."

Gradisher added that senior Naval intelligence officials and aviators, "who reported hazards to aviation safety," have briefed congressional members and staff in response to requests for information.

All three, Space Force and NASA and their partner Blue Origin agree with the president. No E.T.'s

Tune in Sunday at 8 pm ET for an hour-long ABC News special, only on ABC — including "ABC News Live," the 24/7 streaming news channel available on abcnews.com, Roku, Hulu, Amazon Fire TV, and Apple TV.

"What is this *AP* wire? There is no team? No ET?" asked Putin. "You brought 20 million shares of Blue Origin 55% over the original IPO opening price per share and there's not going to be a 'Phone...Home?'

"You spent almost 2 billion American dollars of RDIF on Blue Origin. Foreign investors and pensioners money set aside specifically to support domestic companies developing Artificial Intelligence," yelled Putin pushing an accusing finger towards Siluanov.

To answer correctly would mean their death and their family's disgrace and ruin. Both Siluanov and Rogozin lowered their heads in shame, until finally, Comrade Siluanov spoke out,

"Perhaps you will allow me to sell the shares and recoup the money and no one will be the wiser."

"Recoup? The only coup we'll have will be a coup d'état when the millions of pensioners find out what you did with their money."

"What about all the foreign investors?" asked Siluanov.

"Foreign investors can't destroy Mother Russia — her children can," said Putin. "This is your neck in the nose Comrade Siluanov. You better put it out on Russia-1 and on Pravda.ru that it is a wonderful opportunity and that it is going to make a lot of money for our good men and women who worked all their lives and gave everything to our great Motherland. Where is the stock trading now?" asked Putin.

"It is down slightly from yesterday's trading, but I'm sure it will go back up."

"For both your sakes and your families, I hope you are correct."

Chapter 59

President Trump had an exhausting day meeting with his Cabinet, Joint Chiefs, citizen groups, several meetings with foreign leaders, and a late lunch meeting with most of the U.S. Women's Soccer Team after winning their fifth World Cup. He was tired and wanted to finish up so he could leave Washington for a peaceful weekend in Wolfhampton.

"The stock was now trading at $65, a share and way off but slowly, very slowly trending back to its first day high. It will be a while before it reaches $93 and then Putin will sell and break-even," said Ross.

"Okay, I'll relay that to the boss," said Halsey, acting out his part as a buffer, disconnected and walked across the Oval Office towards the president.

President Trump was listening over the speaker, "I'll make my 'Address to the Nation' before he can sell and that will ruin his day… The kids are doing a terrific job setting everything up, don't you think?"

Halsey agreed, but regardless learned to just go with the flow and to carefully pick his fights, "Yes, they have. They have divested the entire real estate empire, except for your jewels like Trump Tower, and are fully into the markets."

"Melania would never let me sell Trump Tower. Besides, I have to keep my personal real estate out of this, so they don't start screaming collusion again…

"Our economy grew at a faster pace than expected in the second quarter and posted its best growth to start a year in four years. Second-quarter gross domestic product expanded by 3.2%," said the president.

"Democrats in the House have approved funding the wall. Can you believe that? Pelosi came through. Mitch McConnell will get the Senate with Schumer, but it's so nice when the entire Frantic Five were pro wall.

"Acosta, Maddow, the Deep State, the Left, and their 'Fake News Media', are going crazy and don't know what to do. The economy is booming like never before, jobs are at historic highs, two Supreme Court Justices, bi-partisans infrastructure and healthcare. Now the wall!

"You know Peachy, my supporters are starting to demand that I serve more than two terms as president. If I stay in for a second term that could be an option for 'The Man Who Would Be King', right here in America, but they just don't get it; I hate this job and can't wait to get out. With a second or even a third term like FDR, I would still have to put up with the Pelosi and Schumer — a fate worse than Hell for a man like me. I answer to no one. You can't run a company or a country by committee."

Abby, who had been sitting quietly while the president ranted that he had had enough, "Mr. President with all due respect, public, and private companies have a board of directors and the country has the Executive Branch-headed by you, the Legislative Branch-led by Pelosi and McConnell and Judicial Branch-overseen by Roberts, all to keep checks and balances so that we don't have another King George."

"It would be 'King Daniel' and I had a board Abby, but they were handpicked and 100% loyal to me, but I called all the shots. Everything got done on time and on budget and my way. If I could run the country like I ran the Trump Organization, the country would be even greater than we are now. The wall would have been built already; HillBilly would be in jail. I would have to come up with a new slogan. How's MAMB sound?"

"HillBilly—MAMB?" asked Abby.

"Abby, did I ever tell you about the Clintons and the Trumps?

In 1978, after a dispute about the ownership of a hog: Floyd Clinton, a cousin of Devil Bill Clinton, had the hog, but Donald Trump claimed it was his, saying that the notches on the pig's ears were Trumps, not Clinton, marks. The matter was taken to the local Justice of the Peace, Devil Bill Clinton, who ruled for the Clintons by the testimony of Robert Mueller, a relative of the Clinton family. In June 1980, Mueller was killed by two Trump brothers, Don Jr. and Eric, who were later acquitted on the grounds of self-defense.

The feud escalated after one of the Trump boys entered a relationship with Devil Bill Clinton, daughter, leaving his family to live with the Clintons in Arkansas. The boy eventually returned to the Trumps... Anyway, do you see where I'm going with this?" asked the president.

"No, Mr. President. Not a clue. Why don't you cut to the chase?" suggested Abby.

"The HillBilly's, Hillary and Bill Clintons? Well, they both ended up in jail."

"Sounds like a parody of the Hatfield's and McCoy's to me, but MAMB your new logo—what's that stand for?" asked Abby.

"Make American Millionaires Billionaires."

"How about after your 'Address to the Nation' when you desert your base, tank the economy and turn on your country, you hand out MBMA hats instead, Mr. President?" said a resolved Abby.

"I can't wait to hear this," said President Trump.

Abby, who was starting to have second thoughts about her and Tommy's relationship with the president, said, "Make Billionaires Millionaires Again."

Chapter 60

President Trump, Melania, Barron, Halsey, and Abby were back in Wolfhall for the weekend. It was early Friday evening and they were sitting outside by the main pool overlooking the golf course, tennis courts, heliport and the Atlantic Ocean beyond. The president was sitting on a couch talking to Nancy Pelosi over speakerphone while drinking a Diet Coke.

"Yes, Nancy. No, Nancy. Nancy, this is just posturing. I'm going to soon release all the arrested illegals," said the president.

"Posturing? Showboating is more like it. I'm trying my best to hold my coalition together, not to mention my base and the newbies. Just stop it! And what's all this about continued campaigning? I'm reading your tweet now," said Pelosi.

Donald J. Trump
@realDonaldTrump
Big Rally tomorrow night in Orlando, Florida, looks to be setting records. We are building large movie screens outside to take care of everybody. Over 100,000 requests. Our Country is doing great, far beyond what the haters and losers thought possible - and it will only get better!

"Nancy, I told you I'm playing this to the wire, but you're going to see huge crowds and tremendous support for four more years. I'm not going to get into it with you on your unsecured phone. I'm building up the economy and when it hits its high, I'll make my move. How come you didn't mention my tweet this morning about meeting with President Xi Jinping? The market and your portfolio surged."

Ignoring the good economic news Pelosi continued, "I gave you your wall."

"And I gave you infrastructure and healthcare."

"You better be leveling with me about releasing illegals or I will…"

"Nancy, calm down…"

"Don't tell me to calm down, you racist."

"I'm not a racist."

"You're an ethnocentric racist. You're acting like a dictator going after a minority who have no defense."

"You mean potential Democratic voters and I have no idea what that big word means."

"It means you like people just like yourself—old rich dumpy white men."

"Not true. There are plenty of old rich dumpy white men and a few old rich dumpy white broads I would love to punch in the face. But I'm no racist. I like anyone who likes me. Black, yellow, brown, red, white or blue. If you say nasty things about me, I will punch back twice as hard no matter the race or color. I'm an equal opportunity boxer."

"You're a racist. We are having more hearings on reparations for slavery today and a White House source has leaked to the *New York Times* that you were heard saying that slavery was a good thing?"

"Totally out of context and I'm not going to get into it with you over the phone. Now Nancy, sit tight and keep your people together and I guarantee it will be worth the wait." President Trump disconnected from the speaker and looked to his family, Halsey, and Abby for some sympathy.

He didn't get any, not even from Halsey or Barron.

Abby, feeling bold, asked, "What, may I ask Mr. President, was the speaker referring to about you thinking slavery was a good thing?"

"Something she took completely out of context. 'Fake news.'"

"Where there's smoke there's fire," suggested Abby.

"Please Donald, don't," pleaded Melina.

"No. She asked, and she deserves an answer. I'm going to say something that's probably going to upset you,"

"You think?"

"But if you listen. I mean really listen; you have no choice but to agree.

"Slavery was good for our country. There I said it."

"Mr. President, just guessing here, but this will probably go downhill from here," said Abby.

"But," continued the president holding his finger up to emphasize his point, "but it was wrong, bad, horrible and unacceptable. White Europeans and Black Africans captured and sold black men, women, and children in Africa to slavers who sold them throughout the world but primarily in the Caribbean and North America. They broke up families and shipped these poor souls bound in chains deep within the holes of rotten slave ships with little food and water and horrible sanitary conditions. Upon reaching their destinations, families were broken up and sold for the highest price to wealthy white re-sellers and plantation owners. Your family probably owned a few."

"Mr. President, if you're referring to my ancestors, President John Adams and his son, President John Quincy Adams, they were not slave owners. And how can any of this be 'good?'"

The president ignored the rebuke and continued, "Conditions improved but only slightly. Only as long as the slaves performed their back-breaking jobs without complaint and showed respect to their white owners; if not, they were beaten — there were no laws protecting slaves.

Slavery officially ended towards the end of the Civil War, but state laws took over and discrimination, especially in the South continued for another hundred years under Jim Crow until great leaders like Rosa Parks and Martin Luther King Jr. resisted and brought the discrimination to the forefront forcing politicians, like JFK and President Johnson to finally enact the Great Society, the elimination of poverty and racial injustice. Discrimination did not end however but continued into the 21st century only with the election of President Barack Obama in 2008 did America finally relent.

"Do I sound like a racist?"

"No, but I have a feeling it's coming."

"Well, here it comes, and you decide. America has become the greatest nation in the world. The biggest reason for this is the diversity of its people: American Indians, Dutch, Germans, French, English, Africans and then Irish, Scottish, Italian, Asians, Europeans, Latinos, and Western Asians. Forgive me if I left anyone out, but you must agree that we have people from every country in the world living in and making America great.

"But two groups of Americans didn't have a choice. American Indians and Black Slaves.

"Now here's where I seem to upset some people.

"Without slavery, would the blacks in Africa have come to America in the 17th, 18th, or 19th, century on their own? The answer is yes, probably a few, but not in the numbers caused by slavery. They weren't going to row their canoes across the Atlantic Ocean, were they?

"When this country began, we were not yet an industry-driven country that we would become. We were an agriculture-driven, country exporting raw cotton, tobacco, and rice to the known world. Without black slaves to harvest all the crops America would never have gotten off the ground.

"Where would America be today without all the great black men and women descendants from slaves? Rosa Parks and Martin Luther King Jr, all the other great black leaders. Where would America be without black entertainers, entrepreneurs, teachers, business leaders, blue-collar workers, soldiers, politicians, scientists? Where the hell would America be today without black music and black athletes?

"Yes, slavery was bad and possibly because of how bad it was it produced a segment of America that excelled in everything they touched. Without slavery, America would just be a clone of Britain. Instead of Otis Redding, James Brown and Jim Brown, we would have had Herman's Hermits and the Hollies and be watching the NCL on TV."

"NCL?" asked Halsey.

"The National Cricket League!" answered the president.

"Interesting how your thought process works, Mr. President, but how do you feel about reparations for slavery, some form of compensatory payment to the descendants of Africans?" asked Abby trying to keep the president on script.

"If Congress approves it, I'll sign it, but I want it expanded. The brutality of slavery and the war to end it are woven together. I want to add all the descendants of the dead and horribly wounded soldiers who fought to end slavery. Besides, the United States coming up with the compensation, I want the original slavers who perpetrated the 'Atlantic Slave Trade' to chip in. The Arab States, Spain, England, Portugal, Africa, the Dutch.

"I ask you, does that sound like a racist?"

"I'm not exactly sure, Mr. President. It does and it doesn't, but you're touting the positive black experience but what about all the blacks today in poverty and in prison? Their history is slavery, too. That aside I'll tell you one thing Mr. President, never ever start a sentence with 'Slavery was good for our country,'" said Abby.

President Trump, contrary as always, took out his iPhone pressed a few buttons and on came Rita Moreno and chorus singing 'America' from *West Side Story*,

'*I like to be in America, O.K. by me in America, Everything free in America...*'

"Please," begged an exasperated Melina.

"What?" asked the president shrugging his shoulders. It could be Bernie's theme song. You couldn't make that musical today with all the politically correct crap."

"Tell Steven Spielberg that. His new *West Side Story* movie is coming out soon to coincide with the elections," said Abby.

"Bet he'll change the lyrics," said the president.

Halsey could see an argument coming and said, "There's is a new club in the village that we want to try tonight," Looking at the president and first lady Halsey continued, "want to join us?"

Barron raised his hand and said, "I'm in."

Chapter 61

"Please do not waste my time Director Naryshkin," said Putin.

Foreign Intelligence SVR Director Naryshkin was no fool and never wasted anyone's time, especially his own, and he resented Putin's impudence. As the successor to the infamous KGB, Naryshkin ran the SVR like Hover ran the FBI. He held all the secrets of all the famous, the foreign and domestic politicians including Putin's cult of sexuality. He assisted the Russian Justice Ministry in officially banning photoshopped images showing Putin wearing heavy makeup that authorities say hinted of his "alleged" nonstandard sexual orientation, while secretly assisting Aleksandr Tsvetkov post fake photographs of Putin in makeup on the popular Russian social-networking site Vkontakte. He regarded Putin's service in the KGB as nothing more than that of a minor bureaucrat consular official in Leningrad and Moscow.

"The Trump family, his sons, and daughter have been quietly and clandestinely selling off all their real estate. Third-party, anonymous off-shore LLCs are brokering the deals with non-disclosures clauses and strict caveats in place which prohibit the removal of any Trump names or brands from the property until an undisclosed date. No one — not the management or staff of the many properties, know they have been sold, and the buyers can't say a word or take possession until that undisclosed date," said Naryshkin.

"Why all the secrecy?"

"Just after Trump announced new tariffs on Mexico, the market tanked and the family took all the proceeds from the real estate sales, I estimate about six billion and went 'all in' in the depressed stock market. A few days later, Trump announced the tariffs would be lifted on Mexico and talks with Xi Jinping were back on the table and the markets surged. The Trump family made a killing in the market; they made a fortune."

"On paper."

"Yes. On paper."

"So, what is his game Comrade Siluanov?"

"What Trump does or doesn't do controls the market and therefore the economy. I think what we're looking for is right in front of us," said Ministry of Finance Siluanov.

"Continue."

"The 'undisclosed date'. That's the key that will unlock this mystery. After that date, Trump and his family don't seem to care what happens, so whatever they're planning will have already occurred."

"Very interesting and an astute observation Comrade Siluanov. And if you could guess, what do you think will happen on that undisclosed date?"

"Despite all their past discord, there is now un-natural bipartisan co-operation between the Left and the Right. Even Trump's tweets are positive. This love fest coupled with Fed cuts, and favorable international news is fueling economic growth.

"I think their economy will continue to grow at an unprecedented pace. Until…"

"Until what?" Comrade Siluanov.

"Until something really bad happens or some extraordinary disruptive news is announced on that undisclosed date.

"The Ponzi scheme, aka their stock market, will collapse. The news will be so disruptive the economy will be thrown into a massive recession; a depression."

"So, Trump will lose everything? asked Putin.

"Maybe this is a new scheme, a 'Trumpzi Scheme', and he gets out of the market before it crashes," said Siluanov.

"But then the dollar will devalue along with the market."

"Not if he buys something more valuable with his dollars," said Siluanov.

"Gold!" blurted Putin. "Comrade Siluanov you have done well. Now, Comrade Naryshkin use all the power of your SVR to find that 'undisclosed date.'"

Chapter 62

There's a new club in the Hamptons every year. Most originate in Manhattan and pop-up in one of the villages for a few years. Then like everything and everyone in life, they become old, tired, and die.

Dmitriy Volkov was not old or tired and had no intention of dying. Possibly being killed by Putin, yes, but dying of natural causes never entered his mind. His prestige had remained solid since Trump kept him around and let him stay in one of the guest houses with his two wolves Hammer and Sickle, while he continued to be 'Lord of the Manor' and run the village of Wolfhampton with an iron hand.

Volkov and his four partners, two locals, one from Brighton Beach, and one from St. Petersburg, (the cold one) decided to open the most extravagant, decadent restaurant-nightclub ever; right off Main Street in an old brick three-story 20,000 square foot warehouse in the quiet village of Wolfhampton.

The club name, 'Committee for State Security', proposed by Volkov, didn't sound any better when translated into Russian — 'Komitet Gosudarstvennoy Bezopasnosti' but the acronym 'KGB' seemed to work. Club KGB was conceived as a 'what-if' Studio 54 materialized in Moscow in 2020. Dance stages terracing from a huge dance floor into loges then balcony's, and VIP Rooms under an atrium with a retractable roof created an impluvium effect; from which a glass and metal elevator, shaped like Russia's new RS-28 Sarmat (Satan II) intercontinental ballistic missile, completely enveloped within a waterfall, quickly launched hi-rollers up into the cosmos, or naughty boys and girls down to the basement where the infamous 'Black Dolphin Prison' interrogation rooms and prison cells awaited them.

Four men's rooms, six for the ladies, ten inclusive (gender-neutral) and fifteen bars kept the customers happy and drinking. The A/V system was spectacular. No visible speakers or monitors — all the walls were painted with LED paint making the building itself a fourth-dimension IMAX', a trick Volkov learned from FBI Agent Bob Bates during the kidnapping attempt.

There was no Steve Rubell at the door, but there was a no-non-sense, technology-challenged tough guy from Upper Darby Pa. — Brian Fitzpatrick. At six foot, the 50-year-old, former soap opera TV star was tough and up for the job, though some made the mistake of thinking him a bit long in the tooth. Fitzy as he was known, had more barroom brawls than a professional UFC fighter and a security staff of former Rangers and Marines as his crushers and back up. As the gatekeeper in charge of security, he had unequaled power over life and death, fame or rejection to all those souls who wanted to be famous for a night. Fitzy was recruited from a Hollywood club called Lure and gave instructions to his team to keep the peace even if they had to shoot someone.

Main Street aka Montauk Highway, the only east-west two-lane street was clogged with limos, Ubers, Lyfts, and partiers. Cars trying to get to East Hampton or back to Southampton were at a standstill. The police tried to keep the traffic moving but rubberneck gawkers hoping to see a Kardashian or two made it impossible.

Drugs were rampant. Besides the regular suspects, Cocaine and Heroin, recreational party drugs like; Molly, Liquid Ecstasy, Rohypnol, Special K, Spice, and Opana were flowing as fast as the liquor.

The line to get in was around the corner and the crowd watched the lucky few go through an electronic security check before being admitted to the inner sanctum. The hum of the waiting crowd was loud; the bass shook the building, and the treble was so high it sounded as though a Long Island Railroad diesel train was sounding its whistle and rounding the corner. Paparazzi snapped, drunks stumbled, girls screamed, boys postured, and the mayor and police chief looked the other way.

Tom Halsey, Abby Adams, and Barron along with his security am and pm in the Secret Service black Suburban, guided by a Wolfhampton village police patrol car, eased up in front of the main entrance just behind Volkov's black and red Bugatti. They exited the vehicle and were immediately noticed by Fitzy and ushered through the crowd, and into the inner sanctum of KGB.

"I've heard and read so much about Studio 54, but this is even more amazing," said Barron. "Dad's got to see this."

"Wow!" exclaimed Abby. "Nothing close to this out here or in Manhattan."

Halsey, who had been to the club before, wanted anonymity and covered his face as best he could, but the paparazzi were inside and out, recognized him and it was hopeless. Barron fared better with sunglasses and a NY Yankee cap and sandwiched between am and pm. They made their way through the crowd to one of the many bars and ordered a dry 'Hammer and Sickle Martini', a Sam Adams Light, and a dry Pina Colada for Barron. Halsey handed the bartender his credit card to set up a tab, but the bartender refused to accept it and politely said, "Everything's on the house, Mr. Halsey." Halsey thanked her and tossed a twenty on the bar. A lot of money for him but a drop in the bucket towards the $3,000 in tips she would make tonight.

It was 11 pm and the dance floor was packed, the loges and balconies were packed, the VIP rooms were packed. This was an open night, so the crowd was mixed. College kids, rappers, Wall Street, tough guys, Russian wise guys, Brooklyn wise guys, up-town girls, up-island boys. Kids from Queens taking the train out, and Jersey boys escaping the shore, but not many locals. They couldn't afford the $100.00 cover charge, not to mention the cost of drinks and drugs, but when Fitzy was at the door, he always let a few locals in for free.

KGB had something for everyone, but it would cost you. A bottle of Vietnamese "Ba Muoi Ba" beer aka "33" was 30 bucks a bottle. The house champagne, Jay-Z's mirror bottle 'Ace of Spades' started at two grand a bottle, up to the 30-litre 'Midas' bottle for 50k. 'Bottle Service' was where the club made its money. When one VIP room of players ordered 10 bottles of Ace, ten security guys with gorgeous scantily clad fashion models on their shoulders paraded in with sparklers in one hand and the champagne in the other — an absolute spectacle. Not to be outdone, the players in the next VIP room ordered 20 bottles and then a bigger parade appeared. Each group of players outdoing the other until each room ended up dropping a minimum of 100 grand.

Steve Aoki, the highest-grossing dance artist in North America was at the keyboards, with synthesizer and programming turntables blasting EDM while hundreds of partiers danced on the many stages. Barron was in awe until he saw him. It was fleeting, then he was gone. It couldn't be him, but he told Mr. Halsey and Abby who he thought he saw.

"Couldn't be. Are you sure?" asked Halsey.

"Mr. Halsey, it was just a flash. His hair was short on the side with a mop on top and he had a beard. Sort of going for that Conor McGregor look."

"Let's check out another area."

"Wait-wait," said Barron staring off in a new direction, "if he did change his hair and add a beard he could sort of look like that right?"

"Yeah, I guess so."

"Because 'that' is standing right over there," said Barron pointing to the middle of the dance floor.

Halsey envisioned himself Sylvester Stallone in *Nighthawks* looking in the direction Barron was pointing and expecting to see 'Wulfgar', but instead seeing someone as dangerous. Looking directly back at him with a huge smile on his face was Patrol Officer Michael Denison aka Mikhail Denisov.

Chapter 63

Denison or Denisov was involved in the murder of at least two young girls, kidnapping the president's son, extortion, faking his own death, and several other homicides. But here he was hiding in plain sight where it all took place. The sleepy village of Wolfhampton.

"We're outta here," said am as she grabbed Barron and headed for the exit. PM was on his mic making sure the SUV was standing by outside and then notifying base of the incident. Neither knew for sure if it was Denisov, but their job was to protect Prince and that's exactly what they were doing. Getting him out of harm's way. Other agents would arrive shortly to follow up.

Halsey walked closer and hoped the man smiling at him would turn and leave but he held his ground. "Michael?" asked Halsey.

"Tommy, it is good to see you again my friend," screamed Denisov trying to be heard over the pounding dance music.

"You can cut out the friend crap. You did some crazy terrible things: you lied to me, and put me in the middle of a shit storm and left me..."

"Hanging?" interrupted Denisov as Halsey got up to him.

"Yes, hanging. Speaking of which you've got a pair showing up here. This place will be crawling with Secret Service agents in seconds."

"You forget my friend, I have full pardons from President Trump for any and all crimes committed, and that neither the president or any federal, state, private, military or allies' agencies would pursue me."

"All crimes committed, past tense my friend. Showing up here at the same time as the president's son won't be looked at as a coincidence."

"I've got to talk to you, Tommy. It's not as it seems and…"

There was commotion at the entrance and Fitzy, several bouncers and Secret Service agents came rushing through the room looking for Halsey and Abby. They had a good idea where to look because as VIP's they were followed by dedicated ceiling-mounted face recognition cameras.

Halsey turned back to look at Denisov to see what he was going to do but he was gone — disappeared into the crowd. The next thing he heard and saw was the fire alarm and fourteen hundred screaming panicked partiers stampeding towards exits.

Halsey knew there was no fire and turned to grab Abby, but she was gone. Hustled away by the crowd or…

Fitzy and Secret Service SAC Rob Ceretti, recently transferred from the Bangor office, were the first to reach Halsey. "Was it him? Was it Mikhail Denisov?" asked Agent Ceretti who like most of the Secret Service was very up on the kidnapping and aftermath.

"It was, but he's gone. He probably set off the alarm but now Abby's missing."

Fitzy got on his mic and put a BOLO out on Abby and attached a face shot of her from the face recognition cam.

Agent Ceretti nodded to the other agents and they started for the exits and rooms to reconnoiter. Fitzy sent his team to assist.

Fitzy startled Halsey and Agent Ceretti by pulling out a 7" push button knife, pushing the button and releasing the blade, bending down and speared an envelope off the dance floor. He picked up and handed it to Halsey.

"What's this?" asked Halsey.

"Don't know, but it's addressed to you," said Fitzy.

Halsey didn't know chain of custody protocol, took the note, ripped it open and began to read.

> *All is not as it seems. Putin knows everything. He knows the president's tricks. I have been given a message by Colonel Galkin,*

for you. We are not above interfering again if President Trump continues his tricks. Convince him to purchase back the stock before his announcement and all will be forgiven. Don't, and face the consequences. We may not be able to get to him directly, but we can get to his advisors. What did your AT&T phone company commercials use to say? 'Reach out and touch someone'? We can do that. Talk to him. Convince him of his errors. To prove our point and as a token of our esteemed, you will find what you're looking for in prison.

"Abby's in the basement prison. Let's go," said Halsey.

As they turned to go, Fitzy pushed his throat mic and said, "Say again Truck."

He listened, turned to Halsey and said, "My security guys are in the basement prison now. They found Abby. Truck said she's a 'Bond Martini.'"

"What's that supposed to mean?" asked Halsey as he started to run towards the stairs.

"'Shaken but not stirred,'" said Fitzy, adding "she's okay."

Chapter 64

Abby had had enough and left Wolfhampton for the city vowing never to return, but having second thoughts of completely losing Tommy, stopped short at her parents' home in Southampton. Close enough but a million miles away from Wolfhampton.

President Trump caught hell from Melania for allowing Barron, age 14, to go to a nightclub. Especially one as decadent as the KGB. They all flew back on Marine One to NYC and then took a motorcade to Trump Tower. Halsey waited aboard Marine One at the downtown heliport for the president to return.

"Okay," said President Trump to Halsey after buckling up and beginning their lift-off above the East River, "I read the letter from Putin but tell me again your gut feeling."

"Gut, instinct, whatever you want to call it, he knows. He knows everything. There's a leak or he has the White House and the Wolf House bugged."

"Got to be Volkov," said the president. "I've got a lot on my plate this week. You head back and find the leak or bug. Get Haspel, FBI Director Wray and Secret Service Director Murray to help."

"I might need Haspel, but I would prefer to use Secret Service AIC out of Wolfhampton, Rob Ceretti and the guy who runs the KGB security, Fitzy and his team of Rangers and Marines. I trust them. I will work better and faster without the FBI swooping in and taking over."

"Do it your way, but if Putin fucks with our economy before I sell all my stock and make my announcement we're screwed."

After the president and Halsey disembarked, Halsey was assigned the smaller UH-60 White Hawk to take him from Washington back to Wolfhampton.

Halsey, used to riding in UH-60 Black Hawks, moved to the waiting slick and asked the crew chief for a hook up to the pilot, "Captain, I have to get the Secret Service to run me over to my apartment in Foggy Bottom to pick up some clean clothes."

"Wait one," said the pilot.

A few seconds later the pilot came back on the line, "Hop aboard sir. We'll run you down and set down near your apartment. The SS will shuttle you from there and then we'll run you out to the Wolf House when you're ready sir."

It's good to know the king, thought Halsey.

Halsey set up a secret meeting, off-campus so to speak, aboard an offshore fishing boat skippered by Captain Ken Bouse out of Montauk. Halsey, Secret Service Agent Rob Ceretti, Fitzy, and a couple of his trusted security guys, Truck-Hooah and Recon-Oorah boarded the 32-foot Peggy S.

They were not going out far, just off the Montauk lighthouse for striped bass. Halsey had been fishing with Captain Bouse at least once a season for the last ten years and always caught the two keepers limit, plus plenty of bluefish which they tossed back.

With the captain at the helm taking them out, Halsey, Ceretti, Fitzy, Truck, and Recon huddled by the two fighting chairs in the stern of the boat, which looked very similar to the Orca from the movie *Jaws*. Halsey couldn't escape the irony of the president's analogy about his being remembered as either the greatest con artist since PT Barnum or as a Megalodon, the biggest, most feared shark ever. He hoped it would be the former.

"Thanks, guys, for coming. Let's get this out of the way so we can enjoy some early morning fishing. First up. Any tails?" asked Halsey.

Everyone gave a thumbs up and then Fitzy asked, "How about you?"

"All clear," said Halsey.

"We know. Truck was on your tail and Recon on his. They switched back and forth and you're right, all clear," said Fitzy.

Taking the rebuke well Halsey said, "It's been a while. Sorry, won't happen again."

Truck murmured, "Hooah." and Recon followed with. "Oorah." Case closed.

"Okay," said Halsey, "Any thoughts?"

"The letter came back from forensics with only two sets of prints. Yours and PO Denison aka Denisov," said Ceretti.

"I think we found the weak link in this team," said Halsey making a kind of a 'my bad' face.

Ceretti continued, "No postmark because it was hand-delivered but the stationery was local, Dunkerley's Office supplies in Southampton Village. Handwriting confirmed as his. Store cam surveillance has him entering and leaving. We got him on village and later town cams both proprietary and commercial heading east to the 1770 House Restaurant & Inn on Main Street in Easthampton. We have eyes on him 24/7. He's staying local and taking meals in the inn. We also have one of our agents checked in as a guest. But all in all, pretty sloppy based on his track record — like he didn't care or wanted to be found."

"I agree. But where will he go when he decides not to be found?" Looking at Fitzy he continued, "What about Volkov and the gay community. Are there a lot more like him out here?"

"What do you mean?"

"Older gay guys who like em real young. Maybe we could pressure some of them to talk to us."

"There are plenty of older gay guys out here that come to the club but what's that got to do with Volkov?"

"Riana for starters."

"She's hot," offered Recon.

"She's a he," said Halsey.

"What?" asked Fitzy.

"Riana is really a boy."

"I don't know what your smoking Mr. Halsey," said Fitzy, "we get a lot of the LGBTQ crowd here every night. Boys who identify as girls and girls who identify as boys, crossdressers, the TS crowd, we're even starting to get 'Drag Kids' accompanied by their parents. We're like Farmers Insurance, 'We know a thing or two because we've seen a thing or two', and like Recon said, Riana's hot. She ain't no he and Volkov ain't gay."

Halsey, leaning against the gunwale remained quiet and let it soak in then mumbled, "I guess he's right."

"Sir?" asked Agent Ceretti.

"I guess Denisov was right. 'All is not as it seems.'"

Chapter 65

"Hello Mrs. Trump, it's Tom Halsey."

"I know Tom. All calls are screened."

"May I please speak to Barron if he's home?"

"He's not going out clubbing with you if that's what you're after."

"No, Mrs. Trump. I would just like to ask him a question."

"Is it going to upset him?"

"I don't believe so."

"One second, Tom."

After a second or two Barron got on the phone, "Hi Mr. Halsey. How are things in Wolfhampton and how are Hammer and Sickle?"

"Things are pretty quiet until tomorrow night when the early weekend horde heads out. Hammer and Sickle are fine, and they gave me a message for you, 'Tell Barron we miss him.'"

"Mr. Halsey," said a disbelieving Barron.

"No, honestly they did."

"How did they tell you?'

"With their expression. They were moping but when I mentioned your name, they alerted, their ears perked, eyes widened, and they started sniffing the air for your scent."

"Okay. I'll buy that if it will get me out of here. I want to come out to Wolfhall."

"I'm afraid our little escapade last weekend put a damper on things for a while. Let's let things cool down for a while — k?"

"Okay."

"I need to ask you a question."

"Shoot."

"You spent some time with Riana. What was your impression?"

"Are they in trouble?"

"They?"

"Some people have a gender identity that is non-binary, and conventional pronouns have the effect of assigning them a binary identity, so we use the gender-neutral pronoun 'they' instead of 'he or she.'"

"So, you think Riana is…"

"I hear things Mr. Halsey," interrupted Barron, "and that's how Riana is being portrayed in the media. I used the pronoun 'they' out of respect but if you're asking me if Riana is a boy or a girl there is no doubt in my mind or hers. She's hot, she knows it and she's 100% girl."

How could a 14-year-old be so astute; but remembering that the apple doesn't fall too far from the tree this was probably the best assessment he could ask for, "Thank you, Barron."

"This excuse for a man who is a fornicator, a cheater, an accused rapist, racist, bully, a spoiled ten-year-old child. He suffers from multiple personality disorder and treatment or intervention is what he needs — not sneaky deals that he may or may not honor. He has us sitting on pins and needled waiting to see if he will resign or drop out or whatever the hell he's promising to do. You want me to continue to trust what he says? He won't even acknowledge Kamala Harris," said Maxine Waters.

"Don't hold back Maxine. Say what you really think," said Schumer, faking exasperation and adding, "he tells everyone who will listen that he's and I quote, an 'Extremely stable genius.'"

"I have to agree with Congresswomen Waters," said Jerry Nadler.

"I think we all agree with Congresswomen Waters, but what alternative do we have now? We're in for a penny in for a pound. He has us in writing agreeing to this deal," said Schumer.

"I'm getting very disturbing reports from Brennan, Comey, and Clapper," said Schiff.

"Not surprised from those three but please enlighten us," said Schumer.

"This is not a joke Chuck. As co-chair of the House Intelligence Committee, I have access to a lot of stuff. I write off most of it because it's coming from agencies headed by Trump appointees but Brennan, Comey, and Clapper, CIA, FBI, and NIA, still have many loyal insiders willing and ready to leak. The Russians and Putin, in particular, have been communicating with Trump through Dmitriy Volkov. You remember him? He's the 'Wolfman' of the Hamptons. A Russian with deep ties to Putin and Trump's on and off buddy. He…"

"I've got a vote coming up Buzz that I can't miss. Can you please get to the meat?" asked Schumer.

"Putin, through this Volkov character, asked Trump if he wanted his help in the 2020 elections. Trump said he didn't need his help, suggested he help the Democrats instead and was going to report the conversation to Justice."

"Just how in the hell does that help us?" asked Schumer.

"He never reported it," said Schiff with a big smile on his face.

"That's good. But nobody's going to believe the 'three stooges' anymore," said Schumer.

"I heard the tape," said Schiff.

"That makes all the difference." said Schumer, "Who wants to call the *Washington Post*?"

"No! Let's hold off for now. I've got an idea," said Pelosi.

Chapter 66

On the uppermost floor of the KGB Club was Volkov's private office. Unlike Wolfhall's 19th-century Gothic Revival details Volkov's office was austere — spartan-like. Rough cement walls and ceiling, smooth acid washed and polished floor, sort of like Whole Foods. Recessed fluorescent ceiling lights which were really LEDs. The front portion of his office wall and floor were completely glass — smart glass. The floor glass was 2" thick and Volkov could walk over onto the glass look up and down and survey his entire KGB kingdom, from the retractable glass roof to the main dance floor almost 100 feet below. In the middle of the glass floor where he was now standing was a 3x3 score line in the glass which was allegedly a trap door controlled by a *'Dr. Evil'* button on his desk. No one knew if it was real or just part of the act but there have been rumors.

"Putin's after me. Trump is after me and now Halsey's back after me. And do you know who scares me the most?" asked Volkov.

"Trump?" asked the man sitting across the desk from him.

"Halsey, that's who. And I have you to thank for it. I put him off the scent and you led him back."

"Mr. Volkov. I didn't know."

"No matter. He would have found out sooner or later from Denisov."

"Mr. Volkov, I can't help you with Putin or Trump, but I can take care of Halsey."

Volkov nodded and the man got up and opened the office door to leave when Volkov said, "And Fitzy, make it look like an accident."

Twenty minutes later, two young Russian girls who couldn't be more than fifteen years old, and had been sitting obediently at his desk, were asked by Volkov to join him on the glass floor. Many young Russian girls gravitated to the Hamptons each summer on working visas, to supply the many restaurants, nightclubs and rich older men as waitstaff, bartenders, and escorts.

Volkov returned to his desk and said, in Russian, "Раздевать." The girls, without hesitation, began undressing.

From below, service personnel preparing for the early dinner crowd looked up, as they always did, to see if they could catch a glimpse of the mysterious Russian in his office — this time they weren't disappointed.

Volkov then undressed and walked from behind his desk, with only his cell phone in his hand, to join the completely naked girls on the glass floor. He looked down and saw a few staff, two levels below, surreptitiously looking up at him. He told both girls to lay face down on the glass, knelt between them, smiled to his audience then pushed a button on his iPhone and the clear smart glass wall and floor instantly became opaque.

The Oval Office in the west wing of the White House was President Trump's private office and inner sanctum. Unlike Trump Towers brass and glass, the details of the president's office were traditional, and after some effort the president was finally able to get his feet up on the desk.

"I just had another call from Pelosi, why doesn't she tweet like a normal person. She's squeezing me. She says she has a tape of me talking to Volkov about an offer from Putin to help with the 2020 elections. I turned him down and I thought she was going to, you know, congratulate me. But instead, she said I should have never listened and should have reported it to the FBI. How can I report it to the FBI unless I find out first what it is? I forgot to report it, but now we know that fuck, Volkov is wearing a wire. For who? Putin or Pelosi?"

"What does she want in exchange for the tape?"

"I'm impressed Peachy. You're starting to think like a politician. But you could never become one — you're too honest. What she wants is a date."

"She's not your type."

"Funny, but what she wants is my announcement date. But speaking about dating, back in the seventies and early eighties, before the big bookstores like Barnes and Noble, B. Daltons, and Rizzoli's, before Bezos fucked it all up with Amazon, all the young single guys and girls from the Upper East Side would meet up in department stores like Bloomingdale's 'Saturdays Generation'. Well, Bloomingdale's and to a lesser extent fashion stores like Bergdorf's were known pick-up spots on Saturdays. I met so many hot girls, got so many numbers and ..."

"I think you should have stopped in the eighties and you would not be in your current shit storm, and what's Bloomingdale's have to do with Russia?" said Halsey.

"Cute. Nothing. I just thought you wanted to tell stories like girlfriends."

"Putin's after me. Pelosi's after me and now we know for sure Volkov's after me. And do you know who scares me the most?" asked the president.

"Putin?" asked Halsey sitting across the desk from President Trump.

"Volkov, and I kept him around because you and Abby felt sorry for him. All this LGBT crap which, as I found out from your young clubbing buddy, is a crock of shit."

"Mr. President. We were misinformed."

"No matter. We would have found out sooner or later from Denisov."

"Mr. President I can't help you with Putin or Pelosi, but I can take care of Volkov."

President Trump nodded and Halsey got up and opened the office door to leave when the president said with a smile and a chuckle, "And Peachy, make it look like an accident."

Chapter 67

The showdown came quickly. President Trump was in Washington meeting with congressional leaders and then with Vice President Pence and his Cabinet. Halsey was back in Wolfhampton looking for trouble. He found it.

Volkov's throaty red and black Bugatti came roaring up the long driveway to the guest house and skidded to a stop. Halsey was sitting on the porch steps as Volkov and Fitzy got out. Fitzy nodded to Halsey and walked away towards the garage leaving Volkov and Halsey alone.

"Nice car. Bet it set you back a few thousand," said Halsey.

"About one thousand thousand," said Volkov.

"Sit down," said Halsey.

"I like it where I am."

"Suit yourself. I should have known you were lying when I found out Riana went to the Convent of the Sacred Heart. Pretty hard to hide a boy in an all-girl school," said Halsey.

"Where else but in plain sight?" said Volkov.

"Everybody's dead Volkov. Olivia's dead. Zoe's dead. Kahbib's dead. Sally Dunn's dead, as is John Doe, which was supposed to be Denison, but he outsmarted you. A half dozen young girls are missing. You and Putin colluded in kidnapping Barron and offered to get involved in the 2020 elections, which the president declined. You're through Volkov. Today we settle all this business, so don't tell me you're innocent. Admit what you did," said Halsey.

Volkov let out a hearty laugh. "Jesus. You're even starting to talk like Trump. Admit I did what? All those names? I didn't kill them. Olivia and Zoe committed suicide. Kahbib was killed by the SVR — finished off by Hamer and Sickle, yes but while under your command. This Sally Dunn and John Doe were also dispatched by the SVR. Admit to what — that I like young boys? You and Trump are homophobic."

"Cut the shit, Volkov. Riana is a girl and you're not gay. Stop hiding behind the LGBT community. You're out of here, that's your punishment. We're finished. I'm putting you on a plane back to Russia. Only don't tell me you're innocent — it insults my intelligence."

"You bring your cavalry? You forget who runs this village and the police?"

"Who approached you, Putin or Pelosi?"

"Pelosi? What's she got to do with this?"

"She has a recording of you offering Trump, Putin's help in the 2020 elections."

"How the hell did she get that?"

"I was hoping you would tell me."

"It wasn't me. Someone must have planted a bug. Your FBI and Secret Service have been breached or look at the SVR. Putin's behind all this intrigue. President Trump is trying to punch back at Putin for the kidnapping and now Putin is punching back. You send me back to Russia and I'm a dead man…"

That was the last Halsey heard. 'I'm a dead man'. The force and pain smashing into his chest were like nothing he never felt before. Pain and darkness. *But that's good right*, he thought. *Don't know about the darkness, but I feel pain so I'm still alive.*

The *Democratic* Presidential *debate* for 2020 had been over for some time and all the nominees were all friends again except a resentful Joe and a rejected Bernie. Harris was their pick, but it really made no difference because the leaders of the Democratic party knew they were in trouble, even MSNBC host Joe Scarborough called most of the 2020 Democratic debates a "disaster for the Democratic Party." But Pelosi and the other four co-conspirators knew different, but could they hold the party together until the announcement?

"Mr. President, you seem to not be running full steam," said Vice President Pence sitting on the receiving side of Resolute. "Pelosi and Schumer are badgering me constantly on your plans. I'm more than ready to debate Pete Buttigieg, but is there something you want to tell me?"

"Mike, I'm not running full steam because I don't have to. It's been a long fight within the Left. They still don't have their socialist platform nailed down, but Harris is an almost a perfect Democrat. She's from San Francisco, half Jamaican and half Indian – dot not feather. Doesn't matter. I'm gonna win if I run."

Did I just hear him correctly? Did he just say, 'If I run'? thought the vice president.

"And don't worry about Joe Biden and the way he was treated by the Democratic Party. Even his Svengali Barack Obama didn't come through for him. I will never treat you like that Mike. I'll be there for you no matter what, which reminds me, you need to start thinking about your future and…"

A knock on the door interrupted the president, "It's Agent Ceretti from Wolfhall," said Madeleine Westerhout. "He says it's important."

"Give me a second then put him through. Mike, I have to take this but think about what it is you want, and we'll talk again."

"Agent Ceretti," said the president, "This is probably not good news unless you're going to tell me Volkov and Denisov, both have middle seats on a plane back to Russia."

"That was the plan Mr. President, but something went wrong. Halsey confronted Volkov but was shot. We had him wired and wearing a vest, as planned but someone else, a sniper took the shot, not Volkov. Halsey's in Southampton Hospital and in fair condition. Has a nasty bruise and had the wind knocked out of him but otherwise…"

"Where's Volkov?" interrupted the president.

"I said Halsey's been shot."

"I heard you Agent Ceretti, and you also said he was in fair condition. So, where's Volkov?

"I want Volkov and Denisov gone. Dead or back in Russia. They're colluding with Russia and somehow feeding information to the Democratic Party. Putin wants them back and I'm sure once there they will never leave again."

"I'm not sure Denisov isn't on our side," said Ceretti.

"Bring him in."

Chapter 68

Secret Service SAC Rob Ceretti, his team, along with the assistance of the East Hampton Village Police surrounded the 1770 House Restaurant & Inn on Main Street.

Not since British infantrymen, in 1776, were bowled over by a steaming kettle of pudding from a top of Pudding Hill had East Hampton seen so many long guns.

"Better you than the SVR," said Denisov who offered no resistance during the early morning raid. In fact, he was dressed and waiting as if he knew they were coming — he did.

Not wasting any time, Agent Ceretti had him cuffed and placed in the back seat of his black Suburban. Ceretti then got into the shotgun seat turned and asked, "Where's Volkov?"

"Around," said Denisov.

"Around?" asked Ceretti.

"Yeah — around — just not around here."

Ceretti pushed a button on his secure phone and President Trump's voice came over the ear speaker, "Agent Ceretti, you have him."

"Right here, sir."

"Did he tell you where Volkov is?"

"No, Mr. President."

"Put me on speaker... Mr. Denisov, we can do this nice or not so nice; up to you. Where's Volkov?"

"Mr. President, good to speak with you again. I thought we had a deal?"

"We do but you obviously have something to say or you wouldn't be hiding in plain sight."

"You want Volkov? You know the catchphrase from the movie *All the President's Men*, 'Follow the money?'"

"Of course. Lousy, fake movie but a terrific line."

"Well if you follow the money, you'll find Volkov soon enough. He goes through it like a sieve. But if you want to find him now, follow the wolves. He won't leave them. Where Hammer and Sickle go, so goes Volkov."

"Did he shoot Halsey?"

"No. That would be the local branch of the SVR. Putin was sending you a message. He's pissed at you for the 'Con'. You read the letter. He knows everything. He wants you to purchase back the stock before your announcement and all will be forgiven. Don't and face the consequences. He got to Halsey and maybe his girlfriend will be next, and she may not be wearing a vest."

"What's Putin's fascination with Volkov?"

"Volkov was in the SVR under Naryshkin and was on his way up the ladder. He was, is, a stone-cold pathological killer, and Naryshkin recognized talent. Then some skeletons started to surface. Real ones, not the closet kind. Seems some young girls and boys were turning up dead. Seems he was also scamming money from some very wealthy guys. Putin wants him, his money and his expertise back in Russia."

Chapter 69

"Schiff wants to release the tape. You have to give us something," said Speaker Pelosi sitting in front of the Resolute alongside Chuck Schumer during their third réunion secrète in the Oval Office.

"How did Schiff get hold of the tape? We have a tape of Volkov denying he made a tape or released it. He said the SVR recorded the conversation. Somehow, I smell Brennan, Comey, and Clapper's stink on this. Have you and the stooges been colluding with the Russians, Nancy?"

"Mr. President, we need a date for your announcement. Kamala Harris has beat out all the other nominees and she's our party's candidate for the next President of the United States. She's all bent out of shape and telling anyone who will listen that you're ducking her and afraid to debate her. Mr. President, you're either in or out."

"Good thing I'm gonna bow out. Didn't think you would be stupid enough to run another woman against me after what I did to Crooked Hillary."

"Stupid? Let's not discuss intelligence, Mr. President. Did you forget that Hillary beat you in the popular vote?" asked Schumer.

"Who won? That's what counts."

"A date, Mr. President. We more than held up our end and gave you another 300 miles of wall…"

"And your damn immigration reform," interrupted Schumer.

"When are you going to announce you're out?" asked Pelosi.

"New Year's Nancy," said President Trump, "I'll make the announcement then."

"Are you out of your mind? New Year's is after the election," said Schumer.

"Not our New Year — yours," said the president looking at Schumer. Rosh Hashanah, September 19th. Your Jewish New Year."

Schumer shook his head and was about to respond to the president when Pelosi quickly held up her hand and said, "I can live with that and I should be able to placate the group." She had her date and didn't want to lose it.

"Okay. You placate your group but if it leaks this time Nancy, I'll know you and Chucky boy really didn't want a deal and have been just stringing me along."

"And Chuck. You really want to talk about intelligence and immigration reform? Let me tell you about intelligence and immigration reform because I'm a really smart guy.

"Here's a story you might empathize with Chuck. Once during a Senate committee hearing, Senator Ted Kennedy began questioning Defense Secretary Rumsfeld by saying, 'Don't you think some members of the Bush administration should be held legally accountable for the lies they told about Iraqi weapons, and the subsequent cover-up?'

"Rumsfeld was ready and had a reply that shut Ted Kennedy right the fuck up. 'First, with all due respect Senator Kennedy, you're all wet...' Rumsfeld continued, but just the mere mention of water around Ted Kennedy was enough to shut him up. Kennedy knew where it could lead if he continued the questioning."

"What the hell does any of that have to do with me?" asked Schumer.

"Because immigration is your water Senator and you best know when to shut up."

"What does immigration have to do with me?"

"Chuck, you're known as the king of 'Pay to Play' in our corrupt, rigged Washington swamp. You exploited the immigration laws for wealthy real estate developers through the EB-5 visa program, allowing investors to pay $500,000 in exchange for a green card, in return for plenty of campaign cash given back to your coffers."

"All lies."

"All true," said President Trump.

"You're a smart guy alright, Mr. President, I was never charged and you're not smart enough to admit when you're wrong."

"I'm not wrong, you're a hypocrite. And that doesn't prove a damn thing," said President Trump.

"Well, it proves one thing, Mr. President. It proves that you wealthy college boys on your daddy's dime don't have the education enough to admit when you're wrong."

"Pretty good Chuck. Quint taking Hooper to school. Not a bad analogy. I like that. Didn't think you had it in you."

They both seemed to enjoy the back and forth repartee.

"You're a quitter," challenged Schumer.

"I thought you wanted me out, but no, I'm not a quitter I'm a fighter..."

"President Trump," interrupted Schumer, "you're a fighter alright, but you're more George Foreman than Mohamad Ali. You throw a lot of jabs and punches, but you never learned to bob and weave. You might sting like a bee, but you never learned how to float like a butterfly."

"I've still got rope-a-dope and by the way, I was there in Zaire for the 'Rumble in the Jungle' back in '74."

"Yeah, well, that was as close as both Mohamad Ali and you ever got to a jungle. He had a religious deferment you had a bone spur deferment. Kept you out of the jungle, but not out of the sand trap."

"We're close in age Chuck, what were you doing back in the '60s? College or Canada?"

"I was in a similar situation as Muhammad Ali. We both sought religious deferments from Vietnam, but my lottery number was never called; and of course, there was Harvard."

"Harvard for you, Harlem for him. Senator, I knew Muhammad Ali. Muhammad Ali was a friend of mine. Senator, you're no Muhammad Ali."

Schumer was about to respond when Pelosi stood signaling that the meeting was over. They both got up to leave and while walking out the door, President Trump gave them the 'Italian salute' behind their backs, blew a raspberry and forgetting Hooper's third gesture just gave them the finger.

Halsey had only spent a few hours in Southampton Hospital before he felt well enough to be discharged. The Southampton detectives questioned him, and he told them that he was on private property, with the owner's permission, taking a walk when it happened. He told them that it must have been a stray shot from a hunter. They knew whose property it was and that even in Wolfhampton there were no hunters with high power rifles in July. He was lying, but they couldn't prove anything and knew the Wolfhampton PD would be uncooperative. As the detectives were leaving, Det. Kimberley McMahon turned and congratulated him on having the foresight to wear a Kevlar vest while taking a walk.

"You told her the date?" asked Halsey over a new improved secure line from the Wolfhall that Agent Ceretti had set it up."

"I told them September 19ᵗʰ The Jewish New Year's knowing that it will leak back to Putin somehow, possibly through one of the three stooges."

"Yes, but then he knows. Everyone knows and everything tanks before you can get out of paper and into metal."

"Don't mention tanks. It brings back bad memories of my 2019 July 4ᵗʰ Salute to America Parade. They wouldn't even let me roll the tanks down Constitutional Avenue. They put one tank on display like outside a VFW post somewhere. It rained, and tarps were over everything. Our soldiers, sailors and Marines couldn't march. Probably for the better — they didn't look half as cool as the Chinese, or North Korean troops marching. The Marines and the Revolutionary Soldiers looked good but there was no one in the stands watching. I mean I gave a terrific speech, everyone said it was terrific, and I learned a lot. We had a 'Fly Over' of Air Force One, some jets, and helicopters but a typical air show in Podunk would have been more exciting. 'Fly Over. I want a 'Do-Over'. Maybe I should have done it again this year only bigger and without the rain. If I did, I wouldn't be in the mess I'm in now."

Waiting for the president to finish rambling Halsey asked, "Did you find out who shot me?"

"Yeah, Agent Ceretti didn't tell you? Denison said it was Putin sending us another message. He said you were the mailman and Putin may be looking for a mailwoman to deliver the next message."

"That's just great. Abby has been ducking me but she's still at her parent's house on Gin Lane."

"Sorry about that. I'll have Agent Ceretti double security on her."

"Anyway, where was I? Oh yeah, it won't be Rosh Hashanah. The Dow will hit 30,000 just about a week before on Labor Day September 7th. That's the real date. The date I will give up the presidency, become free and propel my family's wealth into the Cosmos."

Chapter 70

Trump jokes Dow 30K will be the next big milestone. Here's how long it could take

PUBLISHED SAT, July 25, 2020, 12:23 PM EST

Keris Kerisalison

The market barely had a chance to catch its breath this week, with the Dow hitting a new milestone of 28,000 and other indices setting new highs.

However, chatter on Wall Street (and in the White House and Wolf House) has quickly turned to the next target. "I guess our new number is 30,000," President Donald Trump teased to reporters on Thursday, after lauding the blue-chip index's run-up to its 28,000 level.

At least one Wall Street analyst thinks the president could be proven correct sooner than some think.

Chris Zaccarelli, chief investment officer at Independent Advisor Alliance, is also expecting the Dow to set its next significant round-numbered milestone, perhaps this year.

Stuart Varney of Fox Business News interviews Donald Trump
July 28, 2020 Varney & Co." on FOX Business Network

Varney: We have a very special guest. President Trump just walked into the studio. I just stood up and shook his hand. He's with us right now. Mr. President, thanks for being with us.

Varney: Well, it's only because I like your show.

Varney: Oh, thank you very much indeed, sir.

Varney: I watch you.

Varney: Really fast, your son Barron had some trouble in Wolfhampton not too long ago. Everybody okay?

Varney: He's fine, they're fine. I just spoke to Melania. They're back in Manhattan, but yes, they had a problem.

Varney: What was the problem?

Varney: Yes, they had a problem but they're fine.

Varney: OK, does anybody ever say to you, you're doing an awful lot of media and you like it?

Varney: Well I don't like it, I like getting the point across, I've heard you say many times that the economy isn't covered properly and it's not. That the economy is not covered properly by the so-called "mainstream media" and it isn't.

Varney: We went up almost 600 points yesterday and they didn't even have it on the major news. You couldn't find it anywhere and the economy is doing probably better than it's ever done in history and they don't even talk about it.

Varney: And that's because they have their opinion and they'd like to keep their opinion going the way they have it. They do not treat us fairly and therefore if I do the news, they all want me on the news, so I can talk about it myself.

Varney: Are you going to keep up this pace of media after the election?

Varney: Probably not, no this is just for the election. We want to win; we want to get the Republicans elected and win back the house.

Varney: Mr. President, If you can stick around, I would like to ask you about a prediction you made about the market, but I'm hearing in my ear we must take a short commercial break and we'll be right back if you…

Varney: Sorry Stuart, I'll be gone by the time you get back.

Varney: Well Mr. Producer can we hold off for a few so we can accommodate the president's schedule. Okay, go ahead? Okay. Mr. President, you told reporters on Saturday and I quote, "I guess our new number is 30,000." You said it with a smile on your face and it's being touted as a joke. If you would have told me in 2016 that we would even be talking about a 30k market I would have said you were crazy, but here we are, Mr. President."

Varney: Stuart, I told you and anyone who would listen that you were going to get tired of winning. I wasn't kidding. The DOW is going to hit 30,000 this year and maybe higher. But what goes up, must come down and if you're in the market now as a speculator, just remember it's all because of me and my policies. If anything happens to me — If the Socialists get in, everything we built together will come tumbling down.

You know Stuart, When your campaign is based on giving teachers huge pay raises, college students free education, forgiving student loans, and mortgages, free Medicare for all, free money for not working, free college education, free benefits and legal status for illegals, you're gonna get a lot of votes. I'll have more to say in my upcoming Address to the Nation.

Varney: And when will that be and what can we expect to hear?

Trump: Mid-September. You'll be the first to know Stuart. What can you expect? You know me Stuart — expect the unexpected.

Varney: Thank you. Can't wait. I just want to thank you very much for being on the program.

Trump: Thank you.

Varney: Yes, sir. Expect the unexpected. There will be more Varney after this short commercial break.

"Are you all there?" asked the president talking into the speaker.

"We are Dad, and yes, the line is secure. We're ready," said Don Jr.

"Gold has dropped to just under $1,100," said Ivanka, "and the DOW is at 28k and moving up. We put 10 billion into stocks and now it's worth just under 17 billion."

"Sell everything just before my speech on Labor Day. As soon as they find out I'm out, the market will crash, and gold will take off. When Gold hits 2k, sell and get back into cash. We'll double our money to 34 billion. Not bad from just 6 billion a few weeks ago."

"They're gonna be pissed off."

"Who's they?" asked Eric.

"Putin, Bezos and the other 2,150 billionaires in the world."

Chapter 71

LABOR DAY

President Donald J. Trump's Address to the Nation

CNN Studios in Washington D.C.
September 7, 2020, 8:45 pm

Announcer: This is the Situation Room with *Wolf Blitzer.*

Wolf Blitzer: In just a few minutes the President of the United States will give the Address to the Nation from Trump Tower, something that has never occurred before, but still carries with it the weight of the Oval Office. This also seems to have been moved up. We were told the president would give the address more towards the middle of the month. Regardless, tonight we'll hear President Trump speak and you'll hear the Democratic response afterward. We will examine what was said and report the facts. We'll have analysis from our panel of experts and hold on a second. Just a minute. I've got Jim Acosta outside Trump Tower with a live report. Jim.

Jim Acosta: Thank you, Wolf. I'm standing just outside Trump Tower and as we pan up Fifth Avenue., you can't see but can hear the president's motorcade heading down Fifth toward us here at between 56th and 57th Streets. There is a large crowd gathered in front of the tower and plenty of security for this unprecedented Address to the Nation from Trump Tower. Why Trump Tower and not the Oval Office Wolf? That's anybody's guess. Back to you Wolf in the studio.

Wolf Blitzer: Thanks Jim, we'll check back in with you as soon as the president arrives. But let's go to our panel of experts this evening. We have Senior Political Reporter Nia-Malika Henderson, *CNN* Politics Reporter Chris Cillizza, *CNN* Political Director David Chalian, and our Chief Political Analyst, Gloria Borger. Thank you all for being here.

Let me start with you, Nia. What is President Trump going to say tonight, and why from Trump Tower and not the Oval Office?

Nia-Malika Henderson: Wolf, yeah, I think he would have tweeted about it by now, but this is the most closely held address I have ever covered. All my sources have come up blank. I'm told the president won't be using a Teleprompter so as he told another news network, we can expect the unexpected. Trump Tower and not the Oval Office. My guess is that he wants to distance himself from the Washington swamp.

Chris Cillizza: If I may add Wolf, Donald Trump tweets and talks a lot. I think this unprecedented president just plain hates Washington and prefers the Wolf House to the White House and is thumbing his nose to the country from his Sanctuary City Trump Tower penthouse instead of from his self-inflicted Washington swamp.

Wolf Blitzer: I think the president's motorcade has arrived, so let's go back to Jim Acosta outside Trump Tower.

Jim Acosta: Wolf, the motorcade is rolling in now and just past the first two Secret Service Suburban's I see the Beast. The president is right in front of the tower now and I'm going to see if I can get a quick word with him as he enters Trump Tower.

Sounds of some jostling for position and sirens in the background as Jim Acosta pushes through the crowd to try and get a word with the president.

Jim Acosta: Mr. President. I was wondering if you could comment on tonight's address to the …

more noise and jostling could be heard and then the screen went black a second before Wolf's image appeared back in the studio.

Wolf Blitzer: Looks like we lost the feed again. The buildings are so tall we sometimes lose our satellite signal. We'll check back with Jim Acosta as soon as we reestablish contact. What do you see so far tonight as the big headline, David?

David Chalian: Well I think the big headline no doubt obviously is that he is venting his frustrations with Washington and going to show America who's in charge.

Wolf Blitzer: Should there be outrage over this? Gloria.

Gloria Borger: First of all, Wolf, there isn't any outrage. I mean if there's such a thing as a narcissistic White House official White House statement. This is it, and…

Wolf Blitzer: Sorry to interrupt you Gloria but I have just been handed a note, Oh my God. I'm just going to read this. Two shots were just fired in front of Trump Tower. First reports say that President Trump has been seriously wounded. I'm also getting more details in my ear from my producer; another person next to the president was also shot. The wound to President Trump, we are being told, could be fatal. He is in route to… One second. we just got our live feedback with Jim Acosta on the scene of the shooting. Jim go ahead, please.

Jim Acosta: Wolf it's been utter chaos here for the last minute or two. I was asking President Trump a question and as he stopped to answer a lone gunman broke through over my right shoulder, tripping my feed, and fired two shots at the president. I have the president's blood splatter all over me. He fell into my arms before his Secret Service agents grabbed him away. I'm scared, shaken and sick to death of what just happened Wolf. It is no secret that President Trump and I were not on the best of terms, but he never backed down from me or ignored me.

The camera focused on Jim's face and there was true shock and sadness evident. Tears were now mixing with blood splatter on his cheeks as he made his final comment before sitting down upon the curb.

Wolf, I almost feel responsible for setting the president up tonight. If the president didn't stop to answer my question, he may have made it into his tower and would be addressing America at this moment. This shot will be, I'm quite certain, heard round the world. I don't know how this will end but I have a bad feeling. Wolf.

Chapter 72

The New York Times

TRUMP WOUNDED IN CHEST BY GUNMAN; OUTLOOK CRITICAL AFTER TWO-HOUR SURGERY; AID SHOT; SUSPECT HELD

Pence Flies Back From Texas Set To Take Charge In Crisis
September 7, 2020, Late Addition
LEFT LUNG IS PIERCED
Russian Billionaire Arrested
Halsey, Presidential Aide Seriously Injured
By LOWELL RAINES

New York, Monday, September 7, 2020, President Trump was shot in the chest just before 9 pm earlier this evening as he was leaving his limousine and walking to Trump Tower to give his Address to the Nation. The White House…

Six hours after the shots were fired, Wolf Blitzer and the Situation Room was still on the air. It was now 3 am September 8, 2020, the day after Labor Day and instead of Americans returning to work after the last big summer holiday most were still glued to their TVs and watching probably for most, the biggest event of their lives. Fifty years from now, 'they' will ask 'who doesn't remember where they were when President Trump was shot?'

Jim Acosta was back in the studio with Wolf playing and replaying the video of the assassination. His face and hands were now cleaned, and his hair was combed but the president's blood was clearly visible on his white shirt collar and cuffs.

Wolf Blitzer: Jim, I know we have been through this before, but can you give our viewers, just tuning in, your personal account of this tragedy. But before you do, I once again want to offer our hearts and prayers to President Trump, First Lady Melania, and the entire Trump family and to Vice President Pence for assuming the responsibility that has been thrust upon his shoulders.

Jim Acosta: Wolf, I was reading the New York Times late addition and have to say that they refer to the 'Suspect Held' but he is no suspect. He's the shooter. I saw who shot President Trump and he is the assassin, not a suspect. He's the president's friend, billionaire, 4th of July host, alleged Russian spy, and friend of Putin; Dmitriy Volkov. Wolf, he was standing right next to me, mingling around reporters with his cell phone out taking pictures. I noticed him and thought at the time why would he be here and why would he need or want to take a photo of President Trump. I should have followed my instinct and notified the Secret Service.

Wolf Blitzer: Jim. Let's roll the tape and if you will talk over it and fill us all into what you experienced. To our viewers, we may have lost the live feed when it happened, but we still have the video.

The video appeared in slow motion, showing President Trump, along with several aides and Secret Service agents exiting the Beast; the president waving and walking towards the glass, black and brass entrance to Trump Tower, just past the Trump Tower clock, you could clearly see Jim Acosta, mic in hand pressing forward.

Jim Acosta: Here is where I get the president's attention and begin to ask the question about the content of his speech. He stops and turns to answer when Volkov, as you can see, he's right behind me looking through the cell phone like it's a camera just before he lunges forward and his cell phone transforms into a gun, which turned out to be a 380 Cal double shot 'cell phone gun' from a company called Ideal Conceal, blasts two shots one directly almost point-blank at Trump and one purposely at an aide who turned out to be Thomas Halsey; the president's aide and reporter friend from Wolfhampton.

Wolf Blitzer: Can you stop the film there and go back to the frame where Volkov is holding up the Cell phone using it as a camera? Okay, there it is. It looks exactly like a cell phone in size and color. Amazing — and this turns into a gun?

Jim Acosta: Wolf can you start the vid again in slow motion. There. See? He folds a handle down which contains the trigger then just points and fires. Two shots. One point-blank into the president's chest the other into the neck of Tom Halsey. He didn't even have to cock it.

Wolf Blitzer: Jim where was the Secret Service when all this happened. How did he get so close?

Jim Acosta: There were agents all over the place Wolf, but I think I saw press credentials around his neck. Regardless, he was on the lam for another shooting in Wolfhampton, and from what I understand there's even a BOLO out on him. He should never have gotten anywhere near the president. Here you see the instant the president turns from me and recognizes Volkov – then the shots. You can see the president grimace and begin to fall. I was so close he fell right into me before Secret Service agents swarmed over me and tackled Volkov and dragged the president away. It is all a blur.

Wolf Blitzer: Was the president cognizant while you held him? Did he recognize you or say anything?

Jim Acosta: I tell folks I'm not a psychiatrist. I can't assess the president's mental state, but I will tell you my sense of it, covering him for a pretty long period of time now, I made it known in an interview, that he's crazy like a fox. I thought he recognized me, but then he whispered something, and I could barely hear him, so I leaned in closer and then he looked at me, smiled and said, "Crazy like a wolf." Then he was gone.

Chapter 73

"Well I guess he did it," said Schumer.

"I'm not sure. He may be near death but he's not out. He could come back and win with the sympathy vote alone. I just don't know," offered Pelosi.

"This was not part of the plan, or was it, Nancy?"

"What are you getting at?"

"Well, remember your comment about 'aiming higher?'"

"Don't be ridiculous Chuck. You sound like Waters. What we need to do is..."

"What we need to do," interrupted Schumer, "is get the 'Hearts and Prayers' thing out, then ramp up Harris and..."

"Yes, on the 'Hearts and Prayers,'" re-interrupted Pelosi, "but we need to continue singing his praises and continue playing nice till we see which way the wind blows. If this keeps him out, then we're in."

"Do we have to? If he croaks all bets are off and we can be ourselves again. We don't have to continue this bipartisan crap and everything we agreed to is out the window."

"Chuck, not so fast. He said he was going to drop out of the election. He didn't say how he was going to do it. Maybe this is what he intended."

"You mean he had himself shot so he didn't have to be president and deal with us? Come on, even Trump isn't that Machiavellian. Besides, nothing could keep Trump from being in front of a camera."

Chapter 74

Varney & Co. on FOX Business Network
September 9, 2020

Varney: "Expect the unexpected." That's what President Trump said to me just over a month ago when I asked him about his up-coming Address to the Nation. Shot in the chest and prevented from making that address. I don't know about you, but something stinks here, and I intend to get to the bottom of it.

While our president clings to life and our vice president assumes the mantel of authority, we need our country to remain vigilant, stay strong, and come together. The world is watching and I for one believe the president will pull through and once again lead us out of what is quickly becoming a self-fulling prophecy.

He predicted and tweeted back on June 19, just over two months ago, that, and I quote "The Trump Economy is setting records and has a long way up to go...However, if anyone but me takes over in 2020 (I know the competition very well), there will be a Market Crash the likes of which has not been seen before! KEEP AMERICA GREAT."

Minutes after the first shot was fired, the world's people reacted with shock. World leaders offered support and condolences and the world's wealthy began selling. That's right, selling. They're getting out now because of what they think is going to happen. The market has come to a crashing halt less than two days after President Trump was shot.

All trading has been suspended until further notice. Stocks skidded Monday night and Tuesday, with the Dow slumping nearly 1,200 points, in the biggest single-day point loss ever, after President Trump was shot.

The day's loss knocked out approximately $3 trillion in market value, the second post-$1 trillion day ever, according to a drop in the Dow Jones Wilshire 5000, the broadest measure of the stock market.

The Dow Jones industrial average lost 1,777.68, surpassing the 684.81 loss on Sept. 17, 2001, and the 777.68, lost on September 29, 2008

The Standard & Poor's 500 index lost 21.8%, its worst day ever on a percentage basis and the biggest one-day percentage drop since the crash of '87 when it lost 20.5%. The Nasdaq composite fell 19.1%, its third worst day on a percentage basis and also its worst decline since the crash of '87.

If the hemorrhaging continues, and I think it will when trading resumes, we could be looking at a 50 percent market drop to 15,000 or worst, while gold has jumped from a low of $1,100 on Labor Day To just under $1,500 an ounce this morning. Expect the unexpected.

Chapter 75

"Peachy — Peachy."

The attractive nurse, startled, jumped from her chair, at the sound of the president's voice, tripping over the dosing Secret Service agent sitting next to her. The president had closed his eyes and was still and silent when she leaned over him to see if she had been dreaming.

"Peachy," barked the president again springing into an upright position, and obviously startled having just come out of an on again – off again medically induced coma.

Nurse Fletcher ran out of the president's private intensive care suite bumping into Rear Admiral Ronny Jackson, Physician to the President and Dr. Aaron, chief of cardiovascular and thoracic surgery, Lenox Hill Hospital, rushing in after having been alerted at the nurse's station.

Jackson rushed over to the president and placed his stethoscope to his chest while Dr. Aaron reached for his wrist and started counting. "Thank God," said Jackson.

Melania, Kellyanne, and Mick Mulvaney came through the adjacent living area of the suite and the first lady rushed right to her husband's side. "Oh, Donald you're back," she said, "never do this again — promise me." She leaned over and kissed her husband, the President of the United States.

Just then, Nurse Fletcher aka Nurse Ratched, her behind her back nom de guerre, came in with a dish of peaches and joined the bedside welcoming committee.

"What is that?" asked Melania.

"It's alright, it's sugar-free," said Nurse Fletcher.

"But my husband doesn't eat fruit, especially peaches."

"But he woke up asking for them," said Nurse Fletcher.

"It's okay, I remember this nurse from when I was first admitted. It's Nurse Ratched right? Like the movie?" asked a weak President Trump. "I asked for Peachy not peaches, but that's okay. By the way, where is he?"

"Who, Mr. President?" asked Dr. Jackson.

"Peachy — Peachy Carnahan." Turning to Nurse Fletcher he asked, "A Diet Coke, please Nurse Retched."

Nurse Fletcher grimaced at her comparison to Nurse Retched from the movie 'One Flew Over the Cuckoo's Nest', but she left to fetch the Diet Coke none the less.

"I believe the nurse's name is Fletcher," said Dr. Jackson.

"Where's Peachy?" asked the president again.

"My husband is referring to Mr. Halsey, I believe."

"He is in another wing recovering from a gunshot wound to the throat. Had trouble breathing for a while, but he's now in stable condition Mr. President," said Dr. Jackson.

"Jesus. Now I remember. Bring him here," said the president.

"I don't think that's advisable at..."

"I don't care. I want him in my room," demanded President Trump.

Dr. Jackson nodded to an agent and nurse, who both scurried out to find 'Peachy'.

"Melania, please let the kids and the vice president know I'm back, and I need to talk to Ivanka as soon as possible."

"The kids were here but left just twenty minutes ago and are now on their way back. Vice President Pence is aware you're awake, sends his, 'Welcome back' and is in Washington awaiting your orders."

"So, Mr. President, while we're waiting for Mr. Halsey and your children, what do you remember?" asked Dr. Jackson.

"I don't recall all the events clearly, but I knew right away, once I saw Acosta sucking on his mic, that both he and I were going to enjoy my Address to the Nation. He asked me something as I passed and stuck his mic in my face. Something caught my eye over his right shoulder then I was hit with a bat. I fell and it felt like I broke a rib. Next thing I know I was being thrown into the Beast by agents, but when I sat up on the seat the pain wouldn't go away, and I was coughing up blood."

"Good recall. Shows you're really on track," said Dr. Aaron, "you're recovering in every way and doing as well as you can possibly be doing. But you must recognize that you don't get well overnight. That's unrealistic, and it's unfair to you."

"You still looked a bit pale and thin in your face and have been in a medical coma for a few days. Since the shooting, you lost 20 pounds and haven't gained back an ounce. 239 down to your fighting weight of 219," said Dr. Jackson.

"I'm gonna do a Nutrisystem commercial. 'You eat the lead you lose the weight' — funny right? The shooting still seems kind of unreal. I have to watch my back the next time I go out in public, but I'm not going to change in the way I do things.

"I thought what the hell's that? That bat that hit me sounded like a firecracker as I got out of the Beast saw Acosta then saw Volkov. My head of Secret Service hurled me back into the Beast and jumped on top of me. Landing on my face, I felt a pain in my upper back that was unbelievable. It was the most excruciating pain I ever felt.

"I remember speeding toward the hospital. I was almost paralyzed by pain, coughing up red, frothy blood in the palm of my hand.

"I told the agent, you not only broke my rib, I think the rib punctured my lung.

"The sight of my blood seemed to make the driver speed here to Lenox Hill. We did the 20 blocks in ten minutes. I walked on my own through the emergency room doors around 9:30 pm, but then I remember dropping to one knee and gasping for air, then I collapsed. That's it, until I was carried to the trauma room. So, what happened after I blanked?"

"It was a close call," added Dr. Aaron, "you lost 50 percent of your blood volume by the time you got here. You were tipsy and lost your blood pressure when you tried to walk in.

"We saw blood in your mouth, and the agents and all news reports said you've been shot but we couldn't see it until your clothing was removed. You were immediately given oxygen and two units of type O Rh-negative blood and other fluids to stabilize you. Your limo had, thanks to Dr. Jackson, a refrigerator full of your own blood type.

"Although we spotted a 3/4-inch, oblong-shaped entrance wound in the lower left chest, we could find no exit wound. Your heart sounded normal, but no breath sounds were detected in the left lung, meaning it had collapsed.

"The team inserted a chest tube, which quickly filled with more than a quart of bloody drainage. They were able to re-inflate the lung. Breathing sounds became audible. However, dark blood continued to drain from the lung - an ominous sign.

"I leaned in and made a six-inch incision into your chest. I knew a bullet was lodged deep in the lower left lung an inch from your heart. Somewhere, an artery must be severely damaged because you were bleeding badly. You had lost about half of your blood.

"If I couldn't find the bullet," continued, Dr. Aaron, "there was a possibility that it had migrated into the heart. Then it could have been ejected into the bloodstream and gone anywhere in the body."

"If that were the case, we were up to our ears in real trouble," said Dr. Jackson. "Fortunately, a few minutes later Dr. Aaron found the flattened fragment.

"The decision to keep looking proved crucial when it was discovered that the .380 caliber bullet had been a 'Devastator,' designed to explode on impact. It contained the poisonous substance lead azide, and had it been left in, probably would have required a second operation.

"After Dr. Aaron found the bullet, it was removed and I handed it over to a waiting Secret Service agent," said Dr. Jackson.

Chapter 76

Halsey was wheeled into the president's room by Nurse Fletcher, and his bed was placed next to the president's. Halsey and his bed had been thoroughly searched. Two Secret Service agents were also in the room and a slew of others outside the door, around the hospital, the grounds and the roof.

Before President Trump asked everyone to leave the room, he said, "Have you met Peachy McMurphy Nurse Ratched?" Now starting to enjoy being singled out by the president, she smiled but left the room with the others.

"Will you please stop getting shot," said the president.

"You should have taken my advice and worn the vest."

"A lot of good it did you — a throat shot — I heard you almost choked to death."

"It could have been worse if I would have ducked."

"Fucking Volkov tried to kill me," said the president.

"Us — kill us, and Putin was behind it. I don't know why you kept him around," said Halsey.

"I told you. To piss off Putin."

"You succeeded."

"Beyond my wildest imagination. Volkov will fry and I'll pull the switch. Then I'll push the button and Putin will implode."

Wanting to wipe both optics from his mind Halsey changed to the subject, "Well, how does it feel to have 30 some billion in gold while the rest of the fat cats are jumping out windows?"

"It didn't happen."

"What?"

"I never was 100% in on this thing, so I had Ivanka have everything all set. Sell orders for all the stocks all set with buy orders in place. All she had to do was watch for my signal, during the address, then press the sell button and the stock would be gone. Then press buy and we would be all-in on gold. You know about 'lag time' right? Stock trades from no delay to one's lasting more than a minute—a huge advantage for top traders. Well, there's also an algorithm called 'cloud time'. That's when they buy what you're selling and it's a totally done deal, but it goes up into the clouds or somewhere and stays there till the seller pushes the button. That was our plan so we would be locked in before I told the world I was not going to go for a second term then Ivanka would push the button. That way if it ever got back to us, we could prove we sold after the announcement like everyone else."

"And the buyers couldn't get out?"

"No, the buyers or their brokers couldn't react fast enough. Doesn't matter. I never got the chance to give Ivanka the signal."

Just then Ivanka, Don Jr. and Eric came into the room and rushed to their father's side. There were tears and hugs. No one seemed to notice Halsey, except Eric, who never got along with Halsey or Volkov, and whispered, "Dad, I think we can afford a private room."

"I'm sorry about this whole mess. This is not what I planned. We were supposed to come out on top not caught up in a free for all," said the president.

"Dad..."

"I'm sorry Ivanka," interrupted the president, "my caution got the best of me."

"We did it, Dad."

"Did what?"

"We did it, Dad. When you were shot, I knew you wouldn't be able to give me the signal, so I did the trade. I pushed the button. We got out of paper and into rocks. Gold is now trading at just over $1,900.00 an ounce," said Ivanka. "We nearly doubled our money to 34 billion."

"My girl. You done good Ivanka. I thought we lost it, but I should have known. What's the DOW?"

"Bad and sinking Dad, said Don Jr. Trading started up again but started to drop like a rock and they halted trading at just under 15,000."

"Shit, I knew it would implode if anything happened to me, but a 50% drop in a few days…"

"Dad, if you don't get out front and reassure the country that you're back, in charge, and going to win 2020 it's going to be a world tsunami — even our wealth won't protect us," said Eric.

"He can't do that."

Everyone turned towards Halsey.

Chapter 77

Lolita Express
September 29, 2020

"Lolita Express." The Little Black Book kept by Dmitriy Volkov, the alleged shooter in the failed assassination attempt on President Trump, pedophile, billionaire, murder suspect, and Russian President Vladimir Putin's pal, was published by the now-defunct website Gawker in 2015 and contains hundreds of names, including those of celebrities, politicians and other A-listers, with their phone numbers and email addresses blacked out.

Notable entries include a former New York City mayor and a New York governor, famous actors, singers, industrialist, a former secretary of state. President Trump's name was not in the book.

Volkov treated some of his rich and powerful pals to trips aboard his Boeing 727. A former president was revealed in 2016 to have flown on the private jet airliner at least 26 times between 2001 and 2003, according to flight logs obtained by *Fox News...*

"My pal," said Putin waving the post article, "how is he my pal? He's Trump's pal."

Comrade Siluanov sold all of Putin's Blue Origin stock just hours before the shot. He sold just as Blue Origin reached $93.00 a share, the break-even mark. All the pensioners and foreign investors in the RSD investment fund money never knew how close they came to losing everything. Ministry of Finance Anton Siluanov knew how close he came to losing his life.

"Well, that takes care of Volkov. America will have a big trial and execute him," said Colonel Galkin, former head of Volkov's security.

"If Trump dies yes, but not if he lives. If Trump lives, and I have no doubt he will, they will throw Volkov in prison for life and he'll write a best seller about the whole mess and smear me. When the trial is over, and he's tucked away have him taken care of," said Putin.

"I'll have Zinovy Bari and his Brighton Beach crew, take care of it," said SVR Director Naryshkin. "We'll make it look like he hung himself."

"I want to go back," said Galkin.

"Why?" asked Naryshkin.

"To take care of Denisov."

"Any other reason?"

"I want something that belongs to me."

"Trump owns Wolfhall. Volkov's nightclub perhaps? Oh, wait. I will be giving that to the Brighton Beach crew for future services rendered. You can have his Bugatti if you can sneak it out of the country?"

"None of the above. I want Riana."

"Ah, said Putin, my 'PYT'. But is she a girl or is she a boy? He then started singing the 60's hit song, *'Are you a boy? Or are you a girl?With your long blond hair, you look like a girlYeah, you look like a girlYou may be a boy, hey, you look like a girl.'"*

"She will my gift to you Comrade Putin, but I would never offer you a gift that would not please you."

Chapter 78

"This is the third time Pelosi was able to get the impeachment resolution dropped," said Ayanna Pressley. "The House Judiciary Committee is preparing to take its first formal vote to define Nadler's "impeachment investigation" of Trump, and this is the third time Pelosi was able to get the impeachment resolution dropped," said Ayanna Pressley.

"The Squad..." began Rashida Tlaib.

"Company," interrupted Ilhan Omar, "and after the election, the 'Squad' will become the 'Company'. If we also take back the Senate, we'll become a 'Battalion'. Our supporters will soon make us an 'Army.'"

Rep. Alexandria Ocasio-Cortez slapped back Sunday at President Trump for suggesting that she and three other freshman Democrats produce their birth certificates, saying he's irked at them because they push back at his version of America. Trump's "go back" to the countries 'they're from' started to get old, so he turned it into a 'Birther Movement' lumping them with former US President Barack Obama.

"But you know what's the rub of it all, Mr. President?", said AOC to the Squad, "On top of not accepting an America that elected us, you cannot accept that we don't fear you, either. You can't accept that we will call your bluff and offer a positive vision for our country. And that's what makes you seethe."

"Harris better start kicking butt. We've given her 100% support, now she's pulling a JFK on us. She forgot who 'brung her to the dance,'" said Rashida Tlaib.

"Why are the speaker and her gang still playing house with Trump? That's the question."

"Maybe it's because he got shot. He seems to be holding all the cards now, but the sympathy will wear off as soon as he starts tweeting again late at night in his 'Tighty-Whities' roaming the White House."

"Late at night is going to get a lot worse for him. We will come to him when he tweets and sleeps. We will become his reoccurring nightmare. His nightmare will be seeing a Somali immigrant refugee rise to Congress. His nightmare will be seeing the beautiful mosaic fabric of our country welcome someone like me as their member of Congress. And so, we are going to continue to be a nightmare to this president," said Rep. Ilhan Omar.

When the two Muslim Squad members, Rashida Tlaib and Ilhan Omar, were alone Omar started laughing. "What is so funny?" asked Tlaib.

"They think we are just socialist and that all we want to make America a socialist country."

"I always thought Americans thought big, but they have no idea."

"We are just the beginning."

"Europe was full of appeasers, France, Germany, and Great Britain. And now look at them. Britain's famous Prime Minister Churchill once said, 'An appeaser is one who feeds a crocodile, hoping it will eat him last.' If the world wouldn't listen to the Churchill the great orator, do you think Americans will listen to Trump the great imposter?"

"Yes. Many will."

"I can't believe you told him about your deal with Pelosi and Schumer," said Eric looking over to Halsey adding, "and not us."

"I told you before. I wanted to keep you out of harm's way."

"How's that working out Dad?" said Eric.

"What if we get socialist countries to back Harris like Moreno of Ecuador or Maduro of Venezuela," said Eric.

"Or Macron of France, or Putin if we want to take it up a notch," said Don Jr.

"Are you kidding me? Putin hates me. He's the one guy I can count on to back me. A little more collusion for the Left to spill out every night at six-thirty," said President Trump. "Look kids, as Halsey said, I can't do that. I'm tired of all this crap. I want to be in charge again. No committees. No more Frantic Five. No Squad. No more kidnappings, and no more assassination attempts."

"You think by 'dropping out' everything will go back to the way it was?" asked Don Jr.

"Look. I made a pact with the devils — we have a deal. Pelosi is holding up her end and Harris is a shoo-in when I drop out."

"Yeah, but what if something happens to Pelosi?" said Eric.

"What are you suggesting?"

"Nothing like that. I'm talking about coup d'état within the Democratic party. You know — out with the old — in with the new kind of thing," said Eric.

"The Squad is just four crazy Congresswomen?"

"The Squad is quickly becoming an army," said Ivanka.

"Dad, you leave office and we're all at their mercy."

"We'll have immunity and I wouldn't call these four ingrates a squad. I'm told in the Marine Corp; a squad is three four-man fireteams and a squad leader. I wouldn't disrespect the Marines or a squad by equating them to these four wackos. Besides, I have the 'Trump Card' so to speak," joked the president.

"You think that will make a difference to AOC and the rest of the Squad, gang or posse or whatever you want to call them? Do you think they care about what you and Pelosi agreed to? They would throw her to the wolves. And you Dad — they would follow you to hell just to watch you burn," said Don Jr.

"Yeah, I like the last one," said the president.

"What last one?"

"'The Pussy's.'"

"'The Posse Dad — please,'" said Eric.

"You thought impeachment was bad. How about treason? They will leak the letter and you Pelosi Schumer and all of them will get sent up for treason, but Pelosi and Schumer will somehow squeeze out of it and turn on you. They did it for 'the good of the nation', and all that crap. It will be you hanging out there in the breeze. Then they will come for us, said Don Jr."

"You?"

"Us. With you behind bars, and that's if they feel compassion, they will come for me. Then they will come for Ivanka, Eric, Melania, and Barron. Then come for the money and claw it back. I'll be in jail with you, but they'll have to get jobs and our kids will have to go to public schools."

"Halsey," said the president inquisitively looking over at his wounded comrade in arms, "will they be my worst nightmare?"

"I think your children are right, and the idiom 'Better the devil you know than the devil you don't' couldn't be better applied than here. But with that said, the Left is in a power struggle and as Napoleon Bonaparte once said, 'Never interrupt your enemy when he is making a mistake.'"

"English."

"The 'Squad' will be your worst nightmare and if there is a going to be a battle between the old and new guard, stay out of it and let them destroy each other."

My family is too important to me. I can't risk another kidnapping, attempted assassination or God forbid something worse. I could never forgive myself if anything happened to any of you. I'm tired of this whole thing and I have made my decision," said the president.

Chapter 79

President Donald J. Trump's Address to the Nation on the Looming Crisis

October 1, 2020
Oval Office9:01 PM EST

THE PRESIDENT: My fellow Americans: Tonight, I am speaking to you here from the Oval Office in the White House because forces beyond my control prevented me from speaking with you on Labor Day.

Every day, since the assassination attempt, I have thought of my duty to my country as president and my duty to my family, as I struggled to regain my strength to resume my presidency and finish my term. For a while, it was touch and go, but I was determined to recover and again lead this great country.

But there are many people who do not want me to continue as your president.

There is a great deal of dissension and hatred emanating from the Congressional House. Threats against myself and my family from inside and outside our government and our country. I and many Americans have come to the realization that this unacceptable behavior cannot be permitted to continue.

I have been called a racist, but I am not a racist. I treat everyone the same regardless of color, or gender or how they may identify. Show me respect and I will respect you.

I have been accused of colluding with the Russians, but they hate and fear me so much they sent assassins against me and threaten my family.

To my detractors that have accused me of tweeting too much, I ask you how else am I to get the truth out to America? You will not put it out. I will stop tweeting if at least one other major news organization begins once again to present the news fair and balanced. Don't take sides, just report the news or take the 'N' for News out of your logo and replace it with an 'O' for Opinion and tell it like it is. For example, if *CNN* were completely honest, they would substitute their "N" for an "O" and become the *Cable Opinion Network. CON* for short — seems to fit don't you think? If I do something wrong call me out for it. I'm a big boy and can take it. But when I do something right, I expect the same amount of coverage.

The Left and the far Left, the Socialist, the Russians and some in my own party have turned on me when I was down. My own party! — they are my biggest disappointment.

My detractors have come at me with mean words, lies, but I have more respect for my assassin who at least did it to my face. The Left has said horrible things about my wife, the First Lady, and my children. I cannot allow that any longer to be acceptable behavior.

The looming crisis is here, and I have to asked myself what I intend to do about it.

There is division in America's house. There is divisiveness among us all tonight. And holding the trust that is mine, as president of all the people, I cannot disregard the peril to the progress of the American people and the hope and the prospect of peace for all peoples.

With fewer American sons and daughters in foreign fields than any time in recent history, with a booming economy and lowest unemployment in our history, safe borders, an improved affordable health care act and massive infrastructure projects, we were the envy of the world. Despite all this progress, one shot changed all that and Americans are hurting now, and America's future is under challenge. With our hopes and the world's hopes for peace in the balance, I do not believe that

I should devote an hour or a day of my time to any personal partisan causes, debating, or to any duties other than the awesome duties of this office — the presidency of this country, Trump intoned, looking earnestly into the camera lens.

Accordingly, I care about America, but I also care about my family. However, I can't let America suffer any longer. To the peril of my detractors here and abroad I shall not sit back and allow them to write America's story and to that end, I shall again take up the mantel and lead my party, my country for another term as your president.

I'm in it to win it.

To every citizen: Help me get Congress back to work for America and not for their own selfish political ideology, even if we have to lock them behind closed doors and not let them out until they create and pass meaningful bills that actually help the country. Tell them that, 'You can't always get what you want, but if you try sometimes, well, you just might find you get what you need.'

This is a choice between right and wrong. Justice and injustice. This is about whether we fulfill our sacred duty to the American citizens we serve.

When I took the Oath of Office, I swore to protect our country. And that is what I will always do from threats from without and from within, so help me God.

Keep America Great!

Thank you and goodnight.

END   9:11 PM EST

"That son of a bitch," said Pelosi as she turned off the TV and prepared to go into the next room to give a Democratic rebuttal speech which would now be entirely different from the 'Kumbaya' speech, she had written.

Chapter 80

"We're going on a balloon ride, Halsey," said President Trump.

"What do you mean?"

"The stock market is shooting up like a hot air balloon and gold is sinking like a lead balloon. We're about to double our fortune again. Give it three weeks and the market will be back near 30k."

"Meaning?"

"Meaning yesterday, before my 'Address to the Nation' Ivanka got out of gold and got back into the stock market."

"Pelosi will come after you with everything she's got."

"Pelosi's finished. I know you're not in the business end of the family, Tom, so I don't want you to be scared. I want you to help the Trumps, and I want you to help me."

President Trump handed Halsey a Diet Coke.

"Yeah, Alexandria Ocasio-Cortez got her inside her office just about an hour after Marine Two picked you up. The coup d'état has begun.

"Drink it," said the president pointing to the Diet Coke.

"So now it's up to you to make the peace between me and AOC. Pelosi was hot for my deal, and you knew it was the right thing to do."

"AOC will come after you with everything she's got," said Halsey.

"That'll be her first reaction, sure. That's why you gotta talk some sense into her. My Cabinet and the military are behind me with all their people. Pence and the Senate will go along with anything that will prevent a full-scale war. Let's face it Tom, and with all due respect,

Pelosi, rest in peace, was -- slippin'. Ten years ago, could I have gotten to her?

"Well, now she's gone. She's as good as dead, Tom, and nothing they can do to bring her back. So, you gotta talk to AOC. You gotta talk to the rest of the Squad, to Schumer and Fat Jerry.

It's good business, Tom."

"I'll try, but even Schumer won't be able to call off Mad Max."

"Yeah, well, let me worry about Crazy Waters. You just talk to Schumer – and the others."

"I'll do my best," said Halsey.

"Good. Now, you can go."

The president started to guide Halsey out of the Oval Office.

"I don't like violence, Tom — you know that. I'm a businessman. Blood is a big expense."

The president's phone rang. He walked back to the desk and picked it up, listened, hesitated and turned back to Halsey.

"She's still alive. Cortez hit her with all the shots, and she's still alive! Well, that's bad luck for me, and bad luck for all of us if you don't make that deal!"

President Trump's Godfather movie mind took complete control and he stormed out of his own office leaving Halsey not to wonder what he had gotten himself into, but how to get the fuck out.

Chapter 81

President Trump, a few of his staff and advisors along with Tom Halsey took Marine One from the White House to the Wolf House for the weekend.

Just as the president was heading out for a golf game, Mick Mulvaney told him he had a phone call.

"Who?" asked the president.

"The Speaker, Mr. President."

Trump's face slumped, but he had been expecting the call ever since his Address to the Nation and hearing Pelosi's and Schumer's scathing rebuttal directly after.

"Madam Speaker, I'm about to play nine holes, the first time since my assassination attempt, part of my prescribed rehabilitation, but for you, I have a minute."

"Mr. President just so we're clear, everything we agreed to is off the table."

"Nancy, it's not what I intended. We had a deal and I intended to honor it, but the assassin's bullet changed all that. You saw what happened to our economy and jobs. It's not only affecting us but the world. You couldn't expect me to sit by and let America go down the drain."

"What do you think would have happened if you had gone on and announced you were dropping out?" said Pelosi.

"Not the same. I would have smoothed the way for Harris, and you would have gone on to take the presidency and Senate. There would have been order."

"You can't hustle a hustler Mr. President, and from what I hear you made out quite well either way."

President Trump thought that if he divided the House it would fall and with Pelosi out, he could deal with the Pussy's as he now referred to the Squad. It didn't work out so well and now he had to deal with both groups even if Pelosi was now able to somewhat marginalize AOC.

The Senate wasn't a problem because he still had control despite Schumer's roadblocks. Mostly because they were hell-bent on getting a quick public trial and public execution of Dmitriy Volkov, at the speed and the scale of Lincoln's assassins.

No one blamed the president for the horrible recession that the country was thrown into immediately after he was shot. Conversely, everyone credited him for the rise back out of the depth depression when he again took up the mantel and returned as their president despite all the odds against that happening.

"Look Nancy, I have to run…"

"You didn't have to run, interrupted Pelosi, you could have let it go and kept to your deal but…"

"No Nancy, I really do have to run," re-interrupted the president. "Do what you have to do, but as a professional courtesy, I was hoping for a Mulligan on this and if I were you, I'd be watching my back. The Pussy's, excuse me, the Posse has their eye on your pie and you and your old guard better close that hole."

"That's disgusting, but it's what we have come to expect from you. No little Donald — no do-overs for you. Put your big boy pants on because we're coming for you. And by the way speaking about pussies and holes — being driven around a park in a go-cart and putting little balls into little holes is for pussies. Get a real man's sport — try parachuting — I'll pack your chute."

"Now that is disgusting Nancy. You stay away from my chute," said President Trump as he disconnected and turned to his golfing partners and yelled, "Fore!"

President Trump was exhausted after just six holes and had to stop. His three partners grabbed a fourth and continued as President Trump and Halsey drove their cart off the freeway towards Wolfhall, followed by Hammer and Sickle.

"The Secret Service doesn't like the wolves running loose and following me," said the president.

"We haven't had one crazy reporter crashing the grounds since the *Wolfhampton Press* printed the story about how we leave the wolves run free on the property.

"What are we gonna do about the club?" asked Halsey.

"KGB?" asked President Trump.

"Yes, sir. It's really bad, disturbing the neighbors, creating mayhem and bringing kids in from all over the island and New Jersey. The Russian mob from Brighten Beach runs it and they take all the cash back to Brooklyn, and our mayor and police chief have a piece of it — Fitzy, and his crew run it.

"The NY State Liquor Authority and the state police keep pulling raids and are taking down tons of drugs, prostitutes and underage drinkers, which our local cops can't seem to find."

"Keep the wolves, lose the mayor and police chief. All four were Volkov hold-overs anyway, but Barron would be devastated if Hammer and Sickle did the Houdini, but nobody will miss the mayor and police chief. Send the Russians back to Brighten Beach and let the party crowd create mayhem in the Southampton Village rat clubs. They don't seem to give a shit over there."

"What about the club and Fitzy?"

"Wasn't he one of Volkov's guys? Didn't you say you thought he was the one who shot you in front of the guest house while you were questioning Volkov?"

"No, he's not the one who shot me. He's the one that warned me and suggested I wear a vest if I was going after Volkov. He later told me that Volkov feared me more than Putin or you, but Putin intervened and had the SVR hit me to send you a message."

"Yeah, I remember now. So, what are you gonna do with this guy? Give him a pass for telling you to wear a vest before his boss had someone shoot you? Look, you do what you want with him and the club, but don't let it come back and bite me in the ass."

Chapter 82

"Are we all in agreement?" asked the Speaker.

Her team: Schiff, Nadler, and Waters were unanimous.

The Squad: Cortez, Omar, Pressley, and Tlaib wanted more but would settle on impeachment if it led to Trump's removal from office. All four nodded in agreement.

"Chuck, I have everyone here," said Pelosi.

Schumer expected the call but dreaded it, "Nancy."

"Chuck, I'm putting you on speaker. It's all up to you."

Unlike Bill Clinton, 18 years previous, who was impeached by the House but failed to be convicted by the Senate, Trump had to go. Impeachment alone was not an option.

"Don't wait on me. You impeach and I'll get a conviction and he'll be gone."

"We don't want gone. We want jail," said Omar.

Schumer didn't acknowledge Omar nor say goodbye — he just disconnected.

"Get me Romney, Paul, Cruz, and Rubio on conference. Get John Thune and put him on hold. If everything goes according to plan, I'll let you know when to patch him into the conference," said Schumer to his secretary.

Mitt Romney is the junior United States Senator from Utah, Ted Cruz is the junior United States Senator for Texas, Rand Paul is the junior

United States Senator from Kentucky, and Marco Rubio is the senior United States Senator from Florida. All four have three things in common: They're senators, they have all been humiliated publicly by Trump, and they haven't forgotten.

John Thune won and is serving his second term in the U.S. Senate in 2010 in a rare unopposed race. He was only the third Republican and the lone South Dakotan to run unopposed for the U.S. Senate since direct elections were created in 1913. He's the Senate Majority Whip, JFK handsome and right out of central casting for the job of President of the United States. He doesn't hate President Trump, but he has an ego, aspirations, and someone has to be the next Republican superstar – so why not him?

"What about the Frantic Five and the Posse?" asked Halsey sitting alongside Kellyanne Conway, Mick Mulvaney, and White House Press Secretary Stephanie Grisham.

President Trump had just finished an early morning Cabinet meeting and had a break before a national security meeting with his Joint Chiefs, Esper, Coats, Haspel, and Pompeo. North Korea was firing rockets again. It seemed the little Rocket Man's feelings were hurt and needed to get attention.

President Trump held court, "They're coming after me. But that's okay. I'll be out campaigning and setting the narrative. They will be spending all their time on impeachment proceedings and their socialist agenda.

"Here's what I want to do. For every day starting tomorrow morning until the election Tuesday, November 3, I want distractions — one after another. Keep them coming. While they're reacting, we put something new out there that's even bigger, that contradicts the previous. Instead of a 24-hour news cycle, we'll make it a 12-hour news cycle."

"Distractions?" asked Grisham.

"Yeah, something big, splashy, something to make their jaws drop — something completely out of the blue."

"Sounds like you want to make 'Jaws 5' The Retribution?"

"Yeah, why not? A Megalodon. I'm the biggest, most feared shark in the water. They can try to catch me, kill me, but it's gonna cost them. They can spend the next month or so on impeachment and we'll spend it on building the economy back up, infrastructure, bringing troops home, campaigning and building my favorability rating and votes.

"What do we have? Twenty-five days or so left? Well then, we need 25 distractions. I'll tweet them out and you guys build the case, get everybody hyper then that night just as the Left is getting all worked up and salivating on the *CNN*, I'll tweet something completely opposite and catch them with their panties down — the girls, too. Day after day till we reach, as my good friend Imus used to say, 'Erection Day.'"

"We'll slam them with racism, Muslim supremacy, anti-Semitism, homophobia, misogyny, xenophobia, fascism. Most of this is completely detached from reality, but it doesn't matter once it's out there. I just read somewhere how can a president whose daughter converted to orthodox Judaism when she married her husband, and who has brought in so many Jews into his administration in powerful positions, and who has moreover repaired relations with Israel, really be anti-Semitic? Can a president who reached out to gays in his nomination acceptance speech, really be homophobic? Is it any more likely that the president is a white supremacist or racist? One can think of many unflattering adjectives that might accurately apply to you but are these the right ones?" asked Kellyanne Conway.

"I'm not sure what you just said but I'll take it as a compliment," said the president.

Chapter 83

"It looks like the American president survived and is back and kicking behinds."

"Butt."

"But what?"

"Butt. He is kicking butt. Not behinds. You can't even talk like an American, how are you going to influence them if you can't mimic them?"

"I don't have to mimic them. I have people for that; which reminds me, we have got to pick a side. Left, or Right?"

"We must first ask ourselves who do we want to win. The crazy left socialist or the crazy right capitalist?"

"Better the Satan we know."

"I agree but it's the Devil, not Satan."

"Six of one, a dozen of the other."

"Please just stop with the idioms, you idiot. Now, if we want to help Trump to get re-elected what do we do?"

"Get the dirt on this Harris person. Ger the emails just like last time but more secretly and turn everything over to the Trump team and WikiLeaks."

"No, you fucking idiot. If we want Trump to win, we must help Harris. Have the IRA put some disinformation out there and see if they'll take it. If they bite, we'll expose them. Trump, after he wins again, can bring back Muller and spend a couple of years witch-hunting the Democrats."

"Who is dumb enough to fall for Russian collusion again?"

"I know just the person."

"We need to pass this by the Pale Moth."

"We are proceeding," said Pelosi over the speakerphone to Cortez, Omar, Pressley, and Tlaib.

"But not fast enough. We only have 25 days until the election and in that time, we have to get an impeachment and get it over to the Senate. If Schumer can't get the votes from the other side of the aisle we might as well just coronate Trump president," said Cortez.

"We're in this with you but we warned you about the time restraints," said Pelosi.

"Yes, you did, and we wanted you to start impeachment this time last year," said Cortez.

"You want to get rid of Trump by impeachment. I want to do it by the vote. We need to keep the pressure on both fronts. Harris and the DNC need our help and I'm going to help her get elected because the House, Senate and Supreme Court are at stake," said Pelosi.

After the meeting was over and the Squad left in a huff, Nadler and Waters had business elsewhere, but Pelosi and Schiff remained behind in the Speakers office.

"I may have something," said Schiff.

"Anything that can get rid of him is on the table. What?"

"I received some good information from a very high-up reliable source that if leaked would be devastating to Trump."

"Reliable."

"I should say so."

"How high up?"

"An insider. Someone high up inside the White House."

"An Obama holdover?"

"Yes."

"Care to tell me who?"

"I promised not to reveal my source."

"Then I don't want to hear it and you better be careful Mr. Schiff."

"The same source that told me that it was the Russians that kidnaped Trump's son."

"Your source was dead on about that. Okay, give me a little taste," said Pelosi.

"That whole deal he made with us about not running for a second term because he was tired of fighting with us and he just wanted to get out. Well, that was true but what he really wanted was immunity and indemnity from indictments, criminal or civil prosecution against him or any member of his family while he's in office or out."

"Because?"

"Because of what he and his family are up to."

"That being what, Buzz?"

"His family made a very secret deal to build the tallest building in the world."

"Taller than One World Trade Center?"

"Where have you been, Nancy? One World Trade Center is only 1,776 feet tall — I'm talking mega tall. Taller even than Burj Khalifa in Dubai at 2,717 feet. He's planning to build a 5,280-foot-high building."

"That's more than double the height of the one you just mentioned in Dubai."

"To use his expression — 'Huge. A mile high.'"

"I thought that was impossible to build that high?"

"That's why he's doing it."

"He's got a pair. He's not doing it is he? It's his family, right?"

"No both, and on our dime, but you didn't ask the most important question."

"What?" asked Pelosi.

"Not what — where," answered Schiff.

Pelosi stopped and stared into Schiff's eyes and thought he reminded her of the Buzz Lightyear's character in Toy Story.

"Moscow — Trump Tower Moscow," said Schiff, not waiting for her to guess.

"Oh my God! Are you positive?"

"Yes, my source is solid."

"If that leaks, he's dead in the water. He'll be impeached, forced out and sent to prison."

"If it leaks — dead in the water. That's funny," said Schiff

"Funny?"

"Yeah, leak, and water! Who does that suggest?"

"Call Maxime."

Chapter 84

"Mr. President, it's Rudy Giuliani on line one," said Madeleine Westerhout.

"Rudy, it's early this is probably not good news," said the president.

"I don't know where they get this shit, but I have my suspicions. They ambushed me this morning in Manhattan on the way to get beagles. I deflected as best I could, but this is gonna blow up. It's all a lie but that's what they do."

"Whoa Rudy. What's a lie and who ambushed you?" asked the president.

"Trump Tower Moscow and BuzzFeed."

"What are you talking about? There is no Trump Tower in Moscow."

"According to the reporter who ambushed me someone high up in the White House leaked the story that you and Ivanka, Don Jr. and Eric are secretly building a skyscraper in Moscow that is huge and going to manifest into Trump Tower as soon as you leave office."

Conway, Mulvaney, Grisham and Halsey were back in the Oval Office with the president for an early morning follow-up 'distraction' meeting, when Mulvaney, who was listening to the president and Giuliani on speakerphone interrupted and said, "Mr. President take a look at this," turning his laptop for the president to see and read.

Trump's Lawyer Said There Are "No Plans" For Trump Tower Moscow. But Here They Are.

Rudy Giuliani claims the Moscow Tower was barely more than a notion back in 2013 and dropped completely in '16. "There were no drafts. Nothing in the file," but documents obtained by BuzzFeed News tell a different story.
Gzeen Amoretti BuzzFeed News Reporter

The plan is dazzling: a glass skyscraper that would stretch higher than any other building in the world, offering ultra-luxury residences and hotel rooms and bearing a famous name. Trump Tower Moscow, originally conceived as a partnership between Donald Trump's company and a Russian real estate developer Dmitriy Volkov, looks likely to yield profits in excess of $400 million annually.

The original tower had completed plans for a bold glass obelisk 100 stories high by September 2015, with the Trump logo on multiple sides. The planned Trump Tower would have been the tallest skyscraper in Europe but was never built and was the focal point of the investigation by special counsel Robert Mueller into Trump's relationship with Russia in the lead-up to his presidency.

The president and his representatives had dismissed the project as little more than a notion — a rough plan led by Trump's then-lawyer, Michael Cohen, and his associate Felix Sater, of which Trump and his family said they were only loosely aware as the election campaign gathered pace.

This morning, his lawyer, Rudy Giuliani, said "there is no current proposal," and he went on to tell BuzzFeed that "no plans were ever made. There were no drafts. Nothing in the file."

However, hundreds of pages of business documents, emails, text messages, and architectural plans, obtained by BuzzFeed News, tell a very different story. The new Trump Tower Moscow is a richly imagined vision of upscale splendor mega skyscraper on the banks of the Moscow River. And it's happening now.

A long-held dream

Trump had for 30 years tried to extend his real estate empire to Moscow. He even wrote about it in his book *The Art of the Deal*. But he never found the right opportunity — until 2013, when he visited Russia to host the Miss Universe pageant. "TRUMP TOWER-MOSCOW is next," he tweeted after the event.

The Tallest Mega Stratoscraper in World

Six years later, a bigger vision had emerged. The new Trump Tower Moscow is to be much more than just another upscale apartment building. It is to be a vast — and vastly lucrative — undertaking that would elevate the Russian capital's skyline and extend the perimeter of the New York company's influence.

By September 2017, the Chicago architectural firm Skidmore, Owings & Merrill had completed plans for a bold glass obelisk 300 stories high, to be topped by a gleaming, cut-diamond–like shape emblazoned on multiple sides with the Trump logo. The tallest building in the world. One Mile high giving a name to a new innovation. 'A Stratoscraper'.

"The building design you sent over is very interesting," said the Russian real estate developer billionaire and friend of both Putin and Trump, Dmitriy Volkov wrote to Cohen, September 2017, "and will be an architectural and luxury triumph. I believe the tallest building in the world should be in Moscow, and I am prepared to build it." Of course, Volkov is now currently awaiting sentencing for an attempted assassination…

Apparently, President Trump was reneging on progress payments for Trump Tower Moscow, something he has been known to do, and that may have been the reason for the kidnapping and assassination attempt.

President Trump closed the laptop. "I can't believe these fuckers fell for that. Putin set them up and they fell for it hook, line and sirloin. It's gonna backfire on them. I'm 'In Like Flynn' for a second term."

"That is amazing. Can I use that?"

"Use what?"

"'Hook line and sirloin'. Fitzy and I are looking for a name for our new waterfront fish and steak restaurant. If it's okay, I would like to use it, regardless of the reference to Flynn, which, by the way, you don't want to be 'in like', at the moment. A lot of folks would like to see you and General Flynn sharing a cell."

"No. Because of the Flynn comment you can't use it," said President Trump and continued, "I all but gave up on Trump Tower Moscow but you know it's not such a bad idea. It would be huge. A mile high. I would have celebrities standing in line just to fuck in the penthouse and get a mile-high club card. In fact, it's brilliant. I think we might have found our kingdom, Peachy. Our Kafiristan."

"It's impossible. You can't build anything that high."

"Really? Picture a sandy beach in Wolfhampton just below the high-water mark. A sand crab burrows into the wet sand and the sand he excavated and creates, what to him is a huge mound, but is only a few inches high.

Twins sit on the beach and scoop wet sand into a small bucket and flip it over and create, what is to them, a huge sand sculpture, but, is only 12" high. An older boy comes over and takes their bucket and adds a few more forms alongside then begins to layer more on top and creates, what is to him, a huge sand sculpture, but is only 36" high. See where I'm going with this?" asked the president.

"It's the same beach only the older boy comes along and showed up the twins after the twins smothered the sand crab," said Halsey.

President Trump ignored the sarcasm and continued, "Then André the Giant comes walking down the beach at 7'- 4" with hands the size of catcher's mitts, bends down and scoops up the three kids, the sand crab and tons of wet sand into an enormous eight-foot-high sandcastle."

"André the Giant is dead."

"He the only giant I know, and you're missing the point."

"That being?"

"It's the same beach only André's bigger, thinks bigger and builds bigger. You just need bigger people, bigger thinkers, and bigger mitts."

"Okay, you're saying it's about one's perspective. Regardless, the weather and winds would make the building sway and cast huge shadows over the whole city."

"Say the college professors, but the doers say the tower would coral and harness the wind, produce energy and part the clouds so it always 'Sunny in Philly' — until, that is, you spike the clouds and make it rain — now that's real 'Climate Change.'

"You forget, Halsey. I'm different than other people. I'm a doer and I ain't afraid of nothing. 'I've wrestled with alligators; I've tussled with a whale - I done handcuffed lightning and throw thunder in jail - You know I'm bad, just last week, I murdered a rock, injured a stone, hospitalized a brick - I'm so mean, I make medicine sick.'"

"That's amazing, Mr. President. Did you just make that whole shtick up or..."

"No. A good friend of mine said that but I can't tell you who because I'm a racist and I'm not allowed to have black or Muslim friends.

"You know Halsey, you think like a little guy looking up, you gotta start thinking like a big guy looking down."

Chapter 85

WASHINGTON (AP)— A half-dozen Democrats on Wednesday introduced articles of impeachment against President Donald Trump, accusing him of obstruction of justice including demanding Quid Pro Quo from a foreign leader and other offenses. If the House votes for impeachment there is little chance of a conviction in the Republican-led Senate.

The impeachment of Donald Trump was initiated on October 8, 2020, when the United States House of Representatives voted to commence impeachment proceedings against Donald Trump, 45th president of the United States, for "high crimes and misdemeanors": Abuse of Power, Advocating Political Violence, Collusion, Profiting from the Presidency, and Obstructing Justice which was subsequently detailed in 5 impeachment charges. Adam Buzz Schiff, impeachment committee chairman said, "I found the allegations both disturbing and credible." The catalyst for the president's impeachment was the Muller Report, a March 22, 2019 report prepared by Independent Counsel Robert Muller for the House Judiciary Committee, and House Speaker Nancy Pelosi. In essence, publicly implied that Trump is too mentally impaired to function as president.

Volume I of the report concludes that the investigation did not find sufficient evidence that the campaign "coordinated or conspired with the Russian government in its election-interference activities

Volume II of the report addresses obstruction of justice. The investigation intentionally took an approach that could not result in a judgment that Trump committed a crime, abiding by an Office of Legal Counsel (OLC) opinion that a sitting president cannot stand trial.

"Our investigation found multiple acts by the President that were capable of exerting undue influence over law enforcement investigations, including the Russian-interference and obstruction investigations," Mueller wrote. Legal Counsel found that "the indictment or criminal prosecution of a sitting President would impermissibly undermine the capacity of the executive branch to perform its constitutionally assigned functions" in violation of "the constitutional separation of powers."

Trump became only the third American president to be impeached (the others being Andrew Johnson and Bill Clinton) when the House formally adopted the articles of impeachment and forwarded them to the United States Senate for adjudication. The trial in the Senate began on October 2020, with Chief Justice John Roberts presiding. On October 15, Trump was acquitted of the charges against him, when the Senate, despite strong pressure from Schumer and the left and a gathering storm of dissident Republicans led by Senators Romney and Thune, failed to convict him on either charge by the necessary two-thirds majority vote...

Conway, Mulvaney, Grisham, and Halsey were back again in the Oval Office with the president discussing and updating the distractions they had been putting out in the morning and President Trump's contradicting tweets in the evening and early morning.

"Well, Pelosi and the Squad finally got what they wanted," said Grisham.

"The Frantic Five and the Pussy's finally got what they wanted, but it backfired on them. Yeah, the president got impeached like Clinton and like him was acquitted," said Conway.

"You're in good company," said Mulvaney.

"Johnson and Clinton," offered Grisham, "a Democrat racist and a Democrat rapist."

"Yeah, and you're a Republican accused of the both," said Conway with a chuckle before she realized her mistake.

President Trump gave Conway a dirty look but let it go, and added instead, "Whistleblowers — who needs them when Pencil Neck Schiff sits in front of the impeachment committee and the fake news media and fabricates an entire bullshit story about my phone call to Volodymyr. Saying the call was made to manufacture dirt on Biden and his son. I don't need to manufacture dirt; they're both dirty as shit. When Schiff gets called out for it, he says his summery was meant to be a parody and couldn't understand why that was not clear to everyone. He makes shit up and lies about me and it's a parody. Well, let's see how he likes it when the tables are turned."

"They wasted a lot of time and effort and it's gonna come back and bite them," said Grisham.

"We got them chasing shadows and with this whole Trump Tower Moscow fabrication their perusing, courtesy of Russia's Internet Research Agency, it's going to sink them once the proof comes out that they have been colluding with Russia to get dirt on us," said Halsey.

"They're saying the leak came from a senior White House source."

"Of course, they are and I'm sure it did, but how and where did that source get it? I'm betting our Russian friends will 'out' their source in a well-timed manner."

POLITICS
10/17/2020 08:37 pm

The Polls — All of Them — Show President Trump Leading Which means Senator Kamala Harris is losing.

President Donald Trump is either slightly ahead or way ahead of Democratic Presidential Nominee Kamala Harris with just 17 days until Election Day, according to new polls released Wednesday.

An AP-GFK poll shows Trump leading by an astonishing 14 points, 51 percent to Harris' 37 percent, in a four-way race. In a two-way heat, Trump's lead narrows to 13 points.

A new Fox News poll finds Trump ahead by a much smaller margin — just 3 points ahead in a four-way race, 44 percent to 41 percent. He also leads by 3 points head to head with Harris.

Other recent polls show Trump with a lead ranging from 2 points to 12 points.

It's best not to freak out just yet over which of Wednesday's polls are right. Instead, consider the aggregate of recent polls for a more sober look at the race.

According to the HuffPost Pollster aggregate, Trump is leading by about 7 points in the four-way race, 46.6 percent to 39 percent...

Chapter 86

Donald J. Trump
@realDonaldTrump
Billions of Dollars are pouring into the coffers of the U.S.A. because
of the Tariffs being charged to China, and there is a long way to go.
If companies don't want to pay Tariffs, build in the U.S.A. Otherwise,
let's just make our Country richer than ever before!

Donald J. Trump
@realDonaldTrump
Tariffs are the greatest! Either a country which has treated the United
States unfairly on Trade negotiates a fair deal, or it gets hit with Tariffs.
It's as simple as that – and everybody's talking! Remember, we are
the "piggy bank" that's being robbed. All will be Great!

Donald J. Trump
@realDonaldTrump
On Trade, France makes excellent wine, but so does the U.S. The
problem is that France makes it very hard for the U.S. to sell its
wines into France, and charges big Tariffs, whereas the U.S. makes it
easy for French wines, and charges very small Tariffs. Not fair, must
change!

The New York Times

Trump Plans More Tariffs for China. You'll Feel This Round.

By Alice Rappeport, John Simanek and Alison Schwartz
October. 18, 2020

President Trump announced another wave of China tariffs this week, essentially saying he would impose a tax on nearly all $540 billion in Chinese goods that come into the United States in a year. And this batch could really bite.

The administration carefully tailored previous rounds of tariffs to pinch businesses in ways that most Americans might not notice. But the 10 percent levy on $300 billion of imports that Mr. Trump announced on Thursday, which would take effect October 20th, is expected to hit consumers where it hurts. From Apple's iPhones to school supplies, a broad swath of everyday products are about to get more expensive.

The latest move is likely to prompt companies to submit exclusion requests to be spared from the tariffs, causing the Federal Reserve to rethink its plans for interest rates and inspire fresh retaliation from China that could compound Americans' economic pain.

Here's what to expect.

Scramble for exclusions Until October 20, the focus will be on the Office of the United States Trade Representative for a final list of the Chinese products subject to the new tariffs…

Slump at retailers' registers Earlier rounds of tariffs mostly focused on industrial goods, but the 10 percent levy announced Thursday is directed squarely at consumer items like clothes, toys, and footwear…

A bite out of Apple The most prominent American company bracing for the tariffs is Apple, which typically unveils new products every September…

Will China hit back? Throughout the trade conflict, Beijing has demonstrated a willingness to respond to the Trump administration's tariffs as proportionately as possible…

Will the Fed cut Trump more slack? The Fed was already laser-focused on the trade war before Mr. Trump's latest tariff announcement. Officials lowered interest rates this week for the first time in more than a decade…

"Is he purposely trying to destroy the economy and his second term bid?" asked Mnuchin, putting *The New York Times* down on the conference table.

"This ongoing trade war with China is producing unacceptable casualties. We had another Monday Meltdown. China is starting to manipulate the currency again and it's escalating the trade war," said Ross.

"We just had a 750-point drop. A global crash. The seventh biggest drop of all times. Worse than the first currency drop last August," said Mnuchin.

"Guys — guys calm down," said Kudlow, "we're gradually shifting the U.S. tax burden from wages, income, and profit to consumption. You know that. Personal and corporate income taxes will be cut, and tariffs are and will be placed on consumer and producer goods.

"We collected $51 billion in tariffs and customs duties in 2018's third quarter, compared with $38 billion in the third quarter of 2017, for a gain of $13 billion.

"We now collect tariffs on Canadian timber products, Chinese solar panels, on some $200 billion of other Chinese goods that range from bicycles to baseball gloves, and on aluminum and steel imports from countries worldwide, with exemptions for the UK and a handful of other favorites.

"The consumers can pay the higher price for a Chinese phone and solar panels or they can buy American. And if we don't make it here, some American entrepreneur will see the hole and fill it.

"We now have a growing tariff-based national sales tax. The nation is moving from taxing income to taxing consumption. How can the Left top that?"

"Free stuff," said Mnuchin.

Chapter 87

WASHINGTON (AP) — The Ambassador of the Russian Federation to the United States of America, Anatoly Antonov, confirmed today that the Trump Tower Moscow story was a complete fabrication.

The CIA has concluded in a secret assessment that Russia is again intervening in the 2020 election to help Senator and Democratic Presidential Nominee Kamala Harris win the presidency, rather than just to undermine confidence in the U.S. electoral system, according to officials briefed on the matter.

Intelligence agencies have identified individuals with connections to the Russian government who provided WikiLeaks with thousands of hacked emails from the Republican National Committee and others, including President Trump's campaign chairman, according to U.S. officials. Those officials described the individuals as actors known to the intelligence community and part of a wider Russian operation to boost Harris's and hurt Trump's chances.

"It is the assessment of the intelligence community that Russia's goal here was to favor one candidate over the other, to undermine President Trump with a false story and to help Harris get elected," said a senior U.S. official briefed on an intelligence presentation made to U.S. senators. "That's the consensus view."

According to White House sources, former Deputy Chief of Staff Patty Welsh was suspected of being a leaker. "The snakes are everywhere," said President Trump of the list suspected White House, leakers...

"Was Patty Welsh your source, Buzz?" asked Pelosi from behind her desk in her congressional office during an early morning meeting.

"Yes," said Schiff eating a bagel while sitting on the couch next to Nadler.

"Oh God, we're so screwed," said Waters nervously walking over to the window and looking out.

"It may have been Schiff's bullshit source, but it was you Maxine, who leaked the unsubstantiated Trump Tower Moscow story to the media," said Naylor.

"Oh, and you didn't want me to leak it? Jerry, you brought into the story just like everyone..."

"Hold on fellas, this is not the time to be pointing dicks," interrupted Schumer.

"Chuck's right. We're all screwed. We were set up and boy did we fall for it," said Pelosi.

Pelosi's COS Terri McCullough came bursting into the office and rushed over to Pelosi's wooden cabinet containing six TVs and switched them on. Each of the six was tuned to one specific station *CNN*, *FOX*, *MSNBC*'s Morning Joe, and Squawk Box on *CNBC*, *ABC*, or *CBS*.

"*CNN's* reporting another mass shooting," said McCullough

"Oh God, where?" asked Pelosi as everyone moved over to the TVs.

CNN was on a commercial break. Joe Scarborough was introducing his eight contributors, which would take 10 minutes, but *CBS* had a banner flash across the screen 'CBS NEWS Special Report'. McCullough muted the other TVs, and everyone focused on CBS as the banner faded and...

> This is a *CBS News* special report. I'm Major Garrett reporting from Washington. Eight people have been killed in a second mass shooting in 24 hours. This time it happened in Wolfhampton New York, out on the eastern end of Long Island in a nightclub called KGB, directly across the street from a residential neighborhood shattering what had been a normally peaceful village until President Trump became a resident. Police say they have killed the gunman. At least sixteen more have been hurt and taken to area hospitals. Twenty-four casualties in twenty-five seconds. Wolfhampton Assistant Police Chief spoke earlier, "We're very fortunate that the officers responded so fast or the casualty number could have tripled. I need to thank all the..."

"Turn it off before he starts thanking everyone and their mothers. Did you see all the police and police cars in the background? There must be several hundred police and SWAT units there policing-up. Had just a few cops been there before the shooting it would never have happened."

"Jerry, you're so cold."

"Look, this is bad, but I think we can turn this to our benefit. Trump has been throwing disinformation and distractions at us full-time, not to mention this whole Trump Tower Moscow fiasco, but this is a game-changer. Now, not only do we have a mass shooting fall into our laps, it happened in Trump's back yard —Wolfhampton," said Schiff.

"If I hear 'Guns don't kill people; people kill people,' one more time, I'm going to kill someone," said Waters.

"Take away his gun and what's he gonna do? Attack a crowded night-club with a knife? Is he going to beat them to death with his fist? I doubt it. That would take a man. A punk needs to kill from afar not up close and personal. Why make it easy for these punks to kill?" said Naylor.

"Don't say that outside this room or we'll have the military, vets, and police saying we're calling 'them' punks and crazies," said Schumer.

"Big difference. The military, vets, and police have bad guys shooting back," said Naylor.

"We should have more police presence in malls, around churches and schools, nightclubs…"

"Everywhere?"

"Yes, everywhere. If we did, we might not have as many mass shootings."

"But that would cost a bloody fortune."

"Better before than after. You see how many cops are running around in combat gear after the shootings? Hundreds! That's all on overtime. Better to have a few positioned before than many after, I say."

"Whoever sells a gun to a crazy, a nut or a punk needs to be held accountable. If there is even a shred of a doubt, pick up the phone and call the police and let them sort it out. Don't sell them guns and ammo."

"Most of these punks have family and friends and teachers that know they're fucked up but don't say anything — they should be held as accomplices. Many punks are reported to officials, but the mental health officials, police, and FBI don't follow through, aren't permitted to follow through, or drop the ball. They too should be held accountable and fired."

"All right, here's where we are. Trump's shot and survives and gets a big jump in the polls. We impeached the bastard, but he survived, and another big jump in the polls. We got hustled and distracted by this bogus Trump Tower Moscow story, of which we haven't even begun to pay the piper for yet, but God intervened with a mass shooting which will save our asses, replace the Trump bump and completely saturate the news cycle for the next 48 hours. Let's get our 'Hearts and Prayers' message out to the shooting victim, then our 'Ban the Guns' message out to the deplorables," said Schiff.

"Don't you blame this on God. I know you all don't think very highly of me. I get it, and I don't really care, but let's not go down that 'Ban the Guns' road again. We'll have as much luck with that as we did with impeachment; and if we don't get the deplorable's to join our respectable's we're going to lose the House, Senate, Presidency, Supreme Court — the whole ball of wax forever. We're not going to beat Trump with Harris; she's too normal — trust me I'm not normal and Trump's not normal. We need someone who can go head to head with Trump and beat him. We need to unnominate Harris and put in our own kind of crazy — the sooner the better," said Waters.

David Axelrod
@davidaxelrod
Oct 22
Polling suggests @kamalaharris currently runs strongest @realDonaldTrump, but Trump doesn't seem to agree, which is why he keeps avoiding Harris. But if Harris continues stumbling her way through the race, anxieties will rise among Dems about her ability not to go the distance, but to win first place.

Chapter 88

"What are you worried about? You're ahead in the polls," said Halsey.

"That's exactly why I'm worried. Hillary was ahead in the polls, re-member?" said the president.

"That was different."

"The difference is that the pollers back then wanted Hillary to win and me to lose. The pollers now want me to win and Harris to lose."

"So?"

"So, so they didn't have their pulse on the country and blew it. They're going to blow it again. Unless they're polling in my favor for a reason. Something's up, I can feel it."

"I'm assuming Wolfhampton is out this weekend."

President Trump looked at Halsey as if studying him. Halsey had seen the president turn on a dime against ardent supporters for the slightest di-gression. He had watched the president turn on Scaramucci, former White House Communications Director and hedge fund manager, who worked briefly for the Trump Administration in 2017, for speaking against his past tweets, which he called "racist." The president tweeted that Anthony Scaramucci had been quickly terminated (11 days) from a position that he was totally incapable of handling. He said Scaramucci now seems to do nothing but television as the all-time expert on "President Trump." He went on to say Scaramucci, like many other so-called television experts, knows very little about him.

President Trump surprised Halsey and reacted normally, "You assumed right. I thought I told you to take care of that club. Send everyone packing and let the "fookin eejit's go party in the Southampton Village rat clubs. Now I have to do a 'Hearts and Prayers' and probably two news cycles on why I allowed a Russian fronted club to operate in Wolfhampton — why I don't institute greater gun controls — why I don't issue a gun 'Buy Back' policy. Criminal and crazies would just break into honest people's homes and rob their guns just to sell them back for a quick buck.

"I thought your guy Fitzy was running the club. Barr's telling me the shooter was a Russian mob wannabe sent by the Brighton Beach mob to shoot the club up as payback and to embarrass me."

It's Official: Harris Out — Sanders In as the Democratic Nominee for President

By Stephen Tupan and Cal Collins,

Updated 10:04 PM ET, Tue October 18, 2020

Cleveland (*FOX NEWS*) Bernie Sanders, the millionaire socialist will go head to head with Donald Trump the billionaire capitalist. With only 16 days till the election, the Democratic Party decided that Harris' disappointing poll numbers and lackluster support would give them nothing on Tuesday, November 3 but absolute total defeat. Sanders, the outsider whose campaign has both galvanized millions of voters and divided the Democratic Party, is now the 2020 Democratic Presidential Nominee.

The Vermonter, embraced by the Democratic National Convention, at this late date, marks a remarkable moment in U.S. political history and validates a campaign that shattered precedence, defied pundits and usurped the party of Jefferson and Jackson.

Tom Perez, the Democratic Party chairman said today "We want to win, and Bernie is the only candidate who, with this short time left, can go right for Trump's jugular and take us to complete victory..."

Sitting in the White House second floor family dining room, President Trump, Melania, Barron, Halsey, and Abby had just finished dinner and the stewards were bringing in coffee and dessert. Warm bread pudding with a whiskey sauce. Everyone including Barron had a slice covered by a delicious creamy, warm whiskey sauce. The president and Halsey had seconds.

"If you're going to have dessert and beaucoup calories it might as well be absolutely the best dessert ever. Nothing can top this — end of story," said Halsey who had had the kitchen prepare the bread pudding according to his recipe.

"Halsey, were you a cook in the Rangers?" asked the president sarcastically.

Abby had forgiven Halsey but not President Trump and had no intention of ever returning to Wolfhampton. They would meet whenever possible in Manhattan on the Upper East Side. She agreed to again return to Washington at the behest of Halsey and was again wondering what she had gotten herself into. She enjoyed being with Melania, Barron, and Tommy but not Donny.

After Melania and Barron left the room to watch a movie with several of Barron's school mates Abby suspected what was coming. The report just out that Bernie Sanders would replace Kamala Harris as the Democratic presidential nominee was a shock to everyone especially at this late date. But apparently, they, the DNC, thought Harris would drag down the House along with the presidency, but Bernie could galvanize and unite the party and Bernie was out on the stump doing just that — fiercely attacking Trump, his policies and the president's mental health.

"I told you something was wrong. I could feel it. Harris was not hacking it. Crazy Bernie is fucking nuts, and funny as a heart attack. No matter how loyal my base is, they love 'crazy' and if that crazy is also giving away free stuff, you start to ask yourself hey, why not me, too?

"The Demos live in a dream world where everyone gets a free ride. The rest of us live in the real world where nothing is free.

Except what you got from your Daddy, thought Abby.

"College-free tuition for all students. Free health care for everyone. Free cash for everyone. Free stuff' to anyone dumb enough to vote Democrat.

"Democrats want to give illegal aliens free welfare, free health care, and free education. Give them a driver's license. Give them a driver's license? Next thing you know, they want to buy them a car. Then they'll say the car's not good enough, how about a Rolls Royce?

"Free healthcare for all. Don't they understand what will happen? The rich, the wealthy will just go to private doctors and private hospitals and get the best care money can buy for themselves and their families. The rest of America may get it free but going to the doctor's office will be like going to the post office — long lines and disgruntled employees going 'Doctal'. Just like grade school and high school — yeah, it's free, but the education is shit. I see all these commercials for after school learning centers that you have to pay just to get your kids a decent basic education.

Those with money send their kids to private schools with the best teachers and the best education — and the poor and blue-collar kids are not invited!

"Well, I've got some free stuff of my own. I'm going to eliminate the income tax. How's that? A consumer tax fueled primarily by tariffs and consumer purchases. You want a Bentley you'll pay out the bum in taxes. You want an American Ford you pay very little in taxes. No more income tax. No more deductions from your paychecks. No more IRS.

"Harris was just a free stuff me-tooer. Bernie's the real deal. He invented the 'free shit for all' movement. He went SMU."

"I believe he went to Brooklyn College and the University of Chicago," offered a mystified Abby.

"SMU — Stalin and Mao University. Crazy Bernie scares me."

A steward knocked, entered, and whispered into the president's ear. "Thank you. Put him through."

"It's Mulvaney," said President Trump pulling the phone over and pressing the speaker button, "Yeah, Mick. What's up?"

"Sander's people just called. They want a debate and they want it now. Want my advice Mr. President?" asked Mulvaney.

"Go ahead, I'm listening."

"This is yours to lose. Don't do it," said Mulvaney.

Halsey nodded in agreement.

"Do it, Mr. President," urged Abby.

Chapter 89

NBC NEWS

October 20, 2020, 9 PM

ANNOUNCER: Live from Hofstra University in Hempstead, New York. This is the first presidential debate between President Donald J. Trump and the United States Senator from Vermont, Bernard Sanders. And here is our moderator, Lester Holt.

(Applauds)

LESTER HOLT: Good evening from Hofstra University in Hempstead, New York. I'm Lester Holt, anchor of "NBC Nightly News." I want to welcome you to the first, and possibly only presidential debate.

The participants tonight are President Donald Trump and Senator Bernie Sanders. This debate is sponsored by the Commission on Presidential Debates, a nonpartisan, nonprofit organization. The commission drafted tonight's format, and the rules have been agreed to by the campaigns.

The 90-minute debate is divided into three segments, each 30 minutes long. We'll explore three topic areas tonight: America's direction, securing America and achieving prosperity. At the start of each segment, I will ask the same lead-off question to both candidates, and they will each have up to two minutes to respond. From that point until the end of the segment, we'll have an open discussion if time permits.

The questions are mine and have not been shared with the commission or the campaigns. The audience here in the room has agreed to remain silent so that we can focus on what the candidates are saying.

I will invite you to applaud, however, at this moment, as we welcome the candidates: Democratic nominee for President of the United States, Senator Bernie Sanders, and the President of the United States, Donald J. Trump.

(APPLAUSE)

SANDERS: How are you, Donald?

President Trump came across the floor and shook hands with the senator adding, Better than you.

(APPLAUSE)

HOLT: Good luck to you both.

(APPLAUSE)

HOLT: Well, I don't expect us to cover all the issues of this campaign tonight, and I remind everyone, there are only 14 days remaining until the election and this whole debate was set-up only just last night. We are going to focus on many of the issues that voters tell us are most important, and we're going to press for specifics. I am honored to have this role, but this evening belongs to the candidates and, just as important, to the American people.

Candidates, we look forward to hearing you articulate your policies and your positions, as well as your visions and your values. So, let's begin.

By a flip of a coin we will begin with you, President Trump. Are you for or opposed to 'Climate Change'?

TRUMP: The concept of global warming was created by and for the Chinese in order to make U.S. manufacturing non-competitive. It used to be called global warming. That wasn't working. Then it was called climate change and now it's actually called extreme weather.

HOLT: Senator Sanders, would you like to respond?

SANDERS: President Trump wants to decimate the EPA. He has questioned science and silenced scientists. He's rolling back key environmental standards. Americans and markets disagree with Trump. Donald Trump believes climate change is a hoax. Donald Trump is an idiot.

(APPLAUSE)

HOLT: Please. Please, let's keep the applause down to a minimum.

HOLT: President Trump you have been labeled a racist. What do you have to say for yourself?

TRUMP: Crazy Bernie recently equated the city of Baltimore to a 'THIRD WORLD COUNTRY!' Based on that statement, I assume that Bernie must now be labeled a racist, just as a Republican would be if he used that term and standard! The fact is, Baltimore can be brought back, maybe.

HOLT: Senator Sanders, would you like to respond?

SANDERS: President Trump's racist tweets about the late House Oversight Committee Chairman Elijah Cummings were a disgrace.

It's unbelievable that we have a President of the United States who attacks American cities, who attacks Americans. Our job is to bring people together, to improve life for all people, not have a racist president who attacks people because they are African Americans. That is a disgrace and that is why I'm going to defeat this president.

HOLT: President Trump, would you like to respond?

TRUMP: Cummings' district, which is majority black, includes parts of Baltimore, are far worse and more dangerous than those at the US-Mexico border. Elijah Cummings is gone but he failed badly!

SANDERS: And so have you, Mr. President.

(APPLAUSE)

The debate continued another 10 minutes on America's direction, and then the securing America phases concluded, with one further question.

HOLT: The final question on securing America. Stay or pull out of Afghanistan. Senator Sanders you first, please.

SANDERS: I have been appalled by the continued presence of the U.S. in Afghanistan, the resulting casualties, and the debt accrued over the long war. This country has a $23 trillion national debt, in part owing to two wars that have not been paid for. We have been at war in Afghanistan for the last 19 years and paid a high price both in terms of casualties and national treasure. This year alone, we will spend about $3 trillion on that war. In my view, it is time for the people of Afghanistan to take full responsibility for waging the war against the Taliban. While we cannot withdraw all our troops immediately, we must bring them home as soon as possible. I appreciate the president's position, but I believe that the withdrawal should occur at significantly faster speed and greater scope."

HOLT: President Trump. Same question.

TRUMP: If we wanted to fight a war in Afghanistan and win it faster, I could win that war in a week. I just don't want to kill 10 million people. If I wanted to win that war, Afghanistan would be wiped off the face of the earth. It would be gone. It would be over in — literally, in 10 days. And I don't want to do — I don't want to go that route.

SANDERS: That's mighty white of you.

(APPLAUSE)

HOLT: I would hope that that would not be a consideration, Mr. President.

Moving on, Lindsey Graham United States Senator from South Carolina recently tweeted that any peace agreement which denies the US robust counter-terrorism capability in Afghanistan is not a peace deal. Instead, it is paving the way for another attack on the American homeland and attacks against American interests around the world.

TRUMP: Graham Cracker (Trump's new nickname for Senator Graham from South Carolina) is absolutely wrong. Osama bin Laden and Al-Qaeda planned 9/11 from a cave, and they can do it again from a cave. They outsourced the hijackers. 15 of the 19 were citizens of Saudi Arabia, two were from the United Arab Emirates, one was from Lebanon, and one was from Egypt. They didn't need an army. They don't need an army; we don't need an army. They can plan another attack from a cave and sub it out.

SANDERS: Mr. Trump, you really need an intervention.

(APPLAUSE)

President Trump was visibility annoyed, fidgeting and beginning a Nixon sweat. He enjoyed sparing but Sanders
was good. This went on for over an hour and President
Trump known for hitting back twice as hard had met his
match. Sanders was smart, well informed and a fighter.
The President knew there was time for only one more
question and he was ready.

HOLT: Let me interrupt just a moment. We're just about
out of time and I want to give each of you one minute to
wrap it up on achieving prosperity. Senator Sanders.

SANDERS: I'm running for president so that, when we
are in the White House, the movement we build together
can achieve economic, racial, social and environmental
justice for all.

Health care for all. Reinvest in public education and
teachers. Immigration reform. Empower the people
of Puerto Rico. Combat climate change and the New
Green Deal. Jobs for all. Revitalize rural America. Get
big money out of politics and restore democracy. Fight
for: working families, veterans, women's rights, racial
justice, LGBTQ equality, tribal nations, those with dis-
abilities, fair trade and workers, and gun safety. Enact a
responsible, comprehensive foreign policy, criminal justice reform, the right for a secure retirement. Fair banking for all and real Wall Street reform. College for all,
cancel all student debt and demand that the wealthy,
large corporations, and Wall Street pay their fair share
of income taxes.

HOLT: President Trump.

The president had been making funny, some would later call them goofy faces all during Bernie's closing statement and finally shook his head in amazement.

TRUMP: I won the election. The markets went up thousands of points, things started happening. If for some reason, had I not won the election, these markets would have crashed. That will happen even more so in 2020. You have no choice but to vote for me, because your 401(k), and everything is going to be down the tubes. Whether you love me or hate me, you have got to vote for me.

He turned and looked at Senator Sanders and said, in my world, you have to work for a living. Create a business that builds the economy and creates jobs. In your world Bernie, how are you going to pay for all your free stuff?

SANDERS: Raising his hands over his head in his trademark optic while turning to President Trump said, I'm gonna make you pay for it.

(APPLAUSE)

Bernie waited a beat then continued.

SANDERS: You and all your flunky friends. On day one in the Oval Office, I will raise the rate all you big wig billionaires pay and make you and all your banking and Wall Street buddies pay more personal and corporate Federal Income Tax and you will all like it. I would think you would want to keep your workers happy by paying a higher income tax. After all, without all the workers you can't do shit.

(LOUD APPLAUSE)

President Trump was smiling and shaking and tilting his head in his iconic optic. He got what he wanted. He had Bernie by his stringy white hair.

TRUMP: You can't do that Bernie. You can't raise income tax on the wealthy or even sneak in a middle-class income tax hike which we all know you're planning. Can't do it.

SANDERS: I can do it and you'll be watching me do it on the TV, in your underwear, from Trump Tower, Mar-a-Lago, Wolfhampton, prison or wherever you land after we throw you out.

(LOUD APPLAUSE)

HOLT: Calm down, please. Quiet please; we only have a second left. President Trump. Last word.

TRUMP: Can't do it, Bernie. You're from Vermont, right? And your state fruit is the apple — you like apples, Bernie? (Bernie begrudgingly shrugged his shoulders and nodded) Well, you can't raise Federal Income Taxes on the wealthy or anyone for that matter to pay for all your free stuff, because less than two hours ago, I signed an Executive Order doing away with Federal Income Tax. No more deep well for you to draw from Bernie. It's now a dry well. We'll replace it with funds fueled primarily from tariffs and a consumption tax. No more deductions from your weekly paychecks, folks. No more IRS. How do you like them apples, Bernie?

(HUGE APPLAUSE)

HOLT: All right. I don't know how that's going to work, but we're out of time and we'll have to leave it there. (Senator Sanders could be seen and heard, behind Lester Holt's close-up, yelling and stabbing his finger at Trump. Trump had his famous Mussolini stance and smug 'I won' smile.)

That concludes our debate for this evening, a spirited one at that.

There is no next presidential debate scheduled, unfortunately, so this is it. The conversation will continue.

A reminder. The vice-presidential debate scheduled for tomorrow night October 21st at Longwood University in Farmville, Virginia has been put on hold until Senator Sanders chooses his running mate. My thanks to Senator Sanders and to President Trump and to Hofstra University for hosting us tonight. Goodnight, everyone.

Chapter 90

For the 13 remaining days until the election, November 3, 2020, President Trump, the Senate and FOX battled Senator Sander, the House, and most the other media outlets.

Senator Sanders, who may not have ended on top at the end of the debate trumped Trump by tweeting,

---

Bernie Sanders
@SenSanders
Oct. 21
Well, President Trump, it took some time, but it looks like we finally won you over. By eliminating the personal income tax, you are now a 'Free Stuff Me -Tooer. Welcome to the Left. Not!

That gave Senator Sanders a huge boost. But knocking out an incumbent, no matter how controversial, would need something more.

The voting demographics, even in the last four years have drastically changed. The World War II generation was all gone except for a few sturdy nonagenarians. The Korean War generation was in their mid to late eighties and the Vietnam War generation aka the Baby Boomers were all in their seventies. Almost 78% of America's population was 64 and under and only a little over 22% of the population, born before or at the dawn of Television, was still alive.

Gen Alpha, Gen Z aka Zeds, Gen Y aka Millennials, and Gen X aka Xennials make up almost 78% of the population. Although 62% were white, almost 38% are black, Latino, Asian and other. Most were not considered Trump voters.

Bernie Sanders and the DNC got that huge boost when they announced his running mate for vice president.

The New York Times

Sanders Chooses Harris as Running Mate

By JEFF JOURNEY and LENY SELENY
October. 22, 2020

WASHINGTON — Senator Bernie Sanders has chosen Senator Kamala Harris of California to be his running mate.

In 2017, Kamala D. Harris, who until a few days ago was the Democratic Nominee for President, was sworn in as a United States Senator for California, the second African American woman and first South Asian-American senator in history. She serves on the Homeland Security and Governmental Affairs Committee, the Select Committee on Intelligence, the Committee on the Judiciary, and the Committee on the Budget.

Kamala has spent her life fighting injustice. It's a passion that was first inspired by her mother, Shyamala, an Indian American immigrant, activist, and breast cancer researcher.

Senator Sanders' selection ended a quick two-day search that was conducted almost entirely in secret. It reflected a critical strategic choice by Senator Sanders, to go with a running mate who could reassure voters about gaps in his résumé, rather than to pick someone who could deliver a state or reinforce Senator Sanders' message of change.

Two recent female nominees for Vice President, Republican Sarah Palin and Democrat Geraldine Ferraro didn't fare so well but it is hoped that Senator Harris will bring out the largely Black and Latino vote and...

Both candidates and their running mates began a full team press. The vice president nominees hit the big cities and both coasts — you can imagine the reception Harris received to that of Pence in Los Angeles, Chicago, and New York City. Harris admitted that she was decimated when she was replaced but decided on the high road when Bernie called. Harris could become the first female vice president and the first black vice president, and it was also not lost on anyone, especially Harris, because of Sanders' age and recent heart attack, that she could go on to become the first female president.

Sanders followed Trump tit for tat into each of Trump's strongholds gaining crowd strength with each rally.

More and more Trump supporters were abandoning him and doing so publicly.

Anthony Scaramucci, former White House Communications Director's off and on-again love-hate affair with his former boss was on again. Scaramucci said to the Washington Post, Vanity Fair, Fox News and to anyone who would listen, "President Trump is disassembling and sounding more and more nonsensical." — "Trump Is In 'Meltdown Mode"—Trump will turn on everyone eventually, then the entire country."

Ann Coulter's book *In Trump We Trust* became *In Trump We Distrust.* "Trump deserves to lose the reelection."

Other one-time supporters or never Trumper's like Joe Scarborough, Bill Kristol, Jeb, George and Laura Bush, Jeff Flake, Lindsey Graham, Mitt Romney, Arnold Schwarzenegger, William Bennett, and Robert Gates rekindled their attacks or flipped on Trump.

Chapter 91

NPR Battleground Map: Donald Trump Is Winning — And It's Not Close

October 23, 201612:59 PM ET
DOMINIC DOMENICO

Let's make one thing clear: Less than two weeks out from this election, Donald Trump is winning — and it's not close.

Yes, people still have to vote, but if Republican groups come out — and the Sanders New Green Deal campaign is more like a white flag than an actual strategy — President Trump will get four more years as president of the United States unless something drastic changes between now and Election Day...

Just how unlikely is it that Sanders will win?

To do so, he would have to take all the toss-up states — Florida, North Carolina, Ohio, Iowa, Nevada, Arizona, Nebraska, and Maine — and win a state leaning in Trump's direction. The likeliest target remains New Hampshire, with its almost all-white population, but

Trump — especially in the past couple of weeks — has maintained what appears to be a durable lead there...

To put this into perspective, Sanders winning would be something like coming back from being down 3-0 in a best-of-seven baseball series. Sure, the Toronto Blue Jays could come back to beat the Cleveland Indians. I mean, the Red Sox did it to the Yankees in 2004, right? Yes, but it's highly unlikely...

"What do you think? Sounds like you're gonna get another four years," said Halsey handing the National Public Radio release back to the president. "If they've got you ahead, they must have lost all hope for Sanders."

"I think that piece is meant to get Sanders voters out and make me complacent."

"You may be right."

"I'm not going to win."

"You said the same thing in 2016. Besides, now you deserve it."

"Yes, but I was the underdog in '16. Hillary was ahead in all the polls just like I am now, but she got cocky, her base got lazy, her advisors got overconfident, they all started to believe in their own press. She thought she deserved it and she lost.

"I didn't think I would win the first time. I never thought I would be president now. I'm TCO — been there done that, but Sanders and Harris are a winning ticket. Left, far Left, women, Millennials, Blacks, Latinos, free shitters — they got them all. And the best part is that they're hoping Bernie croaks in the first term so Harris can take it over and finish it out then run for and win an additional eight years."

"TCO?"

President Trump didn't answer. Halsey thought it was a new acronym for The Commanding Officer or something like that and continued, "With all this new-found knowledge, don't you think you should let someone know your apprehension? Let your staff, the RNC know so they can rally the troops?"

"Troops? I bring the troops home from Syria and Turkey goes after the Kurds. What do we owe the Kurds? They didn't support us in World War II, or at Normandy."

"Mr. President. Neither did the Italians, Japanese or Germans, but we didn't throw them under the bus," said Abby.

The president let Abby's history lesson go and continued, "Like I said. I'm TCO, 'The Chosen One', and if I win it will have already been decided — same if I lose. I wanted out but they pulled me back in — now it's written."

Abby stared at the president in silence and almost felt pity for him. Then her stare turned to a glare.

Chapter 92

Washington (CNN)

President Donald Trump, and Russian President Vladimir Putin in a secret meeting during the G8 summit in Dural Florida last August, expressed their desire to invite China into the G8, in 2021, according to a senior administration official. Making the G8 into the G9.

"I think it's much more appropriate to have China inside the room instead of outside the room, he said during a meeting in the Oval Office with the Romanian President just months after the group of leading industrialized nations convened for its annual summit in Dural Florida.

"If somebody would make that motion, I would certainly be disposed to think about it very favorably," he added. Canada, France, Germany, Italy, Japan, the United Kingdom are vehemently opposed...

"Did you read this?" asked Sanders.

"Last year Russia, now China? He said it's now time to invite China into the group. Threatening to add Mexico and Spain if Canada and Italy don't cow-toe to him," answered Pelosi during a meeting in her office with

Sanders, Harris and DNC Chairman Tom Perez just over two months after the G8 convened for its annual summit in the Dural, Florida.

"He said if somebody would make that motion, he would certainly be disposed to think about it very favorably.

"I heard from some of his staffers that what he actually said, back in '19, was he wanted Russia back in the 'G-String' before that skinhead, shit-head, Dobby tried to kill him again and he now wants Junk Boat Jinping in as payback for Jinping blinking on tariffs," said Harris.

"He's going down. All our polls and media friends have been saying he's out ahead and they're eating it up. He's gonna get a low turnout and we're gonna get a blowout," said Perez.

"Bernie, you need to hit him with the economy. If the economy is so good, why has the debt risen to 23 trillion and why is it not coming down? Why is the deficit still rising to a trillion? If the debt and deficit aren't in a reversal now during his so-called 'best economy ever', then when?" asked Harris.

"Just because Trump, *FOX*, and his talking heads say the economy is great doesn't make it so. The FED doesn't believe him. The markets correct every day with every new "Breaking News" banner," offered Pelosi.

"He's a racist," said Harris.

"He is, but not if you got money. Then he's an elitist. He plays to the proletariat but plays with the bourgeoisie. Who is in his Cabinet? Who are his advisors? Who gets invited to Mara Largo or the White House? Who does he surround himself with? Billionaires-black, white, brown. Makes no different the color of one's skin to Trump, only the color of their money," said Sanders.

"Sell him Greenland. He's pushing to buy it again, but he doesn't know the difference," said Perez

"Difference?"

"Yeah, the difference? The difference is he doesn't know the difference. He doesn't know the difference between Greenland and Iceland. In Viking times, Erik the Red was exiled from Iceland for murder. He set out in ships to find land rumored to be to the northwest. After settling there, he named the desolate, ice-covered island Greenland to fool people and attract them to settle there. Conversely, the much smaller island to the south was beautiful and they wanted to keep people away, so they named their island Iceland. Fucken Donald the Red, a thousand years later, is still falling for the scam."

"Okay. We got things to do and people to see and we're almost out of time. Bernie, Kamala, it's up to you now. You have less than a week to turn it around. No pressure, but the future of America is in your hands," said Pelosi.

Chapter 93

ELECTION NIGHT IN AMERICA
November 3, 2020, 6:38 pm

Amazing graphics and an announcer with a deep bari-tone voice reminiscent of the opening of any UFC event began, "Tonight, voters have the last word in the election of a lifetime. Senator Sanders from Vermont is trying to change the direction where America is heading, while President Trump is determined to hold the course and once again shatter expectations. After months of twists and turns, the first results now just minutes away."

More animated graphics appeared on the screen with the *CNN* logo and a banner 'Election Night in America' The announcer continued, "This is *CNN* coverage of Election Night in America. The fight for the presidency the battle for congress and the issues dividing the na-tion. The people are choosing, the world is watching, and anything is possible till the last vote."

Music and more graphics fill the screen until another *CNN* Election Night in America banner appeared with Wolf Blitzer standing out in front. "We want to welcome our viewers in the United States and around the world. I'm Wolf Blitzer in the *CNN* election center, and we're closing in on our first task to make projections in the presidential race with America now choosing to elect the oldest independent Democrat to lead the nation or a one-time political outsider, some would say still an outsider, the younger presidential incumbent Donald Trump. We're counting down to the top of the next hour and that's when polls close in the battleground states of Georgia and Virginia, they are two of the key races we'll be watching. Also, at the top of the hour voting is ending in Indiana, Kentucky, South Carolina, and Vermont. A total of 60 electrical votes are on the line within the next hour and remember 270 are needed to win the White House.

"Jake Tapper, we have been building for this moment now for nearly two years," Wolf turned it over to Jake Tapper, "That's right Wolf, there's never been a campaign like this, and we can expect many surprises in this very long election night..."

Over the next few hours, Jake Tapper along with David Axelrod, Dana Bash, Sanjay Gupta, Anderson Cooper, Van Jones, John King, Manu Raju, Paul Begala, Jim Acosta, Gloria Borger, and a dozen more *CNN* reporters contributors and analysts will join Wolf Blitzer to produce charts, maps, voice opinions and everything possible to predict the outcome of the 2020 elections. And like 2016, they will again get it all wrong.

Another banner appeared with Wolf stating, "And we have our first projection of the night. Take a look at this. We predict that Donald Trump will win in Kentucky with its 8 electoral votes. Donald Trump also wins in Indiana with its 11 electoral votes.

"More predictions coming in. We now predict that Bernie Sanders will be the winner in Vermont, no surprise there, with its 3 electoral votes.

"Let's take a look where it stands right now. Donald Trump taking a very early lead with 19 electoral votes to Bernie Sanders 3…

"Alright, let's take another look. Too early to call in North Carolina and Ohio. Right now, we have a key state alert, but too early to call.

"Right now, Let's check in with our correspondent Jim Acosta in Palm Beach Florida covering the Trump campaign. Jim, what are you learning?"

"Wolf, a senior advisor from the Trump campaign just told me it would take a miracle for Sanders to win."

"Thank you, Jim, and please stand by. We have another prediction; Donald Trump is projected to be the winner in West Virginia with its 5 electoral votes bringing the total for Donald Trump to 24 – Bernie Sanders remains at 3.

"More projections coming in, Sanders wins Illinois, New Jersey, Massachusetts, Maryland. More wins coming in for Senator Sanders, Rhode Island, Delaware, and the District of Columbia.

"Trump also has some new projections coming in, Oklahoma, Tennessee, and Mississippi.

"We now look at 68 electoral votes for Sanders and 48 electoral votes for Trump. My-my what a difference a few minutes makes."

As the voting in each state closed, more and more projections were made, and the electoral vote total changed back and forth between the two candidates.

Ohio, Michigan went for Sanders but if Virginia turns on Trump things could start to spiral out of control for the incumbent.

President Trump and his family, along with Vice President Pence and his family were in Mar-a-Largo watching the election results on TV. His acceptance speech or concession call would emanate from there.

Senators Sanders and Harris were in their respective campaign hotel rooms watching the results on TV and were preparing for the celebratory memorial or deplorable funeral, later in the ballroom of the same hotel.

Pelosi, Schumer, The Squad, McConnell, McCarthy, Halsey and Abby Adams and millions of Americans and millions of people around the World were at home glued to their TVs, computers, and radios watching or listening to history being made.

Chapter 94

ELECTION NIGHT IN AMERICA
November 4, 2020, 9:00 pm

"Jake, we have another major projection now," said Wolf Blitzer.

"And *CNN* can now project that Virginia will go to Bernie Sanders.

"Now let's take a look at how we stand. Donald Trump is still ahead with 157 electoral votes and Bernie sanders at 142. 270 electoral votes are needed to win the White House.

"Let's go over to Jake. Jake this is a moment that the markets are watching very closely because few people thought Bernie Sanders would be doing so well at this stage."

"The markets don't like instability Wolf, and they're not sure what Sanders is going a do if he keeps up this momentum and wins. The Dow futures were down more than 500 now they're down more than 600. But let's just take a moment here and look at this. Pollsters predicted that Donald Trump would not only have a victory, but he was going to have an electoral landslide. Victory still seems probable, but a landslide is not possible, and it may go to prove that Bernie Sanders is redrawing the map the way he said he was going to. And let's not forget how all this support for Sanders is having a residual positive effect on the House, Senate, and governorships up for grabs. Let's go to David Axelrod for an update. David."

"Jake. What we're seeing in the presidential race is been mirrored in the House, Senate and governorships seats up for grabs. The Democrats are on track to keep control of the House and it looks like they are sweeping most of the open seats of the Senate and a majority of the open governor slots. If Sanders keeps on winning states it looks like Congress and the states are following behind him step by step. Jake."

Chapter 95

ELECTION NIGHT IN AMERICA
November 4, 2020, 2:00 am

Wolf Blitzer appeared again before the large graph-
ic of the United States with the states going for the
Republicans in red, Democrats in blue and 7 states in
undecided yellow. Unlike 2016, where at this time the
map appeared almost all red, this time it was a color
checkerboard across the country with Trump at 247
electoral votes and Sanders at 215.

"Donald Trump has moved closer and closer to the
magic number of 270 electoral votes to win this election.
Let's do a key state alert right now. Trump has the lead
in Michigan, Wisconsin, Arizona, and Pennsylvania and
if he were to win just Michigan and Wisconsin that would
take him over the top. Sanders, if he is going to be president, will have to win all 4 states an unlikely possibility
with Trump ahead at the moment.

"Let's look at the remaining outstanding states. Sanders is ahead in New Hampshire with 4 electoral votes, Maine with 4 electoral votes and Minnesota with 10. If he continues that will bring his total to 232 — 38 electoral votes short. 7 states in yellow remain outstanding.

"Let's go to Jim Acosta in Trump headquarters in Mar-a-Lago, Florida. What do you see Jim What are you hearing?"

"Yeah Wolf, I just spoke with a senior Trump adviser a few moments ago who said that if Donald Trump is declared the winner, and they have every reason to believe that is going to be the case, he's going to deliver a speech calling for the country to come together. You can just hear the crow behind me. The chants are loud and calling for Sanders to go back to Russia and to 'Keep America Great'. There're lots of red hats in this rather large ballroom and adjacent tents. Back to you, Wolf."

"We expect to be hearing more about 'Keep America Great'. Hold on a second, here comes DNC Chairman Tom Perez coming out on stage at the Sanders headquarters in New York City."

"Well folks, we have been here a long time. It's been a long night and a long campaign, but I can say we can wait a little longer, can't we?" announced Perez and the crowd went wild. "They're still counting votes and every vote counts. There are several states too close to call so we're not going to say anymore tonight. Listen to me. Everyone should head home, get some sleep. We'll have more to say later this morning. I want you to know and every person in this hall to know and everyone in

America to know that your voices and your enthusiasm mean so much to Bernie and Kamala. We are so proud of you, and so proud of them. Let's get those votes counted and bring this home. Goodnight and we'll see back here a little later this morning."

And with that, most of America and most of the world went to bed despite Wolf Blitzer, *CNN*, *FOX*, *NBC*, and others attempt to hold onto ratings by hyping the tension and adding pundit's drama. Nothing was going to be settled in the next few hours with seven states still up for grabs.

Chapter 96

On Wednesday, November 4, 2020, after a few hours' sleep aboard Air Force One, President Trump was back in the White House Oval Office sitting astern Resolute. He was grinning ear to ear even though his third attempt to put his feet up on the desk failed. Halsey was on the couch talking on his cell to Abby. A knock on the door announced the arrival of his family having just left Barron upstairs sleeping. Some with no sleep at all, others with just a few hours were all smiles as the went over and hugged and congratulated their Dad.

Melania came in, walked over and gave her husband a kiss.

"We did it," said President Trump.

"We did," affirmed Melania.

"Papers out?" asked Eric.

The president picked up *The New York Times* and tossed Eric *The Washington Post*.

The Washington Post

November 4, 2020

Sanders Sprints to the Finish Line
VOTER SCORN FOR STATUS QUO PROPELS UPSET OF TRUMP

Sanders urges Americans to come together as a nation… He ran a free for all but how will he govern? Markets Tank as the World Buckles Up for a Free Ride…

"We just witnessed one of the most stunning political upsets in recent American history. This is a historic night. The American people have spoken, and the American people have elected their new champion, and it will be an honor and privilege to serve as your Vice President of the United States. So, let me say, it is my high honor and privilege to introduce to you the president-elect of the United States of America Bernie Sanders," said Kamala Harris to an exuberant crowd at 5 am this morning from the Sanders-Harris ballroom in Manhattan's Javitz Center. It has been confirmed that President Trump called Senator Sanders just after 3 am from Air Force One, offering congratulations and conceding…

"Well, how'd we do?" asked the president.

"I'd say we now have more gold than Fort Knox. Goldfinger would be jealous," said Eric.

"Let's hope we don't get accused of committing 'The Crime of the Century' and of bringing economic chaos to the west like Goldfinger did and have James Bond Nadler up our ass," said Don Jr.

"Watch your language," said the president.

Channeling Hyman Roth the president looked at his family and said, "If I could only live to see it, to be there with you. What I wouldn't give for twenty more years! Here we are, protected, free to make our profits without Pelosi, the goddamn Pussy's and the F.B.I. interfering in our partnership with a friendly government. A mile high! It's nothing! Just one small step for the man who would be king and having the cash to make it possible." Looking at Halsey he added, "Tom, we're bigger than U.S. Steel."

"The way everyone's acting here you'd think you won," said Halsey.

"I tried, I really did, but Black and Brown is the new white, and Free Shit Happens."

"What about the frantic Five and the Squad. Now they can come after you."

"Why? They got what they wanted. I'm out. They got the trifecta; House, Senate, and Presidency and if they last two-term they'll get at least two justices. I can handle Pelosi and her crowd, as for the Pussy's I'll do whatever it takes to get them out office."

"How did you end up doing it?" asked Halsey.

"Monday, November 2nd when the polls were predicting me having a 40-state sweep, I had Ivanka pull out of the market and get cash. We made a killing. The market was betting on me taking it all. Last night just before I conceded we brought gold and we are now worth over 150 billion and the richest family on earth."

"Yeah but a lot of people lost a lot of money."

"Oh, Sanders will get it back. It will take a while and he won't be able to get any of his free shit, but it will eventually bounce back the way it did for Obama after Bush proclaimed the sky was falling in '08.

"The economy was headed for a downturn anyway even if I won, but there was nothing I could have done about it except own it and that was not going to happen."

"But you're not a loser how can you take this so well."

"I didn't want another four years anyway. You know that, but now it happened and all above board at that — and I'm finally free."

"So, what are you, what are we going to do now?" asked Halsey.

"You and I, Peachy, are off to Kafiristan."

Chapter 97

Mid-February 2021, Halsey and Trump were sitting in the conference room of Skidmore, Owings & Merrill's Moscow office looking at a scale model of Trump Tower Moscow. The size and scale of the model had to be reduced and the ceiling removed for the mile-high tower scale model to fit into the room.

"So, this is it — our Kafiristan?

"I had to deal with all those asshole politicians and fake news day after day and had to take it. I couldn't stop them, but here in Mother Russia, it's different. The kid from Queens has become 'The Man Who Would Be King' and for now, this is our Kafiristan Peachy, at least for the next four years till we get Trump Tower Moscow built and open. It's going to be the eighth wonder of the world. Only two wonders will last the test of time, Trump Tower at a mile high and four city blocks at its base. A gleaming steel, carbon-fiber and titanium alloy self-sustaining tower that will generate its own energy and create its own weather — it's so high it will affect climate change."

"What's the other?"

"Most of the others no longer exist: The Hanging Gardens of Babylon, Temple of Artemis at Ephesus, Statue of Zeus at Olympia, Mausoleum at Halicarnassus, Colossus of Rhodes, and the Lighthouse of Alexandria are all gone. They didn't last the test of time, only the Great Pyramid of Giza is still standing, and of course the greatest wonder of them all Trump Tower Moscow.

"Trump Tower will put Moscow on the map. A destination and tourist mecca. Who would have thought? And I won't have to deal with lying politicians and fake news — they're not permitted in Russia as long as my friend and business partner holds onto his job."

"How will you get people to buy apartments above the clouds?"

"Elevators."

"Funny. You know what I mean."

"Actually, we're using a pneumatic tubes systems that will propel cylindrical Lexan Polycarbonate capsules containing everything from people, pets, to fast food, groceries, and dry cleaning, through networks of tubes by compressed air and partial vacuum directly into their apartments, health clubs, pools, retail shops, places of work and garages."

"Excuse me? You're going to put Chinese take-out into tubes and Flash Gordon them into the bowels and spires of Trump Tower Moscow, never to be seen or smelled again?"

"You're a comedian now, Halsey?"

"No, but I can see little Ivan and Natasha after school entering your vapor lock when mom's not around and never being seen or heard from again."

"Elevators have been around just a bit longer than elevator music. They're noisy, high maintenance and rightly shut down during fires. Pneumatic Tubes Systems are quiet, safe and virtually maintenance-free, and in case of an emergency can deliver residents directly outside. They have been around since the 19th century. In 1873 a guy named Alfred Ely Beach built a block-long pneumatic transit system in New York City. The demonstration actually sold 400,000 rides during its first year of operation.

"Regardless, it's not a problem. All I have do is tell buyers that they can't have it and they will beat down the doors. I was once having trouble getting customers up to a high retail floor in one of my properties. I hired this design firm FDG out of New York City, where else, and I gave them a two-million-dollar budget to do whatever it took to get traffic up to that level and increase sales. I told them I wanted fast results. Two weeks later,

I heard from the retail manager that traffic to that floor increased 200% and sales were out the roof. I told him I would be right over to see what the design firm did. He told me not to bother — They didn't do anything. I asked him how do you explain the increase in customer traffic and sales? He said the designer had signs made that said, 'Free $100.00 cash to any customer who comes up to the 5th floor.' We had 15,000 new customers onto the floor in less than a week — on schedule and under budget. Brilliant.

"Anyway, what's important is that people don't know what they want till you tell them and sell them."

Halsey had asked before, but now it was real and so many lives were now affected by the election outcome. "Why did you do it? I mean why did you really do it and give up the biggest most powerful job in the world. Why did you do it when you knew America's economy would crash and so many people's lives would be affected?"

"I'll tell you why. Do you know the story about the scorpion and frog?" asked former President Trump and without waiting for an answer proceeded to tell the story.

"One day, a scorpion looked around at the mountain where he lived and decided that he wanted a change. He climbed over rocks and under vines and kept going until he reached a river.

The river was wide and swift, and the scorpion stopped to reconsider the situation. He couldn't see any way across. Suddenly, he saw a frog sitting in the bushes by the bank of the stream on the other side of the river. He decided to ask the frog for help getting across the stream.

'Hellooo Mr. Frog!' called the scorpion across the water, 'Would you be so kind as to give me a ride on your back across the river?'

'Well now, Mr. Scorpion! How do I know that if I try to help you, you won't try to kill me?' asked the frog hesitantly.

'Because,' the scorpion replied, 'If I try to kill you, then I would die, too, for you see I cannot swim!'

Now, this seemed to make sense to the frog. But he asked. 'What about when I get close to the bank? You could still try to kill me and get back to the shore!'

'This is true,' agreed the scorpion, 'But then I wouldn't be able to get to the other side of the river!'

'Alright then... how do I know you won't just wait till we get to the other side and then kill me?' said the frog.

'Ahh...,' crooned the scorpion, 'Because you see, once you've taken me to the other side of this river, I will be so grateful for your help, that it would hardly be fair to reward you with death, now would it?!'

So, the frog agreed to take the scorpion across the river. He swam over to the bank and settled himself near the mud to pick up his passenger. The scorpion crawled onto the frog's back, his sharp claws prickling into the frog's soft hide, and the frog slid into the river. The muddy water swirled around them, but the frog stayed near the surface so the scorpion would not drown. He kicked strongly through the first half of the stream, his flippers paddling wildly against the current.

Halfway across the river, the frog suddenly felt a sharp sting in his back and, out of the corner of his eye, saw the scorpion remove his stinger from his back. A deadening numbness began to creep into his limbs.

'You fool!' croaked the frog, 'Now we shall both die! Why on earth did you do that?'

The scorpion shrugged and did a little jig on the drownings frog's back.

'I could not help myself. It is my nature.'

Then they both sank into the muddy waters of the swiftly flowing river.

Looking Halsey in the eye, Trump smiled and said, "It's my nature."

The End

Epilogue

The Trump family became the wealthiest family in America, surpassing the Walton's; but not of the entire world. Saudi Arabia's House of Saud has a net worth of $1.4 trillion but that is spread out over the entire royal family estimated to comprise of 15,000 souls including a king, multiple princes, brothers, sisters and cousins, compared to a few dozen Trumps.

Melania continued to live in Trump Tower, but had the Trump Clock removed because every time she passed the clock, she saw her husband lying on the pavement with a bullet in his chest. She, to Barron's deep regret, would never go back to Wolfhampton because of the kidnapping and the ilk that built it. She stayed with her husband in Mar-a-Lago, while Barron moved to Philadelphia to begin working on his B.S. degree in economics at Wharton. The other kids, Ivanka, Don Jr., Eric, and Tiffany continued building the family real estate business and/or as fashion designers, authors, reality television personalities, political office aspirants, socialite, and big game hunters.

Tom Halsey spent most of his time in Wolfhampton, married Abby and became a successful businessman. Along with his friend Fitzy, and his new love Riana, they turned Club KGB into a fabulous French steak and fish restaurant called Steak & Poisson. Their delicious House Salad and mustard vinaigrette steak, fish, and pommes frites accompanied by their proprietary mustard sauce, thanks to Trump and the FDA, gave them a Platinum rating in Dan's Paper Best of the 'Best 2023 Bistro Winners'.

Abby relented, returned and became caretaker of Wolfhall. She published a major photographic essay of Wolfhall for Architectural Digest, which became a *New York Times* best seller. Hammer and Sickle eventually warmed up to the two little white dogs, Lucy and Coco. Abby and Halsey, because of his Russia connections, became the sole American distributors of Hammer + Sickle Russian Vodka and Hammer and Sickle the black Siberian wolves, along with their best friends Lucy and Coco became advertising icons of Black, White and Red harmony. The quartet became inseparable and the most photographed wolves and wolf groupies in the world. Abby went on to become mayor of Wolfhampton, promising to clean up Main Street, and make the village more vibrant.

Nancy Pelosi retained her position as Speaker of the House, but Steny Hoyer of Maryland and James Clyburn of South Carolina were nipping at her high heels. Schumer became Senate Majority Leader. Nadler, Schiff, and the Squad continued to attack and blame Trump for the 'Three Rs': Russia, Racism, and Recession, but nobody was listening. One Supreme Court Justice passed away opening an opportunity for the left to somewhat get back in the game while at the same time enabling the right to even the score during the approval process.

Denison aka Denisov went on to become Detective Sgt. of the Wolfhampton Village Police Department replacing Detective Rossi who took early retirement. Volkov's trial was cut short when he was found strangled in his prison cell — his Russian CD lover is being held for questioning. Colonel Galkin was last seen climbing over the Wolfhall estate wall.

Trump Tower Moscow opened to rave reviews in 2023 and was completed ahead of schedule and under budget — and according to Trump it was a huge success. "Nothing bigger or better will ever be built." A mile high in the sky and completely sold out. He never returned to New York City and Trump Tower. Palm Beach is now his primary residence.

Working again with Mark Burnett from *The Apprentice* they launched a new show which Trump hosted called *The Incumbent*, a new TV mega-success, where contestants competed for a chance to run for Congress. The winner's campaign was completely funded and managed by Trump

— and he guaranteed a win. The first four seats they targeted were: Massachusetts's 7th congressional district, Michigan's 13th congressional district, Minnesota's 5th congressional district and New York's 14th congressional district.

Bernie Sanders had the last laugh, well almost. Sanders pounded the recession into remission and got the economy moving forward. Slowly but surely, he was able to start delivering on his 'Free Shit for All' campaign promise, primarily by repealing and reinstating the Federal Income Tax. He raised the taxable income for the rich, as defined as anyone, or family, making over $100,000.00 a year, and from 30% to 75% for billionaires. Unfortunately, Sanders had the 'Big One' in his second term and Kamala Harris went on to become the first female black president of the United States for the next ten years.

Donald Trump's taxes were finally released for the years prior to his presidency showing a less than stellar income. However, his 2022 taxes showed an impressive increase in income of which Bernie took 75%.

"If you wrote this as a novel, nobody would buy it. It would be a failure because it would be too unbelievable," Donald Trump referring to the craziness of the Russia investigation, Muller Report, whistleblowers, and Fake News.